SUMMER OF LOVE

SUMMER OF LOVE

A MUSIC & MURDER MYSTERY

Paul Martin

First published by Level Best Books/Historia 2022

Author Photo Credit: Mark Thiessen/NGS

First edition

ISBN: 978-1-68512-168-6

Cover art by Level Best Designs

This book was professionally typeset on Reedsy.
Find out more at reedsy.com

For my longtime San Francisco comrade, writer Mark Hugh Miller, my fellow Vietnam vets, especially Russ Coughlin and Mike Goodrich, and all the hopeful sixties freaks who are still kicking.

Praise for the Music & Murder Mysteries

SUMMER OF LOVE

"*Summer of Love* follows two brothers, Jack and Bobby Doyle, through the terrifying and wondrous heart of the '60s—one in the darkness of Vietnam and the other in the orange sunshine of the Haight-Ashbury, a tale stitched deeply into the historical background. Martin takes you there and he gets it right."—Joel Selvin, bestselling author and longtime *San Francisco Chronicle* music critic

"A deeply immersing, character-rich plot.... With the skill of an expert storyteller and a special talent for bringing different pieces together to form a harmonious story, Paul Martin weaves together a spine-chilling and intense search for a killer, the brutal scenes of war, the thrilling and sensational moods of romance, and a relaxed and artsy atmosphere." (5 Stars)—*San Francisco Book Review*

"Murder, music, and a tour of '67 San Francisco power this literary mystery.... Martin exhibits a mastery of the city, from the level of the street as well as the cultural significance of its music and art.... The sense of a world spinning out of control pervades the novel.... Readers will not guess the jolting resolution.... A fascinating biography of a particular time and a particular place."—*Publishers Weekly*

"This riveting page-turner set against the colorful backdrop of San Francisco in 1967 instantly absorbs the reader with its beautifully worded descriptions and vivid characterizations.... The author is expert at weaving fiction and reality so tightly they nearly become one."—Lida Sideris, author of the Southern California Mysteries

DANCE OF THE MILLIONS

"The Cuba of legend before Castro re-emerges in all its glamour, seediness and danger. A classic recreation."—James Conaway, bestselling author of *Napa: The Story of an American Eden*

"Gripping from the start.... Heartrending and thought-provoking. A fantastic read all around." (5 Stars)—*San Francisco Book Review*

"A striking work of historical fiction and political drama with a murder mystery tying it together."—*Publishers Weekly*

"An astonishing read reminiscent of Erik Larson's work."—Tina deBellegarde, Agatha-nominated author of *Winter Witness*

KILLIN' FLOOR BLUES

"A fascinating tale of music and race during the Great Depression."—Kelly Oliver, bestselling author of the Fiona Figg Mysteries

"Captures the atmosphere of the period perfectly, and the dialogue rings just as true."—*San Francisco Book Review*

"This rich, atmospheric thriller follows musicologist detectives into the heart of the blues on the trail of a murderer."—*Publishers Weekly*

"An honest page-turner."—*Historical Novels Review*

"Beware of the day when your dreams come true."
–Hercule Poirot, in *Three Act Tragedy*

Prologue

Change had once come slowly along the wild western edge of our continent. The prehistoric nomads who roamed the rugged landscape twelve thousand years ago lived lives of brutish sameness for millennia. At night, they huddled around their campfires, exchanging wary grunts and grimaces as they stared into the darkness, where dire wolves, saber-toothed cats, and other terrifying beasts lurked. About five thousand years ago, the Ohlone—tribes of hunter-gatherers—settled on a hilly, gently curving thumb of land between waters that explorers would later name the Pacific Ocean and San Francisco Bay, cornucopias that provided the Ohlone with much of their sustenance.

The Ohlone lived amid relative peace and reliable plenty until the arrival of Spanish colonizers. In 1776, the Spanish established the Presidio, a military garrison on the headlands overlooking the entrance to San Francisco Bay. They also founded a Franciscan mission, Mission Dolores, whose Christian brothers set about civilizing the Ohlone. In short order, the missionaries civilized the Ohlone into oblivion, ostensibly saving their souls while destroying their lives. The few that survived were subject to disease, slave-like conditions, and the unshakable yoke of hopelessness. As their reward, the native population had the privilege of building their new masters' church, where they listened to incomprehensible Latin Masses.

In the 1820s, Spain's hold on the region was challenged by the newly independent Mexico, and later by the aggressively expanding United States. In 1846, the U.S. went to war with Mexico, acquiring all of California, including the shabby backwater village of Yerba Buena near the northeastern tip of the San Francisco Peninsula. In January 1847, Yerba Buena, which meant "good herb," was renamed San Francisco. When gold was discovered the following year in the Sierra foothills, wild-eyed adventurers from across the country and around the world poured into San Francisco on their way to the diggings. Even the Chinese flocked to "Gold Mountain," their name for the boomtown where many of them would settle.

The ragtag army of prospectors—along with the accompanying swarm of peddlers, prostitutes, gamblers, and grifters—changed San Francisco forever, transforming the sleepy village of a few hundred into a brash commercial crossroads. Young writers Mark Twain and Bret Harte captured that rowdy era in their stories. After the Gold Rush and the Comstock Lode silver bonanza that followed, San Francisco continued to attract a colorful procession of visionaries, eccentrics, and hustlers, its population doubling every few years.

In 1894, the city celebrated its entrepreneurial spirit with the California Midwinter International Exposition. In 1915, the Panama-Pacific International Exposition commemorated the completion of the Panama Canal, and in 1939, the Golden Gate International Exposition marked the completion of the Golden Gate and San Francisco Bay Bridges. The 1894 exposition took place in Golden Gate Park, the corridor of green that stretches nearly halfway across the city from the coast. Ever since it was created in 1870, the park had been a popular location for all manner of celebrations, but no gathering there was ever as strange as the marijuana- and LSD-fueled festival held on January 14, 1967.

Billed as the Human Be-In, the celebration was the brainchild of San Francisco's bohemian community—the beatniks, as they were christened by *San Francisco Chronicle* columnist Herb Caen. The festival brought together more than twenty thousand flower children, artists, activists, and older free spirits the likes of Beat poet Allen Ginsberg. Dressed in their psychedelic outfits, serapes, and flowing robes, the attendees mingled amid a succession of rock music, inspirational talks, and poetry readings. Guru Richard Alpert—later known as Ram Dass—was there, along with his former Harvard pal Timothy Leary, who advised everyone to "turn on, tune in, drop out." Some of the participants assumed the lotus position and uttered the mantra *om* until they reached a state of bliss, while others wandered around the park and stared at the mimes, jugglers, and one another. A promotional poster advised people to bring flowers, incense, and feathers.

The curious proceedings signaled the passing of the mantle of nonconformity from the beatniks to a younger generation. Coincidentally, *Time* magazine announced its "Man of the Year" a week before the Human Be-In. Instead of an individual, the award went to everyone twenty-five and under. About that same time, magazines and newspapers began focusing on the Bay Area's youth culture, notably its laid-back, long-haired hippies, who seemed content to loll around listening to music, making love, and getting high. CBS News sternly warned about the dangers of surrendering to the deadly influence of mind-altering drugs—"the hippie temptation," newsman Harry Reasoner called it.

Most of the stories about San Francisco's hippies carried photos of crowds of young people laughing, dancing, and smoking pot in the streets and parks. Those images had the same galvanizing effect as the 1848 announcement that gold had been discovered in California. For footloose young Americans, the City by the Bay became the destination of their dreams, a welcoming liberal bastion flush with a new type of "good herb"—*Cannabis sativa.*

A few months after the Human Be-In, a hundred thousand flower children descended on San Francisco as the city awoke to the Summer of Love, a storied season commonly portrayed as a time of peace, brotherhood, and rock 'n' roll. That iconic summer might have been remembered solely for its music and youthful optimism had it not been for the unmanageable horde of young thrill seekers that crowded into the Haight-Ashbury neighborhood, the insidious influx of heroin and speed, and a rising tide of serious crime. Love was in the air that summer, but so were greed, hatred, and revenge.

I

~May 1967~

Chapter One

Berkeley, California

People said that Jack and Bobby Doyle were as alike as...well, those two proverbial peas in that familiar old pod. Even their friends had trouble telling the twenty-two-year-old identical twins apart. The "Doyle boys" were both six feet four inches tall, with the well-toned physiques of Greco-Roman wrestlers, which was no coincidence, since they both excelled at the sport. They had piercing hazel eyes and thick chestnut hair, which any number of young ladies had either run their hands through or were dying to do.

Besides being good-looking and popular, Jack and Bobby were intimidatingly brainy. They were the sort of fellows that ordinary guys hated, while secretly wishing they could trade places with them. Conversations occasionally faltered when one of the twins walked into a room and flashed his dazzling smile.

When they were younger, the twins sometimes played tricks on the unsuspecting by switching identities, a ruse that occasionally fooled even their relatives at family gatherings in their Beverly Hills home. They never fooled their parents, of course, or anyone who truly knew them, for Jack and Bobby Doyle's similarity ended with their physical appearance. In terms of personality, they were as different as chalk and cheese, as the quaint British saying put it.

Jack Doyle—John Hardy Doyle, according to the name inscribed on the bachelor's degree he'd just been handed by the chancellor of the University of California, Berkeley—was the older of the twins by seventeen minutes. It was an inconsequential interval, but it seemed to set the pattern for the relationship between the two boys. Jack was always the one who took the lead, as in his frequent campaigns to support worthy causes. It had been Jack who'd decided to venture north to UC Berkeley rather than attend UCLA, which was only a few miles from their house. At Cal, he'd majored in political science, the first step toward his goal of attending law school. After that, he planned either to join his parents' Los Angeles law firm or dive into the shark-infested waters of politics. The sky was the limit for smart, handsome, ambitious Jack Doyle.

Bobby—Robert Lorenzo Doyle—had always been content to ease along in his brother's tailwind. He'd never felt the need to be the center of attention, to seek out honors, or run for every office that came along. And while he'd earned top marks in all of his classes, Bobby didn't really care if anyone knew how smart or accomplished he was. The fact that he was seldom beaten at chess and was a wizard on the classical guitar were private pleasures for him, not something to add to a list of accomplishments for others to admire.

When Jack first touted Berkeley, Bobby simply said sure, why not. He'd heard good things about the highbrow school in the liberal town just north of blue-collar Oakland. For his first two years, Bobby had taken random classes he found interesting. It wasn't until his advisor pointed out the need to declare a major that he'd settle on English, a choice prompted by his love of literature. He'd gradually moved in the direction of writing, which led to a stint on the *Daily Californian,* Berkeley's independent student-run newspaper. He and his fellow reporters covered every issue roiling the campus, from the Free Speech Movement to antiwar protests and draft counseling. He'd also connected with the East Bay music scene, writing about the local bands and making several friends in the process.

As Bobby strode to the podium to receive his diploma, he glanced out at the thousands of parents and relatives packed into Memorial Stadium, home of the Golden Bears. The outdoor setting was a relief from the cramped old auditorium in Wheeler Hall, the fifty-year-old building where Bobby had attended most of his English classes, alternately sweltering or freezing, depending on the season. The steely blue waters of the Bay glittered in the distance above the rim of the stadium. Even if Berkeley hadn't been one of the top schools in the country, the campus views alone would have been enough to warrant coming here.

Bobby even loved the fogs that shrouded the Bay, both the dense, drizzly clouds of winter and summer's billowy drifts, which often seemed thick enough to walk on. He'd always wondered why those famous summer fogs appeared so regularly. It turned out to be simple physics. When warm air rose inland, it created a low-pressure area that pulled cool, moisture-laden air from the Pacific through the Golden Gate, like giant lungs breathing in. The Bay really was a living organism, something you could study all your life.

Bobby had no chance of spotting his father and mother in the crowd. In a smaller setting, Donovan Duncan Doyle and Maria Ricci Doyle would have stood out. In their late forties, they could pass for thirty-five, a prototypical power couple with the smart wardrobes and polished mannerisms of top-tier attorneys. The two had met in law school at Stanford and married soon after graduation. Maria's father, a honcho at Columbia Pictures, had paved the way for their connection with the movie industry. Now, Donovan and Maria spent their time hammering out contracts between the studio and representatives of the stars. In the Doyle household, dinner conversations were often laced with references to "greedy bastards," "prima donnas," and "delusional fools"—attributes applied to agents and actors alike. By the time Jack and Bobby were in high school, Hollywood had lost much of its mystique.

After the members of the Class of '67 received their diplomas, everyone settled in for a half-hour of platitudes courtesy of acting University of California president Harry Wellman. Wellman had recently replaced the dynamic, popular Clark Kerr, a man too lenient with student protestors to suit the state's newly elected "gubnor," Ronald Reagan—the former actor whose very name tended to make Berkeley liberals turn blue in the face. One of Reagan's campaign promises had been to "clean up the mess at Berkeley," a school he regarded as a hotbed of "beatniks, radicals and filthy speech advocates."

The new graduates assumed a look of polite attention as Harry Wellman spoke about their admirable academic achievements and bright futures, although their thoughts were far away. The anxious young folks had their minds on job searches, returning home, avoiding the draft, or continuing their educations. They were also thinking about how they'd be celebrating in a few hours, after the obligatory photo sessions with family members were over. There'd definitely be an abnormal amount of drunkenness and fornication in the East Bay on this cool spring night.

The spectacle of his sons' graduation led Donovan Doyle to recall his own undergraduate years. The tall, handsome attorney had attended the University of San Francisco, a private Jesuit school where he was fondly known as "3D" by his friends, not only because of initials but also because he seemed to stand out from the crowd, just as his sons did now. USF didn't have the cachet of UC Berkeley, but as far as Donovan was concerned, it was on the proper side of the Bay. Donovan was a dedicated San Francisco enthusiast, had been ever since he was a kid growing up in nearby San Mateo. Donovan's connection with the city was forged by his Irish ancestor Hardy Doyle, who landed in San Francisco in 1849 after the discovery of gold on the American River at Sutter's Mill.

Donovan had studied the history of his beloved city at USF. He enjoyed reading about the heroes and rogues of the old days, men like Joshua Norton, an immigrant commodities trader and real estate speculator who made and lost a fortune during the years of the California Gold Rush. Norton not only lost his money, he apparently lost his senses as well. In 1859, he proclaimed himself Emperor of the United States. In 1863, he tacked on the title Protector of Mexico. San Franciscans winked and went along, and from then until his death in 1880, the zany Emperor Norton roamed the streets of San Francisco decked out in a plumed top hat and military uniform with fringed epaulets, issuing proclamations and handing out worthless promissory notes to pay for the free meals and drinks he cadged.

Then there was Sam Brannan, California's first millionaire. Brannan ran a general store in the Sierra foothills near Sutter's Mill. He was the one who trumpeted the news that set off the Gold Rush, and he made a fortune selling supplies to the resulting flood of prospectors. For the next two decades, Brannan lived the high life, gallivanting around San Francisco, opening banks and a flurry of companies, buying up huge chunks of land, and creating the Calistoga hot springs resort. But booze, a bad temper, and lawsuits did him in, and he died a pauper, buried in an unmarked grave. For Donovan Doyle, old Sam Brannan embodied the San Francisco spirit, a rakish attitude of make a million, spend a million—and have a grand time doing it.

One of the city's heroes Donovan remembered reading about was Jonathan Letterman, the Union Army surgeon who revolutionized battlefield casualty management during the Civil War, saving thousands of soldiers who might otherwise have died of their wounds. After the war, Major Letterman settled in San Francisco, where he practiced medicine and was elected city coroner. The army hospital at the Presidio was named in his honor. The Letterman Army Hospital treated tens of thousands of sick or wounded soldiers during the Spanish-American War and World War II. Even now, American boys injured in Vietnam were being treated there.

Donovan also recalled the tragic figure of Ishi, the last surviving member of California's indigenous Yana tribe. In 1911, Ishi wandered onto the grounds of a slaughterhouse near Oroville. The half-starved Indian had been living by himself for years in the surrounding foothills after all the other remaining members of his tribe perished. Anthropologists from UC Berkeley rescued Ishi and escorted him to the Hearst Museum of Anthropology in San Francisco, where he lived out his days in comfort, teaching museum staff about his vanished way of life—the last Stone Age man in America.

For Maria Doyle, this afternoon's ceremony evoked a different set of memories. The statuesque brunette with the Sophia Loren cheekbones and voluptuous lips was thinking of her sons' childhoods. Jack and Bobby's Irish-Italian heritage had blessed them with extended families of loving relatives who gushed over their every accomplishment. Their aunts and older female cousins never failed to pinch their cheeks and tell them what special little boys they were. Maria often thought about how proud her immigrant grandfather Lorenzo would have been to see his American great-grandsons, but the 1918 Spanish flu pandemic took care of that. Her parents, Frank and Gina Ricci, had made up for any lack of attention, showering the twins with presents and praise. It was a blessing that the boys emerged as sensible adults with their egos in check.

Maria reflected on how the different temperaments of her sons had played out at Berkeley. Jack had joined the ROTC, not a very popular organization given the school's polarized political environment. His decision may have been an extension of his Boy Scout days, when he advanced to the rank of Eagle and earned more merit badges than any other boy in his troop. Jack had joined Berkeley's debate team, and he'd captained the four straight-A students who appeared on TV's *College Bowl,* a squad that retired undefeated after five games. Jack had also won NCAA Division 1 All-American honors in wrestling. It was an impressive resume he'd put together, one that would no doubt help him on his seemingly inevitable march to the top.

Bobby, on the other hand, had seemed more interested in having a good time than buffing his credentials. He'd connected with clever individuals instead of networking with members of official campus organizations. Maria smiled to herself as she contemplated Bobby's scalawag personality. While Jack was busy organizing worthwhile projects as a boy, Bobby was usually involved in adolescent hijinks, such as the time he tried to sign up their neighbors in the "UFO Welcoming Committee," a group he started after reading about the flying saucer controversy in Roswell, New Mexico. That was Bobby through and through. Truth be known, though, Bobby had probably made more lasting friends at Berkeley than Jack had, even though Jack's associates were all destined for success.

"Thank God that's over," Donovan whispered in Maria's ear as Harry Wellman wound up his address with a rhetorical flourish. "Let's get a picture of Jack and Bobby in their caps and gowns, and then we can all take a break before we get together for dinner."

* * *

Ernie's was one of San Francisco's top restaurants, a satin-and-pearls eatery where the martini-swilling gent at the next table might be British playwright Noel Coward or the free-spending Maharaja of Baroda. Director Alfred Hitchcock kept a private stock of wine at Ernie's while he was in town filming his 1958 movie classic *Vertigo.* Hitchcock filmed scenes all over the city, from the Mission Dolores cemetery to the Legion of Honor museum in Lincoln Park, although he created a soundstage version of Ernie's plush red interior. That was where Kim Novak swanned through the crowded dining room as Jimmy Stewart ogled her from the bar.

The real-life restaurant was located downtown on Montgomery, a street named for Capt. John B. Montgomery, the officer who raised the Stars and Stripes over the village of Yerba Buena on July 9, 1846, staking America's claim to the fledgling port. Captain Montgomery would probably keel over if he could see his namesake street, with its swarm of pedestrians, honking autos, and ranks of sun-blocking skyscrapers. Since Montgomery's time, the city had spread westward across the seven-mile-wide peninsula, taking in a similar swath north to south—a rumpled patch of land with a diverse population of dreamers, schemers, and average Joes, Josés, and Jiangs. Locked in by water on three sides, the compact forty-nine-square-mile city had avoided the urban sprawl of Los Angeles.

Donovan and Maria Doyle's Yellow Cab navigated the heavy evening traffic and pulled up in front of Ernie's at 7:55 p.m. Donovan climbed out and offered his hand to Maria, who emerged into the soft spring night dressed in a severely elegant black-and-white Geoffrey Beene design. She looked more glamorous than some of the stars she dealt with at Columbia Pictures.

Inside the restaurant, the tuxedo-clad maître d' greeted the Doyles effusively. He wagged a finger at them. "It's been far too long since you paid us a visit."

"Hello, George," Donovan replied. "It's good to be back. The old place looks the same, thank heaven."

The maître d' waved to the head waiter. "Pierre, please show Mr. and Mrs. Doyle to their usual table."

"I'm sorry," Donovan told the waiter, "but first we've got to find our boys. They said they'd meet us here at eight on the dot."

"I think you'll find the two young gentlemen over at the bar." The waiter nodded in that direction.

As they walked past the bar on the way to their table, Donovan slipped up behind his sons and laid a hand on each of their shoulders. "Aha. Gotcha."

"Hey, Pop," Bobby said with a grin, brushing his long, dark hair out of his eyes. "Who's the good-looking chick you've got there?"

Maria Doyle snorted and poked her son in the chest. "I know what you're up to, buster. Trying to score some brownie points, huh?"

Bobby leaned over and kissed his mother on the cheek.

"And what about you, young fellow-me-lad?" Donovan said to Jack. "What have you got to say for yourself?"

"Evening, Dad, Mom. Thanks for inviting us. This place is something else. That's Orson Welles sitting over there, and we saw Mayor Shelley earlier."

Donovan glanced around the room. "Jack Shelley? Where? He's a fellow USF alum."

"He left just as we arrived," Jack said. Unlike his brother, Jack wore his hair short. He looked like one of the Kingston Trio, the clean-cut folksingers who got their start here in the city at the Purple Onion, the tiny Beat-era hangout in North Beach.

The waiter led the Doyles to their quiet corner table. Donovan ordered a bottle of champagne, and after it arrived, he proposed a toast. "To the two of you. You don't know how proud you've made your mother and me. And we want to hear all about your plans now that you've got those sheepskins tucked away."

The twins exchanged glances. "Why don't you go first," Jack said.

Bobby toyed with the silverware for a moment. "I'm thinking of pursuing my writing," he said. "You know that I've always dreamed of becoming a novelist, and I enjoyed working on the campus newspaper. I've made a few contacts here in the city. I'm hoping I can latch on with one of the smaller papers and work my way up. I'd like to write about the music scene. There's a lot going on around the Bay these days. It would be fun. I know there's not much money in journalism, but it would help me develop as a writer. Maybe someday I really could take on a novel, or even give screenwriting a try."

Maria laid her hand on Bobby's. "I think you'll make a terrific writer. You've always been good with words. I remember the poems you used to write in grade school. Some of them were amazing, especially for someone that age."

"Thanks, Mom." Bobby glanced at his father. "What about you, Pop? Do I have your blessing?"

"Good Lord yes, son. You'll only be successful if you do something you love, and we all know how much you love literature. I remember you read *Crime and Punishment* when you were just a kid. Heck, I could barely plow my way through that tome in college."

Donovan hesitated for a moment. "Of course, there's another factor at play. What about the draft?"

Bobby and Jack again exchanged glances.

"Yeah," Bobby said. "The bloody draft."

Maria tsk-tsked.

"Sorry, Mom, but just thinking about the draft gets me going."

Jack leaned forward with an intense look. "Like I keep telling you, you've been hanging out with too many campus radicals."

Bobby rolled his eyes. "Oh boy, here we go again."

"I might as well lay it all out right now," Jack snapped. "I don't care what the naysayers think about the war in Vietnam. As far as I'm concerned, if your country asks you to serve, then it's your duty to do it. That's why I enrolled in ROTC, and that's why I've applied for my army commission. I'm going on active duty next month."

Maria gasped. "Oh, Jackie. Please tell me you won't be going off to that awful war. What's the point of it all?"

Donovan took his wife's hand. "I'm sorry, dear, but if that's Jack's decision, then we should support him. I'm afraid I don't agree with this war either, but I'm certainly not going to try to talk anyone out of it if their conscience tells them they should go."

"Thanks, Dad," Jack said soberly. "Actually, there's no way of knowing if I'll be sent overseas. I could end up at an army base right here in the States."

Maria sighed. "At least that's something to hope for."

"That still leaves my question to Bobby about the draft," Donovan said. "Any notion of where you stand, son?"

"I've been thinking about enrolling in graduate school at USF. They've got strong writing and communications programs. I believe I could handle school while working as a stringer on one of the local papers, especially if I take the minimum course load for a full-time student. That would put off the draft for another year or two. Maybe this lousy war will be over by then. And don't look at me like that, Jack. Not everyone thinks that getting embroiled in a conflict in a miniscule country hardly anyone had ever heard of is vital to our national interests. Besides, I agree with what Muhammad Ali said—'I ain't got no quarrel with them Vietcong.'"

Jack started to say something, but Donovan headed him off, knowing a full-blown argument was in the offing. "If you're interested in writing for San Francisco papers, that fellow over there could give you some advice."

Donovan pointed toward the bar, where *San Francisco Chronicle* columnist Herb Caen had just taken a seat. Caen was a dapper man with a ready smile. He'd been the virtual spokesman for San Francisco ever since he started writing about the city in 1938, churning out daily columns filled with witty insights into goings-on around town. He could also be serious or scathingly critical when the subject called for it, but even his barbs revealed a concern for humanity. He roamed the city of seven hundred thousand by day and by night, gathering anecdotes like a fisherman hauling in his net, and no fish was too small to capture his interest. He wrote about everyone from bigwigs to bootblacks, visiting starlets to local harlots. And always, his love of the multifaceted, multicultural city—his Baghdad-by-the-Bay—shone through. "San Francisco, the gorgeous mess," he called it.

Donovan had read Caen's columns for years. He still subscribed to the *Chronicle,* along with the *Los Angeles Times,* the *Chicago Tribune,* and the *New*

York Times. Donovan had beamed with pride the first time Caen mentioned him in the *Chronicle.* He'd been in San Francisco to confer with Lloyd Bridges and his agent, and Caen had spotted them having lunch at the Old Clam House, the oldest restaurant in the city.

Donovan agreed with nearly everything Caen wrote, except for the man's campaign against calling the city "Frisco." Donovan had never understood the widespread distaste for the nickname among locals. For him, it called to mind the city's bawdy past, when ships from around the world docked along the Embarcadero and slumming gentry rubbed elbows with riffraff in the saloons and bordellos of the Barbary Coast. He could just imagine Dashiell Hammett's cynical shamus Sam Spade tossing out "Frisco" while roughing up a two-bit hood in a gin joint down in the Tenderloin or grilling a gum-chewing floozy in a greasy spoon where people ate with their elbows on the table. Caen could object to the nickname all he wanted, but what did it matter? He was from Sacramento, where the most colorful characters had always been the sleazy white-collar crooks in the state government.

"C'mon," Donovan said to Bobby. "I'll introduce you before we order dinner. It couldn't hurt to know the most famous journalist in San Francisco."

Donovan led the way over to the bar. The ever-alert Caen spotted the pair before they were halfway across the room. "If it isn't Mr. Tinseltown, himself," he said as they walked up. "Long time no see, Don. Your old stomping grounds not good enough anymore?"

Donovan shook the man's outstretched hand. "Hello, Herb. You're right. We don't get up here as often as we'd like." He laid a hand on Bobby's shoulder. "You remember Bobby. He and his brother Jack just graduated from Berkeley."

"Ah, good old Berserkly," Caen remarked with a mischievous twinkle. He swirled his drink and eyed Bobby. "Been in any exciting demonstrations lately?"

"Only to cover them for the *Daily Californian,* although I'm more interested in music than politics."

"Yeah, that's a lot safer. I'd stick with it if I were you."

"Bobby's considering going into journalism," Donovan said. "I thought maybe you could give him a few pointers."

Caen finished his drink and smacked the glass on the bar. "Rule Number One. Don't go into journalism unless you can't find a job on a fishing trawler. The pay's better on those boats, the scenery's gorgeous, you won't get mugged, and you'll never go hungry—unless you happen to hate seafood."

Caen glanced over at the Doyle's table. "I see you brought along the Mrs. If you're busy while you're in town, I'd be happy to squire her around. Show her the sights, you know." He eyed Maria like a lecherous Groucho Marx.

Donovan chuckled. "We're heading home in the morning. Besides, I'm not sure she'd be up to it. She still talks about the place you took us to the last time we got together."

"Hey, I thought that was a sedate nightclub. How was I to know the waitresses would be half naked?"

Caen fished a business card out of his pocket and handed it to Bobby. "If you're serious about this journalism thing, gimme a call. I'll show you around the office, introduce you to a few of my fellow ink-stained wretches."

II

~June 1967~

Chapter Two

Marin County, California

Eddie "The Rat" Ratner liked what he saw. The crowd gathered for the two-day Fantasy Fair and Magic Mountain Music Festival on Mount Tamalpais was ripe for the plucking. To the Rat, the tens of thousands of mellowed-out rock fans, nature lovers, face painters, and kite fliers were just a bunch of chumps looking to get high and get laid. He could accommodate their first wish. He had enough merchandise in his beat-up canvas shoulder bag to get the entire 49ers football team stoned—pot and acid for the candy-asses and coke, speed, and horse for the hardcore.

The slump-shouldered dope dealer with the orange fright-wig hairdo and high-heeled Beatle boots could always spot a prospective mark. He simply looked for anyone with darting eyes, like a drunk searching for his next shot of rotgut. If a pusher couldn't make a good living here in the Bay Area, the Rat said to himself, he ought to consider another line of work. The man's pointy face puckered into an obscene smile, revealing his prominent yellow teeth. He looked like he could gnaw his way through a tin can, just like a voracious rodent.

Eddie Ratner definitely made a good living at his trade, although you couldn't tell it by his appearance. From the condition of his navy surplus bell-bottom dungarees, anyone might think he'd spent the night sleeping in an alley. Despite the wads of cash the Rat had stashed away in his fleabag Haight-Ashbury apartment, he constantly worried about keeping his customers. The competition was tough. The last guy who tried to push the Rat aside ended up in a ditch on a lonely stretch of road in the Santa Cruz Mountains south of San Francisco. The hulking Hells Angel the Rat hired to help him take care of the problem had cut off the interloper's right hand before he tossed his body. Some sort of message, the Rat supposed, or maybe the biker just liked cutting off body parts.

Yeah, the Rat knew how to protect what was his. As he said to the fellow who asked him if he minded his unflattering nickname, "Rats are survivors, baby. Rats and alligators. When humans finally wipe themselves off the face of the planet, the rats and the alligators will still be here. If I was from Louisiana, I'd wanna be called Gator."

* * *

Raul Pitman was far from his usual beat. A reporter for the *Berkeley Barb,* the East Bay's two-year-old underground newspaper, Pitman normally wrote about heavyweight subjects that appealed to the emerging counter-culture—antiwar marches, civil rights demonstrations, Free Speech rallies, and the like. His crusading newspaper was filled with psychedelic art, nudity, profanity, and antiestablishment cartoons. The staff delighted in outraging the straights, and they did it with insightful aplomb. Their mission was simple. They wanted to change the world, and if you didn't agree with them, get out of the way.

Pitman was an authentic intellectual, with the requisite Van Dyke beard, black beret, and black leather sport coat. He was so cool you could almost get a chill standing next to him. He'd decided to cover the fair and music festival after hearing about the stellar lineup of bands. They included a long list of Bay Area groups, headlined by Jefferson Airplane, Country Joe & the Fish, and the Steve Miller Blues Band. Several groups from Los Angeles had made the trek north, including the Byrds, Canned Heat, the Grass Roots, and the Doors. The festival was sponsored by San Francisco's KFRC radio station, and at two dollars a head, the admission was a bargain, with all the proceeds going to a local child care center.

Pitman had a feeling the gathering would be something special—the first big outdoor rock festival—and he wanted to be part of history. Getting here, however, had been an adventure. After driving from Berkeley across the Bay Bridge, traversing the busy streets of San Francisco, and crossing the Golden Gate Bridge to Marin County, he then had to abandon his car and take a yellow school bus up Mount Tamalpais. A fleet of buses had been chartered to haul musicians and fairgoers up the narrow scenic road leading to the Cushing Amphitheatre, an open-air performance space high on the 2,500-foot-high mountain's southern slope.

The trip was turning out to be well worth it. As Pitman looked around, he saw couples strolling through tawny sunlit meadows set off by the intense greens of the surrounding woods. Youngsters and grownups swayed in tree swings and slid down a grassy hillside on sheets of cardboard. Long-haired, bearded artisans from nearby Sausalito were selling handmade rugs, pottery, jewelry, and other craft items. Food stalls were doing a brisk business. A giant inflatable Buddha and a geodesic dome light chamber provided touches of the offbeat. The overall atmosphere was that of a happy, peaceful Renaissance fair.

The organizers of the festival were lucky to have such a beautiful day. The fair was originally scheduled for the previous weekend but had to be put off because of bad weather. That was the Bay Area—sunny and warm one minute and foggy and chilly the next. The region really only had two seasons—winter and summer. The cool, rainy winters lasted roughly from November to March, with April through October being warmer and drier. The cold California Current that flowed offshore usually kept San Francisco below seventy degrees even in summer.

To add to the uncertainty, the weather in different locations around the Bay could vary wildly on any given day, thanks to the region's diverse topography. Even within San Francisco, it could feel like winter in one part of town and summer in another on the same afternoon. Today, the glittering waters of the Bay and the Pacific Ocean vied with the cloudless sky for the purest shades of blue. The clear air bore the fresh, spicy scents of oaks, firs, and madrones. Raul Pitman had lived in the area for five years since moving here from the somnolent Midwest, but he'd seldom experienced a finer day. And there was music and pot to boot.

* * *

Sonny Anders was pissed. He was supposed to be chaperoning the Charlatans, and now the boozy, druggy gang of renegades had disappeared again. This wasn't going to get Anders in tight with his boss, Bill Graham. The impresario of San Francisco's Fillmore Auditorium, Graham was the city's biggest rock promoter and agent. A man known for his tantrums, Graham was liable to toss Anders from a stage—just as he'd once done to the Charlatans when they failed to show up on time for a benefit concert. One of the Bay Area's first psychedelic cult bands, the Charlatans had plenty of talent, but their unpredictable streak was making it harder and harder for them to land gigs. Anders had tried to motivate the band, but they seemed bent on self-destruction. If they don't show up before long, Anders said to himself, they could go to hell as far as he was concerned.

Anders chewed on the ends of his droopy mustache, a sure sign he was agitated. A lanky man with unruly blond hair, he had plans for making it big in the music business, and he had no patience with anyone who held him back. He was one of the earliest to recognize what was happening in the San Francisco music scene. Bands that had once performed for modest crowds in the city's clubs were being elevated to national prominence. Jerry Garcia and his gang of rowdies had helped build their fan base with free jam sessions in Haight-Ashbury. Now, the Grateful Dead, Jefferson Airplane, Big Brother & the Holding Company, and other local bands were being courted by major record labels. Serious money was being tossed around, and Sonny Anders intended to grab his share.

* * *

Bobby Doyle worked his way through the amphitheater's crowded seating area until he was as close to the stage as he could get. He looked up at the intimidating figure of Bob "The Bear" Hite, lead singer of Canned Heat, the L.A. blues group that took its name from a song by early blues great Tommy Johnson. "Canned heat" referred to Sterno, which desperate alcoholics guzzled when they couldn't lay their hands on anything better. The hulking, bearded Hite was belting out the Robert Johnson–Elmore James classic "Dust My Broom," one of the songs the group had just recorded for their debut album. Driven by Henry Vestine on lead guitar, the song rolled along like a runaway freight train. With a backdrop of trees and psychedelic banners, the setting was like nothing anyone had seen before. A rock show amid nature, a new combination.

Bobby tried to scribble a few notes, but after being constantly jostled by the dancing, flailing, head-bobbing crowd, he gave up and decided to enjoy the show and trust his memory when he got back home to write up his account. This was his first outing as a stringer for the *San Francisco Chronicle,* thanks to his visit to Herb Caen's office in the newspaper's venerable gray building on the corner of Fifth and Mission Streets. The columnist had kindly introduced him to Ralph J. Gleason, the *Chronicle*'s music critic. When Gleason learned that Bobby wanted to write about music, he grilled him on his knowledge of every genre from classical to jazz. Bobby must have passed the test, because he came away with a promise that Gleason would take a look at his writing. It was Gleason who suggested that he cover the Marin County festival, so here he was.

After Canned Heat rumbled through a few more blues classics, a procession of other acts followed. Pop singer Dionne Warwick wowed the crowd with her stylish, compelling vocals, although her songs seemed at odds with most of the rock numbers. Eventually, the Doors, another Los Angeles group, took the stage. The Doors had released their self-titled debut album in January, and the LP took off when "Light My Fire" was released as a single. Despite having a hit song, this was the group's first large live show.

Besides "Light My Fire," the Doors performed "Break On Through" and other songs from their album. Bobby was impressed by the band, except for Jim Morrison staggering around the stage like a drunkard. During instrumental breaks, Morrison kept writhing and carrying on to keep the focus on himself. The handsome lead singer gave the impression of being a self-infatuated exhibitionist, someone who stared at himself in the mirror to perfect his bad-boy glower. But you had to give the guy credit. He could put on a memorable performance, even though he was only a so-so singer in Bobby's opinion.

Bobby was exhausted by the time the last of over a dozen groups finished its set. As he made his way toward the parking lot to hop on one of the school buses for the trip back down the mountain, he spotted Raul Pitman up ahead. Bobby had often crossed paths with Pitman when they were both student reporters at UC Berkeley, and he liked the fellow, theatrical getup and all. He knew that beneath the hipster exterior was a friendly, down-to-earth guy who grew up on a Kansas wheat farm. He also knew that Pitman's first name was actually Paul. He'd started calling himself Raul after he arrived at Berkeley, grew a beard, and bought himself a beret.

Bobby caught up with Pitman and grabbed the sleeve of his leather coat. "Hey man, where're you headed in such a hurry? Off to someplace immensely important as usual?"

Pitman high-fived him and flashed a sheepish grin. "You always manage to poke a hole in my image, Doyle," Pitman replied. "I may have to start smoking a pipe to add to my aura. To answer your question, I'm on my way back home to write up the show. How about you?"

"Same thing, although I'm living in San Francisco now. I'm stringing for the *Chronicle,* and I've enrolled in grad school at USF."

"Bravo on both counts. Nice way to hone your writing chops and thumb your nose at Uncle Sam. Lucky for me, I'm 4-F. Weak eyes." He adjusted his rimless glasses and pretended to be feeling his way along.

The two acquaintances continued toward the parking lot, discussing the various performances they'd witnessed. After they'd clambered onto one of the buses and found their seats, Bobby asked if Pitman was coming back for the second day of the festival.

"You bet, man. Jefferson Airplane, Steve Miller, the Byrds, the Grass Roots. Wouldn't want to miss that lineup."

* * *

Jefferson Airplane had already reached cruising altitude by the time the band walked onto the stage on Mount Tamalpais. Their first album, *Jefferson Airplane Takes Off,* had debuted the previous August, but Signe Anderson, their female singer, quit the band shortly afterward to stay home with her new baby. Marty Balin, the band's mastermind, recruited singer Grace Slick as her replacement. Slick brought a new energy to the band, which was on full display when she performed "Somebody to Love" and "White Rabbit," two of the songs that had made the group's second album, *Surrealistic Pillow,* a hit, lifting Jefferson Airplane to international acclaim. "White Rabbit," written by Slick, epitomized the drug-fueled essence of psychedelic rock.

The popular Bay Area band Country Joe & the Fish added notes of strangeness and whimsy to the show before Steve Miller, backed by his old pal Boz Scaggs, shook up the audience with the pulsating "Mercury Blues." The sets by the Byrds and the Grass Roots demonstrated the wide spectrum that rock encompassed, from the Byrds' mind-bending "Eight Miles High," with its jangly Jim McGuinn guitar solos on his twelve-string Rickenbacker, to the Grass Roots' recent hit "Let's Live for Today," a poignant love song that fit the uncertain times. None of the groups imparted greater joy than the 5th Dimension. Their buoyant new song "Up, Up and Away" lifted the crowd along with it. Even the puffy newsboy caps the gorgeous Marilyn McCoo and Florence LaRue both wore added a lighthearted note.

Late in the day, Jefferson Airplane returned for a second set. While they were performing their mellow folk-rock ballad "Today," Bobby noticed a pretty girl dancing by herself off to one side of the amphitheater. Sunlight illuminated the girl's long russet hair and the garland of yellow flowers she wore. The girl spun slowly in time with the music, waving a filmy shawl over her head. Her diaphanous dress floated around her as she moved. She looked like a woodland nymph. It was the most indelible image Bobby would take away from the festival.

A couple of the things that Bobby didn't see would have soured his day. In the staging area behind the amphitheater, Sonny Anders vented his frustration on the hopped-up members of the Charlatans, while in a shadowy, out of the way spot in the woods, the skulking Eddie Ratner plied his trade. With today's crowd, the Rat's hottest sellers were tabs of acid and nickel bags of weed. The sunshine kids at the festival weren't into the hard stuff, to the Rat's disappointment, since he made a greater profit on the coke and heroin he could cut with baking soda or laundry detergent. Most marks didn't know the difference, unless they were dead-enders who failed to get their usual buzz. In that case, the Rat simply blamed the bad dope on his suppliers. "Hey, what can you do?" he would say with a weaselly smile.

Bobby had no time for dope peddlers. It wasn't that he was a prude, but when it came to getting high, he usually stuck with a couple of cold bottles of Dos Equis or a shot or two of pungent Barbancourt rum. He had smoked pot on occasion, and he'd even tried LSD, although he didn't like the experience. He didn't think it was worth surrendering control over his mind just to see blurry colored lights or people's faces melting. And reading about kids on acid leaping to their deaths from buildings because they thought they could fly didn't enhance the drug's appeal. No, what he hated were the scumbags who ruined people's lives with hard drugs.

After the last notes of the day's final song echoed away over the hillsides, one of the festival organizers made an announcement over the PA system. "We'd like to thank all of you for coming out to share in this beautiful event. Bless you, and have a safe trip home. As you make your way down to the parking lot, we ask that you deposit your trash in the receptacles around the grounds. We want to leave this place as pristine as we found it. Peace and love." Surprisingly, the festival-goers did put their trash in the bins, making this not only the first outdoor rock music festival in history but also the tidiest.

Bobby Doyle tried to order his thoughts as he shuffled down the hillside. The two-day barrage of music made it difficult to summarize the festival, although to his mind, the most lasting impression was the sheer variety of musical styles. There was psychedelic intensity of Jefferson Airplane and the straight-ahead rock of the Grass Roots, the foot-stomping blues of Canned Heat and the lilting pop sounds of Dionne Warwick and the 5th Dimension.

He'd have to sharpen his pencil to capture it all in his piece for the *Chronicle.* He was beginning to glimpse how different—and subjective—this new role of music journalist was going to be compared to the unglamorous news reporting he'd done for the *Daily Californian.* It was definitely a challenge, one he was sure he'd enjoy.

Another part of the story was the variety of people who'd attended. Bobby had seen mothers with babies and guys in loincloths, uniformed cops nodding to the music and blissed-out flower children blowing soap bubbles. There were slick Berkeley hipsters like Raul Pitman and scruffy, sandal-wearing artists from San Francisco and Marin. Nowhere among them was there the slightest display of animosity. The festival had been an enchanted island of goodwill. There was a spirit of sharing, of being surrounded by friendly souls who all cared about the same things. Even the rock stars mingled with the crowd, enjoying the show as much as anyone. The fair's organizers had expected twenty thousand people, but probably twice that many showed up.

Bobby thought of the russet-haired girl he'd seen dancing by herself. "The Girl on the Hill," he decided to call her, as if he were naming a painting. He pictured the jubilant, ingenuous smile on the girl's face as she swirled about in the brilliant sunshine. He hoped she'd be able to retain that unaffected joy for as long as possible.

Chapter Three

Saigon, South Vietnam

Jack Doyle could still recall his mother's sharp intake of breath when he told her the news over the telephone. He was going to Vietnam, he'd said. His mother's usual banter had abruptly stopped. "No, Jackie, no," she'd mumbled. She hadn't spoken another word, but he could hear her racking sobs in the background, even though she must have held the receiver to her breast to muffle the sounds. The next voice he'd heard was his father's. When Jack repeated the news about Vietnam, adding that he'd volunteered to serve in the war zone, Donovan Doyle had gone silent for what seemed like minutes. Finally, his dad had told him that they loved him and they'd be praying for his safety. "Don't do anything foolish," were the last words his father said to him.

And now, the vast Pacific Ocean stretched between Jack and his parents, between everything he'd ever known—his home, his brother, his friends. As the chartered Pan Am 707 he'd boarded in San Francisco taxied toward the terminal building at Saigon's Tan Son Nhut Air Base, Jack knew that many people would already regard him as a fool for volunteering to head off to war. That didn't bother him. President Johnson was calling for young people to step up and serve their country, and Jack felt an obligation to do just that. He'd watched the crowds of antiwar protesters at Berkeley and wondered why they seemed to hate their own government. He'd also endured the catcalls of students opposed to the ROTC program on campus.

They had their opinions and he had his. In the end, the only person he had to answer to was himself, and he was confident that he'd made the right decisions about the direction of his life.

Jack heard the rush of air as one of the stewardesses unlocked the 707's forward hatch. Heaving himself out of his seat, he started toward the front of the plane. Among the hundred and eighty army men on board, the highest-ranking officers he'd seen were majors, denoted by the gold oak leaves on their collars. Captains wore two silver bars, first lieutenants a single silver bar, and lowly second lieutenants like himself a single gold bar. The officers and soldiers impressed him as a worthy cross-section of America—men from every part of the country who'd answered the call of duty. A sense of pride welled up in him as he noted their clear eyes and upright bearing. These were men he was proud to be associated with.

Over the past two years, Tan Son Nhut Air Base had become one of the busiest airports in the world thanks to the buildup of troops called for by Gen. William Westmoreland, the commander of U.S. forces in the war zone. Nearly five-hundred thousand Americans were now serving in South Vietnam. The nation of sixteen million had been created in 1954 when the Geneva Accords divided Vietnam into two countries at the end of the war against the French. Westmoreland's plan was to overwhelm the North Vietnamese Army and Vietcong guerrillas with superior numbers and firepower. The military spokesmen who briefed the civilian press on the war's progress frequently cited a ten-to-one ratio of enemy casualties to those of allied troops. It seemed just a matter of time before the communists were routed.

The pretty blond Pan Am stewardess standing by the exit smiled warmly at every passenger getting off the plane, whether they were crusty veterans or bubblegum-chewing teenagers. Jack returned the stewardess's smile and thanked her when she told him she hoped he'd have a good tour of duty. He had no idea that the woman's heart was breaking. She wondered how many of the soldiers walking down the boarding ramp would be returning home on a different kind of flight—aboard one of the frequent military transports filled with flag-draped coffins. For the manufacturers of U.S. flags, these were boom times.

Jack stepped onto the ramp's platform, instantly recoiling from the blast of heat and humidity outside. It was only midmorning, but the summer climate was ferocious. The air reeked of jet fuel and hot asphalt, along with a strange mix of tropical odors—the thick, heavy scents of flowers and prolific vegetation, of rotting garbage and frying food, all overlaid with exhaust fumes from the jeeps and trucks buzzing about. The smells were so intense that Jack could taste them. Overhead, the thump of helicopter rotors vied with the tortured screams of jet engines. The tropical sunshine pressed down on Jack's head like a weight. In seconds, he was sweating through his khaki uniform.

Outside the terminal, groups of small brown men in faded clothing squatted in the shade, smoking and talking in their singsong tonal language. The Vietnamese workers sized up the deplaning Americans as if they were experts at judging men. Some of the workers smiled and nodded, obviously pleased by what they saw, another batch of brave Yankee boys come to save their country from Ho Chi Minh's communist marauders.

A fleet of green military buses waited to haul the new arrivals to their various billets. Some of the buses were bound for hotels in Cholon, the Chinese quarter of Saigon. Others departed for the Long Binh army post northeast of the city. Jack's bus was headed downtown, where he'd be staying overnight at the Rex Hotel before shipping out to his assigned unit the next day. Jack settled onto a seat beside a young second lieutenant as their bus chugged away from the airport. His seatmate smiled weakly and scratched the wire screen over the open window. "That's comforting. Must be to keep someone from tossing a grenade inside."

Traffic on the highway was a free-for-all. Brightly decorated civilian buses and drab green military transports honked constantly as they contested for the right of way. Clusters of dirty stucco buildings with tin or mottled terra cotta roofs clung to the board-flat terrain. Many of them appeared to be on the verge of collapse. There were glimpses of emerald paddy fields in the distance. Sunlight glinted off the water flooding the young rice plants. Gray-barked palm trees grew in profusion, their drooping fronds stirring lazily in the breeze. Jack spotted a peasant woman in a dusty brown side road. She was shuffling along with a heavy load balanced at opposite ends of a long wooden pole over her shoulder. The sight of her *non la,* the conical palm-leaf hat symbolic of Vietnam, drove home the fact that he was in a foreign land.

As soon as the bus entered the city, it slowed to a crawl. Hundreds of motorbikes clogged every street. Aggressive riders gunned their engines and shot through tiny gaps, weaving along with the skill of circus performers. Some of the motorbikes carried entire families, the husbands driving while their wives rode sidesaddle behind them holding an infant or sharing the seat with a toddler. The shops along the streets had colorful signs over their doors, all of them inscribed with the mystifying squiggles of Vietnamese writing. The buildings were linked by the most confused tangle of overhead wires Jack had ever seen. Workmen stood atop rickety bamboo scaffolding erected alongside buildings under repair. Random stacks of bricks and other materials were piled on the sidewalks. Fruit and vegetable vendors occupied almost every street corner. Their constant babble sounded like a flock of songbirds.

Things became more orderly the farther into the city they drove. The confusing jumble gave way to wider streets and taller buildings, a legacy of the French colonialists who'd spent nearly a century extracting the riches of their Indochinese empire, a domain that included Vietnam, Laos, and Cambodia. The French had lined Saigon's boulevards with plane trees, constructed shady parks and comfortable villas. By the time they were sent packing by the communist Vietminh, their customs, cuisine, and language had permeated Vietnamese society. Just beyond Jack's window was a reminder of that cultural influence—the twin-spired Notre Dame Cathedral, a symbol of the Catholic faith embraced by more than a million and a half South Vietnamese, most of whom had relocated from the north when the country was divided. Although a minority in the predominantly Buddhist nation, the better educated, more prosperous Catholics dominated South Vietnam's government, military, and professions.

Other nearby buildings were newer. There was the clunky concrete box of the U.S. Embassy currently under construction, and the grandiose layer-cake of the Presidential Palace, where a democratically elected head of state would reside following the elections coming up in September. In its early years, South Vietnam had been led by the brutal, corrupt Ngo Dinh Diem, along with his callous, edict-issuing sister-in-law Madame Nhu, the infamous "Dragon Lady." A parade of military strongmen ruled following Diem's assassination in 1963, most of them holding power for a matter of weeks or months before the U.S. successfully nudged the country toward democracy.

Here in central Saigon, the streets were filled with well-dressed pedestrians. The ones that held Jack's attention were the slender black-haired beauties in their traditional *ao dais*—long-sleeved, ankle-length silk tunics slit to the waist on both sides and worn over silk trousers. The loose front and back panels of the tunics floated seductively as the women walked along. Most of the women carried parasols to shield themselves from the fierce Asian sun. Schoolgirls wore all-white ao dais, while adults favored pastels or vivid colors. Jack decided that the ao dai had to be the most alluring garment he'd ever seen, even though it covered every inch of a woman's body but her head, hands, and feet.

The young women were small, averaging around five feet tall and a hundred pounds. With their immobile faces and bright lipstick, they resembled dainty porcelain dolls. Jack's impression of the men he saw was mixed. They too were small in stature, and while the older men seemed friendly enough, most of the young men looked tough, with wiry physiques and grim expressions. They had the determined appearance of people under siege, which the South Vietnamese had been since the partitioning of their country. The threat of the military draft was ever-present, although the draft fell hardest on the poor. The sons of wealthy families usually managed to avoid the fighting.

The airport bus stopped in front of the Rex Hotel, now an American BOQ. The hotel was also the site of the daily press updates, the notorious "Five O'Clock Follies," a derisive term hung on the briefings by skeptical journalists. The Rex sat on the corner of Le Loi Avenue and Nguyen Hue

Street, adjacent to the ornate city hall and overlooking Lam Son Square, the aesthetic heart of Saigon. The scenic square was named for the birthplace of fifteenth-century Vietnamese hero Le Loi, the emperor who drove Chinese invaders from the country in 1428.

Two other landmarks overlooked the square, the Saigon Opera House, currently occupied by the Vietnamese National Assembly, and the Continental Hotel, where British author Graham Greene wrote his 1955 novel *The Quiet American,* a story set in the waning days of the French colonial reign. For decades, the Continental's street-level terrace bar had been a gathering spot for foreigners, who sipped their gin and tonics while gazing out at the parade of humanity with the possessive air of conquerors.

Jack and the two dozen other passengers filed off the bus. On the way into the hotel, they passed a soldier in combat gear standing behind a concrete barricade. After commandeering hotels all over the city, U.S. military authorities quickly learned that they'd need to protect them. In December 1964, a Vietcong bomb exploded in the Brinks Hotel, killing two Americans and injuring fifty-eight others. A year later, another terrorist bomb exploded outside the Metropole Hotel, killing eight people and injuring a hundred and thirty-seven. That same month, terrorists gunned down a prominent Saigon editor in front of his home. Popular restaurants and the original U.S. Embassy had been bombed. The attacks sent a resounding message that no one in South Vietnam was safe, not even in the nation's capital.

After stowing their gear temporarily in the lobby, Jack and the other officers were directed to a second-floor meeting room for an introductory briefing. The officers all jumped to attention when a suntanned colonel in starched green fatigues entered the room.

"At ease, gentlemen," the colonel rasped in a cigarette-and-whiskey voice. "Have a seat. We're pretty informal here."

The man sat on the edge of the desk at the front of the room. "My name's Colonel Sullivan. I'd like to welcome you all to the Republic of Vietnam. You gentlemen are arriving at a critical moment. General Westmoreland has stated that this year we'll take the fight to our enemies in a major way. We have the manpower and the weapons to do it, and with the help of officers such as yourselves, we're going to bring this war to a timely and successful conclusion."

The colonel got up and stood beside a map of South Vietnam showing the country's four military regions, from I Corps in the north below the Demilitarized Zone to IV Corps in the south, which stretched all the way to the tip of the Mekong Delta. "Since you gentlemen are all members of the 4th Infantry Division, you'll be flying out tomorrow to this garden spot." Using a wooden pointer, he tapped a region in the Central Highlands. "Pleiku Province in II Corps. You'll be serving there under Maj. Gen. William Peers. General Peers has been running Operation Francis Marion since April and doing a fine job.

"The division's operational goal is to patrol the border with Cambodia to prevent the North Vietnamese Army from infiltrating the Central Highlands from the Ho Chi Minh Trail. I won't kid you. The action has been heating up lately, especially in the last month. Our troops up there can use all the help they can get. I know they'll be glad to see you."

Jack looked at the young second lieutenant to his right, the same fellow he'd shared a seat with on the bus. Both of them raised their eyebrows at the colonel's description of where they'd be going. It sounded like they were being tossed into the fray.

"You've all received orders to your different units, and you have a good idea of what your duties will be, so I don't have much more to go over. And I don't have to tell you that the 4th Infantry has a long and honorable history, having fought in both World Wars. I'm sure that every one of you will do your duty and make your country proud.

"Now, you have the rest of the day to yourselves. I suggest you organize your gear first. You've already been issued your field uniforms, and you'll be assigned weapons, helmets, and flak jackets when you check into your individual units. If you're interested, you can take in a few of the sights here in town, since it'll be awhile before any of you get back to Saigon on R&R. I'd recommend that you stick to the cultural sights. The central market is just down the street, and the zoo and botanical gardens are worth seeing."

The colonel laid down his pointer and smiled at the men. "One final word of advice. If you happen to find yourself on Tu Do Street, you need to be very careful. The bars down there are filled with drugs, drunken enlisted men, and cute Vietnamese girls. The army officially encourages its men to be friendly with South Vietnamese civilians, but as far as those bar girls are concerned, I'd recommend that you steer clear. They've got more kinds of VD in this city than Uncle Ho has whiskers."

When Colonel Sullivan started toward the door, the officers again stood to attention. Sullivan paused and looked over the room. "Good luck, gentlemen. And may God watch over you."

Jack turned to his seatmate as the meeting broke up. "You interested in scouting things out around here?"

"Sure. Let's check into our quarters first and then meet in the lobby. By the way, my name's Vince Tate." He held out his hand.

"Jack Doyle. I'm from California. How about you?"

"Oklahoma."

"Say, a lot of folks from Oklahoma migrated to California back in the Dust Bowl days. Some of your relatives might even know some of mine."

"I don't think so. My dad's a history professor at OU. We moved to Norman when I was fifteen. I actually grew up in Delaware."

"Then you'll have to tell me about the East Coast. I've never been out of California before now."

* * *

Jack and Vince stood in front of the Rex trying to decide which way to go. A steady stream of cars, taxis, and motorbikes whizzed past them on Le Loi Avenue. "What say we visit the central market," Jack suggested. "Like the colonel said, that ought to be a good introduction to the local culture."

Vince nodded okay and turned to the guard next to the hotel entrance. "What's the best way to get to the central market?"

The guard pointed to a gray Chevy Suburban sitting in front of the hotel. "Hop in that shuttle and tell the driver where to let you out."

Five minutes later, Jack and Vince climbed out of the Suburban in front of the Ben Thanh Market, a sprawling ocher building with a central clock tower. Inside, the young officers wandered among rows of stalls selling everything from fresh seafood, fruit, and vegetables to electronics, clothing, and handicrafts. Vietnamese women hunkered beside their offerings, holding up various articles for inspection and laughing when Jack and Vince shook their heads. Often, they had no idea what the women were selling, such as the knobby, football-size jackfruit one woman held out to them. The women wore the informal daily work costume called an *ao ba ba,* a long-sleeved blouse and loose-fitting trousers. Some of the vendors' teeth were stained red from chewing betel nut, an addictive stimulant.

The men passed food stalls where roasted ducks dangled by their long, skinny necks. In a seating area, people were eating steaming, aromatic bowls of *pho,* the Vietnamese noodle soup found on menus throughout the country. Others were eating *banh mi,* sandwiches served on crispy French bread, one of the city's many popular street foods. Jack felt his stomach growling from the sights and smells.

"Here's some nice stuff," Vince said as they passed displays of Rolex watches, Nikon cameras, and French cognac.

"A few Vietnamese must have money," Jack commented.

The two new arrivals hadn't yet learned that U.S. military personnel stationed in the city routinely bought those expensive items on the cheap at the local PXs, selling them on to black marketeers at a considerable profit. The Vietnamese were also adept at pilfering American warehouses. Most of the foreign merchandise sold on the streets had been stolen—just as millions in American foreign aid ended up in the bank accounts of government officials.

Vince stopped in front of a row of garish paintings rendered on black velvet, mostly roaring tigers and coy young Vietnamese beauties. "Better get a couple of those for your quarters, Jack."

"Think I'll pass."

When they'd had their fill of the mayhem inside the busy marketplace, they went back outside to wait for a shuttle heading in the direction of their hotel. They had to cross to the other side of the street, weaving through the heavy traffic—a steady swarm of motorbikes, small cream-and-blue Renault taxis, and the clattering, fume-spouting, motorcycle-powered conveyances called cyclos. Most of the cyclo drivers drove like maniacs.

Vince pointed to the graceful old bicycle-powered pedicabs rolling by at a stately pace. "Those things are pretty neat." Two bashful schoolgirls riding in one of the pedicabs looked at them and tittered.

"As long as you're not in a hurry."

Back at the Rex, they decided to explore Lam Son Square on foot. Circling the square, they passed the Caravelle Hotel, where many of the foreign correspondents stayed. Between the square's central fountain and the Opera House, Jack and Vince stopped to gaze at two giant statues of Vietnamese marines in combat pose. "Looks like the dude in back is hiding behind the other guy," Vince quipped. "Smart fellow."

In the Eden Centre, a commercial and residential building across Tu Do Street from the Continental Hotel, the two men stopped for a cup of coffee in the Givral Café, another hangout of novelist Graham Greene. The young officers sipped their coffee and watched the traffic whizzing around the square. "This place would be a great tourist attraction if it weren't for the war," Jack said.

Vince gave him a look a surprise. "You mean there's a war?"

After dinner in the Rex Hotel's cafeteria, Jack and Vince made their way up to the rooftop bar, one of the favorite watering holes of the Saigon press corps. They watched the sun set in a fiery display while sipping a couple of the local "33" beers, called Ba Muoi Ba in Vietnamese. Lights slowly winked on as the city prepared for another long, sultry tropical night.

A tipsy correspondent with the Associated Press wandered by their table. He wore a jaunty tan safari jacket, like a great white hunter in Africa. The journalist's aviator-style eyeglasses sat askew on his pudgy face. He looked down at Jack and Vince's crisp, spotless uniforms. "Let me guess," he said with a goofy grin. "First day in-country."

"You got it," Vince replied.

"Mind if I join you?" the man asked.

Vince indicated a chair. "Have a seat."

The journalist settled in and eyed the two junior officers. "So what do you young bucks want to know about this godforsaken town? I've been here for over a year, so I know a thing or two about Sin City. You interested in a little female companionship? Just toddle on down Tu Do Street toward the river and take your pick—anything you can imagine. They start out at around fourteen. Rue Catinat, the French used to call the street, and it was every bit as debauched back then."

"I'm afraid we don't have time for that," Jack said. "We're flying out first thing in the morning to our field units. Besides, I'm not sure I feel like adding to the corruption of those young women. It's a shame they have to support themselves like that."

"Ha. You will feel like it, my friend, you will. It won't be long before you're grabbing any kind of fun you can find, once you get a taste of this stinking war. Why do you think those grunts on three-day passes are down there on Tu Do at all hours of the day and night? Getting plastered, smoking dope, screwing their brains out. It's called desperation, my friend. The grunts are desperate, the girls are desperate. Hell, everyone around here gets that way sooner or later. Those girls will sleep with you for the price of a chicken dinner—that's how desperate they are."

Jack shook his head at the man's coarse banter.

* * *

The big camo green C-130 Hercules flew low over the Central Highlands, a twenty-thousand-square-mile plateau region nestled in the Truong Son Mountain Range, the rugged spine of Vietnam. Along South Vietnam's western border with Laos and Cambodia, some of the peaks reached seven thousand feet. Frequent fog, low-lying clouds, and the thick jungle canopy provided cover for North Vietnamese Army convoys of men and supplies traveling south on the Ho Chi Minh Trail. The NVA had even dug underground hospitals and support facilities along the trail. In spite of intense American bombing, the trucks kept rolling.

Long the home of isolated tribes of Montagnards, the Central Highlands region was known for its tea and coffee plantations under the French. Now, it was a hotly contested war zone. In November 1965, three hundred Americans died in the first major engagement between U.S. forces and the NVA, a fierce days-long battle that took place in Pleiku Province's Ia Drang Valley. For the better part of the past year, the men of the 4th Infantry Division had been trying to secure Pleiku and Kontum Provinces from the elusive enemy troops that attacked from sanctuaries in neighboring Cambodia. It had proven a demanding and costly chore. In the last month alone, the division had lost dozens of men in skirmishes with the NVA.

Jack Doyle stared out the cargo hatch at the rear of the C-130, an opening large enough to accommodate vehicles and huge pallets of supplies. The screaming of the transport's four powerful Allison turboprops made conversation impossible for the men strapped into seats around the sides of the cargo bay. Several hundred feet below, the rumpled terrain of the highlands came into clearer view as the plane descended toward the landing strip at Camp Enari, the 4th Infantry Division's headquarters outside Pleiku City, the capital of Pleiku Province. The army installation lay close to Route 19, the main road to the coastal supply depot at Qui Nhon. The camp spread across a patchy brown plain near Dragon Mountain. With its rows of barracks, administration buildings, and other prefab structures, Enari resembled a mining camp from America's Old West days.

The lumbering plane dipped its nose toward the runway. C-130s like this one hauled troops and supplies throughout the country, often at the risk of being hit by enemy ground fire. Jack sighed with relief as the plane touched down and shuddered to a halt. When the loadmaster gave them the okay, the men trudged down the rear cargo ramp, their gear slung over their shoulders. Outside, they got their first glimpse of another mission handled by C-130s. Litters with wounded soldiers filled several trucks parked near the landing strip. The wounded men would be loaded onto the plane for the return flight to Saigon, where they'd receive more extensive medical treatment.

Jack stared at the faces of the wounded, with their bloody bandages and pained expressions. Most of them were no older than he was. Some were still teenagers, not yet old enough to vote but old enough to fight and die in their country's wars.

That night, Jack wrote his first letter home to his brother. His message was brief: "Arrived safely. Interesting place. Tell Mom and Dad not to worry. More later."

Chapter Four

Monterey, California

The song always threw Bobby slightly off balance. "I Feel Like I'm Fixin' to Die Rag"—an irreverent antiwar anthem written by Country Joe McDonald—had become a hit at a time of growing opposition to the fighting in Vietnam. Just two months earlier, massive peace demonstrations were held in San Francisco, New York, and other cities. Country Joe's satirical lyrics expressed the insanity of the war for all those who opposed it, but for anyone who had sons or brothers involved in that far-off conflict, the words could be sobering. As Bobby listened to the song, he prayed that his mother never heard the line "Be the first one on your block to have your boy come home in a box."

The crowd gathered at the Monterey County Fairgrounds certainly reveled in the song. They were singing along with the chorus—"And it's one, two, three. What are we fighting for? Don't ask me, I don't give a damn. Next stop is Vietnam." Country Joe & the Fish was one of more than thirty groups appearing at the first ever Monterey International Pop Festival, a three-day musical extravaganza taking place in the scenic seaside town of Monterey, a hundred miles south of San Francisco. Coming only a week after the Fantasy Fair and Magic Mountain Music Festival in Marin County, Monterey Pop was bigger, longer, and louder. "Music, Love and Flowers" was the motto, and there was plenty of each on display, with Bobby Doyle in the middle of it all on his second assignment for the *Chronicle.*

The festival was the brainchild of a group headed by John Phillips of the Mamas & the Papas and record executive Lou Adler. The planners were hoping Monterey Pop would solidify popular music as a legitimate genre, and they'd produced a slick, professional show toward that end. The sound system dwarfed that of the Magic Mountain Festival, and the lighting system was state of the art. As in Marin County, the musicians were performing for free, with the nominal admission fees going to charity.

A month before the festival, Phillips and Adler released a new song Phillips had written. Sung by Scott McKenzie, "San Francisco (Be Sure to Wear Flowers in Your Hair)" quickly became an international hit. Besides promoting Monterey Pop, the song reinforced San Francisco's image as one of the hippest places to be. Its refrain of "People in motion" described the current youth pilgrimage to the city. That little phrase was as evocative as the title of Jack Kerouac's counterculture novel *On the Road,* a story that lured thousands of free spirits to San Francisco ten years earlier.

Bobby marveled at the size of the crowd on this cool Saturday afternoon, the second day of the festival. There had to be tens of thousands of people milling around the fairgrounds. Most of them carried the free orchids that were handed out—a hundred thousand blossoms had been flown in from Hawaii. People came with backpacks, blankets, and babies, and they wore every combination of street clothes, beatnik regalia, and psychedelic garb. There were even folks dressed up like Wild West cowboys, as well as Indians—the American kind and the Asian kind.

The festival had kicked off on Friday night with eclectic performances by the Association, Lou Rawls, Johnny Rivers, Simon & Garfunkel, and Eric Burdon & the Animals. The members of the Association looked like frat brothers in their suits and ties, while Paul Simon and Art Garfunkel came across as pure folkies, with their turtlenecks and choirboy harmonies. Eric Burdon's grab-bag psychedelic costume made him look like he'd borrowed random pieces of clothing from friends in a last-minute attempt at hipness, but he charmed the crowd with the mellow "San Franciscan Nights."

So far today, they'd heard Canned Heat, Big Brother & the Holding Company, and Country Joe & the Fish. Next up was the Paul Butterfield

Blues Band. Their polished set included the lively "Born in Chicago" and the mournful "Driftin' Blues." They were followed by Quicksilver Messenger Service, a San Francisco group known for its bluesy psychedelic shows in the city's Fillmore Auditorium and Avalon Ballroom. Their stomping rendition of Bo Diddley's "Who Do You Love?"—a shortened take on their half-hour jam session version—was a guitar tour de force.

The music kept flowing when Steve Miller's band revved up Miller's own "Living in the U.S.A.," a catchy tribute to personal freedom in a contentious age. The festival's combination of pop, folk, blues, rock, and protest music was as potent as the clouds of marijuana smoke that filled the air. Bobby must have heard people in the audience use the word "groovy" at least a hundred times.

* * *

Between performances, Bobby wandered the grounds soaking up the atmosphere. The Beatles' new *Sgt. Pepper's Lonely Hearts Club Band* album seemed to be playing continually over the PA system. Inside the exhibition hall where guitar makers displayed their wares, Bobby bumped into his pal from the *Berkeley Barb,* Raul Pitman. After the two compared notes, Bobby headed back outside to grab a snack in one of the many food stalls.

Suddenly, he stopped in his tracks. He couldn't believe what he saw—there was "The Girl on the Hill," the ethereal beauty he'd seen dancing by herself last week at the Marin County music festival. She was sitting on a park bench up ahead, near a giant figure of Buddha. Bobby could only see the girl's profile, but he recognized her deep russet hair and the way she held her head. She had an air of curiosity about her, as if the world was a miraculous flower opening its petals for her inspection. He worked his way over to where she sat and tapped her on the shoulder. She looked up at him, shielding her eyes from the sun with one hand.

"Hello," Bobby said. "We haven't met, but I saw you dancing by yourself last week on Mount Tamalpais. You reminded me of a woodland nymph, with that garland of yellow flowers you were wearing."

"Is that right? I thought I was Tinker Bell. I was totally tripped out on acid. I must have made a proper spectacle of myself."

"I didn't think so. You seemed to be entranced by the music. I remember the song was 'Today,' by Jefferson Airplane."

"That's more than I remember."

Bobby sat down beside her. "My name's Bobby Doyle, by the way."

"Hello, Mr. Bobby Doyle. Do you make a habit of ogling dancing girls?"

"It's one of my favorite pastimes. May I ask your name?"

"You may, although I may not give it to you. My mother told me never to speak to strange men."

"I'm not all that strange. Well, maybe a little, but we're in California."

The girl laughed, a warm, throaty sound. "Lynette Simms."

Bobby looked down at the sketch pad the girl held in her lap. There was a charcoal sketch of Steve Miller. "Say, that's nicely done. So you're an artist?"

"Aspiring."

"I love the way you captured that puckish grin. His personality really comes through."

The girl eyed him suspiciously. "Are you messing with me?"

"Heck no. That's a terrific likeness. Got any others?"

Lynette flipped the drawing over to reveal a sketch of Paul Butterfield playing his harmonica. Bobby could almost hear the music. "May I?" he asked, lifting the sketch pad from the girl's lap and flipping through it. There were drawings of Country Joe McDonald and Bob Hite, each of them rendered in telling detail that caught the personalities of the performers.

"Say, I'd like to buy these," he said. "They'd look great in my apartment."

Lynette took her drawings back and flipped to a blank page. "Sorry. No can do. Got to save them for my portfolio."

* * *

Bobby was eager to hear more music by the time the Saturday evening performances rolled around. They kicked off with Moby Grape, a freewheeling San Francisco band whose self-titled debut album had released days before. The Byrds followed with their usual masterful show. Besides the lyrical "Renaissance Fair" and other of their own compositions, the group performed traditional folk and blues numbers. They finished with "So You Want to Be a Rock 'n' Roll Star," a song from their recent album *Younger Than Yesterday* that poked fun at manufactured bands like the Monkees.

Jefferson Airplane all but stole the show with "Somebody to Love" and "White Rabbit." Grace Slick's powerful mezzo-soprano meshed with the voices of former folksingers Marty Balin and Paul Kantner, producing a rich tapestry of sound. Slick looked like she'd dropped in from outer space in her high priestess robe. The group put on a show worthy of a band riding the crest of fame, sparking a standing ovation and pleas for an encore.

Otis Redding and Booker T. & the MGs closed out the evening with a blast of soul music that made it hard for Bobby Doyle to settle down and go to sleep that night. The joint was definitely jumpin'. And there was another day to go.

* * *

Sunday dawned gray and drizzly, but by noon the rain had stopped. The only musician scheduled for the afternoon was Indian sitar virtuoso Ravi Shankar, a suave international star known for his classical repertoire. Shankar took the stage at around two o'clock and commenced a rapturous performance that lasted over three hours. His scintillating playing was matched by the incredible skills of Alla Rakha on tabla, a pair of small Indian hand drums. Shankar and Rakha's masterful raga improvisations held the audience spellbound, including several awe-struck rock guitarists. At the end of the bravura presentation, the crowd cheered the musicians for five minutes.

The evening's lineup included Big Brother & the Holding Company, Buffalo Springfield, the Grateful Dead, and the Mamas & the Papas—a remarkable finale to a historic weekend. If this was the future of rock, Bobby thought, it was going to be good. After a desultory performance by Greenwich Village's Blues Project, Big Brother & the Holding Company took charge with their signature song, Big Mama Thornton's "Ball and Chain." Lead singer Janis Joplin scorched the crowd's eardrums with her impassioned interpretation of the blues number—nearly six minutes of tortured wailing. She took the stage as a Texas nobody and left as one of the memorable personalities of the festival.

Buffalo Springfield put on one of the best shows of the weekend, even without the mercurial Neil Young, who'd quit the band a few weeks earlier. The recent Stephen Stills hit "For What It's Worth" summed up the angst of the times, when young protestors risked being arrested. The mellow pop feel of "Sit Down I Think I Love You" and the lush harmonies of "Out of My Mind" displayed the band's versatility.

Buffalo Springfield's polished sounds gave way to the pyrotechnics of a relatively unknown group from England called the Who. With Pete Townshend on lead guitar, Roger Daltrey on vocals, John Entwistle on bass, and Keith Moon on drums, the band set out to stir up trouble, like a gang of street toughs. They tore through Eddie Cochran's "Summertime Blues" before spitting out their rebellious "My Generation." At the end of the song, Townshend went berserk, smashing his guitar on the stage as a stunned audience looked on and the stage crew ran for cover.

The Grateful Dead restored a bit of sanity following the Who. At their best when jamming in live performances, the eminent San Francisco group soon had the audience dancing to the sounds of "Viola Lee Blues." The Dead emanated a feeling of mellow good times. Their set turned out to be the calm before another storm, one provided by a second relatively unknown group from England—the Jimi Hendrix Experience. With his British bandmates, the Seattle-born Hendrix sashayed onstage in a yellow ruffled shirt, tight red pants, and a fancy embroidered vest. His music was just as bold. He played his guitar with abandon, coaxing impossible sounds from the instrument as he sang his original compositions "Foxy Lady," "The Wind Cries Mary," and "Purple Haze." Going Pete Townshend one better, Hendrix lit his guitar on fire at the end of his set.

After the shock waves of the Who and Jimi Hendrix, the night's final group was as soothing as a warm bath. The Mamas & the Papas closed out the festival with their perfect harmonies on "California Dreamin'" and "Monday, Monday." Bobby was intrigued by the gorgeous Michelle Phillips. She was alluring in her harem girl outfit, but then she'd look great in a gunny sack. Scott McKenzie joined the group for the last two numbers, "San Francisco (Be Sure to Wear Flowers in Your Hair)" and "Dancing in the Street," songs that summed up the festival's theme of "Music, Love and Flowers."

* * *

As the show wrapped up, Bobby reflected on what he'd witnessed over the past three days, some of the finest live music he'd ever heard. Jefferson Airplane, the Byrds, and Buffalo Springfield were his favorites. Jimi Hendrix was a revelation—as long as he skipped the lighter fluid and stuck to setting his guitar on fire with his virtuoso playing. Big Brother & the Holding Company rocked as hard as any of the groups, although Bobby didn't much care for Janis Joplin's histrionics. She nearly screamed herself out of her shoes at times. A little of her overwrought shrieking went a long way. When she wasn't caterwauling, she had an interesting singing voice, with a raspy edge to it like the voices of the old-time blues singers she admired.

Most of the performers had projected a professional stage presence, except for a few irksome antics. Bobby was appalled by Pete Townshend wantonly destroying his guitar. That wasn't showmanship. It was a cheap trick for the easily impressed. Townshend deserved a swift kick in the butt for smashing his Fender Stratocaster, even if it was an electric instrument, which Bobby regarded as an inferior subset of guitars. To his ear, the rich, woody sound of an old-fashioned acoustic guitar was unbeatable.

One of Bobby's reservations about electric guitars was that too many musicians who played them lived on the treble strings, firing off machine-gun volleys of high-pitched notes to flaunt their chops. Bobby preferred guitarists who employed the entire fretboard, especially those who emphasized melody over pyrotechnics—artists like Paul Simon and George Harrison. Those were guys who could play the guitar the way it was meant to be played. Harrison's languid, understated melody on "And I Love Her," from *A Hard Day's Night,* was musical poetry.

Bobby himself only played acoustic guitars. He'd started with a hundred-dollar Yamaha classical he got for Christmas when he was twelve. In high school, he saved the money he earned from part-time jobs and bought a used Ramirez, one of the finest modern classical instruments. He still remembered the first time he accidentally scratched his Ramirez. He felt like having the entire instrument refinished. He was haunted over having damaged an object of such beauty. Acoustic guitars were alive. They were precious, fragile creations that needed to be protected, like other living things.

He pictured Pete Townshend repeatedly banging his Fender Strat on the stage until it broke apart. If that had been an acoustic guitar, Bobby might have stormed the stage and wrenched it out of his hands. Townshend was a talented guy. Why did he feel the need to cap his performance with a boorish act of hooliganism? Maybe it was supposed to be a nihilistic statement that nothing mattered. But some things did matter. Some things mattered a lot. Bobby tried to imagine Andres Segovia, Carlos Montoya, or Charlie Byrd intentionally damaging their guitars. It was a preposterous thought.

* * *

Bobby joined the slow-moving crowd wending its way toward the parking area. Up ahead, he noticed Lynette Simms standing near the main entrance with her drawing pad under her arm. She was studying the people as they passed by.

"Lost someone?" Bobby asked when he came abreast of the girl.

She gave him a worried look. "My ride back to San Francisco seems to have disappeared."

Bobby hesitated only for a moment. "If you don't think I'm being forward, I'd be glad to give you a lift. I'm headed back to the city myself."

Lynette glanced around nervously.

"I promise I'll deliver you safe and sound. I haven't abducted anyone in several weeks."

"All right then. It's very kind of you. Unfortunately, the girl I rode out here with isn't always the most reliable person. She probably forgot I even came with her."

"Well, you can count on me. I was named Mr. Reliable in my high school yearbook."

"Yeah, I'll bet."

Bobby grinned and reached for her drawing pad. "Here, let me help you with that." He led the way to where his black Triumph TR4 was parked. "Want me to put the top down?"

"Sure, that'd be fun. I've never ridden in a sports car before."

"Then hop in."

Bobby lowered the top and stashed Lynette's drawing materials on the small rear seat. Firing up the jaunty roadster, he pulled into the line of cars inching out of the parking lot. Most of them were headed for Highway 1, which connected with 101, normally the fastest route back to the city at just over two hours.

"So, tell me about yourself," Bobby said once they were humming along 101. "Obviously, you're interested in art...and dancing."

Lynette shook her head. "Please don't remind me of my spaced-out exhibition."

"Sorry. I won't mention it again. Let's start with where you're from."

"The quaint town of Plymouth, Wisconsin—in the land of cows, milk, cheese, and freezing winters."

"I thought you looked like a wholesome farm girl."

"Actually, I grew up in town. My parents run the local hardware store. After a couple of years in school down in Madison, I decided I'd learn more about life by living it instead of studying it in college. I had a former classmate who'd moved to San Francisco, but two months after I joined her, she went back home to Wisconsin. Sort of left me high and dry. I managed to get a job at a clothing boutique, although it barely pays the bills."

"Sounds like you could use a friend."

Lynette smiled at him, the gentlest, most soothing smile Bobby had ever seen. “Now tell me your story.”

“I’m from L.A. originally. I have a twin brother, Jack, and our parents are both attorneys. They work in the film industry. Jack and I both graduated from Berkeley last month. He’s serving in Vietnam. I’m doing a little freelance writing for the *Chronicle,* and I’ve enrolled in a master’s program at the University of San Francisco.”

“My, my. You make me feel like a bumpkin.”

“Hey, never sell yourself short. I’ve seen your sketches. You’ve got real talent. You just need to channel it. Maybe you could go into commercial art. If I ever land a job at the *Chronicle,* I could put in a good word for you.”

Lynette gave him another of her endearing smiles. “Did you major in psychology?”

* * *

Bobby drove down busy Haight Street, the main east-west thoroughfare in the Haight-Ashbury neighborhood. Between Golden Gate Park on the west and Buena Vista Park on the east, Haight Street was lined with café’s, bars, stores, and businesses of all kinds. Ashbury Street intersected Haight roughly midway between the two parks.

Located in the central part of the city, Haight-Ashbury had escaped the devastating fire that followed the Great Earthquake of 1906. Known for being quiet and affordable, the neighborhood attracted artists, writers, and musicians in the late 1950s and early ’60s. They moved into the district’s quaint Victorian row houses, put out their pots of geraniums and begonias, and went about communing with their muses.

Haight Street was busier than Bobby had ever seen it. Packs of young people hung around on the corners and drifted in and out the shops and cafés. People in motion, as the song said. Bobby shook his head. “Boy, this area is hopping.”

“I know. I can hardly walk down the street anymore it’s so crowded. It seems like a lot of kids besides me are looking for their pot of gold in this town.”

Following Lynette's directions, Bobby pulled up in front of a three-story Queen Anne–style row house on Shrader Street, south of the Panhandle, the long, narrow strip of parkland extending east from Golden Gate Park. Japanese spirea bushes lined the front of the tidy white apartment building. The bushes were aflame with pink blossoms. "This is it," Lynette said. "Home sweet home."

Bobby gave the building an appraising glance. "Looks like a nice place to live. This is just a few blocks south of the University of San Francisco campus, where I'll be going to school this fall. I believe the Grateful Dead live together somewhere near here."

"They're over on Ashbury Street. If you stand outside their house, you can listen to them practice." Lynette retrieved her drawing materials from the rear seat. "Thanks for the ride. You really came to my rescue. I don't know how I'd have gotten home otherwise."

"I'm sure you'd have managed. You could have gone to the emergency services people for help, or held up a sign asking for a ride. You strike me as a pretty resourceful person."

"You think so? To be honest, I sometimes feel totally lost out here."

Bobby stared at her thoughtfully. "Um, then maybe I could introduce you to some of the sights. You're living in one of the most interesting cities in the world, so you should get to know it."

Lynette was silent for a moment. "That would be lovely, if it's not too much trouble. I mean, I don't want to put you to any bother."

"No bother at all. I enjoy showing folks around San Francisco. We could visit the De Young Museum. They've got some terrific paintings and artifacts. I'm sure you'd enjoy it."

Lynette's eyes grew big, as if she'd been offered a diamond pendant.

"It'll have to wait a few days," Bobby said. "I've got to write up my story on the festival while it's still fresh in my mind. How about next Saturday?"

"Okay."

"I'll pick you up here at twelve o'clock. We can have lunch and then spend the afternoon poking around the museum. If we get tired of high culture, we can stroll through the Japanese Tea Garden."

"That sounds wonderful." She gave Bobby a hesitant smile before she got out. "See you next Saturday, then."

As the girl climbed the steps of her apartment building, she didn't notice the slump-shouldered, orange-haired dope dealer in the high-heeled boots lurking on the corner, but Eddie Ratner noticed her. What a hot young thing, he said to himself. A future customer? Maybe something more. He stared at her like a hungry rat contemplating a tempting morsel. He had a camera hanging around his neck, but it was getting too dark to take pictures. He'd come back when the light was better and snap a few frames of the chick on the sly.

Chapter Five

Oakland

Jimmy D. had about had it with his hometown. Oakland used to be a great place to make a buck peddling dope. Plenty of action for everyone, and nobody horning in on his little patch of Uptown turf. Now the kids of all those black bastards who'd moved here to work in the shipyards and canneries during World War II were getting pushy. Those two punks Huey Newton and Bobby Seale were stirring up black people with the crazy notion that they had the same rights as white folks. Black Panthers they called themselves, but Oakland's cops were taking care of them. Even the Mexes were getting to be a problem, strutting around with their long greasy hair and cruisin' the streets in those damn lowrider cars of theirs. They seemed to think that just because they'd been in California longer than the rest of us they had some claim to it—but hey, we stole this place from 'em fair and square.

One thing Jimmy still loved about Oakland was the Raiders. Those were some cool cats in their silver and black uniforms with the one-eyed pirate on their helmets. Daryle "The Mad Bomber" Lamonica tossing passes all over the field, Freddie Biletnikoff catching 'em, and big Ben Davidson on defense. Davidson was one mean hombre. Yeah, the Raiders were all right, and they looked to be on top of the heap this season. They represented Oakland to a T—tough as nails and in your face. That writer Jack London had lived here, too, and he was a pretty tough dude himself, going off up north to the Yukon to look for gold. They'd named part of the Oakland waterfront after the guy.

Only trouble was, there were too many tough dudes around today. Jimmy had to deal with hard-ass black pushers and trigger-happy Mex pushers constantly, and he didn't dare set foot in Chinatown or Koreatown. Those crazy mothers would just as soon slice him into little pieces as look at him. Chop him up and put him in one of their nasty dishes. Jimmy D.'s family didn't like foreigners of any kind. Jimmy's old man complained that the lazy bastards kept taking all the good jobs, working long hours for low pay and making white folks look bad.

Maybe it was time to search for greener pastures, Jimmy said to himself. Lately, he'd been eyeing the drug market over in San Francisco. Dumbass college kids were descending on the Haight-Asbury district like a bunch of damn locusts, and they loved their pot and their LSD. Jimmy scratched his patchy beard. It was almost nine o'clock in the evening. Time to get up. The near-sighted drug dealer with the Tom Jones mullet crawled out of bed and reached for his smudged John Lennon granny glasses. After a quick shower, he pulled on his Raiders T-shirt and baggy green cargo pants with the big side pockets. Stuffing his usual assortment of drugs into his pockets, he headed out the door of his studio apartment. The suckers down on Broadway would be getting antsy by this time of night.

Jimmy whistled a ragged tune as he bopped along Telegraph Avenue. He usually came this way to check out what was showing at the Fox Theater. He'd seen *The Dirty Dozen* last week. A lot of good old ass kickin'. That Lee Marvin was bad. A real Marine, decorated in World War II and all. He could scare the crap out of you just with that deep voice of his. Jimmy stopped and stared at the movie poster outside the theater. Hmm. *You Only Live Twice.* Sean Connery. Jimmy could dig a James Bond flick. Always plenty of broads. On the poster, Bond seemed to be surrounded by Asian chicks. Jimmy didn't much care for slants, but, hey, tits is tits. He walked past the ticket booth and stopped in front of the Coming Soon display. There was a poster for a movie called *Cool Hand Luke.* Paul Newman was standing in a field with a shovel in his hand. Must be some lame story about farmers,

Jimmy speculated. He'd miss that one.

Jimmy turned up 19th Street and headed over to Broadway, where he worked the bars and cafés every night. Yeah, maybe it was time for him to look for new opportunities across the Bay, he thought, even though he'd always hated San Francisco. Hell, that place wouldn't have amounted to nothin' without Oakland. Half the damn town was built with lumber from our oak trees, and yet the snooty bastards over in Frisco were always looking down on us. A fellow once told him that some famous bitch named Gertrude Stein had said "there's no *there* there" in Oakland, but what did she know about it, friggin' Jew. His town had plenty going for it. History, for one thing. This is where the Central Pacific Railroad ended, baby—right here in Oakland, not in San Francisco. Anyone who wanted to reach Frisco had to take a ferry. And Oakland's port was way busier than Frisco's. What did those losers across the water have to brag about? Rice-A-Roni? It was high time for those stuck-up smart-asses to start giving us a little respect. They could begin by giving some to one particular Oakland boy.

* * *

What the hell kind of place was this Haight-Ashbury, Jimmy D. wondered. He felt like Alice in Wonderland, as if he'd fallen down a rabbit hole and ended up in a strange country filled with oddball characters. Looking around him, he saw scruffy kids huddled everywhere. They leaned against buildings and parked cars. Groups of them sat right in the middle of the sidewalk like Indians around a campfire, blocking pedestrian traffic. Some of the kids were strumming guitars, while others were drawing things on the sidewalks with colored chalk—flowers, peace symbols, and swirly abstract designs. Jimmy had never seen so much paisley in his life. These wimps didn't look like people in motion. They looked like people going nowhere.

Half of the kids had joints hanging from their mouths, and a few of them were holding out tin cups to the straights passing by. Mostly, the straights just glanced at them with disgust, but occasionally someone dropped a coin or two in their cups. Older women tended to cling to their husbands' arms as they walked past, alarmed by the invasion of young weirdos. White-bread tourists drove by with bewildered expressions. The kids in the backseats were pointing and laughing. Some of the tourists were snapping photos of the hippies to show their relatives back home, like taking pictures of monkeys at the zoo.

The scene reminded Jimmy of the illustrations in his school textbooks about the 1930s, when everyone was broke and roaming the streets looking for work or a handout. Many of the losers here had the same bedraggled appearance. Their scruffy jeans and dirty dresses looked like they'd been slept in for days. How could the bigwigs in San Francisco walk around with their noses in the air with this stuff going on? We sure as hell don't have this mess over in Oakland, Jimmy said to himself. Oh well, he thought, these punks looked like swell customers for someone in his line of work.

Jimmy continued down Haight Street, gazing at the interesting old buildings, which the incoming hordes of hippies were turning into crash pads where people slept on the floors. Earlier, Jimmy had wandered through Panhandle Park, the northern boundary of Haight-Ashbury. Every afternoon in the park, local activists handed out free meals to young folks who'd come to San Francisco with no means of support other than an occasional remittance from mom and dad. Most of those hungry kids had come to the city in search of peace and love, and many of them wore flowers in their hair. Besides being fed for free, they could stop by the Haight's free health clinic for a shot of antibiotics whenever they got a dose of the wrong strain of love.

At 1535 Haight Street, Jimmy stopped in front of the Psychedelic Shop, the city's first head shop. Jimmy knew the brothers who'd opened the store, a couple of dudes from Oakland just like him. The front of the shop was painted bright red and yellow. The windows were plastered with psychedelic posters. Inside, Jimmy high-fived Jeb Tolin, an outgoing twentysomething with a Fu Manchu mustache and a red bandanna tied around his head.

"Hey man," Tolin said, "what brings you to our humble enterprise. Things gettin' boring over on Broadway?"

Jimmy D. grinned. "More like hot than boring." He looked around at the store's collection of clothing, jewelry, records, books, and magazines—all geared to pot-loving hipsters. He went over to a display of bongs and picked one up. "How's business?"

"We can't keep up with it. Me and Buddy are rakin' it in, man. Rakin' it in."

Jimmy set the bong down. "That good, huh?" He walked back to the counter where Tolin stood. He gave his friend a wink. "You know, I'm thinking about relocating myself."

"That right?"

"Yeah."

Tolin gave him a shrewd look. "Exactly where were you thinking of setting up shop?"

Jimmy nodded toward the busy street. "Why not right here in Haight-Ashbury? With all those potential customers, you folks should have room for another pharmaceutical entrepreneur."

Tolin wrinkled up his nose. "I'm not sure that'd be such a great idea, Jimmy. You see, a guy named Eddie Ratner has about got the trade sewed up in this part of the Haight."

"Eddie Ratner? What's he like?"

"He's peculiar looking. Little slump-shouldered dude with spiky orange hair. Wears them Beatle boots to make himself look taller. Everybody calls him the Rat."

"Sounds like a punk to me."

"Uh, I don't know. Word is, he's got some muscle working for him. There's talk that those two may have made a local pusher named Frost disappear."

"Yeah? Well I can hire some muscle myself." Jimmy stared out the window at the passing crowd. "You can't tell me there ain't enough business here to go around." He glanced at Tolin. "Where's this Ratner hang out?"

"He makes his office at the Pall Mall Lounge, a restaurant just down the street, across from Tracy's Donuts."

"Then maybe I oughta pay Mr. Ratner a visit. Size him up, you know."

* * *

Jimmy D. sauntered into the Pall Mall Lounge, a greasy spoon with a chintzy feel—scuffed hardwood floors, fake wood paneling, and a Formica-topped bar with six stools. The overhead lights barely illuminated the place. The room felt like the dim recesses of an old steamer trunk. There were a few scattered café tables and a line of booths along one wall, mostly occupied by local businessmen, office workers, and sales people on their lunch break. The most popular item on the menu was a huge hamburger dubbed the Love Burger. The redhead behind the counter looked like she'd dispensed a fair amount of love in her time.

Jimmy took a seat at the counter. "What'll it be, hon?" the redhead asked, her pencil poised over her green order pad.

"Whatcha recommend?"

"Ya can't go wrong with a good hunk of beef on a bun," the woman said with a wink.

"Then that's what I'll have."

After Jimmy polished off the best hamburger he'd ever eaten, he looked around the room. "Say, ain't that Eddie Ratner at that back table?" he asked the redhead.

"Sure is. Sometimes I feel like takin' a broom and chuckin' him out when it gets crowded. He seems to think that because this establishment is called a lounge he can spend all day lounging around here." The woman shrugged. "But he pays me fifty bucks a month for the privilege of sittin' over there."

While they were talking, Jimmy watched a young dude take a seat at Ratner's table and hand him some bills. Ratner counted the money and nodded, then he reached into his shoulder bag and pulled out a white envelope, which he shoved across the table. Jimmy recognized a drug deal when he saw one. Apparently, this fellow Ratner could just sit there in comfort and conduct his business. Nice work if you could get it, and Jimmy D. intended to get some of it. This punk looked like a clown with that ridiculous orange hair. He belonged in the circus, juggling colored balls and wearing those big floppy shoes that clowns wore.

After the Rat's mark left, Jimmy walked over and took his seat. "So you're Eddie Ratner, huh?" Jimmy said this with a contemptuous curl of the lip. "I hear they call you the Rat, but you don't look like no Rat to me. You look like a little mouse. Yeah, Mickey Mouse. Well, Mickey, there's a new cat in town. And you know what cats do. They eat mice. So better make room for some competition, Mickey, cause this cat's gonna be eatin' your cheese from now on."

Ratner smiled, showing his prominent yellow teeth. "Is that right?"

Jimmy D. reached across the table and poked him in the chest. "Damn straight, Mickey."

The Rat kept smiling. "We'll see about that, pussy cat. We'll see about that."

As Ratner gazed at Jimmy D., he was thinking of a mountainous Hells Angel with no neck, a shaved head, and a prodigious mustache that would have made Joseph Stalin envious. Olaf Svenson was the biker's name. He was a man with a fondness for performing improvised surgeries with a Ka-Bar knife. The Rat called him Olaf the Butcher, although never to his face.

* * *

Jimmy D. found himself a livable walk-up apartment on Masonic Avenue, not far from his new hangout, the Drogstore Café, an eatery on Haight Street where he could keep an eye on the foot traffic and recruit customers. The rent was higher in San Francisco than in Oakland, but he stood to make enough extra dough in Haight-Ashbury to cover his living expenses. He felt good about his new setup, so good that he'd treated himself to a new set of duds at In Gear, a Haight Street clothing store dealing in snazzy outfits. Jimmy had picked out a fringed suede jacket and black porkpie hat. If he was going to be dealing with hipsters, he needed to blend in. He didn't want to look like some Oakland roughneck.

After admiring himself in the bathroom mirror, Jimmy headed out the door. He hadn't gone half a block down Masonic before he ran headlong into a giant baldheaded biker dressed all in black leather. The Hells Angel stood with his massive arms crossed over his chest.

"Good evening, friend," he said in a guttural purr.

Jimmy nodded and tried to step around the biker, but the man laid a dinner plate–size hand on his shoulder and squeezed hard. "Now that's not very neighborly. Here I say 'good evening' and all you do is nod and try to walk away. What's the world coming to when people are so rude that they can't exchange civil greetings?"

"Sorry," Jimmy gasped, wincing from the man's powerful grip. "I guess I was in a hurry."

"That's all right, friend. How about I give you a lift since you're in a hurry?" With that, the biker opened the back door of a red and white '59 DeSoto, a car with huge sweeping fins and fat whitewall tires. The biker tossed Jimmy inside like a rag doll.

"Hey, what the hell?" Jimmy yelled.

The biker climbed into the backseat beside Jimmy. "Sit back and shut up, little man. We're going for a ride in the country."

That was when the driver of the car turned around. Eddie Ratner gave Jimmy one of his obscene smirks. "How you doin', pussy cat?" He indicated the giant biker. "This here's my friend Olaf. He'll keep you company."

Olaf smiled, revealing his gold front teeth. "Pleased to meet you," he purred.

Jimmy had the feeling he was in deep doo-doo.

* * *

The Rat stopped the car as soon as they left the city. By that time, his Hells Angels henchman had tied Jimmy's hands and feet and taped his mouth shut with duct tape. Eddie popped the trunk, and Olaf manhandled Jimmy inside. The big biker slammed the lid and climbed into the passenger seat. Eddie pulled back onto the highway. They were headed for a remote spot in the Santa Cruz Mountains south of San Francisco.

"I always like this drive," Olaf said. "It's real peaceful."

Eddie never knew how to take Olaf's comments. He grinned a sickly grin. "Yeah, peaceful."

"Some nice wineries out here, too," the hulking biker added.

The Santa Cruz Mountains extended down the San Francisco Peninsula all way to the Pajaro River, which emptied into Monterey Bay west of Watsonville. Eddie and Olaf were only going as far south as a small hidden valley west of Palo Alto. They were driving along State Route 35, a scenic highway known as Skyline Boulevard. In the daytime, the views here were spectacular, a rolling green natural paradise dotted with parks and preserves and laced with hiking trails, with the Pacific Ocean and San Francisco Bay in the distance.

By now, the sun had settled into the ocean, turning the surrounding hills and valleys into a shadowy landscape where all sorts of unfriendly critters might prowl for all Eddie knew. He kept his eyes on the highway, trying not to miss their turnoff. The deserted road that Olaf had discovered while riding his Harley with some of his motorcycle buddies was tricky to spot, especially in the dark. Eddie glanced at the DeSoto's odometer. They'd traveled the correct number of miles.

"There it is," Olaf said, pointing to a stand of six Douglas fir trees on the right side of the highway.

Eddie slowed down and turned onto a narrow lane leading into the brush-covered hills. When they were out of sight of the highway, Eddie stopped the DeSoto. He left the parking lights on so they could see what they were doing. The two men climbed out and opened the trunk. Jimmy D. was kicking and squirming around like a Mexican jumping bean. Ratner laughed as he watched the man's frantic struggles.

"What's the matter, pussy cat? Your nest not comfy enough for you?"

Olaf pinned Jimmy to the floor of the trunk while Ratner prepared his syringe. The Rat jabbed Jimmy in the neck, injecting him with enough high-grade heroin to kill a mule.

"Don't worry, pussy cat. This'll make you feel great. For a while."

Jimmy's struggles grew even wilder after Olaf let go of him. Slowly, though, the movements of the would-be Haight-Ashbury drug lord became less pronounced, like a mechanical toy winding down. And then he was very still...and very dead.

Olaf lifted the body from the trunk and carried it down the hill, where he placed it in a dense, shrubby stand of coast live oak. When the body was well hidden, the Hells Angel whipped out his Ka-Bar knife to cut off the dead man's right hand.

"Wait a minute there, Olaf," the Rat said. "Last time you got blood all over my floor mat. How about you skip the souvenir collecting?"

The brawny Hells Angel gave Ratner a gold-toothed grin. "I thought you might say that, after all the bitching you did before, so I came prepared."

The big man pulled a plastic Wonder Bread wrapper from his back pocket and held it up for Ratner to see. "This okay?"

The Rat shrugged in acquiescence, fearing the consequences if he refused. For little orange-haired Eddie Ratner, discretion had always been the better part of valor.

Chapter Six

San Francisco

Bobby pulled his little black TR4 to the curb in front of Lynette's Shrader Street apartment building. He'd been half expecting that the girl wouldn't be waiting for him, that she'd forgotten their date, but there she was, sitting on the top step of the row house. The sun was lighting her long russet hair, which she'd tied back in a ponytail. She smiled when she saw him, a diffident smile that seemed to express both pleasure and relief. Maybe she'd been wondering if he'd show up as well.

She got up and approached Bobby's car. She was wearing a light-blue sundress that set off the color of her hair, and she had a deep-blue scarf tied around her neck. She looked incredibly wholesome, with the girl-next-door allure of a model from *Seventeen* magazine. The delicate sprinkling of freckles across her nose added to the image.

The TR4's convertible top was down. Bobby stuck his hand up and waved. He felt himself grinning a big silly grin, as if he were picking up the prom queen to escort her to the dance. Lynette got in and gave him one of her captivating smiles. "So you remembered."

"Are you kidding? I've been looking forward to this all week."

"Me too."

Bobby laid his arm on the back of Lynette's seat. He had a fierce urge to touch the girl, to stroke her hair and run his hand along her cheek. "You hungry?"

"Not very."

"Then let's walk over to the I and Thou coffee shop and grab a croissant to tide us over. That way we can work up an appetite for later. After we visit the De Young Museum, I'll take you someplace nice for dinner. How's that sound?"

"It sounds terrific."

They strolled over to Haight Street and entered the rundown coffee shop, a popular hippie hangout. Sitting on a stool up front by the window, a long-haired beatnik with thick glasses was reading his free verse. It sounded like an extract from his diary or part of a grocery list. Bobby and Lynette found a table in the back corner and took in the menagerie of customers—guys in jeans and rock show T-shirts, girls in long tie-dyed skirts and halter tops. They were all intently gabbling in each other's faces.

"I love this place," Lynette said. "It's Haight-Ashbury in a nutshell."

"You can't get much funkier than this."

"Did you finish writing your story about Monterey Pop?"

"I did, after about a dozen tries. I wanted to capture the feeling that was in the air, the excitement of the audience. I may be wrong, but I suspect that Monterey Pop will go down as a milestone in music history, a turning point if you will."

"Why's that?"

"Because it seemed to represent what came before and what's ahead. You had stars like Lou Rawls and Johnny Rivers, who've been cranking out slick pop hits for years, and then you had all the newer rock groups, which were edgier and more about today. Even when they were singing traditional blues numbers, those groups gave the impression that they were commenting on contemporary life, all the struggles people face. The music seemed to reflect the rebellion against conventional thinking that's happening in the country today, with the antiwar and civil rights movements. Like Bob Dylan said, 'the times they are a-changin'.'"

"That's pretty deep. I just thought it was great music."

Bobby laughed. "I do tend to get a little pretentious at times."

"I don't think what you said was pretentious at all. You saw things that I didn't. That's what good writers do."

Lynette fell silent for a moment, then she took an envelope from her clutch and hesitantly slid it across the table. "Would you do me a favor? Tell me what you make of this note."

Bobby gave her a questioning look. "Sure. Who's it from?"

"I don't know."

Bobby glanced at the envelope. It was addressed to "The Red-Haired Girl," followed by the street number of her apartment building. Bobby took out the note inside.

"Hello, pretty lady," it began. "I've been noticing you lately. I think you're one hot chick. If you'd like to meet a cool dude, stop by the Pall Mall Lounge anytime. I'll be looking for you." The note was unsigned.

"This is kind of creepy," Bobby said.

"Yeah. Tell me about it."

Bobby put the note back in the envelope and handed it to Lynette. "I wouldn't get too worked up over it. It sounds like it was written by some poor schmuck who's short on social skills."

Lynette tapped the envelope against the table. "You're probably right. The streets are crawling with ding-dongs these days." She tore the envelope in two and tossed it aside.

* * *

"The De Young Museum got its start in 1894," Bobby said, "when the six-month-long California Midwinter International Exposition was held here in Golden Gate Park." He rattled this off as he and Lynette strolled from the parking area toward the museum entrance. "After the fair closed, the chairman of the exposition's organizing committee, Michael de Young—a cofounder of the *San Francisco Chronicle*—suggested that the fair's Fine Arts Building would make a dandy permanent gallery. The new museum opened the following year, and it's been expanded since to house the growing collection."

Lynette smiled in acknowledgment, encouraging him to continue.

"There's an interesting story about the de Youngs. Michael's older brother, Charles, who helped found the *Chronicle* and served as its first editor-in-chief, had a feud with a candidate for mayor in 1879. Charles ended up being shot and killed by the man's son. A few years later, Michael was shot by an angry businessman he'd criticized in print, although Michael survived."

"Oh, my gosh. How awful."

"The history of our other major newspaper, the *Examiner,* is just as colorful. According to legend, George Hearst, a man who made millions from the gold and silver bonanzas, won the newspaper in a poker game in 1880 and gave it to his son after he was kicked out of Harvard. Apparently, the elder Hearst thought that running the paper would straighten out his son. I guess you could say it worked. William Randolph Hearst became one of the biggest publishing moguls ever. He used his fortune to build a lavish estate down the coast near San Simeon. Despite his wealth, he didn't seem very happy. Orson Welles based his movie *Citizen Kane* on the man."

"You make a great tour guide," Lynette said with a laugh.

"I've got an honorary guide's cap somewhere at home," Bobby joked.

A fountain and sculpture garden stood in front of the lofty central tower that marked the main entrance to the sprawling museum complex. Once inside, Bobby asked Lynette which displays she'd like to see first.

"I've got a small confession to make," Lynette responded. "This isn't my first visit."

Bobby threw back his head and laughed. "And here I was trying to show off my knowledge about the place."

"Oh, you know a lot more about the history of the museum than I do, but I've been here several times to see their paintings. They've got some fine American works. That's really their strong suit."

"Then why don't you show me the ones you like."

"Okay." Lynette led the way to the galleries housing works in the permanent collection. She stopped in front of an 1807 painting by John Vanderlyn titled *Caius Marius Amid the Ruins of Carthage.* "This one caught my eye because it looks like a painting from the Renaissance, yet it's by an

American. Apparently, the man in the painting is a Roman general. What I like about it is the way the artist depicted that red robe draped around the man. You don't know how difficult it is to realistically capture folds of cloth. Other than that, the background seems too dark to me and the composition seems a little stiff."

Bobby was impressed by Lynette's analysis. She definitely had an artist's eye.

The next work she showed him was titled *Sacramento Railroad Station,* an 1874 painting by William Hahn. It was a busy street scene with a locomotive, a stage coach, and a crowd of people. "I love this one for the remarkable detail," Lynette said. "Look at all the moments the artist captured. Those two men on the left just dropped someone's trunk and the clothes are spilling out. Beside the stagecoach, families are saying their good-byes to departing passengers. In the background on the right, dozens of people are dashing here and there. You can almost hear the commotion."

They moved on to an 1821 painting by James Peale titled *Still Life with Fruit.* "I think I've heard of this guy," Bobby said.

"He and his brother Charles were both noted artists," Lynette explained. "Peale's use of color is amazing, and look at the texture on those pears."

Bobby leaned in for a closer look. "It must have taken him forever to paint all those bunches of grapes. Imagine having to labor over every single grape to get the color right."

"No one ever said art was easy. If it was, anyone could do it."

Lynette pointed to a portrait of a Victorian lady with a large hat draped with a gauzy veil. "Here's another technical achievement I admire."

Bobby peered at the painting then read the caption out loud. "*The Blue Veil,* by Edmund Charles Tarbell, 1898." He shrugged. "Never heard of him."

"Me neither, but look at the delicate texture of the veil, and the way it's floating on the breeze. Isn't it beautiful?"

"I probably wouldn't have given it a second glance, but now that you point out its merits, I can see why you like it."

Lynette led the way into another gallery. "Here are two of my favorites." She pointed to a pair of vibrant street scenes hanging side by side, *Court in Chinatown, San Francisco* and *Street in Ikao, Japan.* The first was an 1886 work by Edwin Deakin, and the other an 1890 painting by Theodore Wores. "Don't you love them?" The two paintings had a similar composition, and both were done in vivid colors, with interesting uses of light and shadow.

"I do, but probably for different reasons than you do."

Lynette gave him a questioning look. "Like what?"

"You probably like them for all sorts of technical reasons, but I just think the scenes are interesting."

"I hate to break it to you, but that's the main reason people are drawn to pictures. They may not have a clue about what they're looking at, but if they like it, then that's enough."

"It's clear you know a lot about painting, but how much do you know about Asian sculptures?"

Lynette shrugged. "Next to nothing."

"Then let's swing over to the new wing they opened last year. There's a huge collection of Asian art donated by Avery Brundage, the millionaire head of the International Olympic Committee."

Bobby led the way around the new wing, which was chock-full of sculptures from all over Asia, the result of Brundage's longtime passion for collecting. There were dozens of statues of Buddhas and other Eastern religious figures, some of them small enough to hold in your hand and others larger than life size.

"I've always been awed by sculpture," Lynette said. "The artists have to work in the round, and if they make a mistake, they can't just paint over it like I get to do."

"I'll bet you don't make too many mistakes," Bobby said.

"Every artist does. The key is knowing how to fix them."

From the De Young Museum, it was a short jaunt over to the Japanese Tea Garden, another remnant of the 1894 Midwinter Exposition. They sat in the tranquil garden within view of the tiered Buddhist pagoda, surrounded by flowering shrubs and within earshot of the soothing sound of splashing water.

"Thanks for bringing me here," Lynette said. "I've never seen this. It's lovely. I may come back and try my hand at painting some of these scenes."

"You really should. I know you'd create something wonderful."

Lynette stared at Bobby for a long time, studying him carefully, as she would a subject for one of her drawings. "You've got an interesting face" was all she said.

Bobby was slightly disconcerted by her scrutiny. "You're lucky to live so close to the park. You can pop over any time."

"Actually, this was one of the first places I visited after I moved here. I left Wisconsin last January in the middle of a snowstorm, and when I got off the plane in San Francisco it felt like I'd landed in a tropical paradise. The week after I arrived, my friend from Wisconsin brought me here to the park to the Human Be-In. Now that was quite an experience. Talk about culture shock. We heard Timothy Leary talk about dropping out and saw Allen Ginsberg dancing up a storm. It was pretty neat. And the next day, my dad's favorite football team, the Packers, won the first Super Bowl. He called me after the game and told me all about it. He probably drove my mom nuts yelling at the TV set."

"I understand there were lots of drugs floating around at the Human Be-In. You said you were on LSD when I saw you dancing on Mount Tamalpais. Are you a regular user?"

"That was my first time, and probably my last. A girl in my apartment building gave me one of her 'magic sugar cubes.' It took me hours to regain my senses."

"I think Leary and his pal Richard Alpert are frauds." Bobby spoke with an edge to his voice. "They didn't choose to drop out like they advise other people to do. They were kicked out—fired from Harvard because of their experiments with LSD. And they both landed on their feet, with rich patrons, book contracts, and speaking tours. Most of the kids who follow their advice end up living on the street—dirty, broke, and hooked on drugs."

Lynette studied his face again, this time with an expression of fascination. "I've been wondering about something. You said you have a twin brother. What that's like? Do you two have some psychic link like people say? Do you feel things that happen to each other?"

Bobby laughed. "I don't know if you'd call it a psychic link, but we do tend to think along the same lines. More than once, one of us has commented on something the other person was thinking before a word was spoken. We laugh about it, but it is a little spooky."

* * *

"I hope you like martinis." Bobby held the door open as Lynette walked into Aub Zam Zam, an upscale Haight Street bar run by the owner of the Pall Mall Lounge.

Lynette wrinkled up her nose. "Would you think me a total rube if I told you I've never had a martini?"

"Then you have a treat in store. The martinis here are the best in the city. In fact, Herb Caen called this club the holy shrine of the dry martini."

"Ooh, then I'll have to try one. Broaden my horizons."

The couple took a seat in the dimly lit bar, which was decorated in a Middle Eastern motif, with Moorish arches and a mural behind the bar depicting a scene from a Persian fairytale. It was the sort of place Dashiell Hammett might have patronized. Owner Bruno Mooshei came over to take their order.

"Hello, Bruno," Bobby said. "I'd like you to meet Miss Lynette Simms, a local artist."

Nattily dressed in a vest and tie, Mooshei bowed smartly. "A pleasure to meet you, Miss Simms."

"Two of your legendary martinis," Bobby said. When Mooshei left to fix their drinks, Bobby leaned close to Lynette. "You've got to be on your best behavior around Bruno. He's been known to toss people out simply for talking too loud or ordering the wrong thing."

"Then I'll just whisper," Lynette giggled.

After they finished their drinks, Bobby took Lynette's hand. "Come on. Time to eat."

They drove over to Sam's Grill on Bush Street, south of Chinatown. Opened in 1867, Sam's Grill was one of the city's best seafood restaurants.

Bobby and Lynette slid into a curtained booth as the waiter handed them the menus.

Lynette ran her eyes down the list of fresh seafood. "My gosh, look at the prices."

"Don't look," Bobby said, "or else you won't enjoy your meal."

After their appetizers and salads, they tucked into the entrées they'd ordered from the list of the day's catch, swordfish for Bobby and king salmon for Lynette. As they ate, Lynette kept glancing up from her plate. She clearly wanted to ask Bobby something. "Do you eat here often?" she finally ventured.

"Once every month or two. I can't afford any more than that. This meal means I won't be coming back for about four months."

"I'm very flattered," Lynette said with an appreciative look.

For the next hour, they enjoyed one of those companionable interludes that come along so rarely. Bobby told Lynette about his dream of becoming a novelist, and she confided that her ideal job would be to open her own design studio. They discovered that they both liked classical music and ballet but didn't care for opera. They both wanted to ride the trains around Europe, go hiking in Alaska, and take a cruise in the Caribbean. Before the evening was over, they'd begun starting sentences with, "I bet you'd like to…" When the waiter asked them if there'd be anything else for the third time, Bobby got the hint that it was time to go.

"What are you doing tomorrow?" he asked as they got in his car.

"No big plans."

"Then let me show you some of the best views of the city. You can bring your sketch pad. The places I'm thinking of would offer great scenes for you to draw."

* * *

Bobby stopped by Lynette's apartment midmorning on Sunday. She was again waiting for him on the top step. Taking Bobby's advice to wear something comfortable, she had on pale lavender slacks, a lilac-colored blouse, a deep violet scarf, and beige espadrilles—her impeccable sense of color on full display.

"First stop, Twin Peaks," Bobby announced, shoving his TR4 into gear and heading south on Clayton Street. Soon they were buzzing up winding Twin Peaks Boulevard. Located in the center of the city, the two nine-hundred-foot hills afforded spectacular views—the Pacific Ocean to the west, Golden Gate and the Marin Headlands to the north, and the Bay to the north and east. Stretching beyond Twin Peaks to the northeast were some of the city's famous neighborhoods—from the longtime Scandinavian enclave of the Castro to the rough-edged Tenderloin to the Italian quarter of North Beach, each with its own interesting history.

"You probably can't pick it out, but below us in Hayes Valley is the Center for the Performing Arts, and next to it is City Hall. Past that is Nob Hill. That's where rich folks built palatial estates in the 1800s. The four men behind the Central Pacific Railroad lived there. Leland Stanford, Mark Hopkins, Collis Huntington, and Charles Crocker gained control of the railroad when it was being built in the 1860s and made obscene amounts of money. Stanford University is a legacy of the railroad tycoons, and Chinatown grew dramatically after they brought in thousands of laborers to build their railroad. Most of the Nob Hill mansions were destroyed in the 1906 earthquake and fire, and ritzy hotels and condos have taken their place."

"Where did you learn so much about the Bay Area?" Lynette asked.

"From my father. He used to bring us to San Francisco whenever he could and show us around. We would have lived here if it weren't for my parents' jobs in L.A."

"What's your favorite part of the city?"

"Hmm. That's a tough question. I'll have to think about it." He pointed out Coit Tower on distant Telegraph Hill. "That's where we're headed next."

From Twin Peaks, they drove over to Market Street then headed north on Grant Avenue. The Art Deco–style Coit Tower rose two hundred feet above Telegraph Hill, with panoramic views of the city to the south and west and an unmatched view of San Francisco Bay. "The tower was built in the early 1930s with a bequest from a lady named Lillie Coit," Bobby said as they approached the structure. "She was a patron of the city's firefighters and fought a few fires herself as a teenager. It's said the tower is shaped like the nozzle of a fire hose."

Inside, they admired the large murals painted by Bay Area artists. "These frescoes were commissioned by the WPA during the Great Depression," Bobby noted. There were images of farmers, miners, mailmen, policemen, and factory workers, all of them depicting the everyday struggles of working people in that era.

"Some of the murals caused a stir when they were unveiled. Government and business bigwigs said they showed capitalism in a bad light. They claimed the murals were sympathetic toward communism. That was back in the days of red scares, when some Americans thought commies were hiding under every bed." Bobby shrugged. "Maybe they were."

When they reached the observation deck, Lynette let out a gasp. "You can see everything from up here." She pointed to the southwest. "Isn't that where we just were?"

"Yep, that's Twin Peaks, way over there. To the south of us is the Jackson Square historic district. It has some nice old buildings that were saved from the fire that devastated the city after the 1906 earthquake.

"Here's a fact not many San Franciscans are aware of—right down there on Green Street is where a former Idaho farm boy named Philo T. Farnsworth invented television in 1927. And the work of British photographer Eadweard Muybridge here in the Bay Area led to the invention of another visual medium. In the late 1800s, Muybridge took groundbreaking stop-action photos of animals and humans in motion using multiple cameras. The people were stark naked, by the way. Pretty weird stuff, but his work led to the invention of motion pictures."

Lynette laughed and shook her head. "That's pretty weird all right."

Bobby took her by the shoulders and turned her so she faced west. "Most of North Beach lies out there. The neighborhood is filled with Italian restaurants and beatnik hangouts such as the hungry i and the Purple Onion. Poet Lawrence Ferlinghetti's City Lights Bookstore is down there on

Columbus Avenue. West of Columbus is Russian Hill and Lombard Street, the so-called 'crookedest street in the world,' although a section of Vermont Street is even crookeder. The Hyde Street cable car line runs through the neighborhood to the cable car turntable near the waterfront. Some of our big tourist attractions are along the waterfront between Ghirardelli Square and Fisherman's Wharf. And that's where people can catch the ferries to Marin County and other points north of us."

They turned to face south again. "East of Nob Hill are Chinatown and the Financial District, and farther south is Union Square. That's where the St. Francis Hotel is located. Opera singer Enrico Caruso was staying at the St. Francis when the 1906 earthquake struck. It scared the hell out of him, and he vowed never to return to San Francisco. A few blocks to the east is the swanky Palace Hotel. That's where President Harding died in 1923.

"Right behind us is Alcatraz Island, where Al Capone and other dangerous criminals were locked up. They closed the prison four years ago." Bobby swept his arm to take in the entire waterfront. "Just imagine, old wooden sailing ships from all over the world used to anchor out there. During the Gold Rush, hundreds of those ships were abandoned when their passengers and crew caught gold fever. Even the captains left for the gold fields. That tower you see this side of the Bay Bridge is part of the Ferry Building. After the Golden Gate and Bay Bridges were built, ferries became less important, so part of the building was converted into office space."

Bobby held out his hand. "That concludes the nickel tour of San Francisco. That'll be five cents, please."

Lynette spun in a circle as she tried to take in all the sights. "I love it!" she exclaimed.

* * *

Bobby drove west on Geary Boulevard. "You asked me about my favorite part of the city," he said. "I'm beginning to realize that I don't have one favorite place, but this next stop is on my list." As he spoke, they merged onto Point Lobos Avenue, and the Pacific Ocean spread out before them.

A few minutes later, Bobby pulled into the parking lot at Cliff House, a historic restaurant clinging to a promontory on the very edge of the sea. Opened in 1863, the upscale dining spot was damaged when a ship exploded offshore in 1887, and it burned down in 1894 and 1907, but it was always resurrected. One look at the view told why.

"Oh Bobby," Lynette gushed, "how could I have lived in this town for six months and never have come out here to see this?"

"Some people never do. When Cliff House first opened, it was so far from the city that it cost more to get here than to dine. The man who built it was a mining engineer named Adolph Sutro. He made a fortune during the Comstock Lode silver bonanza, then he splashed his money around San Francisco. Besides Cliff House, he built a huge public bathhouse and a mansion near here."

Lynette insisted that Bobby sit for a portrait. He took a seat outside on the terrace that overlooked Seal Rocks, a landmark just below Cliff House. For twenty minutes, Lynette sketched away. When she finished, she handed her sketch to Bobby.

"A small token of appreciation for a wonderful weekend."

* * *

That night, Bobby wrote a letter to Jack, telling him about Lynette. He mentioned a few of the things he'd learned about her, although he left out one of his discoveries about Miss Lynette Simms. She had the warmest lips he'd ever kissed.

III

~July 1967~

Chapter Seven

San Francisco

The alley behind the Grooves record store wasn't a very glamourous place to die. Of course, that didn't matter now to Skeeter Wilson. The wannabe rock drummer lay in a heap of flotsam next to a rusty green dumpster, a short distance away from where he'd made his final drug score. The skinny twenty-year-old with the misspelled Tijuana tattoo on his right forearm had come to the city with forty bucks in his pocket and a smattering of experience in motley smalltime bands. Skeeter's downfall was that his aspirations exceeded his skills by a wide margin. His playing had been good enough to win him a spot with the Visigoths and the Purple Titans—two of the bar bands he'd appeared with for short stints back in his hometown of Fresno—but even those forgettable groups quickly tired of the pothead drummer's persistent habit of losing the beat.

After Skeeter's horizons dimmed in the Raisin Capital of the World, he hopped a Greyhound and headed north. Despite his diligent attempts to latch on with a San Francisco band—any band—he found himself unemployable. That's when his drug habit began to escalate from weed to hard stuff. In his final weeks, Skeeter was shooting up just about every dollar he came by. What he didn't know, however, was that a new supply of killer heroin had found its way onto the Haight-Ashbury drug market. Laced with dangerous additives, the tainted dope could put users where Skeeter was now, flat on his back, staring wide-eyed at the deep blue San

Francisco sky without a care in the world.

The wino who'd stumbled across Skeeter's body the night before had gone through his pockets and discovered a treasure trove of eight dollars and seventy-five cents. The wino immediately staggered down the street to the corner grocery store and bought himself a fistful of Slim Jims and a couple of bottles of sweet, potent, and cheap Thunderbird bum wine, enough to set him up for a day or two. It was only after the Grooves record store opened the next morning that someone in touch with reality came across Skeeter. A young clerk who'd taken some empty cardboard boxes out to the dumpster found the body and called the police.

"Poor schmuck," said detective Fred Chacon, a hulking Jicarilla Apache with glistening black hair and a hard-earned degree in criminal justice. He studied the body while his crime scene team did its work. Chacon had seen about every drug-related abomination on the streets of San Francisco, but as he looked at Skeeter's vacuous face, it seemed to him that the victims were getting younger and younger. Chacon had campaigned for a spot on the drug squad because of his hatred for what dope and alcohol did to Native Americans, especially the young men on the New Mexico reservation where he grew up.

Chacon turned to Raul Pitman, who'd driven over from Berkeley after receiving a tip from one of his sources. The young reporter was doing a story on the recent rash of drug-related deaths in Haight-Ashbury. Chacon's dark eyes narrowed. "If I find the SOB who's peddling this bad dope, I'm gonna personally scalp him." When Pitman recoiled, the big cop laughed. "Just kidding. Us Apaches don't go in for scalping." Pitman gave him a nervous grin. "We're more into torture. Stake guys out on an anthill. That sort of thing."

"So you think tainted heroin is behind these deaths?" Pitman asked.

"More than likely. We confiscated a batch last week that was laced with cocaine and methamphetamine. Too much methamphetamine can kill you for sure. Stops your heart. Did you know we gave that drug to our troops in World War II to keep 'em awake? No wonder we had so many dopers after the war. Same thing's happening today in Vietnam. Kids getting hooked on drugs and bringing their habit home with them." Chacon kicked an empty beer can down the alley. "Really ticks me off."

Pitman glanced down at Skeeter Wilson as the crime scene team zipped him into a body bag. "Any idea where the stuff's coming from?"

"Most of the heroin originates in Southeast Asia. That's where the pure variety comes from, the white stuff. We also see a lot of lower quality brown heroin coming in from Asia. The cheaper black tar heroin comes from Mexico. It's anybody's guess who's mixing in the meth we're seeing lately. They do it to hook users faster." Chacon nodded as his men loaded the body onto a gurney. "But that's what ends up happening way too often."

* * *

Eddie Ratner was having his morning coffee at the Pall Mall Lounge when the ambulance with Skeeter Wilson's body drove past. Ratner was thinking about the night before. Man, business was booming. He'd sold out his entire satchel of goodies before nine o'clock. Most of his regular buyers were looking for their usual weekend pick-me-up, and he'd been getting a slew of new business from all the kids hanging around Haight-Ashbury. He didn't bother to ask their names, especially the last loser he'd dealt with. The jerk had "Helbound" tattooed on his forearm, whatever that meant. The guy was after some speedball, and the Rat assured him the new concoction of coke and heroin he was selling was the best on the street. Guaranteed to give him the buzz of a lifetime.

* * *

Raul Pitman plunked down his dollar and strolled into the newly renovated and renamed Straight Theater at 1702 Haight Street. Opened in 1910 as the Haight Theater, the historic movie palace had been purchased a couple of years back by three hippie entrepreneurs who were intent on providing an alternative to the Fillmore and Avalon concert halls. After raising money from locals and cajoling friends into donating their time to spruce up the place, the masterminds behind the Straight were staging their grand opening over the weekend.

Tonight's lineup of bands included the Grateful Dead, Quicksilver Messenger Service, Big Brother & the Holding Company, Country Joe & the Fish, and the Charlatans, along with some lesser-known local groups. It was the kind of rollicking bash where Raul Pitman hoped to learn more about the Haight drug scene.

By the time the Berkeley reporter arrived, the theater was thick with partiers and swirling clouds of marijuana smoke. Flashing strobes lit up the stage like a battle scene. At the moment, the Charlatans were performing a loping, satirical number called "How Can I Miss You When You Won't Go Away?" One of the first groups to capture the San Francisco sound, the Charlatans sported nineteenth-century garb. With their boots, vests, derbies, and straw boaters, they looked like extras in an episode of *Gunsmoke.* The young musicians had fit right in when they played an extended engagement at the Red Dog Saloon in the old silver-mining boomtown of Virginia City, Nevada, not long after they got together. Despite their local popularity, the Charlatans had never hit the big time. Maybe their sound was too eclectic, with its mix of jug band music, country, blues, and rock. Or maybe the band members were simply too ornery. They continually fought among themselves, and they liked to play with guns.

Raul Pitman spotted the man he was after, the Charlatans' watchdog, Sonny Anders. The lanky blond with the droopy mustache stood at the edge of the stage, observing the members of the band with a critical eye. Anders's job couldn't be much fun, Pitman thought. Working for an autocratic rock impresario like Bill Graham would wear on anyone. Pitman had met Anders during one of his previous assignments. He'd also met Bill Graham, and he'd pegged him as a man who'd explode at the slightest provocation. Pitman was certain that Sonny Anders's hide was laced with scars.

Pitman worked his way through the crowd and approached Anders. After saying hello and exchanging pleasantries, Pitman told Anders about the story he was working on. "You've probably read about some of the overdose deaths here in the Haight."

"Sure have."

"I thought maybe you'd heard something about this bad dope that's circulating."

"Why would I?" Anders said with a touch of irritation.

"I'm not implying anything untoward about you personally. It's just that you're closer to the drug scene than I am because of your association with the music industry. From what I hear, every rocker in the Bay Area is smoking pot or dropping acid nowadays."

Anders sniffed. "If you went by those fellows up on stage, you'd be right. They started using LSD while they were over in Virginia City. That was before Bill Graham took them on." Anders eyed the musicians. "It's too bad, you know. Those guys have what it takes, but they'd rather spend their time goofing off and getting high than putting out a decent record. I'd be better off managing the damned Monkees. They may be a fake, made-for-TV band, but some of their records are outselling the Beatles."

Anders gave Pitman a serious look. "One thing's for certain though. None of the Charlatans or any members of the other bands Bill Graham represents are using the hard stuff. Bill would boot them if he found out. He hates junkies. He says they mess up everything. Not only their own lives, but those of everyone around them. Once the dope takes over, they're completely unreliable."

"Or dead," Pitman said.

"Yeah, or dead."

"So you have no inkling of who's behind this bad dope?"

Anders shrugged. "Maybe the local pushers are doctoring their stuff, or maybe it's the bigger fish further up the supply chain. You're not dealing with a well-regulated industry here. It's really a crap shoot what these unfortunate saps stick in their arms."

Chapter Eight

Pleiku Province, South Vietnam

The words of the Youngbloods' hit song "Get Together" echoed through Jack Doyle's quarters at Camp Enari. "Come on people now, smile on your brother, everybody get together, try to love one another right now." Thanks to the Armed Forces Vietnam Network, Americans throughout the war zone could listen to the latest music from home over the radio, a luxury that kept many a soldier from going crazy. Some people called the Vietnam conflict "the rock 'n' roll war." For other young soldiers, though, the music simply fed their resentment over being stuck in a foreign hellhole while thousands of kids their age were strolling around leafy campuses and carrying on with their lives.

As Jack listened to the lyrics, he considered how difficult it was to love one another in Vietnam. During the month he'd been in-country, he'd learned quite a bit about human nature. The lieutenant he'd replaced had briefed him on the men he'd be leading. It was a disheartening session. Some of the lieutenant's words came back to him. "Watch out for Corporal Jackson. He's about to crack, and once they lose it, anything can happen.... Don't ever turn your back on Private Stooks. He's insolent, resentful, and frankly dangerous. We lost two officers to fragging incidents this year, and Stooks is just the sort to toss a grenade in your hooch.... Some of the men will try to jerk you around because you're an FNG—a 'Friggin' New Guy.' It can be a pain, but you don't have to be a hard ass. Just remember that you're in charge—and never let them forget it. The worst sin is indecisiveness."

The lieutenant had also briefed Jack on the rampant drug use in his platoon. "The men can get anything they want in Pleiku City—grass, coke, heroin. Keep an eye out for anyone smoking Park Lane cigarettes. They're made with pot instead of tobacco." When Jack expressed his surprise at the level of drug use, the lieutenant had grown philosophical. "If we busted them all, there wouldn't be anyone left to do the fighting. Back home, kids take drugs to enhance their pleasure. Out here, they take them to dull their pain, to escape from reality. Hell, I've been tempted once or twice to light up a joint."

Jack picked up Bobby's recent letter and read it again. He smiled at his brother's description of his new girlfriend. Bobby had always been a romantic. He'd fallen in love half a dozen times in high school. This latest romantic interest sounded promising. Jack wished the best for his brother. The two of them had always looked out for each other. There'd never been a trace of sibling rivalry or jealousy. They could thank their parents for that. Donovan and Maria Doyle might be high-powered attorneys, but they'd never missed a single important event in their sons' lives, and they'd supported them equally in everything they put their minds to.

Jack set Bobby's letter aside and picked up his parents' latest letter. Jack detected the forced cheerfulness behind his mother's words. Maria rattled on about daily matters, as if those mundane accounts could convey the homey atmosphere he must surely be missing. Jack's eyes misted over at his mother's desperation. His father's portion of the letter was more pragmatic. Donovan wrote about things going on around the world—Expo 67 was drawing huge crowds in Montreal, and Tennessee's "monkey law" forbidding the teaching of evolution in public schools had just been repealed. Jack chuckled at his father's description of the androgynous British pixie Twiggy, who'd become the latest modeling sensation.

Jack shoved his letters under his pillow when the first rocket exploded. For the third time in the past week, the base was under attack by local Vietcong forces. He grabbed his helmet and flak jacket and headed out the door in the direction of the nearby underground bunker. As he crossed a barren patch of ground, another rocket slammed down next to his quarters, tossing rocks and other debris into the air. The rubble rained down on the building's corrugated tin roof, pinging like hailstones. Jack stumbled down the steps of the bunker and found a seat among the other officers hunkered down in the darkness.

As his vision adjusted to the dark, he saw his friend from Saigon, Vince Tate, sitting across from him. Vince's eyes were as big as saucers. Jack could imagine that his own eyes revealed the terror he felt. The surreal quality of a rocket barrage was gut-wrenching, although the officers who'd been in-country longer seemed unruffled. Some of them were leisurely smoking, heads leaning against the bunker wall as they waited out the attack. One fellow was writing a letter while holding a small flashlight in his teeth.

The boom of outgoing mortar fire shook the air. Soon, teams of South Vietnamese marines would be combing the countryside in search of the attackers. It was probably the same enemy unit that had recently rocketed Pleiku City.

Jack's current fright was nothing compared to what he'd felt the first time his platoon came under fire while on patrol. A raw, visceral fear had surged through him then, akin to what an animal must feel when it's caught in a trap. The enervating realization that this was actually happening had nearly overwhelmed him. All of the theorizing about duty and serving your country meant nothing when angry anonymous men were trying to kill you. It was especially terrifying in light of the fact that the North Vietnamese deliberately targeted officers to sew confusion and panic among the ranks.

Fortunately, Jack's resolve had held, and he'd led his men to the safety of a shallow defile, where they were out of the direct line of fire. A hurried call for air support had produced the heartening sight of a flight of Cobra gunships roaring over the countryside, their deadly Miniguns laying down a field of suppressing fire. Jack and his men had survived that encounter, along with a number of other skirmishes that followed. Sitting in the bunker listening to the sounds of war, he knew that he'd be repeating the same frightening routine again tomorrow, like a science fiction character caught in a time loop.

* * *

"To another day in paradise," Vince said, lifting his glass of Martell cognac in a toast.

"Another day in paradise," Jack echoed, lifting his own glass and draining the shot in a single gulp. "Ah, good stuff," he gasped as the fiery liquor burned a path down his throat.

The two friends sat in Vince's quarters, going through the nightly routine they'd started not long after arriving at Camp Enari. It began as a joke but had become a comforting ritual. Some nights, they weren't able to share a drink due to their duty assignments, but whenever possible, they always got together. Jack had never tasted cognac until Vince purchased a bottle at the camp PX, where the normally expensive French brandy was ridiculously cheap, prompting them to slosh it down like a pair of lords.

Vince's face was flushed from the potent booze. "What do you think about our assignment for tomorrow? I hear our company and Company B are heading over toward Duc Co. That's within spitting distance of the Cambodian border."

"Ought to be interesting." Jack held out his glass for a refill.

After he returned to his own quarters, Jack got out his tablet and began a letter to his parents. He knew they loved hearing from him, and he got just as much pleasure out of writing home. When he concentrated on the page and thought of California, he was temporarily transported from Vietnam. Of course, he never told his parents what things were really like here. That would have traumatized his mom, so he focused on the few positives he could think of—such as the beauty of the countryside and the interesting culture of the people. Once, he told them about how the Vietnamese wove poems into their conical palm-leaf hats, an unexpected touch of artistry in their hardscrabble existence.

Tonight, he set about describing his recent interaction with a family of peasant farmers. Jack was beginning to pick up a few words of Vietnamese, and he wrote about how he'd offered a cute little girl of six or seven a pack of Juicy Fruit. *"Ban be*—friends," he said to her. The girl had hidden behind her mother when Jack held out the gum. She obviously didn't know what it was. Jack took out a piece and popped it in his mouth. The girl watched as he chewed, her dark eyes wide with fascination, then she grabbed the pack and retreated behind her mother, who laughed and said *"Cam on*—thank you," to which Jack replied *"Khong co gi*—you're welcome."

* * *

Jack mustered his men at zero seven hundred. His platoon and Vince's were two of the four platoons that made up Company C. Somewhere close by, a radio blared "Kind of a Drag," by the Buckinghams. The Chicago group lamented the fact that their baby didn't love them anymore. From the attitude of the three dozen bedraggled infantrymen Jack confronted, it was clear that anything he asked them to do would also be kind of a drag.

"All right, men, listen up. We've had reports of increased NVA activity over near Duc Co, and we're supposed to reconnoiter the area. It's a good hike, so let's get going."

"Uh, lieutenant, sir, can I be excused? My head's hurtin' something awful today." The request came from the perpetual complainer and all-around wiseass Jimmy Stooks, one of the men Jack had been warned about. Stooks was tall and lean, with dark hair and a thick mustache. He always had a sulky, furtive look that worried Jack.

"No, Private Stooks. You can't be excused. My head's hurting, too, so the best thing for both of us is to get some fresh mountain air. Now pick up your pack and let's head out."

"Yes sir, lieutenant, sir." The soldier's contempt was palpable.

The men fell into line with much grumbling. The rising sun lit the rumpled green mountains in the distance to the west. The silent hills along the horizon were a picturesque though potentially hazardous destination, with North Vietnamese forces always lurking around, ready to test American defenses. It was a cat-and-mouse game that went on without end, and it was difficult at times to tell which side represented the cat and which the mouse.

Jack marched alongside Staff Sgt. Rob Fisher, a huge black man with biceps the size of hams and an unlit cigar clamped in the corner of his mouth. Sergeant Fisher was starting his third tour of duty in Vietnam. He was a no-nonsense butt-kicker, and Jack was happy to have his company. Though he'd never told Fisher, Jack regarded him as a big brother. Vietnam, like any war zone, was one of the few places where a competent black man could get his due. No white boy would dare smart off to a hardened soldier like Rob Fisher. They feared and respected the man.

As the platoon set off, someone in the ranks began singing the chorus from the Animals' hit song "We Gotta Get Out of This Place." Others picked up the words, and soon most of the platoon was singing what had become the infantryman's unofficial anthem in Vietnam. "We gotta get out of this place," the men bellowed, "if it's the last thing we ever do."

Sergeant Fisher called a halt and turned to face the impromptu performance. "Okay, you sorry bunch of mama's boys. That's enough of that. If you wanna get outta this place, then keep your traps shut and your eyes open. This ain't no holiday excursion we're goin' on."

It took the hundred and fifty men of Company C the better part of two days to reach the rendezvous point with Company B, another of the four companies that made up their battalion. They met outside the village of Duc Co, a scant three miles from the Cambodian border. The trek along Route 19 had taken them through jungle-clad valleys that would have been virtually impassable if not for the narrow, dusty road. Along the way, they passed isolated mountaintop posts manned by squads of shirtless young Americans. Time passed slowly for the half dozen soldiers at each observation post, their tiny sandbagged hideaways dwarfed by the vast forested terrain, like life rafts on the open sea. The men in those posts spent the scorching days keeping watch for enemy troops and the dark lonely nights hoping none were around.

The first night that Jack's platoon spent outside Duc Co, he walked the perimeter of their camp to inspect the security arrangements. Trip wires and explosives surrounded the site, with sentries posted at intervals. When Jack turned in, he smelled the pungent aroma of pot. He could predict who the culprits were, and Jimmy Stooks was sure to be among them. Jack rolled over in his sleeping bag and tried not to think about it.

At first light, Jack's platoon went out on patrol. The rocky, forested hills were spooky in the gray morning light, with ground mist swirling among the trees like in a horror movie. Jungle vines continually tripped them, and frequent streams soaked their feet. Now and then they heard the calls of unseen birds and the chatter of monkeys, but otherwise the hills were unnervingly silent. The smells of the riotous vegetation were heavy on the air—damp leaves, mold, rotting wood. In places, the canopy overhead was so thick that little sunlight reached the forest floor. It was a disorienting green maze where the unwary could become irrevocably lost. They shuffled through the tangled wilderness with every sense alert.

The patrol's point man, a slow-talking Southerner named Earle Boone, led the way. Corporal Boone looked like a halfwit with his mouth hanging open, but he moved through the woods as silently as a ghost, as if he were stalking deer back home in Alabama. If Boone meant to sneak up on someone, they'd never hear him coming. A half hour after they left camp, Corporal Boone spotted a squad of North Vietnamese soldiers. He signaled to the patrol and they ducked out of sight. The enemy troops looked healthy, Jack thought, and their uniforms were clean and new. This wasn't some ragtag mob of underfed, ill-equipped Vietcong. They were disciplined, well-trained professionals. When the soldiers drew closer, Jack's men opened fire, bringing down three of the enemy. The rest scattered deeper into the woods.

Jack fell back against a tree and wiped away the sweat pouring down his face. His knees shook as the adrenaline rush from the skirmish began to subside. He suddenly felt ill. His queasiness was partly due to the chemical tang from spent cartridges, but mostly it came from the realization that he'd just killed a man. He'd seen the NVA soldier he'd aimed his M-14 at crumple an instant after he fired. A flurry of tangled thoughts raced through Jack's mind. Suppose the man had been a teacher or a doctor. What the hell had he done? His pangs of contrition ended abruptly when Sergeant Fisher slapped him on the back.

"Nice shot, lieutenant. You potted that commie bastard good and proper."

Jack gave the man a sickly smile.

A half hour later, nobody was smiling. When observers at Company C's base camp spotted a contingent of enemy soldiers, they called for artillery and mortar fire, unaware that Jack's platoon had moved into the same area. As the incoming fire exploded around them, Jack and his men tried to rendezvous with Company B, whose command post was closer than their own. Instead of linking up with their fellow soldiers, Jack's men found themselves surrounded by a large force of North Vietnamese. They scrambled for cover as bullets ripped through the undergrowth with an obscene sound, the hiss of a thousand vipers. Jack's radioman called for backup, and Company B sent out a platoon in their direction, but that second patrol also became pinned down.

Gradually, the weather closed in and rain began to fall. No one could see anything clearly. Helicopters attempting to locate the two trapped platoons proved useless. One copter was damaged by enemy ground fire and had to withdraw. Then Company B's command post was hit by a mortar round. A series of U.S. airstrikes pummeled the area, allowing a detachment from Company C to rescue Jack and his men. The other platoon was besieged until reinforcements finally arrived by air. Realizing they were now outnumbered, the North Vietnamese retreated back across the border. A hundred and forty-two enemy soldiers had been killed in the fighting. U.S. losses totaled thirty-one killed, thirty-four wounded, and seven missing.

Most of the casualties were from the platoon sent out by Company B, although Jack lost three men—Kowalski, Miller, and Jones. The names sounded like a law firm. Jack watched as the young soldiers were zipped into body bags and loaded onto helicopters. Those men would be providing him with a new challenge. When his platoon got back to Camp Enari, he'd be faced with the task of writing letters to their families. At that thought, he didn't feel so torn up about having killed a North Vietnamese soldier. The mental numbness of war was beginning to set in. No longer would he concern himself with the possible merit of the men he shot at. From now on, they were simply the enemy.

Jack lay awake long into the night. He tried to anchor himself with memories of home, but the mental images that came to him were indistinct, as if he were viewing them through a veil of smoke. He wondered what his brother was doing. He hoped Bobby was safe and happy. Maybe he was with his new girlfriend right now. They both deserved to be happy.

Jack kept flashing back to the day's fighting. He thought about the mighty American arsenal that had been brought to bear in Vietnam, all the planes and artillery and other sophisticated weapons. Unbidden, the image of a paper tiger sprang to mind. The vision was triggered by the sobering knowledge that thousands of the junior officers now serving in Vietnam were just like him—completely inexperienced. He wondered if he was really fit to lead anyone. This was no campus parade ground exercise. How could they win a war led by greenhorns? A moment later, he visualized the paper tiger bursting into flames.

The last words to flit through Jack's mind that night were from the Animals' song his men had been singing. "We gotta get out of this place, if it's the last thing we ever do."

Chapter Nine

Santa Cruz County, California

Lynette craned her neck to look up at the massive redwood tree. "Good gosh, it goes on forever." She held her straw sun hat on her head with one hand to keep it from falling off. "I've never seen anything so big. I've read about these and seen pictures, but I had no idea they were…gargantuan."

Looking up beyond the trees, she saw puffy white clouds drifting across the blue ocean of sky, like the billowing sails of a celestial navy. The vastness of the sky and the immensity of the redwoods made her feel small and insignificant. She realized that the colossal magnificence of nature could be unsettling as well as inspiring. She took Bobby's hand, which felt strong and reassuring.

"Nobody can truly appreciate these trees until they experience them in person," he said. "You can't believe your eyes. It must be what it's like to see the Grand Canyon for the first time. The trees here in Cowell State Park are over two hundred feet tall, but some redwoods up the coast top three hundred and fifty feet. They're the tallest trees on earth, and they can live for over two thousand years."

"If no one cuts them down."

Bobby shook his head. "Yeah. Nearly all of California's redwoods were logged before people had the sense to protect them. The wood was used to build a lot of the houses in San Francisco. Imagine cutting down one of these beauties. It's a sin against nature."

Lynette held out her camera. "Here, take my picture. I've got to send a snapshot to my folks. They'd never believe me if I tried to describe this."

Bobby chuckled at Lynette's enthusiasm. She sounded like a teenager, and she looked like one, too, in her jeans and sneakers. She'd been giddy from the start of their drive to the park, an hour and a half south of the city. Cowell State Park held forty acres of old-growth redwoods, a tiny remnant of the state's once vast stands, which stretched from Big Sur to the Oregon border. Now, dozens of parks and nature reserves protected what was left of the majestic trees.

"You know the difference between redwoods and sequoias, don't you?" Bobby asked.

"Uh, no."

"Basically, redwoods are taller but sequoias are thicker, making sequoias the largest trees on earth. Redwoods only grow along the coast, and sequoias only grow on the western slopes of the Sierras, between four and eight thousand feet."

"You sound like a college professor. Did you learn all that at Berkeley?"

"Nope. My brother and I were Boy Scouts. Our troop went camping in Sequoia National Park once. That's where I learned about the differences between the two species."

"A Boy Scout, huh? You help old ladies across the street?"

"I do. Young ones, too."

Lynette rolled her eyes. "I'll bet."

The couple continued their stroll along the short loop trail that led through the redwoods. The old-growth forest was cool, shady, and peaceful, with a thick understory of greenery growing among the trees. It was a setting of timeless beauty, the kind of place that made you glad to be alive. When they got back to the visitors center, they fetched their picnic lunch from Bobby's car and spread out a blanket on the grass in a patch of shade. A fat blue jay landed on a nearby branch and eyed their food.

"I can't get over how many things there are to do around San Francisco," Lynette said. "I'd love to see the sequoia trees. I saw the Sierras flying in from Wisconsin, but I've never hiked in any real mountains."

"Maybe we can visit Calaveras State Park sometime. They've got sequoias, and the park isn't all that far from the city."

After they'd eaten, Bobby stretched out with his hands behind his head and closed his eyes. Lynette smiled when his breathing slowed, indicating he'd fallen asleep. She let him doze and took in the serenity of the park, hugging her knees to her chest.

When Bobby woke up, he glanced at his watch. "Hey, we'd better get going. Don't want to be late for the concert."

Bobby put the top down on the Triumph, and they packed their things away. They headed out on the highway, the wind tossing their hair. The Beach Boys' "Good Vibrations" was playing on the radio. Bobby turned up the volume, and he and Lynette sang along as they drove.

* * *

Impresario Bill Graham had brought new life to the old Fillmore Auditorium. Built in 1912, the low, boxy building on the corner of Geary and Fillmore Streets had been the site of several black-owned enterprises back when the neighborhood was known as the Harlem of the West. Black workers drawn to the city by the prospect of shipyard jobs during World War II partied in the string of bars along Fillmore Street—Minnie's Can-Do Club, the Long Bar, the Havana Club, the Bird Cage, the Aloha Club, the Encore—and they prayed in the nearby Bethel A.M.E. Church, First A.M.E. Zion Church, and Third Baptist Church.

The Fillmore Auditorium began as the Majestic Hall and Academy of Dancing. In 1936, it was renamed the Ambassador Dance Hall, and in 1939 it became the Ambassador Roller Skating Rink. In 1952, it gained its present name. In the fifties and early sixties, black promoter Charles Sullivan brought in top entertainers such as Duke Ellington, Ray Charles, James Brown, Ike and Tina Turner, and the Temptations.

Bill Graham started renting the auditorium's upstairs ballroom in 1965. Since then, the Fillmore had become synonymous with rock music in San

Francisco, along with the nearby Avalon Ballroom, where hippie promoter Chet Helms produced similar shows. The vibrant posters advertising the two venues' productions defined the visual style of psychedelia, a swashbuckling explosion of luminous colors, wild free-form lettering, and bold, simple images of butterflies, flowers, and peace symbols.

The cloud of marijuana smoke was thick enough to cut when Bobby and Lynette arrived at the Fillmore, which was filled to capacity. The flashing, swirling light show made the gyrating dancers seem like characters in a flickering old-time movie. The strobes and constantly changing photographic images flashing on the stage were nearly as hallucinatory as the drugs coursing through most of the dancers' bodies. Some pundit had written that the crowds packing San Francisco's rock shows were an extension of the Human Be-In, that the hippies and assorted members of the avant-garde came to the shows to be a part of the social phenomenon engulfing the city. It seemed a reasonable assumption as Bobby looked at the blissed-out young people all around him. They were grooving on life as much as the music.

Bobby was dressed in his *Chronicle* reporter's outfit—neat gray slacks, blue shirt, and an oatmeal-colored sport coat. Lynette was wearing a pale green sleeveless jumpsuit of some clingy material, another fashion choice that set off her russet hair. A brass zipper ran from her neckline to her waist. She'd teased the zipper down to expose a hint of cleavage, a purposeful bit of temptation that left Bobby thinking about easing the zipper down the rest of the way.

Bobby was impressed by the music blasting from the stacks of mammoth Marshall speakers onstage. The performers were new to him—the Santana Blues Band, a San Francisco group formed the previous year by Carlos Santana, a skinny twenty-year-old Mexican-American guitarist with a nimbus of curly black hair and a Pancho Villa mustache. Santana's day job was washing dishes at a local Tick Tock Drive In, but the spicy fare his band was serving up was much tastier than any burger.

Bobby recognized the piece the band was playing—"Evil Ways," a song written by jazz guitarist Sonny Henry. Santana's keyboard player, Gregg

Rolie, sang the lead vocal, backed by the energetic beat of conga drums and timbales. During the instrumental breaks, Rolie's Hammond organ filled the auditorium, and Carlos Santana proved he was a guitar wizard on the fast-paced coda. Santana's solo wasn't simply a bunch of repetitious treble runs. He wove a complex, intriguing melody. Together, the band produced an infectious mix of rock and Latin styles that was startlingly original.

"I've *got* to interview these guys," Bobby shouted to Lynette. "They're fantastic."

The band finished its set with the Afro-Latin fusion number "Jingo," a showcase for Santana's guitar mastery and the band's percussionists. As soon as the group left the stage, Bobby grabbed Lynette's hand. "Let's head backstage and see if we can corral those guys."

In the backstage hallway leading to the dressing rooms, Bobby stopped in front of a door marked "Assistant Manager." The door was ajar, so Bobby stuck his head inside. Sonny Anders sat behind a paper-strewn desk with his feet up. Bill Graham's gofer was reading a document, his forehead wrinkled in concentration.

"Excuse me," Bobby said, lightly tapping on the door. "I'm a stringer for the *Chronicle,* and I was hoping to get a backstage pass. I'd like to interview the guys in the Santana Blues Band."

Anders tossed the papers down and shifted his feet from the desk. "C'mon in. Be glad to help you." He stuck out his hand. "Sonny Anders."

Bobby led Lynette into the room and shook Anders's hand. "I'm Bobby Doyle, and this is my friend Lynette Simms. Lynette's an artist."

Anders nodded. "Nice to meet you both." He had the weary appearance of a man worn down by a demanding job. "Doyle, Doyle," he said to himself. "Sure, I've read some of your pieces. That was a good write-up on the Monterey Pop Festival. You really captured the vibe. So how long have you been stringing for the *Chronicle?*"

"I started last month. My twin brother and I both graduated from Berkeley in May."

Anders's face puckered. "A twin brother. That's cool. You from around here?"

"No. We grew up in Los Angeles."

"You know, I met a fellow named Doyle once in Los Angeles. Donovan Doyle, I think it was."

Bobby seemed taken aback. "You're kidding. He's my dad. How did you meet him?"

Anders thought for a moment before answering. He seemed to be casting his mind back to some past event, or maybe he was spacing out. "You know, I can't say for sure. I'll bet it was some PR thing." He snapped his fingers. "Yeah, now I remember. It was a couple of years ago. I was down in L.A. with Bill Graham when he was negotiating a contract for a film production of some sort. Can't even recall what it was."

"That sounds about right. My dad and mom are both attorneys with Columbia Pictures."

Anders tugged on his mustache with a faraway look. "Small world."

Bobby glanced at his watch. "I don't mean to rush you, but I'm worried Santana and his bandmates might wander off. You think I could get that pass?"

Anders sat upright, all business now. "Sure, sure." He rummaged in one of the drawers of his desk and produced a laminated badge. "We can always use more press coverage," he said, handing the pass to Bobby. "Good luck with your interview." His gaze lingered on Bobby and his girlfriend as they left.

Back out in the hallway, Bobby suggested that Lynette might want to bide her time watching the show while he interviewed Santana's crew. "Just hang out here in the wings. I'll be back as soon as I finish."

Lynette found an out-of-the-way spot to watch the band that followed Santana's group, the Sons of Champlin. A lesser-known band popular in the Bay Area, they were performing "Sing Me a Rainbow." The upbeat tune sounded positively tame after listening to Santana's fiery Latin-infused rock, although a horn section set the Sons of Champlin apart from the usual guitar-driven groups. Lynette swayed to the buoyant melody as she watched the musicians onstage.

A short distance away, someone was watching Lynette. Eddie "The Rat"

Ratner had been mingling with members of the audience and some of the musicians and backstage crew, providing interested parties with their drugs of choice from his ever-present canvas shoulder bag. The Rat recognized Lynette as the red-haired chick he'd admired on Shrader Street in Haight-Ashbury. He'd grabbed a few candid shots of her one day with his camera. He smiled to himself, exposing his yellow teeth.

The Rat walked over and stood behind Lynette. He leaned forward and breathed in the scent of her perfume. Lynette sensed his presence and turned around. She jumped back with a start at the sight of Ratner's leering, rodent-like face.

"Hello, pretty lady," Ratner said. "Someone as fine as you shouldn't be all alone."

Lynette moved back another step. "I'm not alone. I'm waiting for someone."

"Yeah, we're all waiting for someone, ain't we?"

Ratner closed the distance between them. He patted his shoulder bag. "How's about you and me having ourselves a party. I got all the stuff we need right here."

"Uh, no thanks. I really am waiting for someone."

Ratner reached out and rubbed Lynette's bare shoulder. "Now don't be like that. I know how to show a girl a good time."

Lynette recoiled from his touch. "Get your hands off me, you little creep. I wouldn't go anywhere with you if you were the last man on the planet. Now get away from me."

Ratner snarled at the girl. "Think you're too good for me, eh? Well I know how to teach bitches like you a lesson."

To Lynette's relief, Bobby reappeared. He didn't realize what was going on between Ratner and the girl. "Hey, babe," he said, "I had a great interview with Santana's band. I tell you, those guys are going places. I've never heard so much about music history in my life. Carlos must know the songs of every blues great."

When Lynette didn't respond, he glanced at Ratner. "Something wrong here?"

"No," Lynette said. "This charming fellow was just entertaining me. I believe he has to be on his way now."

The Rat scowled at her. "See you around, honey."

Bobby put a protective arm around Lynette. Ratner gave him a contemptuous look. "See you both around," he said, then he turned and walked away, his high heels clicking on the hardwood floor.

"What was that all about?" Bobby asked.

"That repulsive little creep was trying to pick me up. He actually touched my arm. I feel like I need to wash it before it becomes infected."

Bobby glanced at the retreating figure of the slump-shouldered, orange-haired drug dealer. "*That* guy was trying to pick *you* up? Ha! Give him credit for being ambitious. He'd have a hard time picking up a dead cat." He gave Lynette a kiss on the cheek. "Come on. Let's go home."

* * *

Bobby's apartment building was a few blocks south of the Fillmore Auditorium in the Western Addition, a centrally located neighborhood north of Haight-Ashbury. After Bobby left Berkeley, he'd settled here to be close to the campus of the University of San Francisco, where he'd be taking graduate classes. His father had recommended the multicultural area, which took in Japantown and an interesting mix of bars and restaurants along Divisadero Street.

Bobby ushered Lynette into his spartan fourth-floor apartment. "Let me show you the place," he said. It didn't take long. The bachelor pad consisted of a living room, kitchen, bath, and a single bedroom. Bobby hadn't lived there long enough to fill the apartment with more than the bare essentials.

Lynette stood looking out his living room window. "This is a great view. What's that patch of green over there?"

"Alamo Square. If you look to the left of the park you can see one of the most photographed features of the city."

"What?"

"See that row of colorful Victorian houses. They call those the Painted

Ladies. They were among the few homes in this area to survive the 1906 earthquake and fire."

Bobby indicated the living room sofa. "Make yourself comfortable while I get us something to drink."

Lynette took a seat and looked around the room. She noticed that Bobby had framed the sketch she'd made of him and hung it over his desk. She nodded toward the sketch when Bobby came back from the kitchen with two glasses of Perrier. "Displaying your great works of art?"

Bobby smiled. "It's my most prized possession."

Lynette picked up a book from the coffee table. *"Robinson Jeffers: Selected Poems,"* she read. "And who, pray tell, is Robinson Jeffers?"

"One of my favorite poets. He lived down the coast at Carmel, in a stone house he built himself with rocks he carried up from the beach. He could be gloomy, but his writing about nature is astonishing. Bobby took the volume from Lynette's hand and thumbed through it. He paused at a page. "This is called 'The World's Wonders.' It's one of his gloomiest poems, but it contains an image that's always haunted me."

He began to read. "I have seen strange things in my time. I have seen a merman standing waist-deep in the ocean off my rock shore, unmistakably human and unmistakably a sea-beast: he submerged and never came up again...."

"That's pretty bizarre," Lynette said.

"It is, but doesn't it make you wonder what he saw?"

"Maybe he was drunk."

Bobby laughed and shut the book. "Maybe he was."

Lynette spotted Bobby's Ramirez classical guitar on a stand in the corner. "I take it you play the guitar."

"Just for my own enjoyment."

"Might I be included in that exclusive circle?"

"Sure. What would you like to hear? Folk, rock, classical? Don't ask me for country, because it's not my cup of tea."

"Surprise me."

Bobby performed a vibrant flamenco number for her.

"I recognize that. It's 'Malagueña,' right?"

"Correct. Cuban composer Ernesto Lecuona wrote it for the piano in 1928, but guitarist Carlos Montoya transcribed the song and recorded it on a live album in 1961. It's becoming a flamenco guitar standard. The basic melody isn't that difficult, but some guitarists speed it up and add a lot of flourishes to show off."

"Very nice. Play something else."

Bobby launched into an exuberant piece that mesmerized Lynette. It was one of the most impressive guitar instrumentals she'd ever heard, far more musically interesting than the screaming, repetitious solos so many rock artists played. "Wow," she said, tapping her chest as if she were out of breath. "What was *that?*"

"Something new. A friend of mine from Los Angeles named Mason Williams composed it. He's the head comedy writer for *The Smothers Brothers Comedy Hour.* He told me he wrote this piece while fooling around in his spare time. He thought of it as 'fuel' for the classical guitar to play at parties, so he's calling it 'Classical Gasoline.'"

"I must say, I'm very impressed by your playing. A skillful writer *and* an accomplished musician. What other talents have you been hiding?"

"I'm a raconteur and a fortune teller."

"A fortune teller? Tell me my fortune."

Bobby set his guitar on its stand and came back to the sofa. He put his arm around Lynette and pulled her close. He traced the curve of her cheek with his finger. "I predict you won't be returning to your apartment tonight."

Lynette's face slowly lit up with an elfin grin.

* * *

Bobby lay in the darkness with Lynette snuggled against his side. He sighed contentedly and took stock of his life. His stories were being published just as he'd hoped, and he'd found himself a wonderful girl. He couldn't get much luckier than that. It seemed that his dreams were coming true.

Chapter Ten

San Francisco

Was it possible she was being followed? Since she'd left work at Fits, the Haight-Ashbury dress shop off Buena Vista Park, Lynette had the sensation that someone was dogging her footsteps, watching her every move. It was ridiculous, she told herself. She was no heroine in distress in some shadowy noir movie. This was broad daylight on busy Haight Street. Still, she couldn't shake the feeling. It was like the sixth sense that prompts you to look across a crowded room, where you spot someone staring at you.

She quickened her pace, glancing behind her periodically. She didn't recognize anyone in the crowd of young people hanging around the neighborhood. No suspicious characters ducking into doorways or hiding their face with their hat pulled down. What the heck was wrong with her, she wondered. Actually, she knew exactly what it was. Ever since she'd found the second anonymous note in her mailbox, she'd been on edge. The message had been brief—"I got my eye on you, bitch"—but it scared the daylights out of her.

Lynette slowed down and took a deep breath. She tried to calm herself by studying the shops she passed. She'd grown used to these sights on her short walks to and from work. The people scurrying in and out of the various establishments reassured her that this was just another typical day. There was the busy Drogstore Café on the corner, and a little farther on, Wild

Colors, with its locally made crafts. The rack in front of the store had some interesting purses for sale. She stopped and examined one.

She passed the Blushing Peony and the House of Richard—boutiques in competition with the shop where she worked. She sniffed the fragrant smells wafting from Tracy's Donuts, where she often stopped on her way to work. On the corner of Haight and Clayton, she passed the Haight-Ashbury Free Medical Clinic. A knot of scruffy kids waited to have their various ailments attended to.

Closer to home, she passed the Straight Theater and the I and Thou coffee shop, where she and Bobby had discussed the first creepy note she'd received. The thought renewed her sense of panic, and she hurried on toward her apartment building on Shrader Street. She dashed up the steps and ran inside, slamming the door behind her. She stood there with her back against the door, catching her breath.

One of the other girls who lived in her building came down the stairs just then. The tall brunette peered over the top of her cat-eye glasses. "Good Lord, girl, what's wrong with you? You look like you've seen a ghost."

Lynette laughed. "I'm a little jumpy today. I think maybe I've had too much coffee."

* * *

Ralph Gleason put down Bobby's story and picked up his favorite briar, filling it from a blue tin of Flying Dutchman tobacco. He struck a wooden match and puffed on his pipe until he had it going. Bobby waited nervously for Gleason's reaction to his story about the Santana Blues Band.

"Not bad," Gleason finally pronounced amid a fragrant cloud of smoke. With his tortoiseshell glasses and handlebar mustache, Gleason looked like a distinguished character from a Sherlock Holmes story, a nobleman from Bohemia perhaps. Gleason hefted Bobby's manuscript. "I've been hearing good things about these guys. I'm glad you came up with this piece. Nice bit of enterprise. We'll run it right away."

Bobby tried to temper his reaction. He didn't want to come off like a gushing amateur, but he was ecstatic over Gleason's comments. Ralph Gleason was the titan of San Francisco music critics, and any word of praise from him was encouraging. Although he was fifty years old, Gleason was about the hippest person Bobby had ever met. Aside from his work for the *Chronicle,* he'd written for *Ramparts,* the liberal, muckraking San Francisco magazine. Gleason appreciated the innovative quality of the city's emerging psychedelic sound, and his writing had helped raise the profile of the Grateful Dead, Jefferson Airplane, and other local groups.

"Thanks a lot," Bobby said. "The minute I heard Santana's band, I knew they were special."

"What else have you got in the works?" Gleason asked.

Bobby had come prepared. "I'd thought I'd focus on some of the free concerts bands are giving in Golden Gate Park and the Panhandle. It's a refreshing concept, all these young musicians sharing their music for no charge. I know the Grateful Dead are big on free shows, and Jimi Hendrix and some of the other groups are getting into it as well. The shows put the slick commercial productions coming out of Los Angeles to shame."

"You hit the nail on the head there. Go to it, my boy."

On his way out of the *Chronicle* offices, Bobby decided to say hello to Herb Caen, the man who'd introduced him to Gleason. Most newspaper journalists were happy to have a desk in a crowded newsroom to call their own, but Caen's celebrity status had rewarded him with a private window office that overlooked the neighborhood bearing the original name of San Francisco—Yerba Buena.

Caen's office looked like a tornado had passed through. Papers and books were strewn on every available surface. The busy columnist glanced up from his cluttered desk when Bobby tapped on his open door. Caen sat in front of his old Royal typewriter. A map of the city hung on the wall behind him. He hardly needed the map, since he knew every street and alleyway, every fancy hotel and dimly lit dive in the city.

"If it isn't Robert L. Doyle, Budding Reporter," Caen said with a grin. "Come in, come in. Take a load off."

"Thanks. I was in to see Ralph Gleason, so I thought I'd stop by."

“I’m glad you did. I’m seeing your byline more and more these days. You’re doing me proud.”

“I can’t thank you enough for paving the way for me.”

“My pleasure.” Caen leaned back and lit a cigarette. “How’s your dad and that beautiful wife of his?”

“I haven’t seen them for a couple of months, but we talk on the phone regularly. They’re both busy as usual. Living the fast life in glittering L.A.”

“Ha. L.A. Better them than me. Don’t get me wrong. Los Angeles is a wonderful place. I just happen to like a city that’s not quite so…amorphous.”

Bobby chuckled. “Yeah, a lot of folks get confused about where L.A. begins and ends. Even some of the people who live there.”

“So what brought you in to see Gleason?”

“I turned in another story.”

“Way to go. Before long, they’ll be offering you a full-time job. Take my advice, enjoy your status as a freelancer as long as you can. Once they get their hooks into you, your time is no longer your own. I have to crank out a column every day, whether I have anything to write about or not. Some days I manufacture things out of thin air.”

“Everyone in town thinks you’re pretty good at it.”

Caen flashed another grin. “I guess I’ve got ’em all fooled.”

* * *

Bobby telephoned Lynette that night and invited her to a free Grateful Dead concert the following Saturday. “It’s in Panhandle Park, so I can meet you at your place and we’ll walk over.”

“Sounds great.” Lynette couldn’t disguise the tension in her voice.

“Something wrong? You sound funny.”

“Oh, it’s just that…I received another creepy note. This one sounds threatening.”

“What? Do you still have it?”

“No, I threw it away immediately, but I remember every word. It said ‘I got my eye on you, bitch.’ Bobby, I’m scared.”

“I can see why. Do you think you should call the police?”

“They’d probably laugh at me. Call me hysterical.”

“Hmm. You don’t think the note could be from that little weirdo we saw at the Fillmore, do you?”

“I have no idea. He seemed more pathetic than dangerous.”

“You never can tell. Do you want me to come over and pick you up? You can stay with me if it would make you feel better. I know I’d feel better.”

“Thanks for the offer, but I can’t hide. I’ve got to go to work, which brings up something else. I can’t shake the feeling that I’m being followed.”

“Damn. We’ve got to do something about this. Maybe I should come stay at your place. I could walk you to work.”

Lynette laughed. “You don’t need to do that. I’m probably being paranoid. Besides, I’m not a child who needs to be walked to school. I can take care of myself.”

“All right, but I want you to promise me something. Promise you’ll call me every morning when you get to work and every evening when you get home.”

“Are you sure that’s necessary?”

“Yes. Promise me you’ll do it.”

“Okay.” Lynette hesitated for several moments. “Bobby, I think maybe I love you.”

* * *

Lynette called twice a day for the rest of the week. Fortunately, she had no further impressions that she was being followed. Immensely relieved, she and Bobby talked about the Grateful Dead concert. They planned to make a day of it, with dinner afterward. And Bobby was planning a surprise. He intended to ask Lynette to move in with him.

When Bobby pulled up in front of her apartment on Saturday afternoon, Lynette was sitting on the steps in a bright yellow sundress, grinning like it was her birthday.

“Hello, beautiful,” Bobby said as he climbed from the car and hugged her tightly. "Ready for some music?"

"You bet."

They set off for Panhandle Park, which was just a couple of blocks away. It was a perfect San Francisco day, clear and sunny, with the temperature in the low seventies and a gentle breeze. They walked hand-in-hand. Lynette was so happy she had to fight the impulse to skip along.

Panhandle Park was filled with a milling throng of Grateful Dead fans. Over the past couple of years, the Dead had become a benevolent Bay Area institution. Today, they stood among a tangled array of microphones and speakers on the back of two flatbed trucks parked end to end, an island of sound in a sea of humanity. Lead guitarist Jerry Garcia anchored the left side of the stage. A stocky man with a dark, wavy mane of hair, he had the playful demeanor of a Labrador retriever. In the middle was Phil Lesh, a slender bass player with a bouffant Prince Valiant hairdo. On the right was baby-faced rhythm guitarist Bob Weir, a perpetually beaming teenager who couldn't read music because of his dyslexia. In back was the squat, disheveled Ron "Pigpen" McKernan on keyboards and harmonica, along with the somber-looking Bill Kreutzmann on drums.

Together, the five friends produced a sound unlike any other local group, a mixture of folk, jazz, blues, country, bluegrass, gospel, and rock. The band's unusual name, which Jerry Garcia had come across in a folklore dictionary, referred to a dead person's spirit being thankful that some charitable person had arranged for his burial. No one, however, was about to bury the Grateful Dead. They'd been riding a crest of popularity ever since they'd gotten together in Palo Alto. Like the Charlatans, the Dead had more success with their live shows than with recording. The free-flowing spontaneity of their extended jam sessions, which fed off the crowd's response, was nearly impossible to reproduce in the studio. Their most loyal fans—the Deadheads—followed the group wherever they played.

Bobby and Lynette joined the crowd as the band cranked up the innuendo-filled "Good Morning Little Schoolgirl," a blues standard made famous in separate recordings by harmonica aces Sonny Boy Williamson and Junior Wells. Sung with gritty intensity by Pigpen McKernan and backed up with his wailing harmonica, the song chugged along to a funky beat. People in the audience were bobbing their heads like a bunch of chickens pecking for food.

Bobby was struck by something as he looked at the faces around him. Every person wore a smile—not the everyday smiles of people saying hello on the street. These were smiles of bliss, the sort of uninhibited, unselfconscious smiles that children wore when playing games under a blue summer sky, their hearts bursting with innocent joy. That was the magic of this time and place, Bobby realized. The music transported the members of the crowd back to their childhood, when pleasures weren't faked or exaggerated but enjoyed wholeheartedly without pretense. At this moment, the people here *were* children. Flower children.

The music went on for almost three hours. After hitting most of their signature songs, the band wrapped up the show with "In the Midnight Hour," a Wilson Pickett number that the Dead stretched to a bluesy, thirty-minute celebration of the things men and women do together late at night. When the song ended, Bobby grabbed Lynette's hand and held on tight as the crowd of laughing young people streamed out Panhandle Park.

* * *

"How about Chinese?" Bobby asked as he and Lynette walked back to her place. "I know a cozy restaurant I think you'll like."

"Lead me to it," Lynette replied.

The Far East Café had been serving Cantonese and Sichuan fare since 1920. It was located on Grant Avenue in the heart of Chinatown, across the street from the Old St. Mary's Church, a Gothic Revival landmark since 1854.

Lynette marveled over the café's antique Chinese murals as they were led to their table. Starting with spring rolls, pot stickers, and fried calamari, they moved on to sweet and spicy General Chou's chicken and prawns with honey walnuts.

"What a feast," Lynette declared, gamely attempting to manipulate chopsticks for the first time.

While they ate, Bobby related the story of a colorful Chinese figure from the late 1800s. "Fong Ching immigrated to San Francisco as a child and became an American success story, owning his own shoe factory over on Washington Street. He also became a successful crime boss. He was known as Little Pete because of his size. He had his hand in every crooked racket in the district. He was the king of Chinatown until he went to a barbershop one day for a shave and two assassins walked in and shot him dead while he sat in the chair."

"He should have stuck to making shoes," Lynette said.

When they'd finished their meal and were sipping their hot jasmine tea, Bobby reached across the table and took Lynette's hand. "There's something I want to ask you."

Lynette gave him a look of uncertainty. "Yes?"

"I change my mind. I don't want to ask you anything. I want to tell you something. Move in with me."

Lynette's mouth fell open. "Wow. This is kind of sudden."

"So what? I know how you feel about me, and I feel the same way about you. What's the point of waiting? We can start moving your things tomorrow."

Lynette stared into Bobby's eyes for what seemed like an eternity. "All right," she said at last.

* * *

Bobby repeatedly told himself to slow down. Traffic was light at eight o'clock on Sunday morning, and in his eagerness to reach Lynette's place, he kept creeping over the speed limit. He'd spent the night before making space in his closet and dresser for Lynette's things. They'd probably need to look for a bigger apartment before long. A bachelor pad would be a tight fit for the two of them.

As Bobby turned onto Shrader Street, he was surprised to see an ambulance and two police cars parked in front of Lynette's row house.

A crowd of neighbors and other gawkers lined the sidewalk on the opposite side of the street. One of the girls must be sick, Bobby told himself, although he wondered why the cop cars would be necessary.

He parked the TR4 and climbed out. "What's going on?" he asked one of the bystanders.

"Someone found a body in the bushes outside that house over there."

Bobby's stomach did a somersault. "A body?"

"Yeah. Some young girl's"

Bobby began fighting his way through the crowd, his mind a complete blank. People stared at him and complained as he blindly elbowed them out of the way. When he crossed the street, he saw several men huddled near the Japanese spirea bushes in front of Lynette's building. Some of the bushes' pink blossoms had fallen to the ground, like a sprinkling of confetti. Bobby couldn't make out what the men were staring at. When he came to the barrier of yellow police tape, he started to duck under it, but a burly uniformed policeman grabbed his arm.

"Where you think you're going, buddy?"

"I've got to see who it is," Bobby yelled. "My girlfriend lives here."

A dark-haired plainclothes cop stepped over. He had the hardened expression of a marine, which he'd once been. "What's going on here?" he growled.

"This guy says his girlfriend lives here."

The plainclothes cop nodded. "Okay, Murphy. I'll handle this."

The uniformed policeman let go of Bobby's arm. "Yes sir."

"I'm Detective Phil Marshall," the plainclothes cop said. "Who are you?"

"Bobby—Robert Doyle. I'm a freelance journalist working for the *Chronicle,* and my girlfriend Lynette Simms lives here."

For some crazy reason, all Bobby could think about was how silly it would be if Phil Marshall were a marshal. Marshal Marshall.

The dour detective flipped open the bright red billfold he was holding. He checked the driver's license and shook his head. "I'm afraid I have some bad news."

Things began spinning in Bobby's mind. He saw the two girls standing on the steps of the building where Lynette used to sit waiting for him to pick her up. They were crying and hugging each other. They had to be Lynette's housemates.

When Bobby glimpsed the jeans and sneakers on the prostrate figure lying behind the spirea bushes, his world collapsed.

"Mr. Doyle. Mr. Doyle." Detective Marshall shook Bobby's arm. "Are you all right?"

"What?" Bobby stammered.

"Look, I know this is a shock. Why don't you go home. There's nothing you can do here."

Bobby appeared not to have heard him. "May I…see her?" he asked.

Marshall considered his request. "Okay. But don't touch anything. The crime scene team hasn't finished yet."

Bobby edged over to the row of bushes and knelt down. Lynette was only three feet away, but she seemed to have already receded into another dimension. She was lying on her left side, so that she was facing him. He thanked God that her eyes were closed. A strand of her beautiful russet hair had fallen across her cheek. She looked like she was asleep—except for the perfect immobility of her features and pallor of her skin.

Bobby reached out to brush the stray hair away from her face, but Marshall touched his shoulder and shook his head. Bobby stood up and continued staring at Lynette. He might have remained there forever if Marshall hadn't broken the spell.

"I think you should head on home now," the detective said. He handed Bobby his business card. "Come down to police headquarters tomorrow and we'll talk. Say two o'clock."

Bobby stared at the card as if it were an artifact from an alien world. He nodded mutely and staggered away. When he reached his car, he climbed inside and broke down. He hadn't cried so hard since his pet beagle was run over when he was a kid.

Among the crowd of onlookers was a slump-shouldered creature with orange hair. Eddie Ratner watched Bobby sitting in his car, then he scurried off like a frightened rodent returning to its nest. Too bad about the chick, he said to himself. Yeah, too bad. Some people just don't have no luck at all.

* * *

Detective Marshall motioned Bobby inside the interrogation room, a brightly lit, timeworn space with a long wooden table and four chairs. One of the chairs was occupied by a man Bobby hadn't met.

"This is Detective Chacon," Marshall said, "head of the drug squad."

The big Apache cop stood up and offered his hand.

"Drugs?" Bobby said in disbelief. "Lynette wasn't on drugs. She'd only used LSD once, and she didn't like it."

"We're not saying she was a drug user," said Detective Chacon.

"Then what are you saying?"

Detective Marshall responded. "When we were at the scene where Miss Simms's body was found, I noticed a red mark on her neck, so I asked our medical examiner to look into it." Marshall hesitated. "Miss Simms was killed by a massive dose of heroin."

Bobby felt like the floor had given way beneath him. "You mean she was deliberately targeted? I thought maybe it was a mugging gone wrong."

"It looks like this was premeditated," Marshall said, "and since drugs were involved, I've asked Detective Chacon to assist with the investigation."

Bobby sat there with a blank look on his face, trying to make sense of what he'd heard. The two detectives gave him a moment to absorb the news.

"Can you think of anyone who might have had a grudge against Miss Simms?" Marshall asked.

"No. No one. Lynette was a sweet, likable kid. I can't imagine she'd ever offended anyone in her life."

The two detectives exchanged glances. With over thirty years of law enforcement experience between them, they knew that few people went through life without creating enemies.

"Well, if you think of anyone," Detective Marshall began.

"Wait a minute," Bobby interrupted. "There was someone we met last week at a concert at the Fillmore. He made a pass at Lynette, and when she blew him off, he got mad."

"Can you describe him?" Marshall asked.

Bobby concentrated, trying to recreate the scene. "He was a homely guy. Not very tall, and he was hunched over. He wore those high-heeled Beatle boots, and he had a canvas shoulder bag like the military use, a messenger bag I think they're called. The guy dyed his hair orange. That ought to be easy enough to spot."

Detective Chacon shook his head. "Do you have any idea how many kids there are on the streets these days with strange colored hair? Orange hair, purple hair, pink hair. They're all over the place. It's like a freaking circus out there."

Bobby shrugged. "I'm sorry, but that's all I can remember about the guy."

Detective Marshall was scribbling notes. He looked up from his pad. "You told me at the crime scene that Miss Simms was your girlfriend. We need to know everything you can tell us about her."

"I know she moved here from a small town in Wisconsin. Plymouth, I think it was. She said her parents run the local hardware store."

Marshall nodded. "That squares with what her housemates told us. They said she had a job at a dress shop in Haight-Ashbury."

"That's right. A boutique called Fits. But she really wanted to become a professional artist. She had real talent."

"Anything else?"

Bobby racked his brain. "Oh, she recently received a disturbing note."

Marshall threw his pen down in disgust. "A disturbing note. And you're just now telling us about it?"

"I just remembered it. I'm sorry. My mind isn't functioning very well."

"That's all right," said Chacon. "We understand. Can you remember what the note said?"

"It said 'I got my eye on you,' and the person called her a bitch."

"I don't suppose she kept the note," Chacon said.

"I'm afraid she tossed it."

Marshall let out a sigh. "Mr. Doyle, do you have any idea why Miss Simms would have had several empty cardboard boxes in her possession? We found them near the body."

"Empty boxes?"

"Yeah. One of her housemates told us she went out that night to see if she could scrounge up some empty boxes at a nearby health food store. Got any idea why she'd do that?"

The news hit Bobby like a thunderbolt. He hung his head for a moment, and he felt himself on the verge of another crying jag. "We'd made plans for her to move in with me. She must have needed the boxes to pack up her things."

"Then you two were in love?" Chacon asked, a note of tenderness in his voice.

Bobby's eyes lost focus. What was love, anyway, he asked himself. Some mystical combination of physical attraction, compatibility, and familiarity? Maybe the surest test of love was the feeling he had right now when he realized he'd never see Lynette again, never again hear her laughter or feel her touch. She was gone forever, and the realization gave him an aching hollowness in his chest that could only be described as heartbreak.

"Yes," he said softly, looking down at his hands. "We were in love."

* * *

Bobby spent the next week with his parents in Los Angeles. When he told them what had happened, his mother hugged him tightly and rubbed the back of his head, saying "Oh, honey." It was a comforting phrase he'd heard innumerable times growing up, each time he skinned a knee or suffered some minor psychological trauma. His father handed him a stiff shot of Irish whiskey, Donovan's fallback remedy when nothing else could be done.

The first night back home, Bobby wrote a long letter to his brother. It was good to state the facts in writing, far better than trying to explain how he felt in person, when his voice kept faltering and his emotions betrayed him. Jack had always managed to say something that made him feel better whenever he suffered a setback, a bit of brotherly advice that was even more effective than his mother's tender embraces or his father's words of wisdom. Jack went directly to the cause of the hurt and put it into perspective, although Bobby knew there was no way his brother could put this wound into perspective. No one could do that.

Chapter Eleven

Pleiku Province

Jack sat on his bunk reading Bobby's letter. He felt a profound sense of sorrow over Lynette's murder, but that feeling paled in comparison to his anger. So much death—so much needless, senseless death. He'd lost several more men from his platoon since he'd taken over. Sometimes, he thought that the soldiers who were killed outright were the lucky ones. The casualties that disturbed him the most were the young men who suffered grievous wounds, some of them maimed beyond recognition. The worst he'd seen was Private Tim Olsen, a poor shambling oaf who'd had the lower half of his face blown off by an RPG.

Olsen shouldn't even have been in Vietnam. Jack was amazed that the slow-witted teenager had passed the draft board's physical and intelligence tests. Jack had often wondered if Olsen actually knew where he was. The soldier always seemed to be in a fog, and every order Jack gave him had to be repeated at least twice. Olsen had probably spent his brief life being told what to do and mutely obeying. Someone told him he was being drafted, and he blankly went along. Someone else told him he was being shipped off to Vietnam, and he grinned his vacuous grin and shrugged.

Olsen had been the butt of constant jokes and pranks. Jack couldn't believe how cruel and callous the other members of the platoon could be to such a simple kid—an awkward puppy tormented by a pack of snarling pit bulls. The worst offender was that bastard Jimmy Stooks. Stooks had teased Olsen relentlessly, calling him Dim Tim to his face. As horrible as it sounded, Jack found himself wishing that Stooks had suffered that hideous wound instead of an innocent lummox like Olsen, who seemed born to be victimized.

But no one was teasing Tim Olsen now, now that the hapless teenager had been turned into an aberration, like so many other horribly wounded soldiers. In the short time that Jack had been in-country, he'd seen far too many formerly handsome young men with unspeakable injuries. Some of them would never return home to wives or sweethearts. Their wounds were too gruesome to behold—and too great a reminder that theirs was the true face of war. They'd live out their days hidden away in lonely wards of veterans hospitals, the years passing slowly as they stared at the TV or played checkers with their fellow outcasts, always wondering what their lives might have been like if they'd never heard of the green hell called Vietnam.

The maiming and the killing had changed Jack irrevocably. Each time his platoon returned from its frequent patrols, he watched his men clinging to their beers or their joints, like drowning men clinging to a life preserver. Once, he might have considered disciplining them when their revels went too far, but not anymore. Not anymore.

* * *

Company C set out early on the relief mission. A Special Forces counterinsurgency camp southwest of Kontum was in danger of being overrun by a massed force of Vietcong. The Green Berets had been under siege for days, and they desperately needed supplies. West of Pleiku City, Jack and Vince's platoons slogged through the damp, tangled vegetation. Tenacious weeds grabbed at their legs as if intent on slowing them down. Some of the luxuriant plants were taller than the men's heads, and they often lost sight of one another. Swarms of insects continually tormented them. At one point, the company had to halt and build a log bridge over a stream so the supply trucks could follow. It was hard to breathe while toiling in the hot, humid air, like exercising in a sauna.

Jack's men were carrying the new M-16 rifle, which was replacing the M-14 in Vietnam. The older M-14 was accurate over a greater distance—up to five hundred yards or more—and it fired a larger 7.62mm cartridge, but the M-16 was nearly three pounds lighter. That made a big difference to a soldier who had to lug his weapon for long distances through rugged terrain. The M-16 was also more suited to jungle warfare, where firepower was more important than long-distance accuracy. On full automatic, an M-16 could spew out its 5.56mm cartridges at over seven hundred rounds per minute. In the confusion of a close-quarters jungle firefight, where visibility might be measured in feet rather than yards, the M-16 was far superior to the older weapon.

Even so, some diehards found it difficult to part with their M-14s. They were tried and true—real rifles with gleaming wooden stocks. "This piece of crap looks like it was made by Mattel Toys," Staff Sgt. Rob Fisher had moaned as he inspected his new M-16's plastic stock. But after he fired the weapon on full automatic on the practice range, he turned to Jack and smiled. "This'll do," he said. "This'll do fine."

Sergeant Fisher and the rest of the platoon would be putting their new weapons to the test today. They could hear the sounds of battle long before they reached the Special Forces camp. The staccato rattle of rifle fire was interspersed with the louder bursts of M-60 machine guns, the hollow thump of grenade launchers, and the boom of heavy artillery. Jack would always remember the looks on the faces of the Green Berets when his company arrived on the scene. There were tight smiles and nods of greeting, but no cheers as if the cavalry had ridden to their rescue. Most of the exhausted men simply went on firing their weapons. To them, the relief troops were just another chaotic element in an unending horror film.

The Green Berets had to brave enemy fire to replenish their dwindling ammunition, dashing toward the supply trucks then racing back to the trenches. A pall of smoke from the continuing barrage hung over the camp like a wispy gray shroud. The Special Forces were dug in atop a ridge that looked out over an expanse of thick jungle to the west. The enemy could be hidden anywhere in that wilderness.

Toward the end of the day, the Vietcong launched an all-out assault on the ridge. With the lowering sun in their eyes, the Americans found it hard to spot the insurgents. Like many VC units, the attackers were more daring—and less disciplined—than North Vietnamese regulars. They flung themselves against the American outpost with little concern for casualties. Their only goal was victory over the foreigners they hated, and if it cost them half of their men to achieve it, so be it. Over the centuries, the Vietnamese had defeated the Mongols, the Chinese, and the French. Fanatical tenacity was in no short supply against their current enemy, invaders who bombed their cities and napalmed their villages.

The Vietcong were unaware of the presence of the relief troops on the other side of the ridge. When the assault began, the men of Company C joined the Special Forces in hurling back the attackers. The Americans mowed down wave after wave of VC as they struggled up the face of the ridge in a blind fury, like berserkers of old. The slaughter continued for nearly two hours. Jack had lain on his belly the entire time, firing round after round as enemy bullets sizzled overhead. At dusk, the VC—what there was left of them—finally called off the assault. A long night followed with sporadic gunfire, but when the sun rose the next morning, all was still.

At zero seven hundred, the Special Forces sent a patrol down the face of the ridge. They encountered no resistance. The enemy had withdrawn. Over the next few hours, the Americans dug pits and buried the enemy dead. Soldiers wandered among the bodies, collecting war souvenirs and confiscating weapons, mostly Chinese-made AK-47s, a Russian-designed weapon that arms experts considered superior to the M-16.

Jack walked among the dead. He had no idea how many, if any, of these men he'd killed. The assault had been a blur of gunfire, shouts, and curses. Jack looked down at one of the bodies, a boy who couldn't have been more than fourteen or fifteen. The boy was curled up in the fetal position. Wearing the typical Vietnamese peasant garb of loose-fitting cotton pajamas, he looked like he was asleep—except for the bloody hole in the side of his head.

Without his weapons, the dead boy would have been indistinguishable from the thousands of other Vietnamese peasants Americans came into contact with every day. That was one of the overriding challenges in this war. American fighting men couldn't tell friendly villagers from Vietcong. The VC were often smiling farmers by day and armed insurgents by night. That deadly confusion caused some soldiers to hate and distrust all Vietnamese. It was one of the reasons for the rampant bigotry among U.S. forces. Jack always cringed when he heard Americans refer to the Vietnamese as gooks, slopes, or dinks. It was a callous dehumanization that had led to more than one atrocity.

* * *

After three grueling days in the field, the men of Company C headed back to Camp Enari. They were a sad-looking lot, unshaven, their fatigues filthy and soaked with sweat. The closer they got to their home base, the more spread out the units became as soldiers began to let down their guard. Jack's platoon was making its way through the hilly remains of a deserted tea plantation. Some of the men were singing Barry McGuire's "Eve of Destruction"—"You're old enough to kill, but not for votin', you don't believe in war, but what's that gun you're totin'?" Sergeant Fisher was so tired he just let them sing.

As usual, Jimmy Stooks was dawdling at the end of the column, ever the incorrigible screw-off. Stooks had never quite crossed the line so that he'd be charged with malingering, the army's quaint term for soldiers who faked injuries or mental problems to evade duty. The worst type of malingering was deliberately wounding yourself. More than one combat-traumatized grunt had resorted to shooting himself in the leg or sticking his hand into some piece of machinery. If an injury was obviously self-inflicted, the soldier could be prosecuted and punished. The trick was to make a wound seem accidental or a mental problem convincing. If no criminal act could be proved, the army often got rid of the soldier with a general discharge, a piece of paper thousands of soldiers would gladly accept—and laugh about all the way home.

As Jack's platoon meandered along, heavy enemy fire erupted from a nearby line of trees. The men scattered for whatever cover they could find. Separated from the rest of the group, the lollygagging Jimmy Stooks was pinned down. Jack ordered his men to give their fellow soldier covering fire so he could retreat, but instead of crawling back to join the others, Stooks decided to pull a John Wayne. He stood up to hurl a grenade toward the trees. Suddenly, he doubled over, screaming in pain. He'd taken a round in the gut. "I'm hit, I'm hit," he kept yelling, as if it were an affront to mankind that he should be wounded.

Jack worked his way down the line of men, closer to where Stooks lay writhing in pain. "Cover me," he yelled, then he ran through thirty yards of patchy vegetation, crouching low. Bullets pinged all around him, raising little puffs of dust. He flung himself across the last few yards and grabbed Stooks by the collar of his flak jacket, which had been hanging open in violation of safety protocols. Fortunately, the lanky Stooks was light enough and Jack was strong enough that he was able to drag the wounded man back toward the rest of the platoon.

While Jack was struggling to reach the relative safety of the line, his radioman frantically called for air support. Jack pulled Stooks into the depression behind the row of tea bushes where his men had taken cover. Jack hadn't expected any thanks from a man like Jimmy Stooks, but he was unprepared for the hostile look Stooks gave him. Being rescued by someone he hated was a bitter pill for Stooks to swallow. Jack left the ingrate in the care of their medic without exchanging a word.

Twenty minutes later, three Cobra gunships came clattering over the horizon. One of Jack's men fired a ground marker round into the trees with his grenade launcher. The plume of smoke directed the Cobras to their target, each of their Miniguns spewing three thousand rounds per minute. The skirmish was quickly over as the enemy troops melted away. It was the typical North Vietnamese tactic—ambush an American patrol, inflict as much damage as possible, then retreat before taking too many losses.

A UH-1 Huey landed to evacuate the wounded. Two other men besides Stooks had been hit.

* * *

That night, Jack sat drinking cognac with his buddy Vince, a classic illustration of the perverse nature of the war they were fighting. In a matter of hours, troops could go from being embroiled in a hellish firefight to drinking cold beer, shooting pool, or watching movies.

"I heard about your heroics today," Vince said. "Tell me something. Why did you risk your life rescuing that worthless jerk Jimmy Stooks?"

Jack pondered the question, which caught him off guard. "I never stopped to think about it. I guess because it was the right thing to do." He knocked back his shot of cognac and held out his glass for another.

IV

~August 1967~

Chapter Twelve

San Francisco

Bobby didn't know what to do with himself. Since Lynette's death, he'd been adrift. He hadn't written anything for the *Chronicle* since the murder. He had scratched out a couple of poems, trying to capture what he and Lynette experienced together and what she meant to him, but everything he wrote seemed maudlin and overly earnest. One of the lines he wrote—"the moths of loneliness flutter about the light of your memory in my unending night"—made him cringe when he read it the next day. He decided that no one should attempt to write poetry while they're grieving. He ended up tossing the poems into the wastebasket.

Bobby kept staring at Lynette's sketch of him and thinking of the talent that would never have the chance to reach its full potential. The drawing that used to give him such pleasure had taken on the melancholy air of an unfinished symphony. Lynette's death drove home the harsh reality that when a person's life ends, their plans for the future become a sort of folktale, something their friends might talk about for a time then gradually forget.

The police hadn't turned up anything on Lynette's killer. They speculated that the person had trailed her home from the health food store and decided to attack her before she went into her apartment building. There was no forensic evidence, and no one saw anything. The greatest mystery was the absence of any discernible motive. Lynette hadn't been robbed or molested. It all seemed beyond explanation. Detective Marshall said that everything pointed to a random murder by a "thrill killer," as he called it. He said that those disturbed individuals were usually the hardest to track down, since they had no links to their victims. Solving the crime seemed hopeless.

In search of a sense of closure, Bobby had returned to some of the places he and Lynette visited. He haunted the De Young Museum to view the paintings Lynette talked about. He sat for hours in the Japanese Tea Garden. He even drove over to Marin County to visit Mount Tamalpais, where he first glimpsed Lynette dancing in the sunlight like a woodland nymph. Nothing helped. Everyplace he went, he kept recalling one of the last things Lynette had said to him. She'd said that before she met him, she was thinking about moving back home to Wisconsin. And now, her body had been returned to Wisconsin. She'd gone home forever.

What made everything worse was that he had nothing left of Lynette but her sketch. On a whim, he tracked down the address of her parents and wrote them a long letter, telling about the things he and Lynette had shared. He asked her parents to send him a copy of the photo he'd taken of her at Cowell Redwoods State Park. He didn't mention the real reason he wanted the photo. He needed it to help preserve his memories, before the passage of time left him with nothing but a blurry image of the girl he'd loved so fleetingly.

Bobby thought of these things as he strolled along Ocean Beach, the three-mile stretch of sand fronting the Pacific between Cliff House and old Fort Funston, a former coastal defense installation now fallen to ruin. Bobby glanced at the thicket of apartment buildings edging the beach. Years ago, there'd been an amusement park where those buildings stood—Playland at the Beach. A roller coaster, Ferris wheel, and other rides offered a temporary escape for people beaten down by the Great Depression and World War II. Bobby tried to imagine the carousel music and laughter echoing from that long-ago park.

Today, there were people playing volleyball, kids flying kites, and fishermen casting their lines into the sea. The sight of couples walking hand in hand gave Bobby pause, until he smiled at the thought that love itself could not be defeated. It would always bubble up amid the hatred, like flowers pushing themselves through cracks in a sidewalk. At that moment, he resolved to not become so mired in gloom that he neglected to live his life. He would never forget Lynette and the time they'd had together, but he needed to carry on. He'd start by getting back to his writing, and he'd enroll in one of the short summer classes at USF before his regular classes began in September. He'd take something fun and interesting. He'd meet new people, and best of all, it would get him out of his lonely apartment.

* * *

The University of San Francisco campus perched on picturesque Ignatian Heights adjacent to Golden Gate Park, a short drive from Bobby's apartment. Founded in 1855 as the St. Ignatius Academy, USF was the city's oldest institution of higher learning. The school's first class consisted of three students. Now, several thousand undergraduate and graduate students attended the private Jesuit university. Among the school's notable alumni was Bill Russell, the basketball great who led the USF Dons to two consecutive NCAA titles in the 1950s. The university's most famous landmarks were the twin spires and dome of St. Ignatius Church, the imposing Italian Renaissance and Baroque edifice where graduates had been handed their diplomas since 1914.

Bobby decided to enroll in a summer class on freedom of the press, which fit in with his goal of earning an advanced degree in writing. The accelerated three-week session met daily. The regular classes he'd be starting in the fall met either two or three days a week, so he'd still be free to continue his work for the *Chronicle.* His master's program would keep him safe from the draft for a year or more, and he told himself that if the damned war in Vietnam was still going on after that, he'd enroll in a doctoral program. The country could make better use of another Ph.D. than one more unwilling soldier.

On the first day of summer class, he arrived on campus thirty minutes early. It turned out to be a wise precaution, since he had to roam all over spacious Kalmanovitz Hall to find the right classroom. Traipsing down the labyrinth of hallways, he was briefly gripped by the panic he'd experienced in dreams about being lost on a college campus. He'd read that researchers had determined those wacky college-related dreams were one of the most common nightmares.

When he finally found the room where his lectures would take place, he was pleased to see that the class was small, only around twenty students. There was the usual mix of ethnicities common in San Francisco, divided fairly evenly between men and women. The syllabus the instructor handed out sounded interesting. They'd be studying the development of the First Amendment and the challenges reporters faced in view of the current political divisions over the war, the emerging Black Power movement, and the issue of freedom of speech on college campuses. It promised to be a lively three weeks.

After class, a petite, attractive girl with short, curly blond hair and a mischievous look in her eyes walked up to Bobby. She was wearing jeans and a bright red T-shirt emblazoned with a white peace symbol, an emblem America's antiwar activists had borrowed from the British nuclear disarmament movement. Aside from being a bold political statement, the tight-fitting T-shirt showed off the girl's impressive bosom. She smiled, revealing two winsome dimples in her cheeks. "Hey, handsome," she said. "My name's Susie Blake. How's about you and me getting together to study? Or, if you'd prefer, we could head over to my place right now and I'll throw a leg lock on you. I'm pretty nifty when it comes to wrestling."

Obviously, Miss Susie Blake wasn't what you'd call a shy girl. Bobby stared at her, his mouth hanging open in astonishment. She had the brightest blue eyes he'd ever seen. Maybe they were cornflower blue, he thought. It was a word that British writers often used to describe a vibrant shade of blue, although Bobby couldn't say if this girl's eyes fit the bill. He didn't recall ever having seen a cornflower. Suddenly, he realized that for the first time since Lynette's death he was laughing. It felt good.

"Let's see," he said, scratching his chin. "Studying or having a leg lock thrown on me. You'll have to give me a moment to decide."

Susie giggled. "Actually, I'm not quite that trashy. I just like to see big macho guys like you blush. Anyway, some of us are forming a study group. You're welcome to join us. We'll be getting together over in the library. It should be interesting, and you might even learn something."

It didn't take Bobby long to make up his mind. "Sounds like fun. Thanks for inviting me."

Susie led the way over to Gleeson Library, a short walk across a sweep of greenery between Kalmanovitz Hall, wisely nicknamed K-Hall, and St. Ignatius Church. The study group met in one of the conversation study areas on the second floor. Dozens of students sat around the room, intently discussing the intricacies of Latin grammar, data science, and something called kinesiology, which Susie said had to do with wrestling.

Susie introduced the three other members of their study group, Bernie Warren, Alison Grant, and Will Taylor. Bernie was a wholesome, cherubic boy with a fledgling beard, thick glasses, and a 49ers cap perched on the back of his head. Alison had long black hair and a deathly pale complexion. She'd gathered her hair and pulled it forward over one shoulder so that it trailed down her chest. She reminded Bobby of illustrations he'd seen of the Lady of the Lake, the ethereal being rising from the waters in the King Arthur tales. Bobby sensed that Bernie and Alison were a couple. Will Taylor was a gawky young man with freckles and a shock of red hair. He looked like a character out of *Tom Sawyer,* or maybe a grown-up Opie Taylor from *The Andy Griffith Show.*

They all took turns telling something about themselves. Bernie and Alison were both communications majors and were both from San Francisco. Bobby didn't ask, but he suspected they'd gone to high school together. Will was a pre-law student from Salinas. Susie was from faraway Missouri and was completing a degree in film studies. After she'd sketched out her background, she turned to Bobby. "So what's your story? And by the way, what the heck's your name?"

"Bobby Doyle. I'm from L.A., and my brother and I recently graduated from Berkeley, where I earned a degree in English."

"Berkeley, huh?" Will Taylor said in a high-pitched voice. "So, we've got a rabble-rouser in our midst, and a poet, too, I'll bet."

"No to the first and yes to the second."

Will laughed. "There's not an English major alive who doesn't write poetry. And I'll bet you want to become the next Ernest Hemingway, too. Right?"

"Whoa," Bobby exclaimed. "You're hitting pretty close to home there, Will."

"Why'd you switch to USF?" Bernie Warren asked.

"My dad went to school here, and he's always had great things to say about the school. I'll be starting a master's program in writing here next month. I wrote for the student paper at Berkeley, and I've been freelancing for the *Chronicle* this summer. I've done a few pieces on the local music scene."

Susie did a double take. "Is your byline Robert L. Doyle?"

"Yes it is."

"What do you know—I've read some of your pieces. I enjoyed them, too. You don't write like other music critics. Too many of them try to sound highbrow, with a string of cheap rhetorical flourishes. Your writing seems to come from the heart. I felt I could believe you."

Bobby didn't know what to say.

"Sorry. I didn't mean to make you blush again."

* * *

When the group broke up, Bobby invited Susie to go for coffee in the student union. He bought them both lattes, and they found seats in the lounge. "I want to thank you for inviting me to join your group," he said. "It's good to make new friends."

"No problem," Susie replied with a smile.

"Mind if I ask why you picked me?"

"You seemed lonely. Like a lost puppy."

Bobby's eyes took on a distant look as he thought of how his world had been shaken. He didn't realize it showed.

"So you're a film major," he said, trying to sound upbeat. "What do you plan to do after you finish school?"

"Move to Los Angeles, take the movie industry by storm, and become rich and famous."

"My parents are both attorneys for Columbia Pictures. Maybe they can introduce you to some people they know."

Susie's eyes became huge. "Are you kidding me? Columbia Pictures. I'd die to work there."

"Well, now you've got friends in the game."

Susie squirmed around in her seat like a little girl anxious to open her Christmas presents. "Wouldn't that be something? Hell, I'd scrub the floors if they'd hire me."

Bobby laughed. "And you came all the way out here from Missouri—the Show-Me State."

"Yeah. They more or less showed me the door."

Bobby gave her a questioning look.

"I was born in Sedalia, Missouri," Susie said, "deep in the Bible Belt. My father's a Baptist minister. I left home at eighteen, right after he told me he would only pay for my college education if I attended Oral Roberts University. I told him I'd rather attend Oral Sex University than to be surrounded by a bunch of emptyheaded evangelicals who believe the preposterous myths that a virgin actually gave birth and people were brought back from the dead.

"After he slapped my face, I went to my room and packed my things. I left that day for California, and I've never been back home since. My mother wrote me several letters telling me my father was willing to forgive me if I'd come home. I wrote and told her that the crux of the problem was that I wasn't willing to forgive him.

"I've worked my way through three years of college without anyone's help. Since I landed in San Francisco, I've worked in a head shop and been a barmaid in Haight-Ashbury. I've cleaned up after drunks and had my ass pinched by every variety of low-life you can imagine. Now I work in a wine shop in the Castro district. Thankfully, they've got a better class of customers than the Haight, and I'm learning about the wine trade. I'm damned proud of what I've accomplished on my own, and I've never told my parents a thing about it."

"That's pretty harsh," Bobby said. "You might feel better if you took the high road and reconciled with your father. You don't have to win him over to your viewpoint. Just be willing to allow him to have his."

Susie gave him a skeptical look. "You don't know my old man. He'd never stop trying to save my soul. He's the one who needs to learn to allow other people to have their own opinions. That's the trouble with zealots—they aren't satisfied unless they can shove their beliefs down someone else's throat. They simply can't understand that what they regard as faith other people see as plain old gullibility."

Bobby could tell his conciliatory advice wasn't achieving anything. But hell, why did he think he knew the right thing to do? He wasn't Ann Landers.

"Now I'm the black sheep of the family," Susie continued. "If you asked my parents what kind of person I am, you'd be shocked. Sedalia is the site of the Missouri State Fair, and one year I went to see Ike and Tina Turner perform. When my dad heard about that he hit the ceiling. He said it was the devil's music. He was mortified when I told them I was moving to California. He calls it 'Californication.'

"He'd probably have a nervous breakdown if he strolled down the street where I work. As you know, the Castro district is becoming one of the city's gay neighborhoods. Like a lot of Christians, my dad thinks homosexuality is blasphemous. I don't know how many sermons I had to listen to when I was a kid in which he characterized gay people as deviates and sinners who were going straight to hell. My boss at the wine shop is gay, and he's one of the nicest, kindest individuals I've ever met. He's got a better chance of making it to heaven, if there is such a place, than half of my dad's congregation."

Bobby had never heard anyone speak so fervently about their lives. "So how did a Protestant girl like you end up here at a Catholic university?"

"I chose USF because it's a great school." Susie reflected a moment. "Maybe there was a part of me that felt like thumbing my nose at my dad. He isn't very openminded about other denominations.

"My first name's really Susannah. When my dad named me, I don't believe he knew that Susannah is the English form of the Hebrew name Shoshana. I hate Susannah. It sounds so prim and proper. It's a name for a tame midwestern housewife whose only goal in life is to please her husband. Cook his meals, wash his clothes, and fetch his slippers. Besides, Susannah means 'lily,' and I think I'm more of a dandelion, a little yellow weed."

Bobby found himself staring at this outrageously frank and rebellious girl, trying to figure her out. He'd never met anyone like her before. It was as if she were from some foreign country with bewildering customs.

When his silent scrutiny went on a bit too long, Susie cocked an eyebrow. "Are you liking what you see, big guy? Or are you dumbstruck in my presence?"

She spoke in the taunting tone she'd used on him before. He decided to answer in kind. "Sorry. It's just that small women with big breasts have always fascinated me."

Susie looked down at her chest. "They're not too big to get in the way when I'm wrestling." She picked up her books to leave. "You know, that offer about coming over to my place still stands."

"You may want to think twice about tangling with strange men. I did some Greco-Roman wrestling in high school."

"Then we could go for the best two out of three falls." She winked and walked away.

Chapter Thirteen

San Francisco

The following week was a welcome change. Attending classes and meeting with his new study group friends proved to be just what Bobby needed. He was beginning to feel more like his old self again. He even wrote a piece for the *Chronicle* about the local club scene. A retro San Francisco band calling themselves the Flamin' Groovies had opened at the Matrix, a hole-in-the-wall club east of the Presidio and south of the Marina district. Bobby did a clever profile of the band, and Ralph Gleason praised the story, which made Bobby feel like he was getting back in the saddle.

"The Flamin' Groovies are certainly out of step with the psychedelic bands," Gleason said, "but you made them sound interesting without mocking them."

Bobby replayed Gleason's words in his mind as he sat in one of his study group meetings. Telling himself not to let Gleason's praise go to his head, Bobby focused on what Will Taylor was saying about the legal aspects of protecting the confidentiality of news sources. The kid was smart, Bobby thought. He was sure Will would make a first-rate attorney.

After the meeting, Susie Blake tugged on Bobby's sleeve. She always sat next to him. He assumed it was because she'd recruited him to the group. When she leaned over, Bobby expected to hear another of her wild, unpredictable comments, but what she said was surprisingly commonplace.

"You like wine?" she asked.

"Uh, sure. I don't know much about it though."

"I could teach you a thing or two."

"I'll bet you could."

Susie rolled her eyes. "I mean about wine. I'm driving over to Sonoma this weekend to visit some wineries. I'll be scouting out the recent vintages for the wine shop where I work. Would you like to tag along?"

Bobby stared at her for a long time. He didn't know if he was ready for this. Slipping into another relationship so soon after Lynette's murder seemed to be rushing things.

"Don't worry, handsome. I won't jump you. I can tell you've got something—or someone—on your mind. I just thought maybe you could use a change of scenery."

Bobby smiled. "Thanks. It sounds like a wonderful outing."

"Great. Give me your address and I'll pick you up at nine on Saturday morning. Wear comfortable shoes, because we'll be doing some walking."

* * *

Susie drove up in a cream-colored Chevy II that could only be classified as a rattletrap. Covered with dust and spattered with bird droppings, it had obviously been parked under a tree for some time. A compact model introduced in the early sixties, the Chevy II was designed for the low end of the market, and it looked it. The boxy, unadorned vehicle could well have been manufactured in East Germany. Bobby climbed in and inspected the cheap interior. "Nice," he said. "I like the plastic seat covers. They add a touch of class."

"You like the body color?" Susie reached out the window and slapped the side of the car. "My boss calls it Barf Beige. He inherited this piece of junk from an elderly aunt who passed away. He considered selling it but decided it might come in handy now and then. If he had a better car he probably wouldn't let me drive it."

She laughed and stomped on the gas pedal. The underpowered four-cylinder engine whined like an overburdened washing machine.

The hour-plus trip to the town of Sonoma took them north on Highway 101 through Marin County, then east into Sonoma County on Highway 37 and north on 121—an up-and-down drive through rumpled hills and bucolic valleys. In the green heart of the Sonoma Valley, they passed several signs advertising wineries. Bobby finally asked Susie when she was planning on stopping. "I thought we came to visit wineries. Something wrong with those?"

"I've got someplace special in mind," she said. "California's first winery to grow premium grapes."

East of downtown Sonoma, Susie turned onto Old Winery Road, which led to the Buena Vista Winery. "This is where the California wine industry began," Susie said as she parked the car. "It started in 1857 when an immigrant from Hungry named Agoston Haraszthy settled here and planted European vinifera grapes. Before then, Californians made wine from the varieties of grapes planted by the Spanish missionaries. The mission grapes were hardy and produced a lot of wine, but it was inferior stuff. Haraszthy planted the grapes that made Bordeaux and Burgundy famous. Nobody thought he could succeed, but Haraszthy proved them wrong."

They climbed out of the car and started down a eucalyptus-lined path toward the tasting room, a large stone structure dating to 1864. "Haraszthy was quite a character," Susie said. "He called himself a count, but that was probably a figment of his imagination. He knew something about viticulture, though, which is why his chose this dry, hilly terrain. Until he came along, vineyards in California were planted in well-watered lowlands. Haraszthy was looking to duplicate the growing conditions of the great European vineyards."

She paused outside the stone building. "It turned out that Haraszthy was a better winegrower than businessman. He lost the winery in the 1860s and moved to Nicaragua, where he tried his hand at growing sugar and making rum. Unfortunately, the poor guy fell in a river one day and got eaten by crocodiles—a pretty dramatic end for a colorful figure."

Inside the rustic tasting room, they sampled the winery's latest vintages of

Chardonnay, Pinot Noir, and Zinfandel. Susie showed Bobby how to check for the proper color by tilting his glass and holding it to the light. "The wine should be clear, never cloudy or showing any sediment. Now—sniff, swirl, and sniff again. The wine should smell fresh, with no chemical or vinegary scents. Finally, take a sip and swish it around in your mouth. Wine experts look for aromas, flavors, and textures. They can name dozens of characteristics. If you want to impress someone, toss out the names of a few types of fruit and flowers."

"Am I supposed to swallow it or spit it out?" Bobby asked.

"Spit it or chug it, whichever you prefer," Susie said with a giggle. "Just don't gargle with it."

After the tasting, Susie bought a half dozen bottles to take back to the shop so her boss could have the final word on which varieties to order. From Buena Vista, they headed a short distance to the south to visit Gundlach Bundschu, the oldest family-owned winery in California, established in 1858. They tried a number of wines, including a full-bodied Cabernet Sauvignon, a fruity Merlot, and a flowery Gewürztraminer.

"Now I know why you shouldn't swill this stuff," Bobby said. "With this many wines to sample, you'd soon get hammered."

After the tasting, they had lunch under a shady arbor with a view of the gently rolling countryside. "I can't imagine anyplace more beautiful," Susie said. "I know that running a vineyard is a tough business, but imagine looking at this scenery every day. Maybe I'll set my first movie here."

Bobby studied the girl as she gazed across the neat rows of vines to the misty hills in the distance. She had a beatific smile, like a small, golden Madonna. He thought maybe he was seeing the real Susie Blake for the first time.

Their itinerary for the afternoon included two more stops, and by the time they were finished, they had two cases of wine in the back of the Chevy II. Bobby sat looking out at the passing scenery as they drove away from the last winery. He seemed to be in a meditative mood.

"Did you enjoy yourself today?" Susie asked.

"I did. Thanks for inviting me."

"Think you're ready for the next step?"

Bobby looked confused. "The next step?"

"Coming over to my place. Listen, I don't want to replace anyone in your life. And I'm not expecting that we'll initiate some grand love affair. It's just that I like you and I think you like me. Hanging out together seems like it would be fun, and if we happen to engage in a little old-fashioned rumpy-pumpy, as the Brits say, what's the harm?"

As usual, Bobby was left momentarily speechless by the directness of this singularly original creature. "Can I have some time to think about it?" he finally stammered.

"Sure. Take your time. The offer will stand for..." Susie looked at her watch. "Fifteen minutes."

They went over to her place.

* * *

Bill Graham wasn't wedded to one type of music. Maybe that came from his multicultural background. The son of Russian-Jewish parents living in Berlin, Graham escaped the Nazis as a boy and grew up in the Bronx. Or maybe the tough-looking, streetwise impresario just liked to put on a good show. After failing as an actor in Hollywood, Graham moved to San Francisco, where he started out by producing benefit performances for the legal defense fund of the Mime Troupe, an activist left-wing theater group. From that modest beginning, he moved on to presenting some of the most memorable concerts the city had ever seen.

Graham loved to combine a variety of acts on the same bill, like the quirky mix that appeared on *The Ed Sullivan Show*. It was no surprise, then, that his lineup for the middle of August was typically unorthodox. Billed as "A Week of Great Music at the Fillmore," the schedule included rock 'n' roll pioneer Chuck Berry, the jazz stars of the Charles Lloyd Quartet, the Steve Miller Blues Band, the blue-eyed soul group the Young Rascals, and Count Basie's seventeen-piece orchestra. There was something for everyone, and Bobby Doyle knew he had to cover it.

In order to see every act, Bobby would have to attend three of the seven concerts. The first night featured Chuck Berry, the Charles Lloyd Quartet, and the Steve Miller band. Chuck Berry led off the show. Bobby had heard that Berry was something of a tightwad. To save money, he traveled alone, without his own backup band. Wherever he played, he depended on local musicians to accompany him. Berry was also a tad conceited, and he expected musicians to be familiar with his work. He was, after all, one of the pioneers of rock music. Some people called him the father of rock 'n' roll.

When Berry walked onto the Fillmore stage, he didn't bother to hand out a set list, so the backup musicians had no way of knowing what to expect. One of the musicians asked him what songs they'd be playing. Berry smiled and replied, "We're gonna be playin' some Chuck Berry songs." With that, he launched into "Johnny B. Goode," and the backup players had to scramble to keep up. The wild ride continued as Berry sang "Maybellene," "Roll Over Beethoven," "School Days," "Rock and Roll Music," and "Sweet Little Sixteen," all performed with Berry's usual verve, right down to his signature duckwalk. The audience wasn't aware of the challenge the backup group faced, but Bobby silently applauded their skill. They followed Berry's lead without missing a beat.

The Charles Lloyd Quartet was an abrupt change of pace, a shift from Chuck Berry's searing guitar to the smooth sounds of Charles Lloyd on tenor sax and flute, Keith Jarrett on piano, Ron McClure on bass, and Jack DeJohnette on drums. Fresh from starring at the Montreux Jazz Festival, the quartet eased into "Days and Nights Waiting," evoking the sounds of a smoky Prohibition-era nightclub. On "Lady Gabor," Lloyd's haunting flute sounded like a shepherd piping in a mystical woodland setting. "Love Song to a Baby" showed off Keith Jarrett's dazzling piano technique. By the time the group wrapped up with a nearly half-hour rendition of their soaring, scintillating showpiece, "Forest Flower," Bobby was hooked. Even the stoned rockers were nodding in appreciation.

When the Steve Miller Blues Band took over, Bobby headed backstage. He'd heard the group often enough to know what to expect. He was more excited about meeting Chuck Berry and the members of the Charles Lloyd Quartet. He was disappointed to discover that Chuck Berry had already taken off. A member of the stage crew told him that Berry was probably in one of the Fillmore Street clubs by now, shooting craps or picking up a lady. Berry didn't tend to hang around to listen to the other acts when his part in the show was done. He collected his appearance fee in cash and vamoosed.

Bobby did get a quick interview with Charles Lloyd and his bandmates. Afterward, he stopped by the office of Sonny Anders to say hello. Anders was beaming over the success of the night's program. "Boy, Chuck Berry really delivered," he said. "That guy has more energy than a kid. I tried duckwalking once and fell on my ass. He does it while playing a guitar."

"He's a force of nature all right," Bobby agreed. "And the Charles Lloyd group blew me away. I got a couple of nice quotes from them for a story."

"Are you coming back for the other shows on the bill?" Anders asked.

"You bet. I'll be here on Saturday for the Young Rascals and Sunday for Count Basie."

"That's great."

As Bobby started to leave, Anders called to him. "Hey, I read that piece you did on the Flamin' Groovies. I don't know if you've heard, but they've put together a self-produced demo record called "Sneakers." Recorded the whole thing on a four-track tape recorder in about eight hours. They're going to be performing it live next weekend at the Matrix. It should be a hoot. Maybe I'll see you there."

Bobby waved as he walked out the door. "Wouldn't miss it for the world."

* * *

Berkowitz Wines, where Susie Blake worked, was located on Market Street, not far from the Castro Theatre. Bobby drove up a few minutes before closing time. He'd invited Susie to accompany him to the Flamin' Groovies show at the Matrix. She'd never heard of the group, but she said with a name like that, they ought to be entertaining.

Bobby found a parking spot on nearby Castro Street and strolled over to the wine shop, an upscale establishment bracketed by an art gallery on one side and an Oriental carpet store on the other. Stepping inside, he saw Susie was waiting on a customer. She was wearing a white blouse and a short black skirt that showed off her shapely legs. Bobby had never seen her in anything but jeans and T-shirts. She nodded to him and went on with her business.

A graying middle-age man with a sad, sweet smile stood behind the counter. "May I help you find something?" Abe Berkowitz asked.

"Actually, I'm here to pick up Susie."

"Ah, you must be her writer friend. The budding wine connoisseur."

Bobby noted that Abe didn't refer to him as Susie's boyfriend. The two of them had agreed that their close friendship—their *very* close friendship—meant no strings attached.

"That's me," Bobby said as he shook Abe's hand. "Although I'm more of a wine novice. Susie was kind enough to teach me some of the basics."

"She's a quick learner. When she started here, she didn't know a grand cru Burgundy from a Beaujolais nouveau. Now, she can talk knowledgeably about wine with anyone."

Susie came around behind the counter to ring up her customer's purchase. After she'd wrapped the wine bottles in paper to protect them on the way home, she turned to Abe and Bobby. "What are you two conspiring about?"

"Oh, just passing the time of day," Abe said, winking at Bobby.

"Are you ready to go?" Bobby asked.

Susie glanced at the wall clock behind the counter. "Mind if I take off a few minutes early, Abe? Looks like things have slowed down."

"Of course. You two go have fun. I can manage fine."

Despite the lateness of the hour, the front door opened and another customer stepped inside.

"Oh, no," Susie muttered.

The man's flashy suit and neat haircut told Bobby he was probably an attorney or a stockbroker. A glance at his gleaming wingtip shoes added further evidence. The man walked up to the counter wearing a smarmy grin. "Hello Abe, Susie."

"I thought I banned you from this store," Abe said angrily.

"You said don't come back for three months, and it's been three months."

Susie let out a groan and came around from behind the counter. She took Bobby's arm and kissed him on the cheek. "C'mon, honey, let's go."

Bobby was surprised by the public display of affection. "Sure. Nice to meet you, Abe."

As the two of them walked out, the unwelcome customer stared daggers at them.

"What the heck was that all about?" Bobby asked as they walked toward his car.

"That pea-brain was Dale Peters," Susie replied. "I made the colossal mistake of dating him for a couple of months. Until he turned weird. He got all possessive, started buying me expensive gifts. I boxed up his trinkets and gave them back. I told him it was over, but he kept coming to the store and hanging around, until Abe kicked him out. Dale's the kind of rich dude who can't comprehend that anyone would reject him."

She laughed. "I should have known better than to date a guy named Dale. I wonder who he was named after. Dale the Chipmunk? Dale Evans?"

Bobby fired up his TR4 and headed north on Fillmore Street. The Matrix was located in Cow Hollow, a neighborhood on the north slope of Pacific Heights where long-ago dairy farmers once grazed their herds. The Matrix had played host to all the top San Francisco bands, ever since folk-rocker Marty Balin converted the former pizza parlor into a performance space for the Jefferson Airplane, back when the group first got together. This evening, the Flamin' Groovies would be playing their own quirky style of music.

Formed in 1965, the Groovies were a throwback group, leaning toward hard-charging rhythm and blues and vintage rock 'n' roll rather than the new consciousness-raising sounds of psychedelia. Their music earned them gigs in some of the bars around the city, but no record labels had shown any interest, which is why they'd put out their new demo record. The locally produced EP sold fairly well in the Bay Area, encouraging the Groovies to hope that a record company might offer them a deal.

The Matrix was only supposed to hold a hundred people, but there were considerably more on hand for the live presentation of "Sneakers." Bobby and Susie shoved their way through the crowd and claimed one of the cocktail tables off to the right of the dance floor. A waitress took their order, returning with two glasses of Chablis. Up on the tiny stage, the Groovies were blasting out "I'm Drowning," a song filled with breathtaking guitar runs.

"So what do think?" Bobby asked Susie afterward.

"Well...they're loud, I'll give them that."

The band followed with "Babes in the Sky," a bouncy, old-timey tune with sardonic lyrics reminiscent of Country Joe & the Fish. "My Yada" had the hundred-miles-per-hour momentum of a vaudeville dance routine. The pace slowed with the mid-tempo ballad "Love Time." "Golden Clouds" thumped along with raw, garage-band energy, and "The Slide" had a funky R&B vibe. Overall, the set was remarkably varied, which was the point of a demo record. The songs displayed the band's more than capable musicianship and obvious sense of humor. Bobby concluded that the Groovies' main goal was to have fun. Instead of aping the attitudes of street toughs or the ultracool, the Groovies laughed and romped their way through the show. Nobody in the Matrix had a better time than they did.

While the band was taking a break, Sonny Anders happened by Bobby's table. Bobby introduced him to Susie, and Anders had the sense not to say anything about Bobby being with a different girl than the sexy redhead he'd brought to the Fillmore. Anders simply said hello, although he did eye Susie surreptitiously for a moment. Maybe he was envious that Bobby dated more than one good-looking woman.

After Anders left, Bobby suggested that they call it a night.

"Fine by me," Susie said. "My ears are ringing, and I'm bushed from work."

On their way out, the couple was observed by a short, homely man sitting in a corner by himself. Eddie Ratner also noticed that Bobby was with a different girl. She was a hottie too, just like the other one, the snooty chick who'd given him the brush-off. That bitch got hers all right. Ended up dead in the bushes. Chalk it up to bad karma for insulting the Rat. He wondered what this other chick was like. She had some nice hooters. Maybe he'd get lucky and bump into her somewhere else.

* * *

It was after midnight when they got back to the Castro district. Susie lived on Noe Street, a couple of blocks from the wine shop. Bobby and Susie's assignations had all taken place in her apartment. Bobby never invited her over to his apartment. He couldn't bear the thought of sharing the bed he'd shared with Lynette with another woman. Susie didn't seem to mind. With her, the *where* wasn't as important as the *what.*

Susie was the most uninhibited, tireless lover Bobby had ever been with. She wore him out. If sexual acrobatics were an Olympic sport, Susie would win the gold in a runaway. Once when they were engaged in a particularly vigorous workout, the clock radio on Susie's bookcase headboard fell off and hit her in the forehead then bounced onto the floor. After they were lying there panting from their exertions, Susie glanced down at the radio and said, "How'd that get there?"

Bobby often wondered what sparked such a fire in a woman. In Susie's case, maybe she was rebelling against her strict Baptist upbringing. Whatever the cause of her insatiable appetites and eagerness to experiment, one thing was certain—her preacher daddy would fall out of his pulpit if he knew what a wildcat his daughter had become.

As startling as some of Susie's sexual predilections were, she surprised Bobby even more when she whispered a question in his ear the morning after the Flamin' Groovies show. "How'd you like to visit a church with me?" she asked. When she saw the look on his face, she qualified the question. "I don't mean a church service, pal. I've sat through all of those I care to. I was just wondering if you feel like taking a walk over to Mission Delores this morning. It's only a few blocks away. I go there sometimes during my lunch hour at the wine shop. The church grounds are one of the most tranquil spots I know of. I like to sit there and think about what life was like two centuries ago."

After breakfast, she and Bobby strolled over to the mission, at Sixteenth and Dolores Streets. The oldest surviving building in the city, the little white adobe church was dwarfed by an elaborately decorated Spanish Baroque–style basilica added in 1918. Susie grimaced at the newer building. "The folks who slapped up that gaudy mess should have paid attention to the maxim 'less is more.'"

They settled onto a stone bench in the cemetery and gardens, a shady patch of greenery planted with varieties of trees, shrubs, and flowers that had grown here when the mission was founded in 1776. "I see what you mean," Bobby said. "This is nice and peaceful. I've driven by the mission hundreds of times, but I've never stopped to visit it before."

"It's fascinating to think that the Spanish settled here the same year the United States declared its independence," Susie said. "Two different nationalities, and yet they had some things in common. The Spanish enslaved the local Indians and Americans enslaved Africans. Do you know why the Spaniards called this place Mission Dolores?"

"Now there's a nugget of local history I'm not aware of."

"They named it after a nearby creek, Arroyo de los Dolores, which means Creek of Sorrows. That's an appropriate name as far as the Indians were concerned. They experienced nothing but sorrows after the Spanish arrived. Besides having to toil on the mission's farms and ranches, they died in droves from European diseases, and they lost touch with their culture. Five thousand of them are buried here in the graveyard. It's sad that so much harm has been done in the world in the name of religion."

Bobby scrutinized the complex, contradictory person sitting next to him. Just when he thought he had her figured out, she sprang something like that on him.

Susie laughed. "But the flowers here sure are pretty."

From Mission Dolores, they walked back down Sixteenth Street to a neighborhood café Susie liked. On a lazy Sunday morning, the outdoor tables were filled with locals sipping coffee and reading newspapers. Several couples had their dogs lying by their feet, a portrait of domestic contentment.

Bobby and Susie found a place to sit and ordered two lattes. Just as their waiter returned with their order, an attractive Asian girl passed by on the sidewalk. She was wearing a pink tank top, revealing the tattoos that covered her chest, back, and arms.

"What's your opinion of tattoos?" Bobby asked as he studied the girl.

"I think that a woman defacing her body with tattoos is the worst form of self-abuse a person can engage in—short of becoming a Republican."

Bobby laughed so hard he spewed his first sip of coffee all over the table.

Susie followed up with another stunner. "Did you know you can tell a future Republican in kindergarten?"

"Really? How's that?"

"They're the ones who hit other kids and take their toys. It's a genetic thing."

"Then I don't have to ask who you'll be voting for next year," Bobby said, mopping up the mess he'd made.

"I don't know. I may not vote at all, even though it'll be my first chance to vote in a presidential election. The choices are always so depressing. You know, Tweedledum and Tweedledee. Look at the fellow you Californians elected as governor—Ronald Reagan, a certified dunderhead. Of course, that seems to be a prerequisite for Republican candidates."

"With opinions like that, I'd think you'd have to vote for Lyndon Johnson next year."

"Hey, he may be a Democrat, but he ain't gettin' my vote. He's a warmonger."

Bobby instantly thought of his brother. "It was really Kennedy who got us embroiled in Vietnam. He and a lot of other politicians were worried about Southeast Asian countries falling to communism after the French left—the old domino theory."

"Maybe so," Susie said, "but Johnson turned Vietnam into a full-scale war. Did you read what he told the soldiers over there? He said they should 'come home with that coonskin on the wall' or some such folksy idiocy."

Bobby took another sip of coffee. "Johnson may have won the last election by a landslide, but his support is sure going up in smoke now."

"Yeah, gun smoke."

"It's too bad, because he's done great things on civil rights, education, and health care."

"I'm trying to think of the last decent Republican," Susie said. "Eisenhower possibly? He was a good leader in World War II, and he always struck me as a kindly grandfather figure while he was in the White House. And how can you not love a gal named Mamie? I'll bet she spends her time fixing casseroles for Dwight." She laughed at the thought. "But tell me something. Who in their right mind would name their kid Dwight? He probably got beat up in school over that."

"Eisenhower did some good things as president. He warned us about the military-industrial complex for one. You have to wonder if we aren't seeing that monster at work in Vietnam. Ike also got the Interstate Highway System built."

Susie snorted. "Uh-huh. Which frigging white supremacists turned into a weapon against minorities. They routed highways right through the middle of prosperous black and Hispanic neighborhoods, shattering established communities, destroying countless businesses, and wiping out years of economic gains."

"I wasn't aware of that. I do know that our double-decker freeway along the Embarcadero isn't very popular. It's the biggest eyesore in the city. Herb Caen calls it the 'Dambarcadero.' Half of San Francisco would like to see it torn down."

Susie shook her head. "Politics, big business, and religion. What a combination. You're lucky to make it through life without at least one of 'em screwing you over."

"If you can't trust those, what's left?"

Susie considered the question for a moment, then she grinned. "You and me, big guy. You and me."

Chapter Fourteen

Pleiku Province

It was great to be home again. Jack had never had so much fun at the Santa Monica Pier. He strolled along, laughing at the clowns juggling watermelons and car batteries. People in gorilla suits were riding the roller coaster, and kids were standing on the backs of the live ponies on the merry-go-round. Would-be marksmen were firing M-16s at targets in the Playland Arcade. It was all just as he remembered it from his many trips here with his parents. Where were his parents? They'd never let him come here alone before. Oh well, he bought a ticket for the Ferris wheel and rode to the very top, where he could see all the way to the Golden Gate Bridge. The fog was rolling in under the bridge, so Jack decided to walk across the fluffy clouds. Walking on the fog was like walking on a mountain of feather pillows. His feet kept sinking in. He laughed and ate his cotton candy.

That's when he heard the cannon going off. It must be time for lunch. Jack hurried back to the campground in the Giant Forest in Sequoia National Park. The other Boy Scouts were already gathered around the campfire, where the troop leaders were handing out box lunches. Jack glanced up at the General Sherman Tree, the largest living sequoia. What the heck was Bobby doing sitting way up there on one of the branches? And why was he wearing his old Hopalong Cassidy outfit? Jack snickered. Bobby always thought Hopalong was the best cowboy, with his all-black clothes, but Jack knew it was Roy Rogers. Jack liked their sidekick Gabby Hayes best of all.

And Bobby would have a fine time trying to get down from that tree.

Boy, was he hungry. Jack held out his plate and his mother gave him a heaping serving of mashed potatoes. Bobby elbowed him and told him not to eat it all. Their dad chuckled and said there was plenty of everything to go around. That's when Jack heard that darn cannon booming again. He tried pulling the covers over his head, but that didn't block the sound.

Jack lurched awake, sitting up in his bunk. Another VC rocket attack. He hurriedly dressed and ran outside to the bunker, where he'd spent so many hot, sweaty hours. Settling back against the wall of the bunker, he closed his eyes. The fuzzy recollections of his dream were quickly fading, but he remembered enough to know that he'd had another of his recurring fantasies about being back home. Safe at home with his family and friends.

* * *

"It's funny, you dreaming about home so often." Vince poured himself a glass of cognac and handed the bottle to Jack. "My dreams are usually about women. Women with humongous boobs and legs about five feet long."

"I guess that's a sign of your priorities," Jack said with a grin. He didn't mention that he'd been thinking about women himself lately. He recalled what the drunken correspondent in Saigon had said that night at the Rex Hotel, when Jack loftily told the man that he didn't feel like contributing to the corruption of Vietnamese bar girls.

"You will feel like it, my friend," the journalist declared. "It won't be long before you're grabbing any kind of fun you can find, once you get a taste of this stinking war."

Jack was beginning to see the truth in what the man said. He had to admit that some of the thoughts he'd had late at night were less than pure. Mr. Hyde could not be kept caged forever.

"So what will you do when you actually do get back home?" Vince asked.

Jack gazed into the middle distance. "First, I intend to go to law school. After that, maybe I'll go into politics. That seems to be the best way to improve things in our country. I'd like to help people make more of their lives. Just think of all the untapped talent in the world. Most people probably only use ten or twenty percent of their abilities, usually because they don't have the means or the opportunity to reach their full potential. I'd like to see what I could do to help unleash some of that talent.

"Of course, I know lots of people are content to cruise through life in low gear. I guess that's why some men stay at home while others sail uncharted waters to discover new worlds."

Vince chuckled. "Boy, with patter like that, you'll make a fine politician. Now me, I'm going to lay around for a year when I get home. Do nothing but have fun. There'll be plenty of time later to save the world."

* * *

Lt. Col. James Sloan wore a pensive expression. A wiry man with a brown, careworn face, he lifted a document from his cluttered desk and flicked it with his fingers. "There's something here that's been brought to my attention, Lieutenant Doyle. Something we need to discuss."

Jack Doyle stood ramrod straight, staring at a point above the colonel's head. He wondered what the hell he—or one of his men—had done that warranted his being called into battalion headquarters? "Yes sir," he answered smartly.

"At ease, man. Take a seat." Sloan laid the document on his desk and tapped it. "It says here that you omitted something vitally important from one of your field reports last month."

"Sorry sir. If I did, I'm sure it was an oversight."

"No, lieutenant, I don't think it was an oversight. I think it was false modesty. You failed to report that you saved the life of one of your men while under intense enemy fire."

Jack flashed back to the firefight in which Jimmy Stooks had taken a round in the gut. "I thought that was pretty much an everyday event. Nothing worth mentioning."

"No, it wasn't an everyday event, lieutenant. It was an act of heroism. And it would have gone unacknowledged if your staff sergeant hadn't told your company commander about it. This letter from Captain Ellison contains Sergeant Fisher's account of the day's action. You acted above and beyond the call of duty, and a man is alive today who might be dead if not for your selfless response."

Colonel Sloan got up from his desk and walked to the window. He stood with his arms crossed, one hand on his chin. He turned to Jack. "Do you have any idea how desperately we need heroes in this war? The damned news media would rather dwell on our mistakes than point to someone like you, someone who's an example of the type of patriot every American should be proud of."

Jack squirmed in his seat, uncomfortable with the notion that he was some sort of hero. "But really, sir, I think..."

Sloan waved a hand. "No, lieutenant. I don't want to hear any demurring about this. Your men know what you did even if you don't seem to." He went back to his desk and lifted another piece of paper. "This is a recommendation that you be awarded the Bronze Star for valor with Combat V. I have no doubt the recommendation will be accepted."

Sloan held out his hand. "Congratulations, lieutenant. You've made me and your fellow officers and soldiers proud."

Jack shook the colonel's hand, not knowing what to say.

"And by the way," Colonel Sloan added, "Captain Ellison signed off on a three-day pass for you. My advice is to hop the next C-130 to Saigon and have a good time. You deserve it."

* * *

Jack was fairly certain this didn't qualify as heroic behavior—lying on a narrow bed in a shoebox-size apartment on a nameless backstreet in Saigon. He was smoking a cigarette and staring at the young bar girl he'd picked up that afternoon in one of the dives down on Tu Do Street. She was sitting naked before her dressing table mirror, combing her long black hair. Jack could see the reflection of her small round breasts rising and falling with each brushstroke.

"You like watch," she said.

"What do you mean?"

"You like watch Vee-na-mee girl. Most GIs, they pay quick then leave after we go boom-boom. You like watch."

"I just think you're very beautiful." It was true. The girl was stunning. A petite twenty-year-old, she seemed as fragile as the blossoms of an orchid, yet she had to be tough to survive the pernicious way of life she'd fallen into. She called herself Michelle, although her real name was probably something like Phuong or Thuy. Most of the bar girls adopted English names, since their own names were often hard for Americans to pronounce.

"There lots of pretty girls in Saigon," Michelle replied. The way she said it made it sound like a curse, which in a way it was. The prettiest girls in the city—at least those who had no other way of earning a living in their war-torn country—usually ended up down on Tu Do Street like Michelle, hustling GIs to buy them watery Saigon tea to benefit the bar and turning tricks in shabby back rooms.

"Why you like me?" the girl asked. She fondled her breasts. "Other Vee-na-mee girls have big titties. They go to doctor and get shots."

Jack thought for a moment. "I like you because you remind me of someone from home."

"You go boom-boom her too?"

Jack laughed. "No, I went to school with her." He was thinking of Betsy Chin, a Chinese girl in his world geography class at Berkeley. She didn't look a thing like Michelle. Betsy was tall and ungainly, with stick-thin arms and legs. She reminded him of Popeye's girlfriend Olive Oyl. But she had a quality he saw in Michelle. She was demure, that was it. While most Caucasian girls spoke up without any hint of bashfulness, Betsy spoke just above a whisper. And instead of cackling like a witch when something was funny, Betsy quietly tittered with a hand over her mouth. She was like the Chinese maidens in old silk paintings, hiding their expressions behind their outspread fans, their eyes modestly downcast.

Maybe that reserve was all an act with Michelle—pretending to be the type of dainty Asian girl all the big American boys wanted to bed. Even if it was a put-on, it had worked with Jack.

The girl turned around to face him. "You stare so much you make me shy."

Jack doubted that. Michelle would have lost all traces of shyness after the first forty or fifty GIs she'd slept with. Some of them had probably slapped her around or subjected her to every kinky sex act they could think of. Jack had been gentle with her, treating her as if she were his girlfriend. And she was for two more days. He'd paid for her services for the duration of his three-day pass. He didn't want to experience the indignity of prowling Tu Do Street again in search of companionship.

* * *

When Jack asked Michelle to name her favorite part of the city, she said the zoo and botanical gardens. The officer who briefed new arrivals at the Rex Hotel had mentioned that the park was worth seeing. Outside her apartment building, Michelle flagged down a pedicab, and she and Jack climbed into the rickety, bicycle-powered contraption. Their quiet, leisurely ride took them along Bach Dang Avenue, the thoroughfare that skirted the wide brown Saigon River, where freighters unloaded war supplies and sampans darted about like water bugs. They passed Me Linh Square, with its heroic statue of Vietnamese general Tran Hung Dao, the military genius who defeated Kublai Khan in two thirteenth-century battles. In the waterfront markets, people were buying fresh fish and the abundant produce of the countryside.

The zoo and botanical gardens were a short distance to the north. On a Sunday afternoon, well-dressed families strolled the grounds, a patchwork of green open spaces and dusty animal enclosures. There were abundant flower beds, a topiary garden, and a display of bonsai plants. Picnickers spread their blankets in the shade of specimen trees from throughout Indochina. The calls of hidden birds echoed through the park. It was a true beauty spot amid the concrete canyons of the city. Jack thought about how the French must have enjoyed the park, back when Saigon was known as the Pearl of the Orient. Even though the gardens were run down due to the war, they were a paradise compared to the sweltering, cratered jungle landscape Jack had grown used to over the past three months.

He and Michelle laughed at the antics of the monkeys scampering about inside their large wire cage. They saw rhinos, elephants, giraffes, hippos, lions, and tigers. A variety of stilt-legged waterbirds waded in several of the ponds. Jack was fascinated by an enormous python wound around the bare branches of a dead tree. The creatures that held Michelle's interest were two ostriches, looking as out of place in Vietnam as an American cowboy in chaps and a ten-gallon hat. "They must be sad," she said.

"Why, because they're in a cage?"

"Because they cannot fly. Birds should be able to fly."

Jack couldn't argue with that.

They crossed a footbridge that arched above a pond where crocodiles floated like scaly logs. At the other end of the bridge, Vietnamese musicians were playing inside a pagoda-like pavilion. Jack and Michelle stopped to listen. The music sounded strangely dissonant to Jack, but Michelle clearly enjoyed it.

As he watched the girl, Jack wondered what she might have become if the war's privations and the presence of foreign troops with money to spend hadn't shaped her life. If you transported an exquisite creature like her to Los Angeles, she might become a model or a starlet. Here, she was expendable, with no chance to make anything of herself—proof that success in life often came down to the sheer happenstance of where you were born. A person could possess all the innate talent in the world, but that meant nothing if they had no chance to nurture and apply their abilities. As Jack had told Vince, when he got home, he was going to do all he could to help people find those opportunities. He just wished he could do something for Michelle.

* * *

Jack got up early on the morning he was scheduled to return to Camp Enari. On his way out of Michelle's apartment, he left a tip of a hundred dollars on her dressing table. The girl was still asleep when he glanced at her for the last time. He knew that a hundred dollars wasn't enough to change Michelle's life, but it might help her survive her current circumstances. If she had any family, she'd probably send them part of the money, but he hoped she'd keep enough to allow her a few weeks of being free from having to sell herself. That would be something at least.

Jack still had a few hours before he needed to report in at Tan Son Nhut Air Base. He caught a taxi in front of Michelle's apartment and told the taxi driver to take him to a place he'd been thinking about lately. A few minutes later, the taxi pulled up in front of Notre Dame Cathedral, the ornate redbrick structure whose twin Romanesque spires loomed over central Saigon. The church sat at the opposite end of Tu Do Street from the city's notorious fleshpots, an ironic juxtaposition that wasn't lost on Jack. Those seedy bars and the venerable church seemed to symbolize the mental turmoil of his last three days, a weekend of carnal indulgence that had left him conflicted.

Inside the church's silent interior, he breathed in the musky perfume of incense, a scent that sparked childhood memories of attending mass with his parents and brother. A rosy light filtered through the stained-glass windows. Jack studied the scenes they depicted—Jesus and the Apostles, an array of benevolent-looking saints, and all the other familiar religious symbols he'd grown up with. He dipped his fingers in the basin of holy water and crossed himself, a gesture that made him wonder if he was fit to be inside this sacred chamber.

Nevertheless, he made his way down a side aisle to the small Lady chapel. He stuffed some money into the collection box below a rack of votive candles. He lit a candle and knelt before the statue of the Virgin Mary, saying a prayer for his family. Then he lit a second candle and said a prayer for Michelle and all the girls like her. The prayer for Michelle was prompted by the story she'd told him when he inquired about her life. She said she'd been engaged to a young man once, an apprentice watch repairman, but he'd been drafted into the Vietnamese army and was killed in his first month of service.

Jack rose and turned toward the sanctuary. He stood gazing at the statue of Jesus on the cross looming behind the altar. An elderly Vietnamese gentleman sat alone in a pew at the front of the nave. He was old enough to have lived through the war with the French. Maybe he'd fought in it. And now he was witness to another foreign power waging war in his country. So much death, so much pain, so much grief. The cycle never ceased. Jack turned around and left.

Chapter Fifteen

San Francisco

Just as they did every afternoon at four o'clock, a crowd of hungry young transients filled Panhandle Park, waiting to be served a free meal. For some of them, it would be their only meal of the day. The scene evoked images of the Great Depression, when out-of-work men and their families lined up at soup kitchens all over the country. The young people in Panhandle Park were being fed by the Diggers, radical community activists who believed that essentials like food, clothing, shelter, medical care—and rock concerts—should be free to everyone.

Operating on a shoestring budget and depending on volunteers, the Diggers served the hordes of summer visitors inundating Haight-Ashbury, an influx that seemed to baffle the straights in the city government. The Diggers also found time to act up—staging demonstrations, guerrilla street theater, and anarchist art displays to promote their anticapitalist agenda. They'd borrowed their name and much of their philosophy from the original Diggers, seventeenth-century English religious dissidents. San Francisco's Diggers, however, were considerably less pious than their namesakes. They weren't above driving a flatbed truck filled with scantily clad belly dancers through the Financial District to get their message across.

It was natural that a free spirit like Susie Blake would identify with the Diggers. That's why she volunteered one afternoon a week to help in Panhandle Park. Having worked as a waitress in high school back in Sedalia,

Missouri, she was used to serving hungry people, although today might not have been the best time to be putting those skills to use. Lowering gray clouds threatened rain. Susie hoped it would hold off, since she'd ridden her bike here from her Castro district apartment. It was a pleasant ride, one she'd made often enough to know many of the shopkeepers along the route, who usually waved or called to her if they happened to be outside.

The crowd in the park didn't seem bothered by the prospect of rain. They were carrying on in the usual way, gathering in groups to enjoy their food while listening to their radios. The Beatles had just released "All You Need Is Love," and the song was getting constant airplay around the world. In the Bay Area, it was fast becoming the summer's unofficial anthem. Love really was all you needed to cure the world's ills. That seemed blindingly obvious to young people. Why was it so hard for older generations to grasp?

Other people in the park were tossing Frisbees or walking their dogs. Young couples canoodled in the shade of the abundant trees—leafy rows of acacias, yews, alders, and dozens of other species planted years ago. A few people were carrying signs, most of them protesting the war in Vietnam. One sign seemed to say it all for the idealistic young Americans who saw a better use for U.S. tax dollars than squandering them in a foreign conflict. "Wipe Out Poverty," the sign read, "Not People."

Susie smiled at everyone as she ladled out a simple meat-and-vegetable stew, which the Diggers prepared each day, along with loaves of wheat bread. The kids she served ranged from young runaways with haunted expressions to hardened drifters who were simply taking advantage of the handouts and couldn't care less about the hippie ethos of peace and love. The sullen looks some of the drifters gave her frightened Susie. It wouldn't have surprised her if they were behind the recent dramatic rise in crime in Haight-Ashbury. Wandering among the mostly trusting, inoffensive flower children, they seemed like wolves sizing up a herd of sheep.

One scraggly beanpole stood looking at the big pot of stew with his mouth hanging open.

"Stew and bread?" Susie asked pleasantly.

"Ain't you got any chicken salad or ham and cheese?"

"Nope. Just stew and bread."

The beanpole seemed put out. "Well, gimme some, I guess."

Another volunteer overheard the exchange. "What's with that guy? He's getting fed for free and he thinks he can order à la carte?"

Susie shrugged. "Hey, you have to accept that human beings are maddeningly irrational. It's a puzzler, huh?" She turned to the next person in line. "Stew and bread?"

Leaning against a tree not far away was one of the most irrational persons imaginable. Eddie Ratner visited the park regularly to check out the chicks. He was watching Susie as she worked. He remembered her from the Matrix. She was with that big dude he'd run into at the Fillmore, he recalled. The Rat was cradling his camera, and every now and then he raised it to his eyes.

Ratner put his camera away and swaggered over to the food line, where he tried out his ladies' man routine. "How ya doin', hon?" he hissed at Susie. He made the mistake of baring his yellow teeth in a frightening smile.

"Fine, thanks," Susie replied noncommittally. "You here for lunch?"

"Sure. Why not?" The Rat rolled his eyes. "And maybe you could provide a little dessert."

It was all Susie could do to keep from retching. "Uh, I think you better ask someone else."

The Rat didn't know when to give up. "But I like cute little blondes like you."

Susie handed him a plate of food. "Sorry, but I'm taken. You might try your luck over there." She used her serving spoon to point to an overflowing garbage can.

The Rat glanced where she pointed then gave Susie a hard look. "Pretty funny. You're a regular Phyllis Diller. But I ain't laughin'." The Rat tossed his plate down and stormed off.

* * *

Bobby handed in his final exam paper and returned to his seat to gather his things. He waited outside in the hallway for the other members of his study group. Now that their summer session was over, the five of them planned to celebrate with a few drinks at a dive on Clayton Street. Will Taylor had discovered the bar, and although he couldn't remember the name of the place, he assured everyone it was far enough away from the campus that they weren't likely to bump into any of their teachers—especially the Jesuit priests who seemed to give the heebie-jeebies to everyone but Susie. She jokingly referred to the black-clad clergymen as the Penguins.

The Clayton Street bar was everything Will said it was—and less. The lighting was poor, the decor shabby, and the clientele looked like the crew from a tramp steamer just back from a long voyage to some destitute Third World country. But the beer was cheap and cold, so nothing else mattered. Susie christened the joint "Will's Café Américain" after the bar Humphrey Bogart ran in *Casablanca.* All that was missing was Peter Lorre lurking in the shadows and Dooley Wilson banging out "Knock On Wood" on an upright piano.

"Here's to freedom of the press," Will said, hoisting his beer. "May it never be compromised."

"To freedom of the press," everyone echoed.

"How are you all spending your break before fall classes start?" Bobby asked.

"Alison and I are going camping in Robert Louis Stevenson State Park," Bernie Warren said, confirming Bobby's suspicion that they were a couple. "The park's just north of Calistoga. It's where Stevenson spent his honeymoon in 1880. From the top of Mount Saint Helena, you can see Napa Valley, the Sierras, and San Francisco Bay."

"Sounds spectacular," Bobby said. "How about you, Will?"

"Going home to visit the folks. And what'll you be up to, Mr. Newspaperman?"

"Polishing up the old prose," I guess. "There are a couple of good shows coming up. Little Richard is opening at the Straight Theater."

Bobby turned to Susie. "You have any big plans?"

She chuckled. "Are you kidding? I'll be working my tail off at the wine shop. Gotta earn all the shekels I can while I have the chance."

She winked at Bobby. "Of course, I'll be free after work."

* * *

At nine o'clock, Berkowitz Wines closed for the evening. Susie helped clean up, said goodnight to her boss, and headed out the door for the short walk home. It was a clear, balmy evening out. The glittering mass of stars looked like someone had scattered handfuls of diamonds on a black velvet cloth. Bobby had begged off on stopping by her apartment this evening since he had a deadline on the story he was writing. Frankly, that was fine by Susie. It had been a long day, and she was looking forward to a hot shower, a cold glass of wine, and a soft bed.

Even so, Susie had Bobby on her mind as she walked along. Her typical no-strings-attached relationship with men was becoming strained with him. What had begun as a purely physical frolic was evolving into something more—at least for her, although she'd never hint at such a thing to Bobby. She preferred to maintain the devil-may-care attitude she'd deliberately affected ever since she left home. She'd been hurt enough there, and she didn't want to risk suffering another kind of hurt by allowing herself to become vulnerable in a romantic relationship. Fun and games, that was what Susie Blake was all about. She was bulletproof. Still, when she pictured Bobby, something seemed to tug at her.

The girl turned off Market Street onto Noe. Usually, she walked home on the opposite side of the street from her apartment building to avoid a dark alley on her side of the block. Tonight, she was so tuckered that she forgot her normal precaution. As she walked by the alley, she glanced into its black depths. There were probably winos passed out in there, she thought, or even worse, rats burrowing through the trash and other debris she could see in the daytime.

Once past the alley, she quickened her step. Just half a block and she'd be home. That's when someone threw an arm around her neck and started pulling her back toward the alley. She tried to scream, but the pressure on her neck was too great. All that came out was a terrified squeak.

Her assailant was obviously taller than she was, since she was lifted off her feet. She fought wildly, her legs flailing the air. Red spots had begun flashing before her eyes by the time she was dragged into the alley. The girl tried to reach behind her and claw her assailant's face, but she couldn't reach her target. Her assailant punched her in the side, sending an excruciating shock through her body. Susie whimpered in pain. With a last burst of strength, she raised both legs and tried to hammer her assailant with her heels. Her puny blow only enraged her captor.

"Hold still, you little bitch," a voice hissed in her ear.

Those were the last words Susie Blake ever heard.

* * *

The knock came early the next morning. Bobby was still in his bathrobe when he opened the door. Standing outside with a grim look on his face was homicide detective Phil Marshall. A uniformed cop stood beside him. Bobby assumed there'd been a development in Lynette's case.

"Detective Marshall. Good morning. Come on in."

Marshall remained outside. "You'd better get dressed, Mr. Doyle. I need you to come down to the station."

"You have news about Lynette Simms?" Bobby asked with a hopeful note in his voice.

"I'm afraid not. There's been another murder. Another person of your acquaintance was killed last night."

Bobby's mind reeled from the news. He tried to imagine who it could be. Someone from USF perhaps...Berkeley...the *Chronicle.*

"Who, for God's sake?" he asked, his voice quaking.

Marshall took his notebook from his coat pocket and read from it. "A Miss Susannah Blake."

* * *

They were in the same interrogation room as before. Detective Marshall sat across the table from Bobby, his pen and notebook at the ready.

Bobby was in a daze. He couldn't believe that Susie had been murdered. What on earth was happening? He still had nightmares about Lynette's death, and now Susie was gone as well. It was too much to comprehend.

"Mr. Doyle, we need to ask where you were last night between nine and ten o'clock."

"*What?* You think I had something to do with this? That's absurd."

"Just answer the question, Mr. Doyle."

Bobby shook his head to clear it. For a moment, he thought he might be dreaming this whole episode.

"Mr. Doyle?"

"I was at home, working on a story for the *Chronicle.*"

"Can anyone corroborate that?"

"Corroborate? What the hell are you talking about? Susie was my friend."

"So was Miss Simms," Marshall said.

Bobby thought back to the night before. He'd been alone all evening. Then he recalled something important. "I was on the phone between nine and ten."

"For a whole hour?"

"Yes, for a whole hour. I was interviewing the manager of the singer Little Richard. I can give you his name and phone number so you can check with him."

Marshall almost seemed disappointed. He shoved his notebook across the table. "Write it down."

Bobby scribbled the information. As he handed back the notebook, he looked up at Marshall. "Was Susie...was she poisoned with heroin?"

Marshall nodded. "Her body was discovered in an alley near her apartment building."

Bobby put his face in his hands. That bright, lively girl murdered. Why? He hadn't loved her the way he'd loved Lynette, but he cared for her deeply. He'd never known anyone so feisty and full of life.

"How in the world did you find out that I knew Susie?"

"We checked with her employer. If it's any consolation, yours was only one of the names he gave us. It seems Miss Blake was a popular girl."

Bobby could have reached across the table and strangled Marshall for his insinuation.

The detective closed his notebook. "You're free to go, Mr. Doyle, unless you have any other information you think might help us with our investigation."

"I can't think of anything now, but if something comes to mind, I'll be sure to call you."

"You do that, Mr. Doyle. You do that."

Bobby was escorted out of police headquarters. Phil Marshall watched him from his office window as he hailed a cab.

* * *

When he got home, Bobby called his parents to break the news. He told them how he'd met Susie at USF, how they'd studied together and gone out a few times, and how she—like Lynette—had been attacked on the street at night. His mother wanted him to come home for a few days, but he told her he couldn't get away at the moment. He didn't tell her that the police seemed to think he had something to do with Susie's death. His father said that he'd read about how crime was on the uptick in San Francisco, most of it tied to the drug trade. The only advice he could offer was for Bobby and his friends to be extra vigilant, especially at night.

The next day, Bobby wrote to his brother. He hadn't even had time to tell Jack about his involvement with Susie before she was gone. Bobby had been distraught over Lynette's murder, but he was incensed about Susie's death. He wanted to find the killer or killers and make them pay. He told Jack about how he'd lain awake most of the night dreaming of ways to punish them—to torture them, maim them, blot out their very existence. It must be the sense of rage that soldiers experienced when they saw a buddy fall victim to enemy fire. He imagined Jack would understand his bitterness.

In his letter, Bobby tried to make sense of why two women he'd been involved with would be murdered. They couldn't both be victims of random killings. The odds against it were infinitesimal. That left him with the conclusion that someone had done these things to get back at him for some reason. Bobby asked Jack if he could think of anyone who might have such hatred for him that they'd do this. He couldn't think of anyone himself. His life had been a cakewalk of easy attainments in school and in sports. He'd never been engaged in any heated rivalries with anyone, so how could something like this happen? It felt like some Greek god on Mount Olympus was toying with a helpless mortal.

* * *

A week after Susie's murder, her friends gathered in St. Ignatius Church for a memorial service. Bobby was stunned to see how many people showed up. Abe Berkowitz was there, of course, along with the members of their study group. But there were also dozens of people he didn't know—friends whose lives Susie had touched. They included other USF students and several members of the Diggers. Bobby reflected that if this were a memorial service in his honor, he doubted if half as many people would show up. He was surprised to see Sonny Anders in attendance, but it came as no great shock to find that Susie's former boyfriend Dale Peters was absent.

A parade of friends gave testimonials about their relationship with Susie. Every anecdote illustrated her kindness, honesty, and generosity. Bobby realized that, in many ways, the people gathered here knew Susie better than her own parents did. That's when he decided to pay her parents a visit, to tell them about her accomplishments—all of the things her father's rigid, unforgiving attitude had kept her from sharing with them. For Bobby, the trip would represent his final tribute to Susie. Her fearless self-reliance was remarkable, and even though she'd been estranged from her parents, it would be a double tragedy for them to bury their daughter without knowing what she'd become.

* * *

The TWA flight from San Francisco to Kansas City was a new experience for Bobby—the first time he'd seen the arid Great Basin, the snowcapped Rocky Mountains, and the vast grasslands of the Great Plains. He was glad he'd booked a window seat. As he listened to the soothing roar of the 707's engines, he drifted into a reverie about Susie, recalling incidents that captured her unique personality. He thought of their last date, when they'd gone to see the new Warren Beatty and Faye Dunaway movie *Bonnie and Clyde.* They'd both enjoyed the film, and as they discussed it on the way back to Susie's apartment, she stunned him with another of her out-of-the-blue comments.

"You know, I think you and I would make good bank robbers."

Bobby had laughed at the absurdity of the idea. "I don't think I'd make much of a Clyde Barrow, but you'd definitely make an excellent Bonnie Parker. All you'd need is her beret and pearl-handled pistol. You've already got her moxie."

Susie had waggled her eyebrows suggestively. "You think so, big boy?" That was pure Susie. Her sense of humor was what he'd remember most.

Kansas City's Municipal Airport was regarded as the most dangerous major airfield in the country by the FAA, but the TWA pilot managed to dodge the downtown office buildings and avoid plunging into the Missouri River at the end of the main runway. Once the plane landed, Bobby rented a car for the two-hour drive to Sedalia. The trip took him through small towns and rolling Missouri farmland. Fields of corn were turning gold, signaling the approaching harvest. It was late afternoon when Bobby pulled into Sedalia. His visit with the Blakes was scheduled for ten o'clock the next morning, so he had time to do some sightseeing.

Susie had mentioned that the Missouri State Fair was held in Sedalia. Bobby had also read that the town was an important nineteenth-century railhead, making it a major destination for cattle drives. That historical tidbit had been the inspiration for *Rawhide,* one of Bobby and his brother's favorite TV shows when they were growing up. Every week, trail boss Gil Favor, wrangler Rowdy Yates, and the cantankerous cook Wishbone braved the perils involved in driving a herd of cattle from Texas to the railhead in

Sedalia, although they never seemed to get there.

Beyond its place in railroading and cowboy lore, Sedalia had another claim to fame, one that was more in keeping with Bobby's interests. The town had once been home to the King of Ragtime—Scott Joplin, the musician and composer who wrote "Maple Leaf Rag" and over a hundred other compositions. Bobby was surprised that a location he'd never heard of before meeting Susie had such an interesting history. He also discovered that Sedalia had the best barbecued ribs he'd ever eaten.

* * *

Susie's mother had given him directions to their home, so he found it with little difficulty. When he knocked on the door of the small white-frame house, a short, harried-looking woman with curly blond hair answered. She was wearing a print dress and a string of imitation pearls. She smelled of peaches, a popular Avon fragrance. She smiled and waved Bobby inside.

"You must be Susannah's friend."

Bobby shook her hand. "Nice to meet you Mrs. Blake. Thanks for agreeing to see me."

The woman led him back to the family room, where Susie's father sat reading a newspaper in a recliner.

"Ron, this is Mr. Doyle, from San Francisco."

The man nodded curtly. "How do." He didn't bother getting up or offer to shake hands. He was a burly, dark-haired man with the permanent scowl of the self-righteous. Bobby could well imagine him preaching fire and brimstone.

"Please, have a seat," Mrs. Blake said, fluttering around nervously. She finally sat down, tugging her dress down over her knees. "We understand from your letter that you want to tell us something about..."—she hesitated, on the verge of tears, although she tried her best to smile—"...about our daughter."

"I do," Bobby said. "I thought you'd like to know some of things she'd accomplished out in California."

Mr. Blake harrumphed.

"Susie was completing a bachelor's degree in film studies at the University of San Francisco."

"Film studies?" Mr. Blake barked. "What kind of films—Hollywood trash, I suppose?"

Bobby thought it would be better to fudge the issue. "I think she was interested in nature films," he said, recalling her comment about setting her first movie in wine country.

"That sounds lovely," said Mrs. Blake. She glanced at her husband with the look of a cowed dog expecting a blow from its master.

"You should know that she worked nights and weekends to put herself through college. She had a job in a little wine shop…"

Mr. Blake exploded. *"A wine shop?* That sounds just like her. Always the party girl."

"Please, Ron," Mrs. Blake pleaded, "let Mr. Doyle finish."

"Susie was a salesperson. Her employer praised her for being exceptionally talented. She also gave of her time generously. She volunteered at a local food bank."

"That's something at least," Mr. Blake said grudgingly.

"I think the most important thing I can tell you about Susie's life in California is that she made lots of friends. People loved her wit and sunny disposition."

"Susannah always had a smile on her face," Mrs. Blake said.

Mr. Blake waved that off. "She never did take things seriously." He gave Bobby a hostile look. "Were you her boyfriend?" He made it sound vulgar, lewd, like an accusation that he'd been part of something unsavory.

"I was her friend."

"I'll bet."

"Mr. Blake, I'm trying to tell you that your daughter was a good person."

"That's Reverend Blake."

"Sorry." Bobby truly was sorry. He was sorry that Susie's father was such a hidebound, small-minded fool that he refused to see the worth of his own child. If the man had lived three centuries earlier, he'd have been one of the petty, ignorant zealots who burned innocent young girls for witchcraft. Looking at the man's stony expression made him realize how lucky he was to have parents who loved, nurtured, and encouraged him. It was one of the greatest blessings a person could have.

Bobby could see that everything Susie had told him about her father was true. There was no use trying to communicate with the man, so he got up to leave. "I'm sorry for your loss," he said in parting.

Mrs. Blake saw him to the door. "Thank you for coming, young man. I know you meant well." She glanced back toward the living room. "And I know that my daughter was a good person, just as you say. I always knew she'd make something of herself."

Chapter Sixteen

San Francisco

The flight home from Missouri had given Bobby plenty of time to think. He'd come away from meeting Susie's parents feeling like a boulder was sitting on his chest, and he had to do something to get it off. The churlish behavior of Susie's father had left him even angrier than he'd been when he was stewing over Susie's killer. The murderer had stolen Susie's life, but her own father was refusing to honor her memory.

Picturing the truculent expression of Susie's father kindled the recollection of something a friend once said to Bobby. "No matter how bad things might be, some folks can always manage to make them worse." The "Reverend" Blake certainly had that ability. He failed to understand that forgiveness didn't mean forcing someone else to accept your views.

Bobby knew that the only thing anyone could do for Susie now was to identify the monster who'd snuffed out the light she brought to the world. The police had failed to find any leads on her death, or on Lynette's, so Bobby thought he might as well give it a try himself. He wasn't sure how he'd go about it, but he vowed to do what he could to ferret out the truth. He had to admit one thing, though. If he did help solve the murders, he still wouldn't be satisfied. What he wanted now wasn't closure. It was revenge. He wanted the killer to be locked away forever—even more than for him to be sentenced to death. He wanted this warped human being to suffer every day for the rest of his life, just as so many people would who'd known

Lynette and Susie.

Bobby also knew that he'd need help if he stood any chance of discovering the killer's identity. He couldn't think of anyone more capable or enthusiastic when it came to digging out facts than his Berkeley friend Raul Pitman. Pitman might affect an easygoing hipster attitude, but he was a bulldog when it came to chasing down leads. Best of all, Pitman loved a challenge. More than once, Bobby had seen him bluff, bully, or charm some reluctant person he was interviewing into telling him everything he was after. The guy never took no for an answer.

* * *

Bobby waited at the Blue Unicorn Coffeehouse on Hayes Street, not far from the dive Susie had dubbed Will's Café Américain. Pitman strolled in looking as debonair as ever in his beret and black leather sport coat. He personified the distinction between Berkeley progressives and San Francisco's flower children. Berkeley liberals tended to be hardcore doers, determined to change society through political protests, organization, and confrontation. Most hippies, on the other hand, were dreamers, a motley bunch of individualists out to change society by changing themselves. There was an easy way to distinguish between the two groups other than by the way they dressed. The hippies were the ones with blissed-out smiles, nodding their heads to loud rock music.

Pitman spotted Bobby sitting in one of the booths at the back of the coffeehouse. The Berkeley reporter had been here before while researching one of his stories. He smiled as he read the familiar signs posted around the long, narrow room. "Impromptu nonscheduled entertainment, no charges.... Chess playing, no charge.... House guitar available to good players.... You may receive mail at the Blue Unicorn free of charge.... Poetry every Wednesday, 9 p.m."

The coffeehouse was run by a musically inclined maverick named Herb Jackson. The word was that he'd purchased the place from its original owner for twenty-five hundred dollars and a kilo of marijuana. The concrete floor was painted battleship gray, the walls were covered with graffiti, and the ceiling was decorated with swirling, hallucinatory designs, a bizarre take on the Sistine Chapel.

The regulars huddled around the wobbly tables up front were just as colorful. They went by nicknames such as Tarot Tom, Pete the Jeweler, Larry the Flute, and Lone Buffalo. No one was too offbeat to fit in here. Aside from the carnival-like atmosphere, people came for the fresh homemade food, the hot drinks, and the live music. Folks were still talking about the night Bob Dylan stopped by. There was also a used bookstore, but—Herb Jackson stated proudly—no jukebox.

Pitman took a seat in the booth across from Bobby. "What's up, my man? You made it sound urgent on the phone."

Bobby toyed with his coffee cup. "I don't know if you've heard, but two friends of mine have been murdered."

"*Murdered?* Holy cow, that's terrible. Anyone I know?"

"I doubt it. They were actually more than friends. I'd been dating both women."

Pitman shook his head. "How were they killed?"

Last month, Lynette Simms, a girl I met at the Monterey Pop Festival, was given an overdose of heroin outside her apartment building here in the Haight. Then two weeks ago, Susie Blake, someone from a summer class I took at USF, was killed the same way while walking home from work in the Castro district. The police haven't turned up anything on either murder." Bobby glanced down at his coffee cup then gave Pitman a determined look. "I'm thinking about investigating the killings myself, and I could sure use your help."

Pitman didn't bat an eye. "You got it. You know me, always a crusader for truth, justice, and the American way. Where do we start?"

Bobby sat back, obviously relieved. "Thanks, Raul. I had a hunch I could count on you. As to how to begin, that's where I need your advice."

Pitman stroked his Van Dyke beard. "You think one person committed both murders?"

"I have no idea, but if one person was behind both murders, it might make it easier to turn up some clues."

"Then let's start with the first murder. You said your friends were killed with heroin. I did a story this summer on the drug trade in Haight-Ashbury. I learned about some of the ugly things that have been happening—pushers selling tainted drugs, teenagers getting hooked on the hard stuff and dying of overdoses. It's a sad spectacle."

"Then you must know some of the creeps who deal in drugs."

"A few. They've all got their little fiefdoms, and the cast of characters changes constantly, sort of like slime mold." Pitman thought for a moment. "I'll tell you who we need to talk to—Blind Cedric. He sees everything that goes on in the Haight."

* * *

Blind Cedric Johnson stood in front of the Drogstore Café, a hulking black man with a wild afro and dark glasses. When Bobby and Raul walked up, Cedric began singing a soulful rendition of Sonny Boy Williamson's "Don't Start Me Talkin'" and backing it up with a mean harmonica. There was an open King Edward cigar box with some dollar bills and coins in it at Cedric's feet, and a long white cane leaned against the window of the café.

Cedric finished his song with a flourish and tapped his harp on his sleeve. A Vietnam veteran, he wore a green army field jacket with the Screaming Eagles shoulder patch of the 101st Airborne Division, a unit that had been in some of the fiercest fighting of the war. Cedric had served in the elite—and controversial—long-range reconnaissance patrol known as Tiger Force, a platoon of hard cases assigned to "outguerrilla the guerrillas." Exactly one year ago, Cedric had been roaming the steaming jungles of Vietnam, and he was still haunted by some of things he'd seen—and done. He'd earned a handful of medals, but they were locked away in a drawer somewhere.

Only a few people noticed that Cedric didn't sing or play unless there were passersby, which indicated that the "blind" street musician could see perfectly well. Whenever the cops questioned him, he answered in nearly nonsensical jive talk, but when he was alone with friends, he spoke with the diction of an educated man. He was a figure with many secrets.

"How goes it, Cedric?" Pitman asked.

Cedric grinned. "You know how it is, man. Still scuffling to get by."

"Cedric, this is my friend Bobby Doyle. He's got something he'd like to ask you."

"Nice to meet you," Bobby said. "Raul tells me you know pretty much everything that goes on in Haight-Ashbury."

"I wouldn't say that, but I do notice a few things from time to time."

Bobby hesitated, unsure of how to begin. "Cedric, a couple of months ago, a good friend of mine, a young lady, was murdered here in the Haight."

"That's harsh, man. Sorry to hear about that."

"Raul suggested that maybe you could help us. You see, someone injected my friend with an overdose of heroin. We wondered if you could think of anyone here on the streets who's crazy enough to do something like that."

Cedric gave it some thought. "There's more crazy mothers running around these days than you can shake a stick at, but if I had to come up with one name, I'd say Charlie Manson. He's an evil-looking son of a bitch. Got a stare on him that would scare the devil. Guy gives me the willies. I hear he makes a living by shaking down drug dealers. There's rumors that he's knocked off one or two of them. If anyone is sick enough to intentionally kill someone with an overdose, I'd put my money on him. He lives over on Cole, just off Haight Street. A couple of young girls hang out with him. Man, I feel sorry for them. They must be messed up."

"Charlie Manson, huh?" Bobby said. "Thanks, Cedric. We'll check him out."

Bobby dropped a five-dollar bill in Cedric's cigar box. Cedric pulled his dark glasses down and peered over the top of them. "That the best you can do?"

Bobby peeled off a twenty and tossed it in the box.

Cedric nodded. "Now you're talking. And here's a little tune you both might like." He played the introduction to another Sonny Boy Williamson song then began singing. The name of the song was "Eyesight to the Blind."

* * *

"Nope. Manson's not our guy," Pitman said. "I buttonholed his landlord and found out that Manson and his harem like to drive up the coast in his VW bus. They were evidently up in Mendocino the week your friend Lynette was killed. I asked the landlord how he could be sure about the date and he said he took the opportunity to bring in an exterminator to treat Manson's apartment that week. He also cleaned out some of the mess, since the tenants in the adjoining apartments were complaining about the smell. Apparently, Manson lives like an animal."

"Which means we've lost our prime suspect." Bobby sounded deflated.

"I'll keep my eyes and ears open," Pitman said. "And I'll ask Blind Cedric to do the same. Meanwhile, maybe we should see what we can find out about the other girl's death. You said she lived in the Castro. Any suggestions of who we could talk to?"

"Susie volunteered with the Diggers. Let's check with them."

"Cool. I know some of the guys who run the group."

* * *

"Have I seen any strange characters hanging around?" Peter Canino sounded incredulous. "This is San Francisco, man. Strange characters are what make this place tick. Now if you're talking about dangerous characters, not so much. We get the usual run of freaks—in all shapes, sizes, and colors. That's part of the fun."

"Do you know if anyone ever bothered Susie Blake?" Bobby asked.

A talented actor and one of the founders of the Diggers, Canino took a moment to search his memory. He was a big, tough-looking man with shoulder-length hair and a drooping mustache. He rode a motorcycle, so people sometimes mistook him for a Hells Angel. "I wouldn't say bothered, but guys were always hanging around her. Can you blame them? She was cute as a kitten with milk on its face, and she loved to joke with guys. She teased the hell out of them."

Bobby knew all about that.

The interview was taking place in the Diggers' Free Store on Carl Street. The location of the store changed frequently, depending on where the Diggers could find cheap space. The first Free Store was in someone's garage. The interior of the current store was painted all white, like a hospital ward, or maybe a mental institution. Its shelves, racks, and bins bulged with donations of clothing, kitchen items, toys, and other cast-offs. Anyone who wandered in was free to take whatever they wanted. More than once, a down-and-outer had stuffed some item under his coat in a needless attempt at shoplifting. If one of the Diggers happened to notice, he'd ask if there was anything else the person needed. How such a store stayed in business was a mystery, but then everything the Diggers did had an air of mystery about it. Perhaps their success was due to providence, or maybe it was sleight of hand. Some of the Diggers were adept at liberating whatever the group needed.

"Let me give you a word of advice," Canino said. "Don't limit your inquiries to the Haight or the Castro. This city has its share of misguided souls. Susie's killer might live in a penthouse downtown."

* * *

Peter Canino's comment prompted Bobby and Pitman to see what they could find out about Susie's disgruntled ex-boyfriend Dale Peters. They discovered that he had a job with a big-deal law firm in the Financial District. Raul also discovered that Peters had a nice little wifey and two kids living in a swishy condo on Nob Hill. He and Bobby agreed it was unlikely that Peters would be creeping around at night murdering young women.

Bobby could only think of one other likely source of information—Sonny Anders. He'd seen Anders at Susie's memorial service, so the man was aware of the girl's death. With his connections in the drug-addled world of rock 'n' roll, Anders might know if there were any violence-prone dealers or users worth checking out.

* * *

The Doors were holding forth when Bobby arrived at the Fillmore Auditorium the next night. Since the release of their debut album in January, the band had been on a steady upward trajectory. "Light My Fire" had hit number one, and although the group missed out on the exposure of the Monterey Pop Festival, they'd become regulars at the Fillmore, the Avalon Ballroom, the Matrix, and other San Francisco nightspots. They'd already been on *American Bandstand* and were scheduled for *The Ed Sullivan Show.*

Bobby marveled that in the three months since he'd seen Jim Morrison at the Magic Mountain Music Festival, the singer had gone from being a little-known Los Angeles hell-raiser to being famous throughout the country. From what Bobby had read, Morrison's fame was going to his head, along with copious amounts of alcohol, marijuana, LSD, and cocaine. In the countless newspaper photos Bobby had seen of him, Morrison seemed to have two expressions—his brooding bad-boy glower and the dull, vacant-eyed look of a hopeless drunk. This evening, Morrison was lurching about while he sang "When the Music's Over." In the middle of the song, he fell down on the stage and started rolling around like a wino with the DTs. A stagehand helped him up, but as far as tonight went, the music was over.

Bobby shook his head at the spectacle onstage and headed for Sonny Anders's office. As usual, Bill Graham's assistant was sitting behind his desk with his feet up. Tonight, he was reading a copy of the *San Francisco Chronicle.* He looked over the top of the paper when Bobby knocked on his door.

"Hey man, come on in," he said, laying the paper aside. He stood up to shake Bobby's hand. "I saw you at the memorial service at St. Ignatius, but it was so crowded I didn't get a chance to say hello. I wanted to tell you how sorry I was about your girlfriend. I remembered her from the Matrix. She seemed like a sweet kid."

"Thanks," Bobby said. "I was surprised to see you at the service. I wondered how you heard about Susie's death."

"One of the stagehands mentioned it. I don't know how he got wind of it, but he told me that the other girl you dated—the one you brought to a show here—had also been killed. What a tragedy. Must make you feel like you're cursed or something."

"It does, now that you put it that way."

"Did you stop by to catch the Doors?"

"Not really. I've seen them before. Actually, I came by to see you."

"Me? That's flattering. Something to do with one of your articles?"

"No, nothing to do with work. This is personal. I wanted to pick your brains."

"What about?"

"It concerns the deaths of Susie and Lynette Simms."

Anders seemed surprised. "Gee, what can I tell you about that? I only met each of the girls one time. I wouldn't have known either of them if you hadn't introduced them."

"I realize that, but I'm wondering if you can recall anyone suspicious that you've come in contract with through your work—someone who strikes you as a bit out of kilter. I'm thinking of a drug supplier or heavy user in particular. The person who murdered both girls had access to drugs. They were each killed with an overdose of heroin."

"No kidding?"

"Yeah. The killer has to be a real sicko." Bobby remembered something from the night he and Lynette attended the concert at the Fillmore. "When I brought Lynette here with me, some orange-haired freak hit on her while I was interviewing Carlos Santana and his bandmates. Do you have any idea who he is?"

Anders tugged on his droopy blond mustache. "Orange hair? Was he a kind of a runty guy?"

Bobby perked up. "Yeah, that's him."

"I've seen him hanging around once or twice, although I have no idea who he is. I haven't seen him in quite a while."

Bobby's shoulders slumped in disappointment.

"Tell you what, though," Anders said, "I'll ask some of the stagehands, see if anyone does know him. And I'll stay on the lookout."

"Thanks, Sonny. I appreciate your help."

"No problem. If we've got a killer lurking around the Fillmore, I want to know about it as much as you do."

"Anyone else you can think of who seems a little off?"

"We always have problems with pickpockets and general troublemakers, but we either call the cops on them or our bouncer gives them the heave-ho. No one I'd categorize as a maniac."

"Well, thanks anyway. Let me give you my address and phone number in case something comes up."

After writing down his contact information, Bobby left, feeling dejected and emotionally exhausted. He'd given it his best shot, but he hadn't come close to the killer.

V

~September 1967~

Chapter Seventeen

Pleiku Province

Jack was almost envious of Pfc. Tony Parker. The young soldier lay in a bed in Camp Enari's field hospital, his leg wrapped in bandages from ankle to thigh. He'd been wounded by a VC grenade two days earlier. The blast had taken the life of another member of Jack's platoon. Happy-go-lucky teenager Leonard Amparo died instantly, his body shredded by the blast. It looked like hamburger meat. Parker had been standing nearby and was struck by some of the shrapnel.

Parker's wounds weren't life-threatening, just serious enough to lay him up for a while, which was why Jack felt a twinge of envy. For Tony Parker, the war was over. He'd be kept here in the field hospital for another week or so then assigned to light duty around Camp Enari. Parker's DEROS—Date Eligible to Return from Overseas—was two months away. He was approaching the glorious state of being an official short-timer. By the time he was fully recovered, he'd be on a transpacific flight back to the States. He might go home with a limp, but he'd be going home alive.

Every serviceman in Vietnam knew his DEROS, the most important date of his life. Many soldiers kept DEROS countdown calendars, with blocks numbered from 365 to 0. At the end of every day, they marked off another block to show how many days they had left. The calendars were simple mimeographed sheets. One of the favorites featured a drawing of a naked Asian girl in a come-hither pose. The numbered blocks covered the girl's body, starting at her neck and ending with the sweet numeral zero over her crotch. Some soldiers x-ed out the days with a pen or pencil, but the more artistic ones colored them in with a felt-tip marker. The colored blocks stood out more—although for new arrivals in-country, all of the uncolored blocks staring at them was a depressing sight. Officers, of course, didn't indulge in countdown calendars, which would have been unseemly. They simply kept the numbers in their heads.

"How're you feeling today?" Jack asked Private Parker.

Parker scooted up in bed. "Better, sir. Thanks for stopping by again." A strapping towheaded boy from Texas, Parker tapped the pile of *Playboy* magazines on his bedside table. "The fellows have been keeping me supplied with...reading material."

Jack glanced at the curvaceous figure of Miss September on the cover of the magazine on top. He winked at Parker. "Yeah, I hear there are some great articles in that issue."

Jack chatted with the soldier for a few minutes longer. He was dreading what he knew he had to do afterward. He had yet to write the parents of the soldier who'd been killed by the grenade blast. It was a task he'd faced too many times in his short stay in Vietnam. It was an agonizing process, trying to convey to grieving parents that their son's death was somehow worthwhile, that he'd died in a noble cause. The task was made more difficult because Jack didn't know if he believed those rationalizations any longer.

Jack had developed a list of stock phrases to help him compose the letters—hollow sentiments such as "he served his country with honor"—but he was becoming increasingly embarrassed to use them. Most embarrassing of all was delivering the news that their dead son would receive the Purple Heart, as if that could make things better.

***

After lunch in the officers' mess, Jack returned to his quarters. It took him an hour to compose the three paragraphs in his letter to Leonard Amparo's parents. When he finally finished, he got out Bobby's latest letter. He'd read it a dozen times, but the news about the murder of Susie Blake still rattled him—just as much as the account of Lynette Simms being killed. It seemed that Bobby was embroiled in his own war, only the casualties were harder to bear because Bobby was so close to the victims. In Jack's mind, Susie's murder was another link in the chain of senseless deaths that were happening all around him.

In his letter, Bobby asked Jack if he could think of anyone who might have a reason to hate him, reason enough to harm his friends. Jack cast his mind back to their high school and college days. If anyone had made any enemies, Jack said to himself, it would be me. He knew he'd always been the overly competitive brother, the one who had to win at everything. Naturally, he'd have bruised some egos in his quest to be the best. Bobby, on the other hand, had always been a good sport, never wanting to embarrass anyone by showing them up in any sort of competition. Even when he won—which he usually did—Bobby would make a point of congratulating the other competitors. Jack recalled the time Bobby intentionally allowed another runner to win one of the races in a high school track meet simply because he felt sorry for the kid, who came from a poor Hispanic family. Jack knew that if he'd been in the same race, he'd have blasted home to victory and danced around with his arms in the air.

As Jack took up his pen to answer Bobby's letter, he began to ponder what it was that turned people into bitter enemies. The petty slights of daily life didn't seem sufficient to make anyone hate another person, and yet he knew that people often despised each other for the silliest reasons. Someone might dislike his neighbor because of where he parked his car, or because he strayed over the property line when he mowed his lawn. And office life was filled with animosity over trivial matters. The way someone looked or dressed or talked—even the way they walked—could irritate a coworker.

But what was it that made someone dislike another person so much that they'd want to kill them, or kill someone close to them? Jack couldn't think of any explanation besides revenge for some horrible wrong the other person had committed. Suddenly, Jack wondered why that logic shouldn't apply to his own situation. How was it that soldiers could be made to regard the Vietnamese as enemies, to hate them even? They hadn't attacked the United States, and the idea that such a miniscule, faraway country could be vital to America's interests was a stretch at best, as Bobby had pointed out. And yet, Jack realized, he'd allowed himself to be swept up in the flag-waving and patriotic arguments that Americans should travel halfway around the globe to kill these people.

Those disturbing thoughts provoked another question. Could anyone be considered a hero for having taken part in a war of choice, a war with so little justification? Was he a hero, as his battalion commander insisted, or merely a glorified mercenary? Beyond that, he wondered why so many people placed wartime valor on such a lofty plane? Weren't the fathers who toiled for forty years in steel mills and coal mines to support their families also heroes? Firemen who rushed into burning buildings and people who saved drowning strangers were every bit as heroic as he was. He almost felt like a fraud. Could he really go marching home with a Bronze Star pinned to his chest?

Jack pushed those thoughts aside and began his letter. Regrettably, he had to tell Bobby that he had no idea who his enemy could be. Even worse, just as he was at a loss to come up with any meaningful words to ease the pain of grieving parents, Jack couldn't think of anything to say to ease his brother's sorrow.

***

A night patrol was Jack's least favorite assignment. As his platoon fanned out to scout the area west of Camp Enari, his mind kept drifting back to the letters he'd written to Bobby and Leonard Amparo's parents. When Sergeant Fisher asked him a question, he had to have the man repeat it. This isn't good, Jack told himself. He needed to stay alert. The lives of his men could depend on it. Patrolling the VC-infested hinterland was dangerous enough without the officer in charge losing himself in existential uncertainties for which he had no answers.

The Central Highlands was the darkest landscape Jack had ever seen. With no lights other than the moon and stars, the patrol moved slowly lest someone fall headfirst into one of the defensive trenches that pitted the countryside, some of them dug by the VC and some by American troops. Tonight, it was even darker than usual because of the heavy cloud cover, and it was eerily silent as well. It felt like they were walking through an immense cavern, or trapped inside a medieval dungeon from which there was no escape. There seemed to be no up or down, only a limitless black void all around. From time to time, the soldier on point briefly switched on his flashlight to get his bearings. The rest of the time, it was the blind leading the blind.

Jack was worried about something worse than having one of his men fall into an abandoned trench. The Vietcong laid primitive but effective booby traps using sharpened, flame-hardened bamboo spikes called punji stakes. The stakes could penetrate the thick soles of combat boots. Hard to see in the daytime, the traps were impossible to see at night. The VC often coated the tips of the stakes with feces or other substances that caused infections. Besides burying punji stakes in the ground to be stepped on, the VC sometimes created deadfall platforms bristling with the bamboo spikes. If an unwary soldier set off the trip mechanism, he could be impaled with multiple stakes.

Although the odds of falling victim to the insidious traps were small, their psychological impact was tremendous. They seemed sneaky and underhanded, one more nightmarish thing to fear in a land that had proven particularly inhospitable to Americans. "Come on out and fight like a man" was a favorite Hollywood cliché, but the Vietcong weren't making movies. Jack's men kept shuffling forward in the darkness, uncertain of where they were going.

* * *

Jack lifted his third glass of Martell and drank it down.

"Better take it easy there, buddy," Vince said. "I don't fancy carrying you back to your quarters."

Jack set his glass aside. "Sorry. This stuff is starting to go down too easily. If I'm not careful, I'll be spouting French before long."

Vince eyed his friend over the rim of his own glass. "Want to talk about it?"

Jack snapped out of a moment of woolgathering. "What's that?"

"I asked if you want to talk about it."

"Talk about what?"

"Whatever it is that's on your mind. You're not here half the time tonight."

"Oh." Jack ran a hand over his face. "Do you think someone who's killed an enemy soldier in combat would ever be allowed to become a priest?"

The question was so extraordinary that Vince choked on his cognac. *"What?"*

"It's just a theoretical question. Do you think it's possible? I mean, if someone knew for certain that he'd killed an enemy soldier, would that prevent him from becoming a priest?"

"First of all, I'm a Presbyterian, so I have no idea what the Catholic rules are, but aren't you fellows big on forgiveness? I suppose if a former soldier confessed his sins and asked for forgiveness, he could become a priest. Weren't the Knights Templar supposed to be warrior monks? Some of them may have even been priests, and they butchered Moslems right and left."

"I think you're right. A person probably could be forgiven." Jack was gazing off into the middle distance.

"Listen, my friend, I know this isn't a theoretical question. What the heck's going on? I thought you had your sights set on becoming an attorney, helping people find opportunities to improve their lives."

"Sure. That's right. I was just thinking that priests can do the same thing. Maybe more so than attorneys." Jack added something in a low voice, as if he were talking to himself. "Of course, there's always the Peace Corps."

"Wait a minute. My guess is you're feeling guilty. Do you think you're the only one who questions what we're doing over here? My God, every time I look down the barrel of my M-16, I wonder if I'm doing the right thing. But until we both make it out of here, we've got to keep doing what's expected of us. It's way too late for second-guessing."

Jack looked into the middle distance again. Vince was right. There wasn't room for personal feelings or moral choices in a soldier's life. You forfeited those when you signed on. Duty always came first, even if your conscience tormented you for what you were doing. You couldn't simply throw down your weapon and walk away—not unless you felt like facing a firing squad or spending years in a military prison. All you could do was keep moving ahead, putting one foot in front of the other. Left, right, left, right.

Jack poured himself another glass of cognac.

Chapter Eighteen

San Francisco

His fall classes had finally started, which Bobby was thankful for, since they offered the distraction he needed. Aside from school, there was nothing else for him to do but lose himself in his work, but he needed a change of pace. The last thing he wanted to hear right now was another loud rock band. He was weary of musicians setting their guitars on fire or smashing them into kindling. And he hoped that he never again had to witness a singer wallowing around on a stage in an embarrassing display of public drunkenness.

Bobby checked the concert listings in the newspaper and discovered that classical guitar virtuoso Andrés Segovia would be performing the following week at the Center for the Performing Arts. He telephoned Ralph Gleason to ask if he could expand his work for the *Chronicle* to include classical music. Bobby told Gleason about the master class he'd taken under Segovia when he was studying guitar, and that sealed the deal. Gleason hooted when Bobby told him how Segovia had become enraged when one of the other students showed up with a bootleg edition of his compilation of transcriptions for the guitar. Segovia grabbed the student's unauthorized edition and threw it across the room.

"The assignment's yours," Gleason said. "I'm sure you'll be the only writer there who's actually studied under Segovia. You should have no problem getting an interview with the master, even if he is a prickly old cuss."

* * *

San Francisco's Center for the Performing Arts comprised two large performance spaces, the Veterans Building and the War Memorial Opera House. Both had hosted countless thrilling concerts, ballets, and operas since opening in 1932. In 1945, the United Nations Charter had been drafted and signed at the center. The opulent Opera House could accommodate an audience of more than three thousand. As a soloist, Andrés Segovia would be performing in the smaller Veterans Building auditorium, a space seating nine hundred.

Bobby loved coming to the center. Lit up at night, the Beaux Arts–style buildings took on a fairytale quality. His front-row seat in the balcony section of the Veterans Building auditorium gave him a bird's-eye view of the main floor, the side galleries, and the tall murals of classical scenes decorating the walls. He felt like he could reach down and touch the stage, with its backdrop of crimson curtains.

As he sat admiring the scenery, a tall, slender, attractive young woman in a sleek black designer dress made her way along the row where he was sitting. She had straight, raven-black hair that brushed her shoulders. When he stood to let her pass, he saw she was nearly as tall as he was. She took the seat next to him.

"I was worried I'd be late," she said with a dazzling smile. She casually brushed her hair back behind her ear "You wouldn't believe the traffic on Market Street tonight."

The woman looked like she'd stepped from the pages of *Vogue* magazine. Her dress must have cost a packet, Bobby thought, and the long string of jade beads she wore was obviously the real thing. Must be an heiress, he told himself. Or maybe she's a princess who escaped her minders to enjoy a night out on her own, like Audrey Hepburn in *Roman Holiday.* Whoever she was, she had sophisticate written all over her. She made Bobby feel like a rustic sitting next to her.

"Looks like you made it just in time," he said.

At that moment, Andrés Segovia walked onstage and took a bow. The audience greeted him with a standing ovation, which the seventy-four-year-old musician accepted as his due. The solemn, gray-haired, bespectacled Spaniard was widely regarded as the finest classical guitarist in the world. He'd been astonishing concertgoers for over half a century with his expressive technique. He'd played for the royal family in Spain, increased the appreciation of the classical guitar as a concert instrument, and given new life to many forgotten works. The world knew of his towering stature—and so did he.

Segovia took his seat and positioned his guitar. He sat in silence for a few seconds, composing his thoughts, then he began playing J. S. Bach's *Chaconne,* a haunting meditation that Bach wrote following the death of his wife. A master of phrasing and tone, Segovia captured every nuance of the powerful emotions expressed in the composition, which he'd transcribed from the original violin solo. After a thunderous round of applause, he changed the mood with Bach's charming, lyrical *Gavotte en Rondeau,* another Segovia transcription. Following several other selections, a short intermission was announced.

Bobby drifted down to the austerely decorated foyer outside the performance area, where refreshment kiosks had been set up. He stood in line to buy a glass of oaky Urbina Rioja, a Spanish red wine that was being sold in honor of Segovia's roots. Looking around for a quiet spot to stand and observe the crowd, he noticed the tall, elegant woman who'd been sitting next to him. She was standing by herself under one of the foyer's archways. Bobby strolled over and joined her.

"Enjoying the music?" he asked.

"It's absolutely divine," she said. "Segovia transports me to some magical place whenever I hear him play."

Bobby hadn't often heard anyone use the word "divine" in a conversation. It was one of those pretentious adjectives, like "intoxicating," but coming from her, it didn't strike him that way. She simply expressed herself differently from most of the people he'd met. Maybe she actually was a princess. Her high cheekbones and the way she stood with her chin slightly raised gave her an aristocratic air. She reminded him of Ava Gardner. She would have looked natural wearing a tiara.

"My name's Bobby Doyle, by the way."

"It's a pleasure to meet you." She gave him a strange smile. She almost seemed embarrassed. "I'm...Deneige Leblanc."

"Deneige Leblanc? Doesn't that mean..."

"Yes it does. Snow White. My parents have a sense of humor. I have a sister named Bianca, which, if you don't know, means 'pure.' You can imagine the fun the other girls at the Hamlin School had with our names. In my case, someone was always leaving an apple on my desk like the Wicked Queen."

"The Hamlin School? So you grew up in the city."

"Born and bred."

Bobby noticed her glass was nearly empty, as was his. "Could I get you another drink?"

She finished her drink and held out the glass. "That would be lovely. A Stolichnaya martini, please." She pronounced the difficult Russian word correctly. "Very dry," she added.

Yep, Bobby thought. Definitely a princess.

* * *

The remainder of the program was devoted to Segovia's own compositions. Though more well known for transcribing and popularizing the work of other composers, Segovia had written fifty or sixty short pieces. Tonight, he played the twenty-minute suite of songs called *Canciones Populares de Distintos Paises,* his own interpretations of popular songs from around the world. The audience was also treated to his lively "Variations for Guitar on a Theme by Mozart." When Segovia stood up to take his final bow, Bobby joined in the five-minute standing ovation. Finally, the audience began filing toward the exits.

"A bravura performance," Deneige Leblanc said.

"It was. He never disappoints." Bobby glanced at his watch. "Sorry, but I have to run. I have an interview scheduled with Señor Segovia."

"An interview?"

"Yes. I write about music for the *Chronicle.*"

"I've heard Segovia is very particular about who he grants interviews to. I'm told he doesn't suffer fools gladly."

"I have an in. I studied under him a few years ago. A master class in Los Angeles."

Deneige raised her eyebrows. "How did you manage to get into a master class with Andrés Segovia? That must be pretty competitive."

"I had to audition. It was the most nervous moment of my life. All of the other candidates were professional musicians or star students at top conservatories. I was just a kid who loved the guitar."

Deneige gave him an appraising look. "Very enterprising. And a bit audacious."

Bobby shrugged. "Like they say, you can't win if you don't get in the game. Besides, I had nothing to lose. The worst thing Segovia could have done was to tell me to go home and practice some more."

Deneige laughed. "The thrill of a challenge?"

"I guess you could call it that. Anyway, it was nice meeting you."

Deneige watched him make his way through the departing crowd. What an interesting man, she said to herself.

* * *

Bobby managed to extend his break from the rock scene into the following week. Young British classical guitarist Julian Bream was in town. One of the many guitarists inspired by Segovia's trailblazing career, Bream was promoting the release of his album *20th Century Guitar,* a collection of pieces by modernist composers. His performance took place in the elegant Venetian Room at the Fairmont Hotel, the supper club where Tony Bennett first sang "I Left My Heart in San Francisco." Glittering with crystal and gilt, the ballroom was filled to capacity.

The highlight of the show for Bobby was Benjamin Britten's landmark composition *Nocturnal,* a mysterious suite evoking various states of sleep and dreams. He also enjoyed Frank Martin's "Quatre pièces brèves," four short pieces that sounded like music from another galaxy, leaping and prowling along with a persistent strangeness. None of Bream's selections were anything like the traditional works played by Segovia.

When Bream's performance was over, Bobby finished his glass of wine and got up to leave. Three tables away, a tall, raven-haired woman stood up at the same time. As if it were scripted, Deneige Leblanc turned his way. She did a double take, then waved to him.

Bobby stepped over to say hello. "We've really got to stop meeting like this," he said. "People will start talking."

Deneige laughed. "I think we were fated to meet again. At least we know we have the same taste in music."

"May I buy you a drink at the bar?" Bobby asked. "Stolichnaya martini, I recall. Very dry."

"I'm flattered you remembered, and yes, I'd love a martini. They're the only civilized drink other than champagne."

"I detect that you have expensive tastes."

"I just enjoy the good things in life."

They settled in at a table in the cocktail lounge. After the waiter took their orders, Bobby asked Deneige how she enjoyed the music.

"It was like being on another plane of existence," she said. "About halfway through the program, I discovered it was better to listen with my eyes closed. I swear, at different points, I was soaring through outer space, walking in a secret garden, and floating down a peaceful river like a fallen leaf. I'm definitely buying Bream's new album. It's got to be the least expensive way to get high anyone ever came up with."

"What do you actually do in life," Bobby asked her, "besides listen to classical guitar music?"

"I have my own literary agency. I've only been in business a short time, but I'm building up a respectable clientele. I specialize in novels, short story collections, and poetry. I represent novels and short story collections for the money and poetry because I happen to like it. Sadly, there's not much money in poetry, just a smidgeon of prestige."

"Don't I know it. I've had a few poems published, but I haven't earned enough to pay for these drinks."

"So you write about music for the *Chronicle*, you play the guitar, and you write poetry. What else do you get up to?"

"I just started a master's program at USF, and I hope to write a novel someday."

"Then do it," Deneige said forcefully. "The world is filled with people who hope to write a novel someday. Most of them don't have the talent or the dedication. Long-form fiction is the hardest type of writing there is. You're starting from scratch, with only your imagination to provide the inspiration. It's not like nonfiction, where you have a body of facts to work with."

"I've never given it much thought, but what you say is true. Nonfiction largely depends on taking good notes, being able to organize your material, and having the skill to turn a phrase. With fiction, there's that proverbial blank page staring back at you."

Deneige sipped her martini. "Have you written enough poetry to make a book? I could take a look at it."

"Not really. I scribbled lots of poems as a Berkeley undergrad, but when I go back and look at them, they often strike me as overly dramatic. It's the curse of the young."

"If you'd like to hear some truly fine poetry, you could come by my office next Thursday evening. One of my authors is bringing out a new work, and she's giving a reading to a group of friends. She might inspire you."

"That sounds tempting."

Deneige dug one of her business cards out of her purse and gave it to him. "The author's name is Diane di Prima. I have to warn you. She's a bundle of dynamite."

* * *

Bobby was staggered by the poetry of Diane di Prima. An associate of Timothy Leary, Allen Ginsberg, Jack Kerouac, and other icons of the avant-garde, the sensuous, dark-haired poet was a dedicated feminist and antiwar activist. The brilliant imagery of her spiritually tinged free verse left Bobby's mind wandering in realms of uncertainty and wonder. She made his own attempts at poetry seem ploddingly conventional. A bundle of dynamite indeed. She'd just blown up some of his old ways of thinking and planted the seeds of a new direction he intended to explore. It came as no surprise to learn that di Prima was a member of the free-spirited, socially conscious Diggers.

Deneige's eighteenth-floor office in the Shell Building was everything Bobby might have expected—a swanky decor, loaded with books, and offering a terrific view of the Financial District. The group gathered here was a cross-section of the city's literati. They ranged from bearded, long-haired Beats in guayaberas to society matrons in Parisian designs. Deneige wore what appeared to be her trademark all-black attire. She glanced at Bobby across the crowded room and lifted her martini glass in salute.

When the reading was over, Deneige said goodnight to her guests with abundant air-kisses and many a "wonderful to see you again, darling." Diane di Prima gave her a big hug and thanked her for everything. She leaned in and kissed Deneige on the cheek, then whispered something in her ear.

Bobby was standing close enough to hear what di Prima said. "Did she just call you Lady Leblanc?" he asked Deneige afterward.

Deneige laughed. "It's a private joke. I have an uncle who's big on genealogy. He traced our ancestors back to the eighteenth-century French nobility. I happened to share that one day with Diane, and every now and then she taunts me with that 'Lady' business. It might be flattering if it weren't for the fact that most of our French ancestors lost their heads in the Revolution."

"You're probably not going to believe this, but when we first met, I thought you were some sort of royalty. It's the way you carry yourself, the way you speak."

"Ha. You're absolutely right. I don't believe you. I think you're trying to butter me up."

"I swear I'm not...your ladyship." Bobby bowed, pretending to sweep a hat from his head.

Deneige held out her hand to be kissed. "You may rise."

* * *

Bobby sorted through his morning mail, the usual collection of bills and letters promoting every cause imaginable, from saving the whales to protecting Canadian harp seals. One letter solicited his support for the agricultural workers strike against grape growers in Delano, California, an action promoted by Cesar Chavez and other labor and civil rights activists. Bobby set that appeal aside to read later.

Among the other letters, a small cream-colored envelope caught Bobby's eye. He sniffed it and detected the faint floral-woody scent of Shalimar. Smiling, he opened the envelope and found a notecard inside engraved with the name Deneigh Leblanc. Addressed to "Mr. Doyle," the handwritten note invited him to the opening of an art exhibition featuring the work of rising California painter Michael Bowen, one of the masterminds behind last January's Human Be-In.

Bobby immediately thought of Lynette. She might have had her own exhibition one day, if only.... He knew he couldn't attend Michael Bowen's opening if it was being staged at the De Young Museum, which held too many memories, but as he finished reading the invitation, he saw that the event would be at a gallery downtown. It was one he'd never heard of, undoubtedly an exclusive showroom patronized by well-heeled collectors.

He picked up the phone and called Deneige's office. "Leblanc Literary Agency," a familiar voice answered.

"Hello, Deneige. I just received your invitation to the Michael Bowen opening."

"I hope you're free that evening. I know the gallery owner, and he said I could bring a friend."

"I am free, but before I accept, I have to ask you something. What kind of paintings does he do?"

"He calls them visionary art."

"I know I'm being old-fashioned, but can you tell what they're supposed to depict? You see, I tend to prefer artists who can actually draw."

"So you don't like abstract art?"

"I'll admit that the designs in some abstract paintings are clever and interesting, but then so are the designs on Christmas wrapping paper."

"My, my, aren't we being provincial. Abstract paintings can reveal things beyond what the mind recognizes. They depict the artist's emotional view of reality, which doesn't always hew to the rational world. That's why they're called abstract."

"Then by that logic, a writer who jots down random thoughts would be considered a major talent."

"Bobby, you're being difficult. Haven't you had your morning coffee? Besides, the style of writing you just described is called stream of consciousness. I believe James Joyce, Virginia Woolf, and Marcel Proust managed to express themselves adequately with that technique."

"Ouch. I surrender to your superior logic. Lead me to the mystical swirling colors."

"For your information, Michael Bowen isn't an abstract artist. He does some of the most interesting, original paintings I've ever seen. No, they're not strictly representational. They're more interpretive. I'll bet you a dinner at Alfred's Steakhouse that you'll like them."

"You're on. But you have to agree to something first."

"Oh, no. Why do I sense something excruciatingly embarrassing in the offing?"

"It won't be embarrassing. If Lady Leblanc would deign to mix with the hoi polloi, I'll escort her to a concert by Buffalo Springfield next week. I know rock music isn't your thing, but these fellows aren't ear-blasters. Their musicianship is superb, their lyrics are thoughtful, and their vocal harmonies are amazing."

"With that buildup, they'd better be good. All right, Lady Leblanc assents to your proposal."

* * *

Michael Bowen's paintings turned out to be surprisingly good. Bobby would have purchased one of the colorful, phantasmagorical portraits if he could have afforded it, but after the show, he had to shell out for an expensive dinner at Alfred's Steakhouse since he'd lost the bet with Deneige.

The following week, it was his turn to surprise her with the music of Buffalo Springfield. The Fillmore was packed with the usual menagerie of shaggy flower children, middle-aged music lovers, and clean-cut Berkeley strivers. Bobby had politely suggested that Deneige might want to dress down for the show so she wouldn't rile up the peasants.

"You think they'd lead me to the guillotine?" she joked, but when he picked her up, she was wearing an understated black pantsuit with a bright red scarf around her neck. The outfit probably cost a bundle, but at least she didn't stand out—other than for being nearly six feet tall and strikingly beautiful.

The opening band for the evening was Quicksilver Messenger Service. They performed their popular rendition of "Who Do You Love?" and other recent hits, but Bobby was glad when they finished their set. He'd promised Deneige Buffalo Springfield, and the undercard didn't hold much interest. As the band filed off the stage, Sonny Anders came out to introduce the main attraction. Looking out over the audience, the lanky blond promoter noticed Bobby, who stood half a head taller than anyone around him. Anders also noticed the tall, dark-haired girl by his side, a regular Amazon. Aside from the surprise of seeing Bobby with yet another good-looking woman, Anders was startled to recognize someone standing a short distance off to their right, a runty figure with fright wig of bright orange hair.

Anders announced that Buffalo Springfield was currently putting the final touches on its second album and would be debuting some of their new material tonight. The group led off with "Mr. Soul," an edgy, evocative song written by Neil Young, who was back with the band after one of his intermittent absences. They also played the lilting "Bluebird" and the shimmering "Rock & Roll Woman," folk-rock pieces by Stephen Stills, both with brilliant guitar work and soaring harmonies. Bobby watched Deneige out of the corner of his eye to gauge her reaction. From the way she was bobbing her head to the beat, it was clear the music hadn't disappointed her.

During a break in the set, Sonny Anders sought out Bobby. "Hey man," he said, "I spotted you from the stage."

Bobby introduced Deneige, but Anders hardly paid her any attention, other than a nod and a brief "How you doing?"

"Man, I gotta tell you about someone else I spotted. I saw that guy you were asking me about—the little orange-haired dude. He was standing not ten feet away from you, and boy, was he giving you the stink eye. Lemme tell you, if looks could kill, he was committing murder."

Bobby hurriedly scanned the room, but he saw no sign of the suspicious oddball. "Looks like he's gone."

They couldn't have known that tough guy Eddie Ratner had left early to catch the first episode in the new season of *Star Trek.* The Rat had a thing for the gorgeous Lieutenant Uhura.

"I just wanted to give you a heads-up," Anders said. "I told you I'd keep an eye out for him. If I see him again, I'll chat him up, find out his name and what his game is."

"Thanks, Sonny. I'd appreciate that."

"No problem." Anders headed off as the members of Buffalo Springfield came back onstage.

"What was that all about?" Deneige asked. "He made it sound like someone is after you."

Bobby reluctantly told Deneige about the murders of Lynette and Susie, explaining how they'd both been attacked while walking home at night.

"Good Lord," she exclaimed. "That's unbelievable. And you think this person who was glaring at you might have had something to do with it?"

"I really don't know, but he was hanging around Lynette one night here at the Fillmore, and when I showed up, he made some nasty comments and slunk off. He definitely looked like someone capable of murder. A real low-life."

Bobby suddenly realized that if Orange Hair actually was the murderer, it could be worrisome that he'd seen Deneige with him. "You need to be extra careful," he told her. "If this little creep has some vendetta against my friends, you could be in danger."

Deneige shivered at the thought. "That's not very comforting, but I should be safe enough. I certainly don't walk the streets at night by myself."

"All the same, you need to stay alert. I hate to think that just being around me could put you in harm's way."

Deneige tried to make light of the situation. "You do strike me as a dangerous man." When Bobby didn't smile, she brushed his cheek with her fingers. "I promise I'll be vigilant, Mr. Doyle."

Chapter Nineteen

San Francisco

Bobby hadn't heard from Deneige for a couple of weeks, which was fine by him. Maybe she'd taken his warning to heart and thought it better to keep her distance. He'd been inclined to put some space between the two of them himself. There was nothing implied about any further get-togethers, no romantic overtures on either side. They weren't a couple, just two friends who'd enjoyed a few cultural events in each other's company. That's the way Bobby wanted to leave it. He wasn't ready for any more emotional entanglements for the foreseeable future.

That's when he received another Shalimar-scented notecard in the mail. He opened it with misgivings, already imagining how he'd frame his regrets if it was another invitation. Then he read the card. Deneige was inviting him to a celebration to mark the publication of a new biography of Dashiell Hammett by one of her authors. Like his father, Bobby was a huge fan of Hammett's work. How could anyone connected with San Francisco not be? What made Deneige's invitation hard to turn down was the nature of the celebration. The author would be leading guests on a tour of Hammett's haunts in the city, along with places connected to his stories. He couldn't say no.

* * *

Bobby learned something new about Hammett from the first few sentences author Stanley Ferguson uttered. Ferguson was giving the guests gathered in Deneige's office a summary of the sights they'd be visiting, and he kept pronouncing Hammett's first name "dah-*SHEEL.*" Bobby had always heard it pronounced "*DASH*-ull." When he asked Ferguson about his pronunciation, the distinguished gray-bearded author peered at him over his half-frame reading glasses.

"It's the surname of Hammett's mother," he explained, "an anglicized spelling of the French name, 'de Chiel.'"

"Then I've been saying it wrong all my life, and so has my father."

"You and millions of others," Ferguson said with a chuckle. "Don't worry, '*DASH*-ull' has become so widespread that most authorities simply shrug and go along with it. They consider it an Americanization. Since Hammett's friends usually called him 'Dash,' there's some justification for it. I just prefer to pronounce it the right way. Actually, Hammett's first name was Samuel. He went by 'Sam' for years, but he thought 'Dashiell' looked more distinguished in his byline. Made him sound foreign and a bit mysterious."

Ferguson was dressed in a dark, double-breasted pinstripe suit, much like the one Humphrey Bogart wore as Sam Spade in *The Maltese Falcon,* John Huston's 1941 noir classic based on Hammett's novel. Ferguson even had the round paper tag from a bag of Bull Durham tobacco dangling from his breast pocket, a nod to the hand-rolled cigarettes Spade smoked in the movie.

Before they left for the tour, Ferguson sketched his subject's life and career. "Hammett was born in 1894 on a farm in St. Mary's County, Maryland, a peninsula on the Chesapeake Bay south of Washington, D.C. I think it's an interesting coincidence that he ended up living on another peninsula in California. After dropping out of school at fourteen, he held a variety of odd jobs in Baltimore and Philadelphia before going to work for the Pinkerton Detective Agency." Ferguson grinned. "Yes, he really did know something about being a shamus.

"During World War I, Hammett enlisted in the army, which broke his health. He contracted the Spanish flu, leading to tuberculosis, a disease that would plague him for years. After he left the army, Hammett worked for the Pinkerton Agency here in San Francisco. Although he married and had two daughters, the marriage eventually fell apart. In 1922, Hammett quit Pinkertons to focus on his writing. During the eight years he lived here, he wrote several stories about a nameless detective he called the Continental Op. In 1929, he began *The Maltese Falcon,* the novel that made him famous, and he created another classic with his final novel, *The Thin Man.* During his brief career, Hammett became the recognized master of the hard-boiled detective story. Shall we go visit some of the places that inspired him?"

As part of the evening's festivities, everyone had been encouraged to come dressed as their favorite Hammett character. Not everyone went along, but the ones who did added to the fun, even if they needed to explain who they were supposed to be. Since most of the tour related to *The Maltese Falcon,* two or three women came dressed as Brigid O'Shaughnessy, the slinky, deceitful dame who killed Sam Spade's partner, Miles Archer.

One of the men had fattened himself up with a pillow to imitate the novel's overweight villain Casper Gutman, a man who'd chased the legendary "black bird" for seventeen years. A fellow on the short side came dressed as Gutman's undersize enforcer, Wilmer Cook, and another smallish man came as the perfumed grifter Joel Cairo. It was a colorful group that filed out of Deneige's office on the way to the first stop on the tour. Stanley Ferguson led the way, wearing a dark-gray fedora pulled down low over his eyes, just like Bogie.

Deneige had hired a tour bus to ferry the group on its circuit around the neighborhoods where Hammett lived and his fictional creations went about their frequently dangerous, often sordid affairs. They began at 891 Post Street, on the northern edge of the Tenderloin district. The no-frills brick apartment building was where Hammett stayed after he'd left his family and quit his job with the Pinkerton Detective Agency.

"Right here in apartment 401, Hammett developed his skill as a writer," Ferguson said as they entered the top-floor flat. "I'm sure he appreciated the privacy of this hidey-hole. Sitting beside those double windows, he had a view of the streets where the poor and the privileged alike hustled for a buck. He pounded out his stories on an old manual typewriter, most likely with a glass of whiskey at his elbow. He sank into alcoholism and became a womanizer during the years he lived here, but he always managed to keep writing." Bobby imagined the ghosts of Sam Spade and the Continental Op hovering over Hammett's desk.

"It's generally thought that Hammett had this building in mind when he wrote about Sam Spade's apartment," Ferguson said. "Some key scenes in *The Maltese Falcon* play out in Spade's rooms. That's where Spade told Brigid O'Shaughnessy he was turning her over to the police for murdering his partner. 'When a man's partner is killed he's supposed to do something about it,' Spade said." Bobby felt a twinge of uneasiness at those words. They made him think of Lynette and Susie. Yeah, you are supposed to do something about it when your partner is killed, he told himself. And he hadn't been able to do a thing.

On nearby Sutter Street, to the north of Hammett's apartment, Ferguson pointed out the antique-looking Hunter-Dulin office building. "That's where Hammett set the Spade and Archer Detective Agency. Brigid O'Shaughnessy sashayed into Spade's office one day and told him a cock-and-bull story about her sister being in trouble and how desperately she needed his help. In the movie, Mary Astor, who played Brigid O'Shaughnessy, talked in quick, nervous little bursts, like shots from an automatic weapon. Spade took her money, but as he told her later, he didn't believe her story. 'We believed your two hundred dollars,' he said. It's one of the great lines in the movie. It captured Spade's cynical nature perfectly. Hammett's dialogue was so good that director John Huston lifted large chunks of it directly from the novel."

The tour bus parked near the corner of Sutter and Stockton Streets, and Ferguson led the way into a dim passageway between Sutter and Bush. The backs of anonymous brick buildings seemed to close in on them. "This is called Burritt Street, but as you can see, it's more of an alley. It's where Brigid O'Shaughnessy shot the unsuspecting Miles Archer. In Hammett's day, not all of these buildings were here. When Archer was shot, he rolled down the hill toward Stockton. Sam Spade came here after learning his partner had been murdered. He realized that Archer must have known his killer, since his gun was still inside his coat. That's what led him to suspect Brigid O'Shaughnessy."

They climbed back onto the bus and headed over to the waterfront, parking just off the Embarcadero. Late-day traffic surged along the sweeping roadway bordering the Bay. Standing on the broad sidewalk in front of the Ferry Building, Ferguson pointed to the north. "One of those piers was where the freighter *La Paloma* was tied up when it arrived from Hong Kong in *The Maltese Falcon.* The freighter's skipper, Captain Jacobi, was carrying the black bird to deliver to Brigid O'Shaughnessy. Casper Gutman tried and failed to get the falcon from him, and in the process, his trigger-happy gunsel, Wilmer, set fire to the ship, and he later shot Jacobi."

Ferguson turned to the group. "For those of you who might not know, the actor who played Captain Jacobi was John Huston's father, Walter Huston. He only got about thirty seconds of screen time, when he stumbles into Sam Spade's office with the falcon. In another John Huston masterpiece, *The Treasure of the Sierra Madre,* Walter Huston was one of the stars. He won an Academy Award for his role as the wily old coot who led Bogart and Tim Holt to the gold."

The line of weathered gray piers jutting into the Bay looked sinister as Bobby pictured the scene with the blazing ship in *The Maltese Falcon.* Overhead, querulous seagulls squawked and wheeled in the erratic wind. It buffeted them about like children's kites. Chop churned up by the wind slapped against the pilings, filling the air with a briny scent. Ferries bound for points north and east plowed foamy furrows in the water. To the south of where they stood, the abandoned warehouses, rundown storage yards, and dilapidated piers of South Beach conjured up the seedy atmosphere Hammett captured in his stories. Rusting cranes loomed like artifacts from a forgotten war.

The sun had ducked behind the tall buildings downtown. It would be dark soon, time for the denizens of Hammett's world to come out and play. Night was the best time to visit the mysterious, often menacing locations Hammett described in his stories. After dark, the neon glow of hotel and bar signs reflected in the fog-dampened streets as strangers shuffled along the sidewalks with collars raised, looking slightly wary, as if they suspected someone was following them.

From the waterfront, they headed southwest on Market Street. Ferguson pointed out the Palace Hotel as they passed by. "Hammett mentioned several places where Sam Spade ate in *The Maltese Falcon.* Most of them were unpretentious eateries, but one was the Palace Hotel's luxurious Garden Court. It made sense for a tough gumshoe like Spade to grab a bite at an ordinary café—in one joint he ate pickled pigs' feet—but I've always thought the Garden Court seemed too refined for him. It's as fancy as the Palace of Versailles, with its crystal chandeliers, marble columns, and domed glass ceiling. Most likely, Hammett himself frequented the Garden Court. He'd have been at home there. A slender, handsome man who dressed to the nines, he looked like a banker or diplomat—or a slick gambler who'd made a bundle at cards."

A few blocks farther on, they stopped in front of the ponderous gray Flood Building, the ornate San Francisco landmark that once housed the Pinkerton Detective Agency. "The building was completed in 1904," Ferguson said, "just in time for the Great Earthquake, although it survived. Hammett only worked there for a short time after he arrived in the city. He already had other things on his mind. San Francisco was working its magic on him.

"From here down to Van Ness, Market Street marks the southern boundary of the Tenderloin," Ferguson added. "We're heading north on Powell up to Geary, the district's northern boundary. The fifty square blocks of the Tenderloin include some of the roughest parts of the city. Hammett lived here during Prohibition, when the town was filled with speakeasies, brothels, and gambling parlors. Right next door in Chinatown, they had opium dens, and rival tongs were still hacking each other to pieces with hatchets. Hammett had plenty of material to draw from. All he had to do was walk out his front door to find it."

Ferguson laughed as they pulled to a stop on Geary Street. "You can still get just about anything you want here in the Tenderloin. It's pretty much the drug capital of the city. You might even get a tip on where to find the black bird." He led the way off the bus and the group strolled down the busy avenue toward Mason Street. Ferguson stopped beneath the arched marquee of the grand old Geary Theater.

"Geary Street has two or three settings Hammett is believed to have used in *The Maltese Falcon.* This is where Joel Cairo purchased tickets to see *The Merchant of Venice,* and down on the corner is the Clift Hotel. From things Hammett referred to in his book, he may have had the Clift in mind when he wrote about Casper Gutman's hotel, which he called the Alexandria. On the corner opposite the Clift is the Bellevue Hotel. That's probably the model for the hotel where Cairo stayed. Hammett called it the Belvedere." They walked to the end of the block to see the two hotels, gingerbread palaces that dated to the early part of the century.

"Sam Spade visited Gutman twice," Ferguson said. "The first time, he and Gutman sparred over who actually had possession of the black bird. The second time, Gutman revealed the legend behind the golden, jewel encrusted falcon statue, telling Spade its value was incalculable. Gutman drugged Spade's drink, and Wilmer Cook kicked him in the head when he passed out. They left him lying unconscious on the floor and rushed off in pursuit of the falcon, which they thought Brigid O'Shaughnessy had located. The entire story pitted thieves against thieves, with Sam Spade in the middle of it all—although you never knew whose side he was on."

As they headed back to the bus, Bobby glanced across the street. He was surprised to see Sonny Anders coming out of a shabby apartment building. Equally shabby people were milling around on the street, like extras in *The Maltese Falcon.* Bobby wondered what Anders was doing in this part of town, although maybe he lived here. Rents were cheap in the Tenderloin, and Anders might need to cut expenses. He probably wasn't getting rich working for Bill Graham.

Now that he thought about it, it was more likely that Anders was visiting a band that Graham was interested in working with. The neighborhood was an area where struggling musicians might live. Anders stood a moment talking to an iffy-looking character wearing an overcoat that was several sizes too big, a homeless person from the looks of him. Maybe he was one of the Vietnam vets who were living on the streets these days, Bobby speculated, someone who'd brought his drug habit along with him when he returned to the States.

Bobby noticed that Anders handed the man some money. It appeared that beneath his seemingly unsentimental exterior, Sonny Anders was a soft touch. Good for him, Bobby said to himself, although Anders would probably deny his generosity if anyone mentioned it. Some folks liked to keep their true nature to themselves. It proved that you could never be sure you knew someone completely. They often had a secret or two that would floor you.

"I guess it's time to wrap up Dashiell Hammett's career," Ferguson said. The group had settled in for a nightcap at John's Grill, the final stop on their tour. A steak and seafood restaurant near Union Square, it was one of the places where Sam Spade ate in *The Maltese Falcon.* With its polished mahogany bar, hardwood floors, and dark paneled walls covered with celebrity photos, the spacious old restaurant looked like a man's domain, the type of hangout Spade—or Hammett—would have favored.

"In 1929, Hammett left San Francisco for New York." Ferguson made it sound like an old friend had abandoned him. "In 1930, he moved to Hollywood. Warner Brothers had paid him eighty-five hundred dollars for the film rights to *The Maltese Falcon.* It may have seemed like a lot of money at the time, until you consider how much the movie earned over the years.

"In Hollywood, Hammett found work on a number of film projects. He was well paid, but he drank up most of his money. By the time his novel *The Thin Man* came out in 1934, Hammett was just about finished as a writer. He should have written much more, but booze, bad health, and his affiliation with the Communist Party did him in. He died of lung cancer in 1961 and was buried in Arlington National Cemetery. I prefer to remember him as he was during his years in San Francisco, when he was at the height of his creative powers."

Hammett's connection with Hollywood made Bobby think about how central the movie business was to his own life. His grandfather had worked at Columbia Pictures, and now his parents worked there. Susie Blake's goal had been to work in movies, and he'd toyed with the idea of trying his hand at screenwriting someday. It seemed as if most of his life revolved around a business built on fantasy. It was an amazing notion, making a living out of weaving dreams. It was easy to get lost in the world of fantasy. It could be better than the alternative. In Hammett's case, his career as a detective and his mystery writing sometimes blurred the line between reality and make-believe.

Looking across the table at Deneige, Bobby pictured her with Lynette and Susie. They would have liked one another, he was sure. All three of them were such vibrant women, each of them clever, talented, and attractive. He recalled Stanley Ferguson's comments about Sam Spade eating at the Garden Court in the Palace Hotel. He visualized Lynette, Susie, and Deneige having tea together in the sumptuous old dining room, discussing art, films, and books while feasting on warm scones, clotted cream, and jam. Then his vision altered as Lynette and Susie faded from the scene, leaving only Deneige seated at the table. Just as she was sitting across from him now, smiling enigmatically.

"Did you enjoy the tour?" she asked.

"I did. I learned quite a lot. It's interesting to find out where a novelist gets his inspiration and his raw material. With Hammett, it came from his own experiences."

"Yes, but like all great writers, he made something more of his experiences. He shaped and embellished them to create art."

Bobby wondered where his own stories would come from. Would they be colored by grief over the deaths of his friends? He hoped not. The lives of too many people were defined by tragedy. He didn't want to be one of them.

At least for tonight, he'd been able to forget about those calamities. The tour had transported him to another era, an escape into a far-off world of excitement, romance, and mystery. He finished his drink. It was fun while it lasted.

Chapter Twenty

San Francisco

John Fogerty sounded like a poor country boy singing about his unending troubles. And he looked the part too. Standing on the stage of the Fillmore Auditorium in his jeans, plaid flannel shirt, and shaggy pageboy haircut, he could have just stepped out of a Louisiana bayou. In a piercing tenor that was something between a shriek and a wail, he bemoaned the fact that he couldn't go back home to Porterville, where he risked being hanged as the son of a jailbird daddy. Despite his problems, he kept vowing that he didn't care.

The story of persecution in a vengeful San Joaquin Valley town was a product of Fogerty's fertile imagination. He and his brothers had grown up across San Francisco Bay in friendly suburban El Cerrito, north of Berkeley. Fogerty's countrified twang was his own invention as well, the result of his fascination with all things southern. As a boy, he read the Uncle Remus stories and soaked up the atmosphere in films such as *Song of the South* and *Swamp Water.* In his teens, he discovered pioneering country blues and rock artists the likes of Lead Belly, Little Richard, and Bo Diddley. The folklore, imagery, and music of the South got his creative juices flowing, even though he'd never caught a catfish, seen a live gator, ridden the rails, or been within a hundred miles of the Mississippi River.

Fogerty shared the stage with his brother Tom and school friends Stu Cook and Doug Clifford. They'd been playing together for several years, performing at Berkeley fraternity parties, seedy small-town bars, and anywhere else they could land a gig. They'd started out calling themselves the Blue Velvets and had recorded a few mostly forgettable singles. In 1964, they signed with Oakland's Fantasy Records. Fantasy's boss changed the band's name to the Golliwogs, which they all hated, but even with the new name, their records still didn't sell.

When the group walked onstage this evening, no one realized that John Fogerty and his bandmates were on the cusp of a breakthrough. They'd recorded a high-powered version of the rockabilly classic "Susie Q," which was getting airplay in the Bay Area. They'd also decided to drop the insipid Golliwogs label and rechristen themselves Creedence Clearwater Revival, a name they hoped would "revive" their lackluster career. Best of all, the new owner of Fantasy Records had offered them the chance to record a whole album. The band may have been second on the bill tonight, but it appeared to be just a matter of time before they were headliners—despite having a throwback sound with only a passing resemblance to psychedelic rock.

The audience at the Fillmore certainly liked what it was hearing. And that included Bobby Doyle. Bobby had seen the group a few times at Berkeley's Monkey Inn during his years at Cal. Back then, they sounded like a hundred other struggling, middle-of-the-road bands, with uninspired pop songs like "Where You Been" and "You Better Be Careful." Now they had a raw energy they'd lacked before. When they launched into "Susie Q," Bobby felt like he was hearing a different group. John Fogerty's bluesy, swamp-rock vocals and guitar solos were down and dirty. He sounded like a cocky bad boy strutting along Bourbon Street on a Saturday night. This was no longer a tame, predictable suburban band. They were kicking butt.

After Fogerty and his bandmates finished their set, Sonny Anders came onstage. His first few comments were drowned out by the raucous ovation for Fogerty and company. When the audience settled down, Anders introduced the star attraction of the evening, the Paul Butterfield Blues Band. Bobby caught Anders's eye and waved to him. Anders nodded and gave him a tired-looking smile of recognition.

Bobby smiled himself, thinking of the act of generosity he'd seen on Geary

Street, the side of Anders he hadn't expected.

Bobby stayed for the Butterfield Blues Band's set, a flawless performance filled with the spontaneous jamming the group was known for. As he drove back to his apartment, Bobby mentally roughed out the article he'd be writing. Paul Butterfield's group was good, but Bobby knew that John Fogerty would be getting the most space in his piece. It was clear that Fogerty had stumbled upon a new formula, one that set his band apart. Bobby kept humming the catchy guitar hook in "Susie Q." He couldn't get it out of his head.

By the time he turned into the underground parking garage at his apartment building, Bobby had begun thinking about another Susie. His Susie. She would have loved tonight's concert. The renegade quality John Fogerty projected suited her own nature. Bobby suddenly felt like making a pilgrimage to wine country in Susie's honor—a sentimental journey to revisit the places she'd introduced him to. The beautiful fall weather they'd been having lately would be perfect for a drive up to Sonoma, and maybe he'd explore Napa as well. Susie had told him about some of her favorite wineries there.

Bobby pulled into his designated parking spot and switched off the TR4's engine. He didn't bother to put up the top. The car would be safe here in the building's private garage.

* * *

Thefts in the Western Addition weren't a serious problem, nothing like the rising tide of crime down in Haight-Ashbury. Bobby's apartment building hadn't yet installed security cameras, and the entrance to the underground parking garage was left open at all hours. That made things easy for the figure who entered the garage at three in the morning. Dressed all in black, with a matching stocking cap pulled low on his head, the intruder was nearly invisible in the dimly illuminated garage. He flitted through the shadows like a specter, his head swiveling constantly as he searched the rows of cars. It was clear he'd never been here before, but he apparently knew what he was looking for.

When the intruder spotted Bobby Doyle's black Triumph parked in a far corner, he smiled. The fool left the top down, he said to himself. No need to jimmy the door. He crept up to the sports car and knelt beside it. Reaching into his canvas shoulder bag, he removed a small package wrapped in brown paper. He checked quickly to make sure no one was around, then he leaned over and shoved the package under the passenger's seat. The intruder wore gloves to insure he left no fingerprints.

His mission accomplished, he stood for a moment, staring at the car. He wanted to do something more—key the side of the vehicle, maybe, or slash the red leather seats, but he knew any damage would spoil the purpose of his visit. Instead, he patted the door, satisfied with the cleverness of his plan. Retracing his steps, he disappeared into the dark streets outside the building. After he'd walked a few blocks, he stopped and glanced over his shoulder. He threw his head back and laughed. It was an unhealthy sniggering sound.

* * *

At ten in the morning, Detective Phil Marshall lit his tenth Marlboro of the day. He leaned back in his antiquated swivel chair, causing its ancient springs to screech in protest. The milky light filtering through the grimy window of his office at police headquarters highlighted the detective's craggy features. If he'd been wearing a cowboy hat, he'd have been a dead ringer for the Marlboro Man.

Marshall scanned the headlines in his morning *Chronicle.* Same old bullshit, he thought. Kids acting up again at Berkeley, Columbia, Harvard, and all the other usual places. They kept protesting the war and the draft, but he'd heard that Lewis B. Hershey was about to put an end to that nonsense. As head of the Selective Service System, General Hershey was planning to cancel deferments for any college student who interfered with military recruiting. About damn time, Marshall said to himself. He'd put his butt on the line in Korea, so why couldn't this generation step up and do its duty without all the whining?

Marshall slurped his bitter black coffee and sighed with pleasure. He noticed a headline that said the U.S. population had hit two hundred million. According to Marshall's way of thinking, that would include a hundred million hardworking Americans and a hundred million deadbeats. He didn't know what the country was coming to. Welfare queens driving Cadillacs while average Joes struggled to make ends meet. And the bleeding-heart liberals kept making things worse. Great Society my ass, he muttered.

The detective saw a headline about China exploding its first hydrogen bomb. That was just what the planet needed, another lunatic nuclear power. Fed up with the real world, he flipped back to the sports section. Mickey Mantle had hit his five hundredth homer earlier this season, which Marshall applauded even though Mantle played for the damn Yankees. Marshall's Giants were having a good year, but they were still trailing the Cardinals. Maybe the Cards would collapse in the home stretch and the Giants catch fire. He could always hope.

Marshall finished his coffee and folded up the newspaper. Before he set the paper aside, his eye fell on a front-page headline about some groundbreaking advances in heart surgery taking place in Cape Town, South Africa. The first paragraph said that Dr. Christiaan Barnard expected to perform a human heart transplant soon.

Marshall stopped reading at that point. He swiveled around in his chair and stared through the window's smeared panes at the patchy morning fog, a rarity at this time of year. It wreathed the streetlights like smoke rising from a Wild West shoot-out. A heart transplant would have been just the ticket for Officer Charlie Murphy, Marshall thought. The beat cop had taken two .45 slugs in the chest last week while investigating a robbery at a convenience store in the Tenderloin district. Murphy was a good egg, too, and he left a wife and four kids behind. Marshall lit another Marlboro from the butt of his old one. His wife kept nagging him to quit smoking, but he figured he'd probably die like Charlie Murphy before cancer got him.

Marshall looked up as his secretary brought in the morning mail. Maggie Brimble had the pale, knobbly complexion of a day-old biscuit, and she wore her hair in an unflattering 1920s bob. A cigarette dangled from the corner of her mouth, and her glasses had slid down to the end of her nose. The woman was mannish, middle-aged, and utterly devoid of a sense of humor. Marshall couldn't recall ever having heard her laugh. A thin smile seemed to be the best she could manage. She'd worked at police headquarters for the past ten years, and she looked the same as the day she walked in. She might have been wearing the same dress, too.

"Anything interesting?" Marshall asked.

"You oughta take a look at that note on top. Some concerned citizen is offering a tip on who committed a couple of murders this summer." Her cigarette bobbed up and down as she spoke.

Marshall lifted the typewritten letter and quickly read it. He'd grown used to crackpot tips about all sorts of crimes, but this note held his attention. The letter was brief, and he read it a second time.

"If you're still looking for the person who killed Lynette Simms and Susie Blake, check out the dude who was sleeping with both of them. Bobby Doyle pretends to be an upright citizen, but he's a dope-dealing criminal. Look under the seat of that sports car he drives if you want proof."

A smile slowly spread over Marshall's face. He picked up the phone and called Detective Chacon of the drug squad. "Looks like we've got a little unfinished business to attend to, Fred. I just got a tip about that bright boy Bobby Doyle. He may have had something to do with his girlfriends' deaths after all. I'll put in for a search warrant, then we'll pay Mr. Doyle a visit."

"I thought Doyle had a solid alibi for the time of the second girl's murder," Detective Chacon said.

"I'm going to get back to the man he was interviewing that night and try to pin down the exact time of the call. And we never bothered to ask Doyle to account for his movements on the night of the first girl's death."

There was a long silence before Chacon spoke. "Yeah, I guess that all makes sense."

* * *

Bobby sang the words to "Susie Q" to himself as he finished getting ready for his drive up to wine country. He'd been looking forward to the trip for the past few days. Now that he'd turned in his story on the show at the Fillmore, he was free to head out. He was checking to make sure all the lights were off in his apartment when he heard a knock at the door. He opened it to find Detective Marshall and Detective Chacon standing outside.

"You look surprised to see us," Marshall said.

"I am. It's been awhile since we last talked." Bobby stood back and held out an arm. "Come on in."

"Not quite yet," Marshall said. "First we'd like to take a look at your car. I understand from the building manager that you have an assigned parking spot down in the garage."

"That's right. But why on earth do you want to look at my car?"

"You let us worry about that." Marshall pulled the search warrant from his coat pocket. "In case you're wondering, we have a warrant to search your car and your apartment."

Bobby stood gaping at them. "A search warrant? What the heck's going on?"

Marshall motioned for him to follow them. "Grab your keys."

Downstairs in the garage, Marshall eyed the sporty little TR4. "Nice wheels. Just the sort of car a guy like you would drive."

"I didn't know you could categorize people by the cars they drive," Bobby said, still trying to sound cordial.

"Oh yeah. Flashy guys tend to prefer flashy cars." Marshall leaned over and felt beneath the passenger's seat. "Well, what do you know?" He straightened up holding a package wrapped in brown paper. He held it out to Detective Chacon. "I think this is your bailiwick, Fred."

Chacon slipped on a pair of rubber gloves and took the package. He laid it on the hood of the car and tore open the wrapper. Inside was a plastic bag filled with white powder. There were also several syringes. Some of them appeared to have been used.

"I have no idea what that is or how it got there," Bobby said.

"Uh-huh, sure," Marshall said. "What you got there, Fred?"

Chacon opened the bag and tested the contents. "Heroin. And pretty high-grade stuff, too."

Bobby couldn't believe what was happening. "I swear, I have no idea how that stuff ended up in my car. I've never even seen any heroin before."

"Maybe it flew in there," Marshall said. "C'mon, let's go back upstairs."

The two detectives took their time going through every closet and drawer in Bobby's apartment. A half-hour later, Marshall called off the search. "Looks like he kept his goods in his car, Fred."

Chacon turned to Bobby with a sad expression. "I never would have expected this of you, son. You sure had me fooled."

"I keep telling you, I have no idea where that stuff came from."

Marshall cut him off. "We've got everything we need to convict you of possession and probable dealing. But that's only the tip of the iceberg. We're going to test all this stuff. I don't imagine we'll find any fingerprints. A smart customer like you wouldn't leave any. But the boys in our lab are exceptionally thorough, and this will get top priority. If there's any DNA on those needles...well, let's just say your future may be all mapped out for you."

* * *

Bobby sat alone at the long wooden table in the interrogation room. He occupied himself by counting the cigarette burns around the edge of the table. The two detectives were absent, but a uniformed officer stood silently beside the door. He was as immobile as one of the Queen's Guards at Buckingham Palace. Bobby didn't bother speaking to him.

Marshall and Chacon finally came in and sat down opposite Bobby. Marshall spoke first.

"Robert Doyle, we're arresting you for the possession of an illegal substance with intent to distribute."

Bobby started to say something, but Marshall held up his hand.

"We're also arresting you on suspicion relating to the murders of Lynette Simms and Susannah Blake. There's DNA on two of the used syringes we found in your car. Once the lab finishes comparing those samples to the DNA collected from the victims, we'll know if you'll be facing charges of murder one."

"This is insane," Bobby shouted. "I'd never harm anyone, let alone two of the most wonderful women I've ever met."

Marshall gave him a sour look. "Funny how often I've heard someone say something like that. I've arrested rich kids like you before, Doyle. Your kind always thinks they can get away with anything, but you're not getting away with this."

"I told you earlier I was conducting a telephone interview when Susie Blake was killed."

"We looked into that. Our medical examiner definitely fixed the time of death between nine and ten in the evening. Turns out when we doublechecked with the fellow you were interviewing, he couldn't pinpoint the time of the call. He just said it started sometime shortly after nine.

"Since you only live a few blocks from Miss Blake's apartment, you could have waited for her in that alley, murdered her, and hightailed it home in under ten minutes."

Bobby's head slumped forward. He couldn't think of anything else to say.

"And we never questioned you regarding your whereabouts the night Miss Simms was killed," Marshall added.

Bobby looked up with glazed eyes. "I was at home getting ready for Lynette to move in with me." His voice sounded hollow, as if it were echoing from the bottom of a deep hole.

"So you've got no alibi there either." Marshall nodded to the officer standing beside the door. "Please escort the prisoner to his cell."

"Can't I telephone my parents first?" Bobby pleaded.

Marshall shoved the telephone across the table. "Sure, you can call your mommy and daddy."

Chapter Twenty-One

San Francisco

Bobby stared at the institutional gray walls of his cell, thinking about the call he'd made to his parents. His mother had begun hyperventilating when she heard he'd been arrested. His father took the news calmly, outwardly at least. He said they'd be in San Francisco the next day to see him. Donovan told Bobby not to worry. He intended to hire a friend of his to represent him, San Francisco lawyer Jake Ehrlich. "Jake's the best criminal defense attorney in the state," Donovan said. "His peers call him 'The Master.'"

Bobby had started writing a note to his brother right after the police escort closed the door to his cell, but he hadn't gotten very far. He kept replaying the sounds of the bars clanging shut and the metallic scraping of the key turning in the lock. He felt like the Count of Monte Cristo, shut away for a crime he didn't commit with no hope of escape. He was glad he didn't suffer from claustrophobia. The six-by-eight-foot cell was hardly larger than his walk-in closet at home in L.A., and the only light came from the feeble fluorescent bulbs in the corridor.

He shivered at the sight of the open toilet in the corner. The odor of urine and Pine-Sol was revolting. Welcome to the nightmare of incarceration, Bobby told himself. It wasn't just the loss of personal freedom that prisoners were made to suffer. They had to endure the loss of their dignity as well. He decided he'd rather be hanged than live through a prison sentence.

Bobby returned to his letter to Jack. He described the situation as objectively as he could. There was no use indulging in self-pity, even though he wanted to scream. He told Jack that since he'd been framed, the surest way to win his freedom would be to find out who'd set him up. It was clearer than ever that the person who murdered Lynette and Susie had an abiding grudge against him. The girls were simply innocent victims. He doubted if the police would bother to investigate along those lines. They thought they already had their man. That meant he needed to find someone on the outside who was willing to help him.

The first person that came to mind was Raul Pitman. Bobby described Raul's previous efforts to help him search for the killer, and he said he'd be contacting him right away. In other words, he told his brother, as of now his fate was in the hands of others—his friends, his attorney, and of course their mom and dad. "Don't worry, Jack," he wrote at the end of the letter. "We'll be laughing about this over a couple of beers one day." He hoped that was true.

* * *

Donovan and Maria Doyle flew up from Los Angeles that night. They'd started packing for the trip the moment they hung up after talking to Bobby. At nine the next morning, they appeared at police headquarters and asked to see their son. They were escorted to the visiting room and asked to wait. Ten minutes later, an officer escorted Bobby in. Maria rushed to embrace him, clinging to him so tightly for so long that she almost squeezed the breath out of him. When she stepped back and wiped the tears from her eyes, Donovan hugged Bobby as well. It was all Donovan could do to keep from joining his wife's tear-fest.

"I spoke with Jake Ehrlich," Donovan said, his voice nearly cracking. "He's looking forward to representing you, son, and this guy is relentless. His slogan is 'Never plead guilty.' He's the attorney they modeled the TV character Perry Mason on. Raymond Burr actually shadowed Ehrlich for a couple of weeks to see how he handled himself in the courtroom."

"Maybe he'll bring Della Street and Paul Drake with him," Bobby joked.

Bobby's comment broke the tension. The three of them sat down to talk things over. Maria held her son's hand the entire time, not wanting to lose contact with him.

"You can joke about Paul Drake," Donovan said, "but Jake told me he'll put his best private investigator to work digging up everything they can about the lunatic who did these things."

"That's great," Bobby said. "I feel helpless locked up in here, unable to do anything to prove my innocence. I've written a friend of mine from Berkeley to see if he'd mind doing a little investigating on my behalf. He's a top-notch reporter I met at school."

"That's smart," Maria said. "Someone your age might be able to go places and find out things an older PI can't. And of course your dad and I are available to help in any way we can."

Bobby laid his other hand on top of hers. "Thanks, Mom."

Donovan opened the briefcase he'd brought with him. "We'll see about getting you out of here on bail as soon as possible. Meantime, we brought you some reading material." He held out the latest editions of the *Chronicle* and the *Los Angeles Times.* He also produced a hardbound book. "This is Norman Mailer's new novel. It's getting good reviews."

Bobby read the title aloud. *"Why Are We In Vietnam?* I'm surprised you'd pick this."

Donovan laughed. "Don't worry. From what I've read, it doesn't seem to be about Vietnam at all. It's about a hunting trip in Alaska. Some rich Texas businessman wants to kill a grizzly bear, and he brings his son along. It sounds pretty wacky. Maybe Mailer picked the title just to be provocative."

"This ought to take my mind off things." Bobby was silent for a moment. "Actually, it would be great if you could swing by my apartment and pick up my textbooks. If you're able to get me out of here on bail, I should only miss a week or so of classes. I can read ahead to keep up. I sure hope I'm not forced to drop out of school."

"We'll get your school books," Donovan said, "but I can do better than that. I know the chancellor of USF. I've met him at several alumni functions. I'll give him a call, explain the situation. I'm sure he'll be happy to speak to your professors. You shouldn't miss any more classes than someone with a bad case of the flu."

"Thanks, Dad."

Maria had become quiet. She had a pained look. "Bobby, are you sure you can't think of anyone who might do something like this? We've racked our brains, but we haven't come up with a soul. It's such a horrible, horrible thing to do to a person. Killing their friends then trying to shift the blame. It's inexplicable."

"I have no idea who'd stoop to such a thing. The person behind this is obviously crazy, and crazy people do crazy things."

* * *

J. W. "Jake" Ehrlich had become a living legend long before he walked into Bobby Doyle's life. Born in Rockville, Maryland, Ehrlich attended Georgetown University before gravitating to San Francisco. To help pay for his night classes at San Francisco Law School, he boxed professionally, transforming himself from the impoverished young Jacob Ehrlich to bust-you-in-the-chops Jake Ehrlich.

In the half century he'd been in practice, Ehrlich had defended people from every walk of life, from captains of industry, movie stars, and sports figures to mobsters, prostitutes, and bigamists. He'd represented billionaire Howard Hughes, singer Billie Holiday, stripper Sally Rand, and drummer Gene Krupa on criminal charges. Errol Flynn, James Mason, and other Hollywood high fliers relied on him in their divorce proceedings. A decade earlier, he'd defended Lawrence Ferlinghetti in the obscenity trial resulting from the sale of Allen Ginsberg's controversial book *Howl and Other Poems* at Ferlinghetti's City Lights Bookstore. Most impressive of all as far as Bobby Doyle was concerned, Ehrlich had kept more than fifty people charged with murder from receiving death sentences.

Ehrlich marched into the meeting with his new client two days after Bobby's parents had visited. The famous attorney wore a dark, expensive suit, with a carmine silk handkerchief in his breast pocket and a matching tie. His gold cufflinks and wristwatch looked like they cost more than most Americans earned in six months. He was frankly scary. He had a grim expression on his hawk-like face, and he spoke in a forceful, self-assured manner. Even at sixty-seven, he seemed like a man you wouldn't want to step into a boxing ring with, let alone face across a courtroom.

After brief introductions, Ehrlich got down to cases. "Let's start with the bad news," he said. "First, the DNA on the needles the police found in your car matches the DNA of the two murder victims, which suggests that the heroin they found was used in the killings. That's what the police are assuming. Second, the presiding judge has denied you bail because of the severity of the crimes and the weight of the physical evidence."

The color drained from Bobby's face.

"That's the bad news," Ehrlich continued. "The good news is that I know you're innocent. I'm positive that no son of Donovan Doyle could be guilty of murder, and I intend to prove it. Donovan has told me about all you and your brother have accomplished, and I've read some of your stories in the *Chronicle.* It's clear that you're an intelligent, responsible young man. Even if my investigators aren't able to find out who actually committed these crimes, I'm confident we can create sufficient doubt in the minds of jurors to clear you of the charges. The evidence may seem damning, but it's all circumstantial."

Bobby managed a weak smile. "I'm glad you think that I've got a chance."

"Now, tell me about your relationships with the two women."

Two hours later, Ehrlich knew everything about the case that Bobby could think to tell him. By the time they'd finished, Ehrlich had filled several pages in his notebook and changed the cassette tape twice in his recorder. Ehrlich asked him for a list of character witnesses. Bobby also gave him the contact information for Lynette and Susie's parents, who'd be called on to testify at the trial. He hoped that Lynette had written her parents about him, and he also hoped that Susie's mother might put in a good word for him. He knew that her father wouldn't. He was better at talking about Christian charity than practicing it.

During Ehrlich's interview, Bobby felt like he was sitting in the witness box. Ehrlich probed relentlessly, asking him for details about things he'd done with Lynette and Susie, what they'd talked about, their plans, their physical relations. It was embarrassing at times, but Ehrlich assured him that the prosecuting attorney would spare no effort to put him on the spot and find contradictions in his testimony.

"It's better for me to grill you now than for you to make some inadvertent gaffe in front of the jury. The old saying that you only get one chance to make a first impression is more appropriate in a court of law than anyplace else on earth."

Bobby returned to his cell filled with hope. If anyone could prove his innocence, it would be this pit bull attorney his father had hired. When Donovan and Maria came back to visit him that afternoon, Bobby thanked them profusely for hiring Ehrlich. "I can see now why they call him 'The Master.' He said he'll be back as soon as he's had time to interview the character witnesses I gave him and organize his thoughts about his line of defense."

* * *

Across the Bay, Raul Pitman opened the letter Bobby had sent him. Raul had two reactions to the news. The first was a feeling of anger that his friend could be charged with the deaths of two women he so clearly cared about. The second was a sense of determination to do everything he could to find the rotten bastard who'd taken innocent lives and was now trying to frame the least likely person in the world for the crimes.

* * *

In her downtown office, Deneige Leblanc also read a letter from Bobby. She had a hard time accepting the fact that he'd been arrested. She immediately phoned police headquarters to find out when she could visit him.

* * *

A week later and eight thousand miles away, Jack Doyle read his brother's horrifying account of being held behind bars for crimes he didn't commit. Jack's hands shook as he held the letter—not just because of the devastating news, but also because it made him realize that, in much the same way, he was a prisoner himself. He looked around his spartan quarters, which were essentially the same as a cell. The bars may have been invisible, but there was no escape from his incarceration until his sentence had run its course.

Thinking of jail, it dawned on him that his responsibility for leading reluctant draftees into the field was not much different from a guard leading a chain gang to a rock quarry to swing sledgehammers all day. The pointless task of breaking big rocks into little rocks mirrored the futility of what his men were being asked to do in Vietnam. Jack also realized that even though he was the boss of his hypothetical chain gang, he suffered just as much as his men. One thing was undeniable. Unlike his brother, Jack couldn't make the claim of innocence in his ordeal.

Jack reached for his bottle of Martell cognac and poured himself another glass. He'd begun drinking by himself of late. The second time he read Bobby's letter, the writing seemed to be blurred. Jack set the letter aside and stared at the wooden walls of his room. He lapsed into a long spell of silence, something between a catatonic trance and a drunken stupor. He was jolted to his senses by the thunderous crash of a rocket outside his quarters. It sounded like car had been dropped from the roof of a tall building.

Jack jumped up from his bed and started for the door. He paused then went back and grabbed his bottle of Martell. Stumbling down the steps of his quarters, he headed for the nearby bunker, but instead of descending into the safety of its black depths as other officers were doing, he plopped down on top of the bunker. He took a swig from his bottle and looked up at the night sky. Flares, outgoing rockets, and tracers lit up the darkness like a Fourth of July display.

Jack laid back on the roof of the bunker and enjoyed the light show. Closing his eyes, he was transported back home to California, where he was watching a fireworks show with his family. He and Bobby were ten years old, and they kept shoving each other to get what they considered the best viewing spot. The show was taking place beside a lake in a tree-dappled county park. The bursting skyrockets reflected in the water, creating a double display of shimmering colors. The burning embers trailed down the black night sky like raindrops on a windowpane—or tears on the face of a person in mourning.

Jack started sobbing as he recalled an accident that had happened in front of their house that same summer. A passing car had run over his brother's pet beagle. The dog's rear end and back legs were crushed, and Jack had watched the injured animal scoot itself down the street with its front legs, howling piteously.

The memory of the maimed dog gave way to the image of a severely injured Vietnamese peasant. The frail old farmer had been caught in a U.S. bombing attack on a village suspected of harboring Vietcong guerrillas. Jack's patrol had been assigned to sweep the village to assess the damage and search for prisoners. Both of the farmer's legs had been blown off in the attack, but the man was still alive when Jack found him. He was frantically dragging himself along the ground, just as Bobby's injured dog had done. They both seemed to be trying to escape the hideous pain by scrabbling away from it.

Jack sat up and took another swig of cognac. He wondered if he'd ever be able to purge his mind of the horrors he'd witnessed. Suddenly, Vince was at his side, tugging on his arm.

"What the hell are you doing out here?" Vince yelled.

Jack gave him a drunken grin. "Enjoying the fireworks."

"Come on, man. Let's get inside where it's safe."

"Haven't you heard? It's not safe anywhere. Bobby's dog was killed and now he's been arrested for murder."

"For killing a dog?"

"No, for killing his girlfriends."

"Jack, you're drunk. You're not making sense."

"None of it makes any sense."

Fifty yards away, another VC rocket crashed to the ground. The deafening explosion tossed a cloud of debris into the air, like a mini mushroom cloud.

"For God's sake, Jack. Stop fooling around and get inside. This is insane."

Jack threw off his buddy's hand. "That's the problem."

Vince left him sitting there, a solitary island in a storm-tossed sea.

VI

~October 1967~

Chapter Twenty-Two

San Francisco

Raul Pitman's conference with Bobby didn't take long. He already knew the circumstances and details of the crimes. All he needed were some fresh leads to investigate. Bobby was embarrassed to tell him that he'd failed to mention what could be the most promising lead of all—the orange-haired weirdo who'd hit on Lynette and stared daggers at him the night he took Deneige to see Buffalo Springfield at the Fillmore Auditorium.

"I'm afraid I allowed myself to get sidetracked when we followed up on Blind Cedric's tip about Charlie Manson. I should never have forgotten this other character. Sonny Anders told me the little creep looked like he wanted to kill someone when he saw us at the Fillmore. I don't remember ever running into him when I was with Susie, but I did take her to a couple of shows, and this guy seems to frequent rock concerts. He's definitely worth checking out."

"Then I'll get back with Blind Cedric and see what he can tell me. If Orangey hangs out in Haight-Ashbury, Cedric will likely know something about him."

* * *

This was one of Eddie Ratner's favorite doorways. Located on busy Haight

Street, the shadowy recess gave him a great view of the chicks going in and out of Tracy's Donuts. Eddie fiddled with his camera, making sure it was focused on the shop across the street. He'd been trailing a hottie for the past couple of days, snapping candid shots while she went about her daily routine. She always stopped at Tracy's for breakfast before going to work at the Drogstore Café.

The Rat lifted his camera to his eye when the pretty brunette emerged from the donut shop. She was a stunner. She'd tied back her long hair in a ponytail this morning. Ratner figured she must be Italian, since she looked a lot like that Claudia Cardinale chick he'd seen in *The Pink Panther.* Big dark eyes, great legs, and world-class gazoombas. Yeah, she was hot all right. Just the way Eddie boy liked them.

Ratner followed the girl down the street, snapping away. He must have taken five or six rolls of her by now. At night, he developed the film in the makeshift darkroom in his apartment, picking out the best frames to make prints from. The brunette made a fine addition to his photo collection, a display that papered one wall of his bedroom and fueled his midnight fantasies. Sometimes, he stood in front of the mirror and worked on his patter, pretending he was putting a move on one of his girls. It was a good thing the walls in his old rooming house were thick. If his neighbors overheard him, they'd have had nightmares.

The Rat snickered. His mom didn't know how helpful she'd been when she told him he should take up a hobby. She'd given him her old Kodak Instamatic on one of his infrequent visits to her squalid tenement across town. He ditched the crappy little camera after realizing he needed better equipment to get the shots he was after. He bought himself a nice Minolta 35mm SLR. His best investment had been the telephoto lens. With the 135mm zoom, he could grab close-ups without getting near enough to his subjects to be spotted. The ladies never knew they were being immortalized. He'd added a couple of dozen chicks to his gallery since he started his "hobby." He'd briefly considered becoming a professional photographer, but he didn't feel like taking a pay cut by giving up the dope trade.

* * *

Blind Cedric started playing "Don't Start Me Talkin'" as soon as he saw Raul Pitman coming his way. It was almost the lunch hour, and the foot traffic was heavy in front of the Drogstore Café.

"Morning, Cedric," Pitman said. He glanced down at the street musician's King Edward cigar box, which was nearly filled with cash. "Looks like business is picking up."

"It's fair to middling, fair to middling."

Pitman tossed a tenner into the box. "Got a couple of questions for you, Cedric. There'll be another ten-spot if you have any answers."

Cedric eyed the crisp ten-dollar bill in Pitman's hand. "Ask away."

"You remember Bobby Doyle, my friend whose girlfriends were killed?"

"How could I forget? Sorry my tip about Charlie Manson didn't pan out. I heard that crazy mother skipped town. They say he's living with his dollies down in Topanga Canyon outside of L.A. They can have him far as I'm concerned. He's got bad news written all over him."

"I guess that's one less freak for San Francisco to deal with." Pitman paused for moment. "Cedric, something terrible has happened to Bobby."

"He sick?"

"No. He's been arrested for the murders."

Cedric did a double take. "You think he did 'em?"

"I know he didn't, and I'm trying to help prove it."

"So what is it you wanna ask me?"

"I'm looking for a suspicious guy Bobby bumped into a couple of times. He's a little orange-haired creep. Bobby said he slinks around like Uriah Heep."

"Who the hell is Uriah Heep?"

"A nasty character in a Charles Dickens story."

"Hmm. Ain't read that one. Must be my limited juco education." Cedric rubbed his chin. "You say this fellow has orange hair, huh? There's a runty dude I see around here all the time. Name's Eddie Ratner. He's supposed to be the biggest dope dealer on Haight Street. They call him the Rat, and he looks like one too. Got a pointy face and nasty teeth, and he's got a sneaky way of walking. Maybe that's what your pal meant by calling him Uriah Heep."

Pitman tossed the other ten into Cedric's cigar box. "Cedric, you're the man. What else can you tell me about this Ratner?"

"He hangs out down the street at the Pall Mall Lounge. And he's a pervert. I've seen him trailing good-looking chicks and taking pictures of them on the sly. He's followed Gina Lollobrigida a couple of times."

"Gina Lollobrigida?"

Cedric jerked a thumb toward the Drogstore Café behind him. "She's a gal who works in there. Her name's Nicole Parente, but I think she looks like Gina Lollobrigida."

"Ratner sounds like the kind of guy Bobby described. Thanks, Cedric. I'll check him out."

"You oughta stop in at the Psychedelic Shop first. It's across the street from the Pall Mall Lounge. It's a head shop run by the Tolin brothers. They've been talking about a friend of theirs who went missing this summer. They think Ratner may have had something to do with it."

* * *

The Tolin brothers were quite a pair. If you saw them together from the right angle, they could have passed for Sonny and Cher. Jeb Tolin had the hairstyle and drooping mustache of Sonny Bono, and his brother Buddy had Cher's slender build and shoulder-length black hair. Raul Pitman wandered about in their store, examining the merchandise. He picked out a couple of records and walked over to the sales counter to pay for them.

"How goes?" Jeb Tolin asked as he rang up Pitman's purchase.

"I'm doing fine, thanks." Pitman glanced around the shop. "Nice place you've got here. Blind Cedric told me about it."

Jeb Tolin laughed. "Good old Cedric."

"Yeah, not much gets by him. He's got the eyes of a hawk and the hearing of a fox."

"I see you know him pretty well."

"I always stop and talk with him when I go for lunch at the Drogstore Café. He's the best source of gossip in the Haight."

"You got that right."

"You know, Cedric told me an interesting story the other day. He said a friend of yours went missing this summer. Did you ever find out what happened to him?"

Tolin shook his head. "Nope. His name's Jimmy D'Angelo. He walked in one day and told me how he planned on relocating here from Oakland. That's where we're all from. Next thing we knew, Jimmy had vanished. Haven't seen or heard from him since."

Pitman leaned closer. "Cedric says a drug dealer named Eddie Ratner may have had something to do with your friend's disappearance."

"That's what Buddy and me think happened." Tolin gave Pitman a conspiratorial wink. "Jimmy told me he was planning on getting into pharmaceutical sales here in Haight-Ashbury. I told him he needed to watch out for Eddie Ratner. The Rat doesn't take kindly to guys moving in on his turf."

"But I've heard Ratner's a little scrawny guy. How could he scare anyone off?"

Buddy Tolin had eased over to the sales counter and was listening to their conversation. "I can tell you how," he said. "He's got a big ugly Hells Angel working for him. And the word on the street is that Jimmy D. wasn't the Rat's first competitor to go poof. There's lots of lonely places in the hills outside the city. Who knows what the cops would find if they bothered to go out there and take a look."

Pitman picked up his records. "Maybe your friend will turn up one of these days."

"Yeah," Buddy said. "What's left of him."

* * *

Pitman looked like a different person when he returned to the Haight the next day. Instead of the beret, leather coat, and spiffy slacks, he wore an old ballcap, baggy gray sweatshirt, and faded jeans. He'd neglected to shave and had carefully mussed up his hair. He carried an old gym bag to give the impression he was a drifter. If he was going to approach Eddie Ratner, he didn't want to go in decked out like a narc.

He spotted Ratner the moment he walked into the Pall Mall Lounge. The orange-haired dope dealer sat in his usual spot at the back of the room. A scruffy young man shared his table, a disheveled slacker who looked much like Pitman. When the slacker shoved some money across the table, Ratner reached into his canvas bag and produced a nickel bag of grass. The slacker grabbed his weed and left. Ratner went back to his newspaper.

Pitman slouched over to Ratner's table. "I hear you're the guy they call the Rat."

Ratner looked up with a smirk on his rodent-like face. Cedric's description of the fellow was dead on. "So what?"

Pitman dropped his gym bag and took a seat. "Name's Mick. A friend of mine said I could score in this joint. Told me to ask for you. The gal over at the counter pointed you out." He tried his best to sound desperate. "I'm in need of a little medication, man. I got a case of the jitters. Got 'em real bad."

Ratner leaned back and bared his yellow teeth. "I might be able to fill your prescription. If you can pay for it."

Pitman pulled out the worn, crumped twenties he'd selected for the occasion. "I got dough, man. Don't you worry about that."

"What was you lookin' for?"

"My buddy said you got some of the best horse on the streets."

"Your buddy's a smart guy. I happen to have just what your heart desires."

Pitman's hand shook as he shoved forty dollars across the table. "That's all I got."

Ratner took the money. While he fumbled in his satchel, Pitman admired the camera sitting on the table. "You into photography?"

"Yeah. I'm what you might call a nature photographer. I like to capture the local birds."

Pitman cringed inside. What an unadulterated creep this guy was.

Ratner produced a plastic bag from his satchel and tossed it on the table. "There you go, my friend. Have yourself a good time."

Pitman grabbed the dope and left without another word, like a desperate junkie in need of a fix. Outside, he examined the bag. It looked like the one Bobby had told him the cops found in his car, a sandwich bag with a blue plastic zipper across the top.

Pitman concealed himself while he removed his grungy sweatshirt and stuffed it into his gym bag. Underneath, he was wearing a navy polo shirt. He exchanged the ballcap for a tan bucket hat and added a pair of dark glasses to complete the transformation. He intended to follow Ratner back to his apartment, and he didn't want to be spotted. Pitman went across the street and found a window table in Tracy's Donuts. He was prepared to wait all day if necessary.

Two hours passed before Ratner emerged from the Pall Mall Lounge. Pitman left a hefty tip for taking up a table for so long. Fortunately, it was the middle of the afternoon, and the donut shop wasn't crowded like at breakfast time.

The Rat walked to the end of the block and turned south on Ashbury Street. Not far from the Grateful Dead house, he turned left on Waller and headed toward Buena Vista Park. He entered a rundown Victorian apartment building, precisely the sort of dump where someone like Ratner would make his home. The small yard was neglected, and two overflowing garbage cans sat to the side of the steps by the entrance. Pitman wrote down the street address and left. He planned on returning the next day while the Rat was busy plying his trade.

* * *

Pitman peered in the front window of the Pall Mall Lounge. At ten in the morning, Eddie Ratner was enjoying a cup of coffee and reading a tattered paperback with a nude woman on the cover. Pitman headed for Waller Street.

The geezer who managed Ratner's apartment building was nearly as seedy as the building itself. Pitman told him he was a friend of Ratner's and that he wanted to see his rooms so he could decide on a surprise gift for his buddy's birthday, which was coming up. The old rascal made a pretense of objecting, but when Pitman waved a twenty-dollar bill in front of him, his objections melted away. He grabbed the twenty, holding onto it as if it were a coded message containing a state secret.

"I'll have to watch to make sure you don't steal anything," he said. "We take our tenants' security very seriously."

Yeah, I'll bet, thought Pitman. "That's fine. I just want to take a quick peek, get an idea of what Eddie might need."

The manager led the way to the second floor and unlocked the door to apartment 201. The old man followed Pitman inside. Ratner's place was a genuine rat's nest. Piles of crap teetered precariously everywhere. None of that mattered to Pitman. The only thing that held his attention was the wall opposite the window in Ratner's bedroom. It was covered with eight-by-ten black-and-white photos of young women. Pitman studied every one. Several of the photos matched the descriptions of Lynette Simms and Susie Blake that Bobby had given him. Pitman took out a camera of his own and documented everything he saw.

Pitman put his camera away and turned to the manager. "That's it," he told the old man. "Like I said, a quick peek is all I needed. And please don't say a word to my pal Eddie. I want him to be surprised by the present I have in mind. I'm sure he will be."

* * *

Pitman spread out the photos he'd taken in Ratner's bedroom. Detectives Marshall and Chacon eyed them without much enthusiasm. "Look," Pitman said, pointing to the photos of Lynette and Susie. "This fellow Eddie Ratner was obviously stalking these women. He's a known drug dealer in Haight-Ashbury."

"How come we never heard of him?" Detective Chacon asked.

"You'll have to ask yourself that question. If you need proof that he's a dealer, here's forty bucks' worth of heroin I bought from him. His fingerprints will be all over this." He tossed the plastic sandwich bag on the table. "Ratner operates out of the Pall Mall Lounge on Haight Street. You can pick him up there or at his apartment on Waller. I can give you the address. You can't miss the guy. He's got bright orange hair."

"Oh, the mysterious guy with the orange hair," Marshall said. "We've heard about him before, but no one besides Doyle seems to know anything about him. So you're telling us you found this photo display in Ratner's apartment and you bought this dope from him, and now we're supposed to believe that he murdered Miss Simms and Miss Blake and framed Doyle?"

"That's right."

"And just why would he do all that?"

"Bobby told me that Ratner made a move on Lynette Simms one night at the Fillmore, and he got mad when Bobby showed up and scared him off. Later, Ratner was at another concert Bobby attended with a woman named Deneige Leblanc. Ratner was seen staring at Bobby like he hated him. And it's a good bet that Ratner's dangerous. He's suspected of bumping off a drug dealer named Jimmy D'Angelo who encroached on his territory, and possibly a second dealer as well. Add it all up—Ratner's hatred of Bobby, his reputation for violence, the photos of the girls, the dope. It all points to Ratner being the guy you're looking for."

"Any witnesses to any of this?" Marshall asked.

"You can corroborate Ratner's hatred of Bobby by checking with a man named Sonny Anders. He's Bill Graham's assistant at the Fillmore. He's the one who saw Ratner staring at Bobby like he wanted to kill him. And Bobby had talked with Anders earlier about Ratner hitting on Lynette Simms. He didn't make any of that up. As for Ratner's reputation, I heard about that from the Tolin brothers at the Psychedelic Shop in the Haight. They were friends with this D'Angelo. They even warned him about how dangerous Ratner is."

Pitman was getting worked up over the cursory investigation the police had conducted. "And another thing. Didn't it seem suspicious to you that someone would tip you off about drugs in someone else's car? How the hell would this person have known about that unless he put them there himself? I bet if you test this bag of dope, you'll find it's from the same batch as what you found in Bobby's car."

Detective Chacon looked at Marshall. "We ought to at least check into these things, Phil."

Marshall hesitated but finally gave in. "Yeah, I guess you're right. Just to put this silly business about the orange-haired phantom to rest."

* * *

Eddie Ratner yelped like a rodent caught in a trap when he opened the door to his apartment and found two uniformed officers waiting outside. The burly cops showed him their search warrant and went through his rooms. They found a large cache of assorted drugs, more than enough to book him on possession with intent to distribute. The cops removed all of Ratner's photos from the wall in his bedroom, along with the rolls of film he'd processed.

The officers clamped the cuffs on Ratner and read him his rights. The Rat hung his head as he was led down to the waiting patrol car and shoved inside. A train of twisted thoughts raced through his devious little mind. Who the hell had squealed on him? How could he weasel his way out of this? Who could he blame everything on? Ratner had never been very keen on loyalty to his friends. Self-preservation ranked far higher on his list.

* * *

Sonny Anders's stomach fluttered when the uniformed police officer knocked on the door of his office at the Fillmore Auditorium.

"Mr. Anders?" the officer inquired.

"Yeah, that's me. Can I help you?"

The cop walked into the office and took out his notebook. "I'm here to ask you a couple of questions regarding Mr. Robert Doyle. Do you know this individual?"

"Of course I do. Why?"

"Mr. Doyle had been arrested and your name came up in the investigation."

Anders seemed startled. "Arrested? What on earth for?"

"He's suspected of murdering two women he'd dated."

Anders shook his head. "I find that hard to believe. And what do I have to do with it?"

"Mr. Doyle has stated that he spoke with you about a man who may have had some animosity toward him." The cop showed him a mug shot of Ratner. "This man. Do you know him?"

"I don't know his name, but I've seen him around."

"His name is Eddie Ratner. Do you have any reason to suspect that he might have held a grudge against Mr. Doyle?"

"All I can tell you is that the fellow pestered one of Bobby Doyle's girlfriends here at the Fillmore one night. And another night, I saw him giving Bobby a real hard look. He sure didn't appear to be a friend of Bobby's."

The cop was writing in his notebook. When he finished he snapped the notebook shut and tucked it into his pocket. "That's all, Mr. Anders. We'll be back if we need to ask you anything else." The cop touched the bill of his hat. "Thanks for your time."

"No problem." The expression on Anders's face was hard to read.

* * *

Detective Marshall hovered over the table in the interrogation room. He was staring at the cringing figure of Eddie Ratner, and he didn't like what he saw. The Rat looked particularly unhealthy today. His blotchy skin was the color of old parchment, and his twitching eyeballs were eggnog-yellow. With his spiky orange hair, he could have played one of the characters in the old horror film *Freaks*. Marshall would have been all for locking him away based on his appearance alone, although he told himself that if he started locking up every oddball in this town, the jails couldn't hold them all.

"We don't need to bother talking about the drugs," Marshall said. "You're busted on that charge and you'll be doing time for it. What we're interested in are the murders of two young women you apparently had some connection with. On the first charge, you'll be getting a stay at Folsom Prison. If the other one sticks, it'll be the gas chamber at San Quentin."

"Whoa, hold on. I didn't kill no women."

Marshall laid down the photos of Lynette and Susie that Ratner had taken. "We found these photos of the victims in your room. How do you explain that?"

Ratner snickered. "Oh, them. They're just a couple of chicks I noticed and took some shots of. My hobby is photographing pretty girls."

Marshall sneered. "Yeah, we noticed that."

"But I never killed those chicks," Ratner protested.

"Then how do you explain the fact that the heroin we confiscated from your apartment matches the heroin that was used to kill these girls?"

Ratner's mouth hung open. "I…I can't explain it. Must be a coincidence."

Detective Chacon spoke up. "There seems to be a lot of coincidences in this case, Mr. Ratner. It's beginning to look like what Mr. Doyle told us about you is true."

"I don't know what he said, but if he accused me of killin' his girlfriends, he's lyin'."

"Then you knew they were his girlfriends," Marshall said.

"I might have seen 'em together. But that don't prove nothin'."

Marshall sounded tired. "Mr. Ratner, we've been told that you may have been involved in other homicides. We've spoken to several people in Haight-Ashbury who voiced that suspicion."

The Rat wiggled around in his seat. "That's bullshit. You ain't got no proof about any of this."

"Do you know a Mr. Olaf Svenson?" Marshall asked.

Ratner almost passed out. Holy crap, he said to himself, they know about Olaf. "Uh, I might have bumped into him once or twice. But he ain't no friend of mine. He's downright crazy. You never know what that guy will do."

"One of our sources in Haight-Ashbury described your relationship with

Mr. Svenson a little differently. We were told that he functions as your enforcer. That's why we visited Mr. Svenson's apartment. It seems that, like you, Mr. Svenson has a hobby. He likes to collect hands. We found two of them in his freezer. The fingerprints we took from one of the hands belong to Jimmy D'Angelo, a small-time crook from Oakland who moved to Haight-Ashbury this summer and has since gone missing. The other hand belongs to an upstanding fellow named John Quincy Frost. You probably knew him by his street name, Jack Frost."

"Hey, I didn't have nothin' to do with either of them guys gettin' whacked. Olaf made me tag along when he got rid of 'em. I tell you I'm innocent. I'm the victim here. Olaf is behind everything. He made me sell drugs for him, and he threatened to get rid of me if I crossed him. I only went along because I was scared."

Phil Marshall smiled. "Mr. Ratner, I'm feeling generous today. I was going to put you in a cell by yourself, but if you'd like, I could let you share a cell with your friend Mr. Svenson instead. You two must have lots to talk about."

Ratner's eyes darted around the room. He looked like a terrified rodent searching for a hole to crawl into.

* * *

Bobby sat in his cell picturing the shocked expression on Deneige's face when she came to visit him. She'd held his hand and asked if there was anything she could do to help. There wasn't, of course, but he told her he'd let her know if he thought of anything. He was startled when she got up to leave and kissed him hard on the lips. At least he knew she believed him when he told her he was innocent.

Bobby looked up when he heard the rattle of a key being inserted into the door of his cell. Phil Marshall wore a sheepish look as he unlocked the door and swung it open. "You're free to go, Mr. Doyle," he said.

Bobby nearly fell off his bunk. *"What?"*

"I said you're free to go. We've arrested a man named Eddie Ratner for the crimes. He's your orange-haired antagonist. Your friend Raul Pitman convinced us to look into Mr. Ratner, and it turned out that he had the means, the motive, and the opportunity, and he has no confirmable alibis for the nights your two friends were killed. There's sufficient evidence to connect Ratner to both of the murders. For one thing, the stash of heroin we found in Ratner's apartment matches the dope we found in your car. He has to be the one who put it there.

"We've also arrested an accomplice of his, a Hells Angel named Olaf Svenson. We've got them dead to rights on dealing drugs and on two unrelated killings." Marshall chuckled. "We're told that Ratner is known as 'the Rat' on the street. It's a good name for him. He ratted out Svenson as fast as he could. He claims Svenson was behind everything, and he only went along because he was afraid of the guy. Sounds like a cover-your-butt story to me."

Bobby just sat there, staring at the man.

"You need to buy Mr. Pitman a steak dinner." Marshall held out his hand. "Sorry for everything, but at least we finally got the right guy."

Bobby could never forgive Marshall for what he'd put him through, but he shook the man's hand. "I suppose it's like they say—all's well that ends well."

Raul Pitman was waiting in the lobby of police headquarters. He looked supremely cool in his Berkeley hipster outfit. Bobby gave him a bear hug and thanked him for everything he'd done.

"I may consider becoming a private eye," Pitman told him. "Going undercover was a blast."

Bobby slapped him on the back. "If you do, you can count on me for a five-star endorsement."

Chapter Twenty-Three

San Francisco

Bobby sat with his parents at their usual table in Ernie's restaurant. The muted laughter and murmur of voices around them was a balm to Bobby's frazzled nerves. Maria Doyle looked stunning in a frilly new design by Halston. Deneige sat by Bobby's side, dressed every bit as fashionably as his mother. Her black sheath dress set off the double strand of pearls she wore. The two women had taken to one another from the start, kindred spirits in their taste for fine things and in their affection for one particular member of their dinner party.

Donovan held up his glass of champagne. "To justice. Sometimes it actually happens."

The others raised their glasses and echoed the toast. "To justice."

Donovan set his glass down and laughed. "I called Jake Ehrlich as soon as we heard the good news. Your mother and I were doubly relieved. Not only was our son free again, but we were also free of a potentially enormous legal bill. Ehrlich claims that when he defends someone in a capital case, his fee is everything the person owns. He figures that if he gets the defendant off, it's worth it, and if he doesn't, the defendant won't need it anyway."

"Oh, Don, that's just an urban legend," Maria said.

"I don't know. Ehrlich had to pay for that fancy house he designed up in Marin County. I hear it's got a sliding glass roof. Apparently, Ehrlich tells his visitors it's powered by clients who couldn't pay their bills."

Donovan took another sip of champagne. "I wish Jack was here to share this moment. We need to write him tomorrow to let him know what's happened."

Maria was overcome with a stricken look at the mention of her son in far-off Vietnam. She struggled to put on a smile. "Tell us more about your work, Deneige."

"There's not a lot to tell. I have a one-woman agency but it's growing steadily. I represent some very talented writers." She looked at Bobby. "Maybe someday I'll represent Mr. Robert Doyle. He tells me he's thinking of writing a novel."

"And he will," Donovan said. "I've never known him to not go after something he wants."

Deneige gave Bobby her enigmatic smile. "I certainly hope that's true."

Bobby's face turned red, and he hurried to shift the focus from himself. "When are you planning on heading back home, Dad?"

"Your mother and I are now enjoying our stay at the Mark Hopkins. Nothing like sipping a martini in the Top of the Mark. You can see forever from up there. We're thinking of hanging around for a few more days, visiting some old friends."

"What about you, dear?" Maria asked Bobby. "What's on your agenda?"

"First thing in the morning, I'm going to check in with the administration at USF to make sure I can continue my classes."

Donovan waved a hand in dismissal. "Don't worry about it, son. Father McGloin assured me there'd be no problem if you only missed a few days."

"That's great. Thanks, Dad. And after I stop by USF, I'm going shopping for the most expensive thank-you gift I can find for Raul Pitman. You really discover who your friends are when you're in trouble, and Raul came through for me. I might actually owe him my life."

* * *

Bobby pulled to the curb in front of Deneige's apartment building. He turned off the TR4's engine, and they sat in silence for a bit. "Thanks for coming with me tonight," Bobby said. "I need all the friends around me I can get until I manage to decompress."

"I was honored that you'd ask me to share the occasion with your parents. They seem like terrific people." She laid a hand on Bobby's shoulder. "And they raised a terrific son."

Bobby took her hand. He didn't say anything. It was enough just to touch another person.

"Would you like to come up for a nightcap?" she asked.

"More than anything in the world."

Bobby got out and came around to open the door for her. At nearly six feet tall, Deneige struggled to extricate herself from the low-slung sports car.

"There's one favor I'd ask you to do for me, Mr. Doyle," she said.

"What's that?" Bobby asked as he closed the door.

"Buy yourself a bigger car."

Upstairs in Deneige's apartment, Bobby felt as if he'd entered an artsy Aladdin's cave. Her living room was filled with books, paintings, and sculptures. She asked him to excuse the mess, but as far as he could see, there wasn't a thing out of place. Everything was arranged as it might be in a gallery.

"How can you afford all this?" he asked in amazement.

"It helps that my mother's a sculptor and several of my friends are artists. The books are all mine. I've been collecting them since I was in junior high. I never seem to be able to let go of any of them. They're like old friends."

She motioned to the couch. "Have a seat while I get us something to drink."

While Bobby waited, he thought of the emotional roller coaster he'd been on this summer. From falling in love with Lynette to his passionate dalliance with Susie to his encounter with the sophisticated beauty who was walking toward him holding two glasses of white wine. Toss in being accused of murder then unexpectedly being set free, and he was left wondering how to make sense of it all. Maybe the best way would be to write about it, he told himself. Art had helped people put life's mysteries into perspective ever since Stone Age man began scrawling images on the walls of caves.

Deneige sat close to him and handed him his glass. She touched her glass to his and took a sip, then she sat her wine on the coffee table. She looked into Bobby's eyes with a serious expression. "Your father said something interesting tonight. He said that you always go after something you want." She took Bobby's glass from his hand and sat it on the coffee table. "I hope that includes me."

* * *

The scene at the Fillmore Auditorium was wilder than ever, a tribute to the appeal of the night's lineup, which included Jefferson Airplane, the Charlatans, and Blue Cheer. Bill Graham had helped whip up interest by announcing that the entire proceeds from the show would be donated to the Haight-Ashbury Free Medical Clinic. Bobby and Deneige were in the crowd, although their reason for being there wasn't related to the benefit performance. Bobby was there to thank Sonny Anders for telling the police about the two encounters with Eddie Ratner at the Fillmore, a testimonial that had helped Bobby win his freedom.

The first band on the bill this evening was the local power trio Blue Cheer. Bobby wasn't familiar with the group's music, although he'd heard they were managed by a Hells Angel and had named themselves after a variety of LSD. As soon as the band erupted into a cover of Eddie Cochran's "Summertime Blues," he knew that they weren't for him. Their music was a brutal, angry assault on the senses. Deneige instantly covered her ears. She turned to Bobby and screamed, "Get me out of here!" He nodded silently and led her through the crowd.

Backstage, they found Sonny Anders in his office, sitting with his feet on his desk as usual. He was staring at a poster for the evening's concert, a burgundy, purple, and yellow montage of the three featured groups. The sonic barrage of Blue Cheer was shaking the walls. The combination of the deafening music and the swirling psychedelic imagery of the poster was like an LSD trip. Maybe that was what Anders was thinking.

Bobby had to knock twice before Anders heard him. When Anders turned around and saw who was standing in his doorway, he looked stunned. "Hey, man," he stuttered, "I thought they'd locked you away for good." He got up and held out his hand. "How'd you manage to get out?"

"The police have arrested a fellow named Eddie Ratner for the crimes. He's the orange-haired creep we talked about. That's why we're here." He indicated Deneige. "You remember Deneige Leblanc."

Anders waved them in. "Sure, sure. How you doing?"

Deneige smiled and took the seat opposite Anders. Bobby had to stand. "Sonny, I want to thank you for vouching for me when the police came by to see you. The fact that you corroborated my account of running into Ratner helped convince them I was telling the truth."

"No problem, man. Always glad to help out a friend." He spoke in a detached manner, as if his mind was somewhere else.

Anders gave Deneige a once-over. "What's your line of work, Miss Leblanc?"

"I'm a literary agent."

"Here in town?"

"Yes. I have an office in the Shell Building."

Anders thought for a bit. "That's down in the Financial District, isn't it?"

"Yes it is. It's at 100 Bush Street."

"Yeah, I think I know the place. Must be interesting work."

"It has its moments."

Bobby put his hand on Deneige's shoulder. "We won't take up anymore of your time, Sonny. I just wanted to make sure you knew how grateful I am for your help. I might not be standing here if it weren't for you and another friend who believed in me."

"Like I said, always glad to help out."

* * *

Deneige read through the contract from Houghton-Mifflin, the old-line Boston publisher. She'd recently sold them the debut novel of Sean Timothy, a San Francisco writer she'd been cultivating for the past two years. Timothy was a royal pain to work with, but he had talent. Deneige had run across one of his short stories in *Ramparts* magazine and encouraged him to try his hand at a novel. The result was a brilliant antiwar satire titled *Liars Poker,* which she sold to Houghton-Mifflin for a hefty five-figure advance, one of her biggest sales.

Satisfied that the contract was in order, she laid it aside. She got up from her desk and walked to the window. She stood there, thinking about the past few weeks, an onslaught of highs and lows such as she'd never felt before. She'd always been an organized, level-headed businesswoman—until she met Bobby Doyle. When she first met him, she'd been intrigued. When she got to know him better, she was impressed. When he was arrested for murder, she'd been plunged into a blue funk. When he was freed, her spirits soared. And after the night they'd spent together, she was smitten for the first time in her life. He was the tender, passionate, intelligent man she didn't think existed.

Previously, she'd focused solely on her agency, driven to be a success in a business that—like every other business—was dominated by men. She had to admit that her devotion to work and her sense of independence had given her a reputation for being a loner. She'd always been content to take her pleasures by herself, whether it was visiting a gallery on her own or going to a concert, but talking with Bobby about art and music made those experiences infinitely more enjoyable. Now, when she considered going out for the evening, she automatically pictured him beside her. It shocked her to realize that if he asked her to drop everything and move with him to Tahiti to live on the beach in a grass shack, she'd do it without hesitation.

Deneige turned from the window, smiling at the thought of becoming a beachcomber. She glanced at her watch. Time to pack up and head home for the evening. She stuffed the documents she intended to read overnight into her briefcase, turned out the lights, and locked up her office. Downstairs, she said goodnight to Toby Gray, the night watchman. When she stepped outside to hail a cab, she was surprised to see an acquaintance walking past her building.

"I'll be darned," the man said. "What are you still doing here this late in the day? Can I give you a ride home? My car's just down the block."

* * *

The call came at nine o'clock that same night. Bobby picked up the phone in his apartment. The voice he heard was odd. It sounded like the caller was speaking through a filter of some kind.

"Doyle," the voice said, "I've got something that should interest you. Her name's Deneige Leblanc, and unless you come up with fifty thousand dollars pronto, she's going to be dead. I'll call back tomorrow afternoon with instructions on where to bring the money."

The caller hung up, leaving Bobby in a daze of disbelief. Lynette and Susie murdered and now Deneige kidnapped? How could this be happening? Eddie Ratner had been arrested. His tormentor could no longer get at him.

Bobby's thoughts flew off in all directions. What should he do? Who should he call? Why would anyone kidnap Deneige? When he finally calmed down enough to think rationally, he telephoned his parents at the Mark Hopkins.

"Brace yourself, Dad," he told his father. "The nightmare isn't over."

* * *

The next morning, Bobby and his father went to withdraw the ransom money at the Bank of America headquarters at 1 Powell Street. Founded as the Bank of Italy in 1904, the financial institution had helped the city recover from the Great Earthquake and Fire of 1906. Now, it would be helping Bobby Doyle free a woman who was becoming increasingly important to him.

After withdrawing the fifty thousand dollars, Bobby and Donovan went directly to police headquarters to discuss the situation with Detective Marshall.

"Good Lord," Marshall said to Bobby. "You do seem to attract more than your share of problems, but I'm glad you both had the sense to come to us. We've seen too many kidnapping cases where the victims' loved ones try to handle everything on their own, and it usually doesn't turn out well. By the way, where are Miss Leblanc's parents?"

"They're in Europe," Bobby said. "Unfortunately, we have no idea how to contact them. Deneige also has a sister, but she's working in New York."

Bobby showed Marshall the briefcase with the ransom money. "I'm supposed to hear from the kidnapper this afternoon about where to meet him. My father and I think the best plan would be for me to meet with him and assess things before the police storm in. Deneige could be killed if the kidnapper gets spooked."

Marshall nodded. "We'll fix you up with a wire so we can monitor the exchange, and we'll be right outside the meeting place. If the kidnapper simply takes the money and leaves, we'll grab him. If things start to go sideways, all you need to do is yell. Operations like this are always dicey, but from what I've seen of you, I think you can pull it off."

They agreed that Bobby would alert the police about the time and location of the meeting once the kidnapper called. Beyond that, there was nothing to do but wait. And pray.

* * *

The second call came at six o'clock that evening. The muffled voice instructed him to bring the money to an abandoned warehouse in South Beach's old waterfront district at ten o'clock. The building was the last one on the right at the end of Brannan Street, the street named for the wily old hustler who made and lost a fortune in the Gold Rush days. Bobby hoped he had Brannan's good luck instead of the string of misfortunes that plagued him at the end of his life.

After telephoning Detective Marshall with the kidnapper's instructions, Bobby spent the next three hours pacing the floor in his apartment while his mom and dad fretted over everything that could go wrong. Maria was terrified at the thought of her son putting himself in danger, but Donovan reminded her that her other son did the same thing every day.

"That doesn't make me feel one bit better," she said.

At nine o'clock, Bobby took the briefcase with the money down to the underground garage. He drove to police headquarters so he could be fitted with a microphone that would pick up his conversation with the kidnapper.

"We'll be listening to everything and tape-recording what's said," Phil Marshall told him. "One hint of trouble and I want you to scream bloody murder. We'll be inside before you can blink. My men have already stationed themselves around the building, and I'll be there shortly. I guarantee you the kidnapper will have no idea what hit him."

Marshall patted Bobby on the shoulder and told him to avoid any heroics. Bobby gave him a tepid smile and left for the rendezvous.

Driving through the old warehouse district wasn't something Bobby would have chosen to do at any time of day. The place was creepy enough when it was light out. At ten o'clock, the black warren of tumbledown buildings reminded him of the scenes of postwar Vienna in the noir thriller *The Third Man.* Bobby felt like Joseph Cotten trying to ensnare the heartless black marketeer played by Orson Welles. All that was missing was the eerie zither music that played throughout the film.

Bobby parked at the end of Brannan Street. There were no lights in any of the buildings, and the glow from the streetlights along the Embarcadero didn't reach this far. Grabbing the briefcase, Bobby headed toward the last building on the right. Fifty years ago, this area would have been the scene of constant activity as longshoremen unloaded ships at the adjacent piers and stowed their cargoes ashore. Not even winos hung out here now.

Bobby saw a light flash on and off at the main entrance of the building. He walked up to the door, which was partially open, and stepped inside. While waiting for his eyes to grow accustomed to the murk, he was struck on the back of the head, and everything went blacker than before. When he came to several minutes later, he was seated on a rough wooden bench along the side of the warehouse. His feet were bound and his hands tied behind him. Deneige was sitting a few feet away, similarly trussed up, and she had a gag in her mouth. She looked at Bobby with a terrified expression.

Her mascara was smeared from all the crying she'd been doing. She tried to scooch closer but couldn't move. All she could do was whimper.

For some reason, Bobby hadn't been gagged. He tried to give Deneige an encouraging smile, although it looked more like the rictus of a terminally ill patient. "Don't worry, babe," he said, "we're going to get out of this."

A gas lantern sat on the filthy concrete floor a few feet away. It cast a weak pool of light on the bench where they were tied up, little more than the glimmer from a campfire. Beyond that, the warehouse was a cavern of black. Someone just beyond the light laughed at what Bobby had told Deneige. Bobby gasped to see Sonny Anders step out of the darkness.

"So you think everything's going to be all right, do you?" Anders said. "Well so do I. For me, that is." He hefted Bobby's briefcase, which he held in his left hand. In his right hand he held a revolver. Anders stepped closer.

"What the hell are you playing at, Sonny?" Bobby shouted. "Untie us and let us go."

"No can do, my *friend.*" He made the last word sound like an accusation. He came closer. The look on his face was frightening.

"Just sit back and relax while I tell you a story. It's about a boy who grew up in Los Angeles. His name was Lars Anderson. Unlike you, Lars wasn't blessed with a rich daddy. His old man was a plumber who didn't earn enough to put his son through college, so Lars had to fend for himself. He worked two jobs between classes at Cal State. He was barely getting by until he started selling some weed on the side. Before he knew it, he was making enough dough to pay for school, living expenses, and a decent car.

"Lars put himself through law school at USC thanks to pot, acid, and coke, but after he finished his law degree, he promised himself he'd never mess with that stuff again. When Lars landed a job in your parents' law firm, he thought he was set. He was making a good living and had a great future ahead of him. Then an old friend asked him for a favor. His friend was having a party and needed a few things. Lars was dumb enough to get him what he wanted. Somehow, your father found out about it, but he didn't turn Lars in to the cops. Oh no, he did something much worse. He fired him and wrote a letter to the state bar association. Lars Anderson ended up losing his law license."

The man waved his revolver in Bobby's face. "What do you think of my story? Pretty sad, huh? Well, that poor sap was me. After I lost my license, I moved up here and found a job working for Bill Graham. I don't make a quarter of what I was making in L.A. It's scut work, scurrying around doing whatever crappy errands Graham doesn't feel like doing himself. I hate it, and it's all because of your holier-than-thou father. He ruined my life."

Bobby shook his head. "Did you ever stop to think that you might have ruined your own life?"

"Shut up, you privileged brat. Your father ruined my life, and now I'm going to ruin his. I thought that getting rid of your girlfriends would do the trick. The first one went down like a lamb, but the little blonde fought like hell. I was sure the cops would arrest you for their deaths, but they kept giving you a pass, I guess because of your squeaky-clean image, or maybe it was your daddy's money. That's why I had to give them a nudge with the dope and the needles."

"You bastard." Bobby struggled to get up from the bench. Lars Anderson laughed and poked him in the chest with the revolver.

"What better way was there to punish the Doyle family than by having one of their precious boys convicted of murder? It was so perfect. How the hell was I to know that bottom feeder Ratner would end up taking the rap? I nearly fainted when the cop showed up with the creep's photo. Then the next thing I know, you waltz into my office a free man."

"But I heard that the heroin the cops found in Ratner's place matched the stuff they found in my car," Bobby said. "How was that possible if you were the one who put it there?" Bobby was simply trying to keep Anderson talking now. The fool had used nylon nautical cord to tie Bobby's hands, and the rope had just enough give to allow him to work it loose. Another minute and his hands would be free.

"Nothing but a coincidence, my man. Must have come from the same local source."

"Let me guess. You buy your drugs on Geary Street in the Tenderloin."

"Now how the hell do you know that? You psychic or something?"

"Never mind how I know. What are you planning to do with us?"

"Your body's going to be found here alongside your girlfriend's—a classic case of murder-suicide. Won't that be tragic? I even took the precaution of using a blackjack to put you to sleep so the cops wouldn't find any marks and get wise."

"You're very clever."

Deneige whimpered at what Anderson was saying. She struggled in vain to get up and flee from this madness.

"There's no reason to harm Deneige," Bobby said. "She has nothing to do with any of this."

"What, let her go so she can tell the cops everything I've just told you. Don't make me laugh. It'll be written up as the final desperate act of a tortured mind. Poor little Bobby Doyle. He had so much promise. No one ever suspected he was a psychopath at heart."

There's a psychopath here all right, Bobby said to himself, but he's the one holding the gun. "You know, your plan won't work."

"And why's that, smart guy?"

"First of all, you can't combine a kidnapping with a murder-suicide. Where do you think I got all that money? From my parents, of course. They know about Deneige being kidnapped."

Anderson seemed taken aback. He clearly hadn't considered all the angles.

"The other reason your plan is bound to fail is that if I really did decide to shoot my girlfriend and then commit suicide, I wouldn't bother to drag her down to someplace like this. I'd do it in her apartment or mine. The police will be suspicious if they find us here. No, Sonny, or Lars, or whoever you are, your plan is about as well thought out as your legal career."

Anderson scrunched up his face in concentration. He looked like the class dunce trying to come up with an answer to a question the teacher asked him. He gave up and brandished the revolver. "Then I guess I'll just shoot you both and let it go at that."

"Hey, you've got the money. The smartest thing for you to do is walk out the door and leave us here. By the time we get loose, you can be on a plane to Mexico."

"But if I shoot you, I don't have to go anywhere." A smile slowly spread over Anderson's face. "And I can take my time before I pull the trigger. Have a little fun beating the crap out of you first. I'd love listening to you whine."

Anderson set the briefcase down and switched the revolver to his left hand. He drew back his right arm to deliver a blow, but by now, Bobby had managed to work his hands free. He caught Anderson's arm, spun him around, and clamped both his arms against his sides in a vise-like grip, one of the body-locks he'd learned in Greco-Roman wrestling.

Anderson instinctively fired a shot, which pinged off the floor. Bobby knocked the gun away, and it skittered out of reach. Anderson struggled, but Bobby easily overpowered him. He felt like crushing the life out of the man, and perhaps he would have if the police hadn't come bursting through the door at the sound of the shot.

Chapter Twenty-Four

Pleiku Province

Vince Tate was dead. Without his best friend in Vietnam—his only friend to be truthful—Jack Doyle was unmoored, disoriented, like a castaway adrift on a trackless ocean. Jack no longer had anyone to share his thoughts with, no one to share a drink with, no one to slap some sense into him when he was close to going off the rails. In addition to Vince being killed, half of Vince's platoon had been wiped out when a company of North Vietnamese regulars ambushed and overran them while they were on patrol northwest of Pleiku City.

When Jack heard the news, he rushed to the field hospital at Camp Enari to talk with some of the survivors. He met a young private named Malone who'd been shot three times and was about to be airlifted to Saigon for further treatment. Malone told Jack that the North Vietnamese soldiers appeared out of nowhere.

"All of a sudden, they were all around us," Malone said in a quaking voice. "There was no place to take cover. There were four of them for every one of us, so we didn't have a chance. It was a slaughterhouse." Malone's eyes glazed over as he recalled the ambush. "We were fighting hand to hand, sir. I could see their faces, their expressions of hatred. The noise was awful…the gunfire and the cursing and the Vietnamese jabbering things we couldn't understand."

Jack poured Malone a glass of water from the carafe on the bedside table.

It seemed to calm him down, but then he started crying.

"Sir, I only managed to survive by hiding under some of my dead buddies." In his agitated state of mind, Malone tried to sit up. "Am I a coward for doing that, sir? Am I a coward?"

Jack wanted to embrace the soldier, to comfort him the way his mother had comforted him when he was a child. Given the soldier's wounds, all Jack could do was urge him to lie back down. Jack took his hand. "No, soldier. You're not a coward. You did the best you could under terrible circumstances."

Another traumatized survivor started yelling from a nearby bunk. "They've got Ted," he shouted in delirium. "They've got Ted."

Malone glanced at the other soldier. He gave Jack the most pitiable look he'd ever seen. "They were cutting them, sir." Malone covered his eyes as if he could blank out the memory. "My God, sir, they were dragging them off and cutting them. Some of them were still alive. Oh God, I can still hear them screaming."

Jack didn't have to ask what Malone meant. He'd seen the bodies of soldiers that had been unspeakably mutilated. It didn't bear thinking about, but as horrible as those atrocities were, they were nothing that Americans hadn't done to their Vietnamese enemies. Sometimes, Jack was embarrassed to be a member of the human race. It was the dilemma of a principled man caught up in an unprincipled war.

The delirious soldier began yelling again. "They've got Ted. They've got Ted."

* * *

Jack visited the camp's interdenominational chapel after his conversation with Private Malone. He had the little room to himself. The chapel was a simple wooden structure like the enlisted men's barracks and the officers' quarters. There were rows of folding chairs for the services held there, and a table up front served as a sort of altar. There was a Bible and a vase of flowers on the table. A lectern stood beside the table for the priest or preacher to use while addressing the attendees. A framed print of Jesus hung on the rear wall. It was religion stripped to its bare essentials, which seemed fitting for the location.

Jack lost track of time as he sat there thinking. It was almost dark when someone flipped on the lights in the chapel. Jack looked toward the back of the room in surprise. A gray-haired officer stood in the doorway.

"I didn't mean to startle you," he said. "I've looked in on you several times this afternoon, but I didn't want to disturb you. You seemed to be deep in your meditations."

"That's all right, sir. I've just been thinking things over."

"Anything you'd like to talk about? I don't know which religion you follow, but I'm the Protestant chaplain here at Camp Enari. I'd be happy to chat with you if you feel like it."

Jack saw the silver eagles on the man's collars. He was a full bird colonel, which meant he'd been ministering to soldier's needs for twenty years or more.

"I don't think denominations make much difference over here," Jack said.

The colonel smiled and walked into the room. He sat across the aisle from Jack. "I suppose you're right. We're all hoping to achieve the same thing, whether we're Protestant, Catholic, Jewish, or whatever." When Jack didn't reply, the chaplain elaborated on his comment. "We're trying to help people find spiritual comfort in the midst of war. It's a tricky proposition."

"Do you think you've ever accomplished that?" Jack asked.

"It's hard to say. Some young men seem to feel better after coming to services or speaking with one of the chaplains. What about you? You appeared to be finding a bit of comfort sitting here today."

Jack looked at the officer and then at the illustration of Jesus. "I have to admit that my thoughts weren't very comforting."

"Care to share them?"

"I suppose I should be confessing these things to a priest. I'm Catholic, you see, but like I said, I don't think it matters much here."

Jack stared at the floor in front of him. "I don't know if I can go on. Leading men to their deaths, taking part in the killing. It all seems so pointless. I feel like I'm losing touch with everything that gives life meaning. I'm certainly not upholding the Ten Commandments."

The chaplain nodded. "I know it's difficult to reconcile the Bible's teachings with the demands of war, but what we're doing over here does seem worthwhile. We're helping a country avoid the contagion of godless communism, one of the curses of the modern age. That's nothing to be ashamed of. When people turn away from God, they're lowering themselves to the level of the beasts in the field. Man's only path to salvation is through the teachings of Our Lord and Savior, Jesus Christ."

Suddenly, Jack felt like crying. He wanted to ask this well-meaning man if he'd ever been in the field himself, ever experienced combat. There wasn't much spiritual comfort to be had out there. Jack had heard too many unanswered pleas of dying men asking God to save them. "I suppose you're right," he said, not wanting to give offense.

The chaplain stood up. "I'll leave you to your thoughts, lieutenant. Maybe you should speak to Father Mallory about your concerns."

"Thank you, colonel." Jack was relieved when the man left. Everything he'd said seemed so divorced from the ugly reality confronting every fighting man in Vietnam. If you asked most soldiers what they were in need of, chances are not one in a thousand would say spiritual comfort. More than likely, they'd say they needed a quick ticket out of here. Or a weekend pass so they could forget their troubles for a while with a Vietnamese whore. Or a cold beer or a long slow toke on a joint or a snort of cocaine. Spiritual comfort could come later, when they were safe at home. That's when they could go to church and sing songs about brotherly love and toss a dollar in the collection plate.

Jack got up and left. He wandered back to his quarters to find comfort in the oblivion of Martell cognac. He'd drink several toasts to Vince Tate, a young man who dreamed of women with humongous boobs and legs about five feet long. Maybe Vince was with one of them now. He hoped so. Vince would find plenty of comfort there. Jack laughed at the thought.

Before he settled down to a bout of serious drinking, he took a few minutes to write some letters. Although it wasn't his official responsibility, Jack wrote a personal letter of commiseration to Vince's parents in Oklahoma. Vince had mentioned that his father was a history professor at the University of Oklahoma. Jack wondered how he'd handle teaching the history of the Vietnam War in years to come.

The letter Jack wrote to his parents was filled with the usual smokescreen of upbeat news. Things were fine. He'd soon be halfway through his tour. He was looking forward to seeing them before long. His letter to Bobby was more honest. It was impossible to hide his feelings from his twin brother. He didn't want to alarm Bobby, but there were things he needed to say. When he finished the letters, he poured himself a tall glass of cognac. He tried to recall his most treasured memories of home, but all he could think about was the delirious soldier he'd heard shouting earlier that day. The words kept coming back to him.

"They've got Ted. They've got Ted."

* * *

That night, Jack dreamed he was standing atop Hai Van Pass, the Pass of the Ocean Clouds—the mountainous dividing line between the steamy southern half of Vietnam and the cooler north. Jack could see the entire thousand-mile-long country from his scenic vantage point, all the way from the ghostly limestone formations dotting Ha Long Bay east of Hanoi to the watery maze of the Mekong Delta south of Saigon. He felt as if he were standing on the peak of Mount Tamalpais in Marin County, but instead of San Francisco Bay and the Pacific Ocean, he saw the Truong Son Range and the South China Sea. The view was breathtakingly beautiful—a painterly landscape of lush green mountains, powdery white beaches, and sparkling blue waters.

In his dream, Jack was frantically waving his arms, attempting to capture the attention of the millions of people in Vietnam. He was signaling for the fighting to stop throughout the country. None of the faces that turned his way paid any attention to him. They continued their bloody struggle as if he didn't exist. All around him, Jack saw burning villages. The flames lit up the sky then slowly flickered out, just as his own hopes were flickering out. At that moment, Jack realized he'd become invisible.

Chapter Twenty-Five

San Francisco

Bobby was the one who proposed the toast the night following their escape from the murderous Lars Anderson. He and Deneige met Bobby's parents in the Top of the Mark, the nineteenth-floor cocktail lounge in the historic Mark Hopkins Hotel, a San Francisco landmark whose guests had included notables from Judy Garland and Elizabeth Taylor to Charles de Gaulle and Nikita Khrushchev. Named after one of the tycoons who founded the Central Pacific Railroad, the storied hotel sat atop Nob Hill, with spectacular views of the city and the Bay.

Tonight, everyone ordered martinis, and when the waiter set their glasses in front of them, Bobby picked his up and held it out. "May our trials finally have come to an end."

"Amen to that," Donovan added.

Bobby took a drink and set his glass down. "I got a call this afternoon from Detective Marshall. He told me the police not only had Anderson's taped confession, they also found heroin in his apartment and discovered that the anonymous note they'd received about my car had been written on the typewriter in Anderson's office at the Fillmore. Marshall said that two of the murder charges against Eddie Ratner and his partner would be dropped, but they'd still be tried on two other murder charges related to their drug activities. Anderson and those two fellows will be lucky to avoid the gas chamber."

Maria turned to Deneige. "And how are you faring?" she asked, attempting to steer the conversation away from talk of murder.

Deneige put on a brave face. "I'm doing all right, considering." She looked at Bobby. "Thankfully, I've got someone to lean on."

She didn't relate how she'd cried on Bobby's shoulder for ten minutes after the police stormed into the warehouse and nabbed Anderson. Once she'd run out of tears, she'd sniffed, wiped her eyes, and announced in a business-like tone, "I'm glad that's over."

Maria smiled at the image of her son as a guardian angel.

Deneige laid her hand on Bobby's. "At least something good came out of the ordeal."

"How could there possibly have been anything good about it?" he asked.

"When we were back there in that horrible old building, you called me your girlfriend."

Bobby squeezed her hand.

Donovan had a befuddled look. "I'm still trying to digest the news that the man who was out to get you used to work for our firm. I remember him, of course. How could I forget him? He was intelligent enough, but he was lazy. He seemed to have a sense of entitlement, as if the world owed him something. He'd been with us for about six months when we fired him, still in his probationary period. He was on thin ice even before I learned about his involvement with drugs. Once that came out, we simply had to get rid of him. He didn't threaten us in any way at the time, but I suppose when he met you, he saw a way of getting back at us. It's really too bad. He could have had a decent career if not for that genetic defect or personality trait or whatever it is that causes people to go wrong."

As before, Maria was determined to change the subject. "Your father and I are checking out tomorrow. It's back to the old grind for us. What about you young folks?"

"After all that's happened," Bobby said, "I plan on taking some time to think about the direction of my career."

"You're not giving up on writing already, are you?" Donovan asked.

"No, no. It's just that I'm getting a little tired of writing about rock 'n' roll."

"Hooray!" Deneige exclaimed.

Bobby smiled at her. "It's not that I think there's anything wrong with it. Most of the groups I've covered this summer feature amazing musicians. But there are so many other kinds of music to write about. I love Charlie Byrd's latest album, *Brazilian Byrd.* Sérgio Mendes & Brasil '66 are terrific, too. In fact, they're appearing next week at El Matador in North Beach."

"Ooh, take me, take me," Deneige said.

Bobby chuckled. "Don't worry. We're going." He took a sip of his martini. "I've also got a new outlet for my writing. Next month, the first issue of a new magazine called *Rolling Stone* is coming out. It's being published here in San Francisco. Ralph Gleason told me about it. He and Jann Wenner, one of my fellow Berkeley students, are behind it. And it's not going to be just about music. It'll also cover politics and popular culture. Ralph's encouraged me to write for the magazine, which already has a stellar lineup of contributors, including Hunter S. Thompson. I think it could be a chance to spread my wings."

"And don't forget about that novel," Deneige said.

"I haven't. I've got some ideas floating around in my head." Bobby laughed. "But first I've got a funeral to attend."

His mother was incredulous. "You're laughing about a funeral?"

"Don't worry. It's a mock funeral being put on by the Diggers. They've decided the Summer of Love is over, and that all the visiting flower children should go home. They're staging a parade tomorrow called 'Death of Hippie,' and I'll be covering it for the *Chronicle.*"

* * *

The Death of Hippie funeral began at sunrise in Haight-Ashbury's Buena Vista Park. Notices posted in shops the week before the funeral described "Hippie" as the "devoted son of Mass Media," a clear indication that the Diggers and like-minded thinkers blamed the constant news coverage of the Summer of Love for the hordes of young people that had overrun the Haight. The funeral's sponsors declared that it was time for the media's fixation to end and for visiting hippies to pass on the spirit of peace and love by taking it back home with them—a polite way of saying "get out of town." San Francisco didn't want to be under the microscope any longer.

Bobby followed the funeral procession down Haight Street. A group of Diggers carried an open casket on their shoulders. The coffin was filled with trinkets symbolizing the public image of hippies. The pallbearers stopped at the corner of Haight and Ashbury Streets, and onlookers added to the collection of hippie paraphernalia. When the procession reached Panhandle Park, participants made a bonfire of underground newspapers, hippie clothing, and related items. Some people brought their own fake caskets and took turns lying in them and having their pictures taken. A grand time was had by all.

In the notes Bobby was scribbling down, he described the event as a humorous send-off for "Hippie," although he observed that many of the kids in the crowd failed to understand that they should have been packing their bags for home. They didn't seem to realize that the funeral's message was directed at them. They acted as if the ceremony was just another wacky happening in a wacky summer in a wacky town. Like far-out, man.

Bobby left and went home himself. He thought that if this actually was the end of the Summer of Love, its conclusion had been unimpressive—more of a whimper than a bang.

* * *

Bobby picked up Deneige at eight o'clock for the show at El Matador. They were both looking forward to hearing Sérgio Mendes & Brasil '66. Deneige was surprised when Bobby drove up in a silver BMW 2000 CS, a racy coupe with enough legroom even for her. Bobby opened the passenger door and held out his arm indicating for her to get in.

"Your car, madam," he said.

"Bobby, I was only kidding about your cute little Triumph. This must have cost you a fortune."

"Luckily, I bought it from a gentleman in the Foreign Service who's been posted to Ankara. He was anxious to sell the car, so I got a sweet deal."

Deneige slid in and sighed as she settled into the spacious leather seat. "Now this is what I call riding in style." She was wearing her long black hair up, the first time Bobby had ever seen her wear it that way. He could hardly take his eyes off her.

"You look lovely tonight. More than lovely. Radiant. You really do look like a princess."

"Oh no, not that royalty line again."

"Sorry, I get carried away sometimes."

She leaned over and kissed him. "Don't stop on my account."

Bobby switched on the radio as they headed toward Broadway in North Beach. "Nights in White Satin" was playing, a just-recorded single by the British progressive rock group the Moody Blues. The haunting love song featured a symphonic accompaniment by the London Festival Orchestra.

"That's a nice song," Deneige remarked. "Very lush."

"It's a pretty complex recording," Bobby said. "Songs like that are hard to duplicate in live performances, unless the band is willing to haul around a busload of backup musicians and special equipment. I've read that's one of the reasons the Beatles have stopped touring and become a studio band. They'd also had enough of life on the road. By the time they put on their final live show at Candlestick Park last year, they'd grown tired of the whole crazy concert scene—all the screaming and pandemonium. Can't say that I blame them. Besides, their tour of the U.S. had become a fiasco after John Lennon's 'we're more popular than Jesus' remark."

Deneige toyed with the back of Bobby's hair. "Poor John. Open mouth, insert foot."

* * *

Sérgio Mendes and his group were just taking the stage when Bobby and Deneige stepped inside the dark confines of El Matador. A favorite hangout of the city's jazz lovers, the elegant nightclub was the brainchild of San Francisco bon vivant Barnaby Conrad, a man who at various points in his career had been a diplomat, a painter, an author...and a bullfighter. He'd actually had forty-seven bullfights—and lived to tell about them in his bestselling book *Matador.*

Sérgio Mendes's previous group, Brasil '65, had recorded a live album at the nightclub, *In Person at El Matador!* The new iteration of the band featured the limpid vocals of Lani Hall and Bibi Vogel, Americans who could sing in Portuguese as well as English. The moment they began the infectious, jazzy samba "Mas Que Nada," Deneige grabbed Bobby's hand. "Come on," she cried, "let's dance." She led him to the floor and began showing off her Latin dance moves. Bobby struggled to keep up as Deneige cavorted around him with her head thrown back and a look of ecstasy on her face. She was enjoying herself so much that he could have stood still and she'd have been happy.

Brasil '66 had released its first album a year earlier under the auspices of Herb Alpert, the trumpeter who'd cofounded A&M Records in the midst of his successful career with the Tijuana Brass. Alpert could spot talent, and he saw plenty of it in the group Sérgio Mendes had assembled. A native of Brazil, Mendes was steeped in his country's musical traditions. Earlier in his career, he'd played with Antônio Carlos Jobim, the father of the jazz-influenced samba music known as bossa nova. Bossa nova had sparked a worldwide craze, largely thanks to Jobim compositions such as "The Girl from Ipanema," "Corcovado," and "One Note Samba."

Bobby had a chance to rest when the group followed "Mas Que Nada" with "Going Out of My Head," a powerful rendition of the hit by Little Anthony and the Imperials. When they played the mesmerizing Jobim composition "Água de Beber," Bobby looked over at Deneige. She wore a Mona Lisa smile, transported by the music to some dreamy realm of contentment.

Brasil '66's version of the Beatles hit "Day Tripper" demonstrated the group's incredible creativity. They made the Lennon-McCartney song their own with an arrangement that showcased the vocals of Lani Hall and Bibi Vogel, along with the jazz piano technique of Sérgio Mendes. Bobby and Deneige got up to dance one last time to the smooth, soothing samba "Berimbau." It only took a little imagination to picture themselves dancing under the stars on a beach in Rio.

* * *

When they got back to Deneige's apartment, Bobby enjoyed one of the most sensual scenes a man can witness—watching a beautiful woman take down her long hair and shake it loose. He wished he'd had a video camera to record it so he could play it over and over.

Deneige left Bobby sitting on the sofa while she went into the bedroom to change. She came back into the living room wearing a filmy negligee.

"Don't sit there staring at me," she said. "Come here and kiss me."

Bobby did as he was instructed. When they finally broke for air, Deneige suggested that he put a record on the stereo while she went into the kitchen for some wine. Bobby flipped through her collection and chose Ravel's *Boléro.*

"Ah ha, I see what you've got in mind," Deneige called from the kitchen.

"Is it that obvious?"

After they drank their nightcap, they made love to Ravel's seventeen-minute masterpiece. The arc of their passion tracked the tempo of the composition, including the rousing crescendo.

"Whew," Deneige said afterward. "That just became my favorite piece of music."

They lay together in companionable silence, enjoying the warmth of their entwined bodies, the enveloping darkness, and the mysterious sounds of the city coming from outside the window. Occasional sirens reminded them of the daily strife that took place everywhere in the world, but they were safe. They were together. It was the special joy that only a couple can experience, a feeling that nothing else matters.

Deneige kissed Bobby before she said good-night. "Thank you for a wonderful evening."

Bobby's last thought before he drifted off to sleep was that it had been a wonderful evening. A night to remember.

* * *

Bobby awoke the next morning with a feeling of unease. Deneige could tell he was agitated as they ate breakfast. "What is it?" she asked. "You seem nervous."

"I don't know. I feel like...something's wrong."

Bobby drove back to his apartment after breakfast. When he walked in, he saw that the call-waiting light on his telephone was blinking. He listened to his messages, one from Ralph Gleason wanting to talk to him about his first assignment for *Rolling Stone,* along with a couple of nuisance calls from telemarketers. The final message was from his father, asking Bobby to call him back.

Bobby dialed the familiar number. It rang several times before his father answered. "Hey, Dad, what's up?" Bobby asked.

"Hello, son." Donovan sounded grave. There was a long silence before he spoke again. "Bobby, I have some terrible news." Another long silence followed. "Jack's been killed."

Bobby couldn't speak. He started to pant. He felt like throwing the phone down and running—running away as fast as he could from the unbearable news, from the ugly reality of his brother's death. When he began bawling, he heard his father start crying, too. For at least five minutes, that was the only sound either of them made.

Finally, Bobby croaked out a few words. "I'll call you back, Dad."

"Sure, son. I'll be here."

A half hour later, Bobby called again. His voice sounded like he had a head cold. "What happened?" was all he could get out.

"The telegram was from Jack's battalion commander. It started with the words 'I regret to inform you.'" Donovan said it with a note of bitterness. "My heart nearly stopped at those words. It went on to say that Jack had been killed in action and that his body would be returned to us for burial. Jack's CO said that he was a hero, that he'd be receiving the Purple Heart and the Bronze Star. He said that we should be proud of him." Bobby started crying again, which triggered Donovan's own deluge of tears.

"How's mom?" Bobby finally managed to rasp out.

"She's under sedation," his father told him.

Chapter Twenty-Six

Los Angeles

Jack's final letter arrived after the telegram about his death. Bobby clutched the piece of paper as if it were a holy document, which in a way it was. It was the last vestige of his brother while he was still alive. The letter had a strange and ominous tone. Jack told Bobby to look after their mom and dad, as if they needed protection because of some unnamed calamity. Bobby realized that Jack may have had premonitions of his own death. Either that or he'd settled into a fatalistic view of the future in general. When Bobby read the part about Jack's friend being killed, he was certain that was what caused his brother's gloomy outlook. Jack's final words were the most unsettling of all.

"You were right about this war," he wrote. "Nothing good can come of it."

Bobby stared at those words with tears in his eyes.

Donovan joined Bobby in the family's living room. "You all right, son?"

Bobby swiped at his eyes. "I'm okay. I was just reading Jack's letter again. How's mom today?"

"She's resting."

It had been five days since the family received the telegram from Jack's CO. Jack's casket had finally arrived back home, one of dozens of other flag-draped coffins carried aboard a giant C-141 Starlifter on the long, silent journey across the Pacific. Yesterday, an army representative had come to the house to inform the family of their son's repatriation. He'd also told them they'd need to hold a closed-casket funeral due to Jack's wounds. The news had sent Maria Doyle into such a frenzy of grief that she had to be sedated again. Not only was her dear Jackie gone, but she would never see him again, never be able to touch his face or give him a farewell kiss.

After Donovan had helped Maria to their bedroom, he returned to thank the army officer for stopping by. The officer presented him with Jack's Purple Heart and Bronze Star. The medals were in fancy silk-lined cases. Donovan had simply stared at them. It was all he could do to keep from breaking down himself. What good were those little pieces of ribbon and metal? They couldn't replace his son. Still, he thanked the officer and set the cases on the mantel next to the photograph of Jack in his uniform.

Before he said goodbye, the army officer shook Donovan's hand and offered his condolences. "If it's any help, you can take pride in knowing your son died a hero."

Bobby had sat silently throughout the entire visit. The fact that Jack was a hero made no difference to him. His brother's absence created a void in his life that could never be filled. He no longer felt whole. His world was out of balance.

And what about all the others who'd died in this needless war, he'd wanted to ask the army officer. Were they heroes, too? The ones killed by a sniper's bullet while reading a letter from home, by stepping on a land mine during a tedious routine patrol, by being blown up by a Vietcong rocket while they slept. Where did heroism begin and end in a pointless conflict? Maybe those who resisted the call to war were the real heroes, Bobby told himself, the ones who risked being labeled traitors and cowards by going to jail or giving up their homes and moving abroad rather than take part in a blood-drenched folly that no one could justify.

Bobby recalled an essay by Sir Arthur Conan Doyle about the joy to be found in books. Sir Arthur said that voices from the past lived on in the written word as a collective memory. The essay was called *Through the Magic Door,* and in it, Sir Arthur used the phrase "the dead are such good company." That phrase had always stuck with Bobby. When this divisive war was finally over, he said to himself, untold numbers of Americans would be keeping their dead loved ones alive through the letters they'd written, although no one would think there was anything good in that sort of companionship. What a waste. What a horrible waste.

* * *

Jack's funeral Mass was held at the Church of the Good Shepherd, the Beverly Hills church attended by many Catholics in the movie industry. Dozens of celebrity weddings and funerals had taken place in the forty-year-old Mission Revival–style building, an oasis of tranquility on busy Roxbury Drive. The grounds were landscaped with palms and pine trees, agaves and cactuses, orange trees and flowering shrubs. Inside, the intimate house of worship was austere, its plain white walls relieved by rows of saints depicted in stained glass. It had been the Doyle family's church ever since they moved to Beverly Hills. It was where Jack and Bobby had been baptized, and now it would be where Jack's loved ones came to honor him and say goodbye.

Jack's casket sat before the altar in the chaste white sanctuary. The Doyles sat at the front of the nave. Maria was dressed in black, including a black veil to hide her tear-ravaged face. She had to lean on Donovan's arm to make it down the aisle. Behind the family, the pews were filled with relatives, coworkers, and friends, including many of Jack's local teachers and classmates and several fellow students from Berkeley. Deneige had flown down from San Francisco to attend the service. At Bobby's insistence, she sat beside him at the end of the family pew.

As the priest recited the eulogy, Bobby happened to think of Wilfred Owen, a British poet whose work he'd studied at Berkeley. Owen was about Jack's age when he was killed amid the horrors of trench warfare in World War I. Bobby wondered how many poets had died—and would continue to die—in Vietnam. It seemed to be a universal curse that young men like Jack and Wilfred Owen had to fight old men's wars. If the ones who started the wars were forced to do the fighting, Bobby told himself, universal peace would break out.

Bobby should have received a measure of solace by the time the service was over and they stood for the recessional, but he hadn't. The drive to the cemetery was bleak. The slow procession through neighborhoods he and Jack had grown up in reminded him of too many experiences they'd shared. The family could have buried Jack in Los Angeles National Cemetery, but Maria refused. The army had taken her son from her, and she would never allow him to lie in a military grave. They chose Woodlawn in Santa Monica instead, a history-rich cemetery just eight miles from their home, close enough for Maria to visit Jack often.

The graveside service was brief. Afterward, a military honor guard stepped forward and offered Maria the folded U.S. flag that had covered Jack's coffin. She turned her head away, and Donovan accepted the flag. The ride home after the service took place in strained silence.

* * *

The next day, Bobby took Deneige to the airport for her flight back to San Francisco. As they sat in the terminal waiting for her boarding call, Deneige asked Bobby when he'd be returning.

"Not for a few days."

"Staying on to spend time with the family?"

"Actually, I'm flying to Washington, D.C., tomorrow. Artist Michael Bowen and some of his San Francisco and Berkeley friends have organized a protest against the war, and I want to be part of it. We'll be marching from the Lincoln Memorial to the Pentagon. It's meant to bring together the entire spectrum of Americans who oppose the war, from college kids to middle-class professionals to Vietnam veterans. They're expecting over a hundred thousand marchers, including members of the clergy and celebrities such as Norman Mailer. It's supposed to be the largest protest ever against the war."

"Good for you," Deneige said. "I hope a million people show up."

"Speaking of Norman Mailer," Bobby said, "I just finished the Mailer novel that Dad gave me to read while I was in jail. It's called *Why Are We in Vietnam?* Dad didn't think it had much to do with the war, but the story implies why we ended up there—a lethal combination of hubris, deceit, naivety, and stupidity. The story gave me an idea for a novel I might try to write. It begins with a family that loses a son in the Revolutionary War and falls apart because of their grief. Throughout the rest of the novel, descendants of the same family lose sons during the Civil War, the First and Second World Wars, the Korean War and Vietnam. The families in each generation are torn apart by the loss of their children. What do you think?"

"It sounds awfully dark."

"Ask my mother what darkness feels like. Or the parents of Lynette Simms and Susie Blake. Or the soldiers who make it back safely from Vietnam only to be jeered instead of welcomed home."

Deneige sighed. "And this was supposed to be the Summer of Love. What did it all mean, Bobby—the hippies, the drugs, the music, all the needless deaths?"

"I don't know. I really don't know."

Deneige stood up when her boarding call was announced. "I'll be waiting for you when you get back." She headed off to catch her flight. After a few steps, she turned to wave goodbye. "Maybe we can go to Tahiti and walk on the beach."

Epilogue

Of all the traumas that Bobby Doyle suffered during the Summer of Love, none was greater than the death of his brother. Jack Doyle's hopes of returning home from Vietnam—to lead a full life dedicated to helping others improve theirs—turned out to be a mirage. It was a tragedy shared by more than eleven thousand other young Americans who died in the war in 1967. In a telling international development, the Nobel Peace Prize wasn't awarded that year. How could it have been?

The following year, the drive to end the divisive conflict would take center stage in the national elections, costing Lyndon Johnson his presidency. Martin Luther King, Jr., and Robert F. Kennedy would fall to assassins' bullets before Richard Nixon was elected with the tantalizing promise of ending the war, although America's involvement in Vietnam would drag on for four more years.

Bobby Doyle refused to take part in the war. No family should have to lose a son in a meaningless conflict, he reasoned, let alone two sons. He was determined to spare his parents that additional heartache. After earning his master's degree, he stayed on at the University of San Francisco to pursue a Ph.D. He also completed his first novel, which was published to wide acclaim. He and Deneige Leblanc continued their relationship after his return from the March on the Pentagon, a protest that rocked the nation. Soldiers were called in to quell the huge crowd with tear gas. The most enduring image of the march was the photograph of a young man placing a flower in the barrel of a rifle wielded by a member of the military police.

Bobby's parents took a six-month leave of absence from their law practice following the death of their son. When they returned, Maria Doyle did volunteer work at the L.A. Veterans Hospital.

In San Francisco, the celebrated months of peace, love, and brotherhood passed quickly, like a butterfly that emerged from its chrysalis and fluttered away. People began leaving the city as the good times were increasingly strained by the aimless crowds inundating Haight-Ashbury. Some young people left to return to school or jobs, while others drove off in their psychedelic buses in search of the next nirvana. The unluckiest among them were those drafted to serve in the war so many Americans opposed. One person who left town that summer was the monstrous psychopath Charles Manson, who even then was assembling the gang of misfits that would later commit their grisly murders.

When the city's remaining flower children held their mock hippie funeral on October 6, 1967, the symbolic end of the Summer of Love had arrived. Of course, the hippies' free-spirited lifestyle and nonconformist ideals lived on, having spread far beyond San Francisco by then. The counterculture movement lasted well into the seventies, although by the eighties, most of the flower children had settled down to regular jobs, moved to the suburbs, and produced their 2.5 children like ordinary Americans.

Still, in enclaves across the country, a scattering of hardcore hippies clung to their ideals even as they reached middle age, despite the fact that the sight of their beads, long graying hair, and increasingly inappropriate youthful dress elicited more snickers than admiration. In their time, they'd experienced free love, free speech, and—thanks to the generosity of San Francisco's Diggers—free lunches. The uninhibited psychedelic spectacle they'd provided had been entertaining while it lasted, but, as George Harrison sang following the break-up of the Beatles, "all things must pass," a fitting epitaph for both the Fab Four and the era. It almost seemed fated that the Beatles' last live concert would take place in San Francisco.

Perhaps the final word on the hippies rightfully belongs to *San Francisco Chronicle* sage Herb Caen, who wrote this appraisal in his October 15, 1967, column: "The most interesting thing about the hippies is not whether they are dead or alive—but, as always, the reaction they elicit (or provoke) from so-called established society.... What really bugs the critics is what the hippies are saying without saying a word: 'What are YOU doing, brother, that's so damn important?' And this is the question—with its ghostly overtones of Vietnam, taxes, bigotry, hypocrisy, corruption, cancer and all the other ills of established society—this is the question that has no answer except fury."

With its crosscurrents of war and social upheaval, the Summer of Love shaped the trajectories of millions of lives. Whatever else it might have been, that long-ago summer was undeniably a time when young people everywhere dreamed of a better world. That may have been unrealistic, naive even, but what a wonderful dream it was.

Author's Note

The Summer of Love has provoked no end of debate. Was it really a cultural milestone or simply a brief confluence of young people looking for a good time? The popular conception of that famous happening is one of idealistic students turning away from materialism and war to embrace equality, peace, and love, a feel-good movement that took root in the nonconformity of the beatniks and blossomed to the sounds of a new strain of socially conscious rock 'n' roll—with an ample supply of marijuana and LSD to ease the way. There's certainly evidence to support that characterization. It's seen in the photographs and films of dancing long-haired beauties and their laid-back, guitar-strumming boyfriends, most of them wearing blissed-out smiles and flowers in their hair.

That mellow image may well have grown rosier over time, like a folktale that becomes more captivating with each retelling. Some accounts, in fact, offer a starkly different interpretation. One opinion is that peaceful, idealistic flower children did gather on the streets of San Francisco, but their ranks were soon overwhelmed by wannabes and hapless drifters, some of them underage runaways who were preyed on by big city thieves and pimps. The most cynical accounts say that the beatific image of the Summer of Love was largely a media-created myth, that the massive gathering was tainted from the outset by hard drugs, rampant crime, and a tsunami of sexually transmitted diseases. Hunter S. Thompson wrote that many of the original hippies were already lying low by 1967, when the news media latched onto the notion that hordes of idle, bizarrely dressed young people represented a BIG story.

Whether the summer was glorious or notorious, important matters definitely took place in and around San Francisco during that time. The

Magic Mountain Music Festival and the Monterey International Pop Festival—two landmark events that helped kick-start the Summer of Love—introduced many of the future megastars of rock to a wider audience, and they heralded similar rock festivals to come, including Woodstock. Also, thanks in part to the flower children's pacifist ethos, politics and music became ever more intertwined, a trend manifested by the founding of *Rolling Stone* magazine by UC Berkeley firebrand Jann Wenner and San Francisco music critic Ralph J. Gleason. The first issue came out in newspaper format on November 9, 1967, featuring a photo of John Lennon on page one.

Aside from influencing music and politics, the unbridled creativity of the Summer of Love still resonates in the worlds of fashion and art. The bright, joyful images of Flower Power are just as evocative today as they were in 1967, when they appeared on clothing and posters, on the sides of cars and vans, and painted on the smiling faces of frolicking hippies.

In setting my story amid the actual events of the Summer of Love, I've necessarily included many of the familiar figures from that time, some of whom are still alive. I've tried to portray these people as accurately as possible, and I apologize for any inadvertent misrepresentations. The principal characters in the story and all of those associated with the murders are purely fictional. None of them are based on actual persons. For anyone interested in the historical figures of San Francisco, I've written about four of those mentioned in the story in works of nonfiction. *Secret Heroes* (William Morrow, 2012) includes biographies of Civil War surgeon Jonathan Letterman and the noteworthy Native American Ishi. *Villains, Scoundrels, and Rogues* (Prometheus Books, 2014) includes an account of Chinatown gangster Fong Ching. And *American Trailblazers* (Gemini Originals, 2018) includes a profile of inventor Philo T. Farnsworth.

The music history in the story is as accurate as I could make it, with a few notable exceptions. Mason Williams did begin writing "Classical Gasoline" in the summer of 1967 as I describe in Chapter Nine, but he didn't have it ready to record until the following year. In an interesting footnote, during the recording session, the music copyist inadvertently shortened the title of the song to "Classical Gas," and the name stuck. In Chapter Sixteen, I describe a drunken Jim Morrison falling down during a performance at the Fillmore Auditorium. Morrison's alcoholic escapades actually took place elsewhere. In New Haven, Connecticut, he was arrested onstage and charged with inciting a riot. In Miami, he was charged with exposing himself during a show. In Amsterdam, he staggered onstage in the middle of a Jefferson Airplane performance, whirled around like a flamenco dancer, and passed out. He had to be carted off to a hospital.

In Chapter Eighteen, I describe performances by classical guitarists Andrés Segovia and Julian Bream. Both accounts are purely fictional. I set Bream's performance in the Fairmont Hotel's famous Venetian Room simply because I wanted to mention the supper club where Tony Bennett first sang "I Left My Heart in San Francisco." My final tweak of history occurs in Chapter Twenty, where I advanced the timing of Creedence Clearwater Revival's appearance at the Fillmore. In the fall of 1967, the band was still struggling along as the Golliwogs, although John Fogerty had just written the song "Porterville," in which he discovered the songwriting style that would make the band famous. CCR rose to prominence the following May with the release of the group's self-titled debut album.

As for my own ties to the Summer of Love, I came of age in 1967, a newly minted English and Journalism B.A. unleashed upon the world with Hemingway-inspired dreams of becoming a writer. And though I lived nearly two thousand miles from San Francisco and had never worn flowers in my hair, I grooved to the same music as the hippest hippies in Haight-Ashbury. That summer, I first listened to the Beatles' seminal *Sgt. Pepper's Lonely Hearts Club Band* in a friend's campus apartment, vaguely aware that a watershed moment had arrived in the history of music.

A week or two after my graduation from tiny Central Missouri State College, now the University of Central Missouri, I received a notice to report for my draft physical. I wasn't looking forward to an all-expenses paid vacation in Southeast Asia, so I hurriedly joined the U.S. Navy. My basic training and my first duty station were both in California, an eye-opening experience for a midwestern kid who'd grown up in a town of eight thousand. In the Golden State, I got my first view of the ocean, which thrilled and intimidated me. I went backpacking often in Yosemite and Sequoia-Kings Canyon National Parks. I hit the beaches at every opportunity. And I attended my first rock concert, a smoky Moody Blues spectacle that still seems surreal.

I'd gotten married shortly before I joined the navy, and my wife accompanied me to California. During the three years we lived in the San Joaquin Valley town of Hanford, near Naval Air Station Lemoore, we drove our little red Volkswagen Beetle all over the state, including a white-knuckle trip along the precipitous, landslide-plagued Coast Highway from Morro Bay to Carmel. Another memorable excursion was the long weekend we spent in San Francisco. We stayed at the St. Francis Hotel on Union Square, where scenes in the classic noir thriller *D.O.A.* were filmed. The city's hippie heyday was largely over by the time we arrived, but that didn't matter to us. Our interests were those of most first-time visitors—riding the cable cars and taking in Ghirardelli Square, Fisherman's Wharf, Golden Gate Park, Chinatown, and all the other famous sights.

Even though I was just a gawking tourist, I felt a special link to what I saw. My paternal grandfather, Walter Lee Martin, and his brother Charles had been in San Francisco when the Great Earthquake and Fire of 1906 destroyed much of the city. They were in the army at the time, having served in the American occupation of the Philippines. Their quarters were leveled by the quake, and according to family legend, the only thing my grandfather was able to recover from the shambles of his room was a demijohn of whiskey. In one of those quirks of history, I would watch the powerful Loma Prieta Earthquake jolt the city during the television broadcast of the 1989 World Series between the San Francisco Giants and Oakland Athletics.

I made one other journey to the San Francisco area during my stay in California, a flight from NAS Lemoore to NAS Alameda aboard an aging A-1 Spad, a single-engine prop plane designed at the end of World War II. I don't recall why I flew to Alameda, which is located directly across the Bay from San Francisco, but I certainly remember the flight. The pilot was a cocky lieutenant commander who went by the nickname of "Ace" and sported a white silk scarf, like some World War I daredevil. As we approached the airfield, Ace asked me if I'd ever "pulled any Gs," meaning experienced extreme gravitational forces. When I replied only on carnival rides, Ace said, "you ought to enjoy this then," and he turned the plane into a gut-churning barrel roll. After we landed, I wobbled from the plane and puked on the tarmac. Ace erupted in laughter. Two weeks later, that same antique Spad developed mechanical problems and crashed in the Sierra Nevada.

After my navy assignment in California ended in 1970, I received orders to a new duty station. It was an ironic turn of events in light of my plan to avoid Vietnam. Having advanced to the enlisted rating of Journalist Second Class, I was assigned to the public affairs office of the U.S. Navy's headquarters in Saigon. My yearlong stay in South Vietnam allowed me to get to know the friendly Vietnamese people, to travel around their exquisitely beautiful country, to enjoy their wonderful French-influenced cuisine, and to narrowly escape being blown to bits by a Vietcong rocket in the seaside town of Nha Trang. Two of my senior high schoolmates died in Vietnam. Both were missing in action, the most horrible sort of tragedy for their loved ones—never knowing what happened to them and imagining the worst.

My service in Vietnam provided other ties to the San Francisco region. I shipped out for Southeast Asia from Oakland International Airport aboard a World Airways jetliner, and it was to the Bay Area that I returned a year later on my way back home to Missouri. Twenty-five years after those alternately terrifying and joyous flights, I flew through San Francisco International on my way to revisit Vietnam on assignment for National Geographic. As I waited for my boarding call, I watched a lingering crimson sunset while reminiscing about my long-ago days in California, and San Francisco in particular. Although my connections with the city were all short-lived or tangential, they were memorable nonetheless, for San Francisco etches itself in the minds of all those who experience it, no matter how brief their stay. To my good fortune, conducting the historical research for this novel was like an extended return to the endlessly fascinating, always beautiful City by the Bay.

Selected Sources

Caen, Herb. *The Best of Herb Caen, 1960–1975,* selected by Irene Mecchi. San Francisco: Chronicle Books, 1991.

Clarke, Jeffrey J. *Advice and Support: The Final Years, 1965–1973, The U.S. Army in Vietnam.* Washington, D.C.: U.S. Army Center of Military History, 1988.

Cohen, Katherine Powell. *Images of America, San Francisco's Haight-Ashbury.* Charleston, S.C.: Arcadia Publishing, 2008.

Cole, Tom. *A Short History of San Francisco,* 3rd ed. Berkeley, Calif.: Heyday, 2014.

Evanosky, Dennis, and Eric J. Koss. *San Francisco Then and Now,* rev. ed. London: Pavilion, 2018.

Hammond, William M. *Public Affairs: The Military and the Media, 1962–1968, The U.S. Army in Vietnam.* Washington, D.C.: U.S. Army Center of Military History, 1988.

Hansen, Gladys. *San Francisco Almanac: Everything You Want to Know About Everyone's Favorite City,* rev. ed. San Francisco: Chronicle Books, 1995.

Karnow, Stanley. *Vietnam: A History,* rev. ed. New York: Viking, 1991.

Kubernik, Harvey. *1967: A Complete Rock Music History of the Summer of Love.* New York: Sterling, 2017.

MacGarrigle, George L. *Combat Operations: Taking the Offensive, October 1966 to October 1967, The U.S. Army in Vietnam.* Washington, D.C.: U.S. Army Center of Military History, 1998.

McGloin, John Bernard, S.J. *San Francisco: The Story of a City.* San Rafael, Calif.: Presidio Press, 1978.

Olson, James S., ed. *Dictionary of the Vietnam War.* New York: Peter Bedrick Books, 1987.

Pennebaker, D. A. *Monterey Pop* [documentary film]. The Criterion Collection, 1968.

Perry, Charles. *The Haight-Ashbury: A History.* New York: Random House, 1984.

Selvin, Joel. *The Haight: Love, Rock, and Revolution, The Photography of Jim Marshall.* San Rafael, Calif.: Insight Editions, 2014.

------. Photographs by Jim Marshall. *Monterey Pop: June 16–18, 1967.* San Francisco: Chronicle Books, 1992.

------. *San Francisco: The Musical History Tour.* San Francisco: Chronicle Books, 1996.

------. *Summer of Love: The Inside Story of LSD, Rock & Roll, Free Love and High Times in the Wild West.* New York: Plume, 1995.

Solnit, Rebecca. *Infinite City: A San Francisco Atlas.* Berkeley, Calif.: University of California Press, 2010.

Urdang, Laurence, ed. *The Timetables of American History.* New York, Touchstone, 1981.

San Francisco in Movies and Television

San Francisco has long been one of the most popular settings for movies and TV shows. Here are a few memorable examples from each medium. Since the number of films set in the city stretches into the hundreds, the movies listed here focus on classic mysteries and crime dramas, subjects that seem particularly suited to San Francisco. Maybe it's the fog.

Movies

Barbary Coast (1935): Historical melodrama directed by Howard Hawks depicting the lawlessness of the Gold Rush era in San Francisco. Starring Miriam Hopkins, Edward G. Robinson, and Joel McCrea.

After the Thin Man (1936): The second Thin Man movie but the first set in San Francisco. The mystery-comedy continued the incomparable pairing of William Powell and Myrna Loy—along with their scene-stealing dog, Asta.

The Maltese Falcon (1941): The blockbuster hit came after two previous attempts—*The Maltese Falcon* (1931) and *Satan Met a Lady* (1936). The Bogart classic, directed by John Huston, is still considered one of the greatest movies of all time.

The Lady from Shanghai (1948): Classic film noir written and directed by Orson Welles, who starred alongside his real-life estranged wife, Rita Hayworth. Notable for Welles's abominable Irish brogue, Hayworth's short blond hair, and the famous hall of mirrors scene at the end.

D.O.A. (1950): Told almost entirely in flashbacks, this film noir classic stars Edmond O'Brien as a small-town accountant who travels to San Francisco to have a good time but ends up having a very bad time when he's poisoned in an incredibly convoluted criminal cover-up.

Vertigo (1958): Alfred Hitchcock's eerie mystery in which Jimmy Stewart becomes obsessed with an enigmatic Kim Novak. That same year, Stewart was again paired with the lovely Miss Novak in the romantic comedy *Bell, Book and Candle,* proving Stewart was a lucky man.

Bullitt (1968): Cop Steve McQueen takes on the mob and wears out the tires and shock absorbers on his Ford Mustang during a hilly high-speed car chase, an impossible-to-duplicate ten-minute tour of the city in which he passes the same green VW Beetle three times!

Dirty Harry (1971–88): Five cop films in which Clint Eastwood gets all Clint Eastwoody. You got a problem with that?

The Conversation (1974): Francis Ford Coppola thriller in which surveillance expert Gene Hackman records dangerous conversations that could lead to murder—or him going crazy.

48 Hours (1982): Buddy film featuring Nick Nolte as a police inspector and Eddie Murphy as a convict serving time for robbery. Murphy is released from prison for 48 hours to help Nolte catch two killers, leading to general mayhem and much bloodshed.

Basic Instinct (1992): Michael Douglas and Sharon Stone get pally in this steamy thriller remembered chiefly for Stone crossing her legs.

Zodiac (2007): Jake Gyllenhaal stars in this creepy tale about the hunt for the serial killer who spread terror in the Bay Area in the late 1960s and early '70s, a murderer who was never caught.

Television

Have Gun–Will Travel (1957–63): Deadly but compassionate gentleman mercenary Paladin (Richard Boone) ventures forth from late nineteenth-century San Francisco to solve his clients' problems with words, fists, or bullets. One of the few Western good guys who wore black.

Ironside (1967–75): Raymond Burr followed up his successful run in *Perry Mason* as a gruff wheelchair-bound police consultant who puts away crooks with brains rather than brawn.

The Doris Day Show (1968–73): A somewhat schizophrenic sitcom showcasing America's perky singing sweetheart as a widow who goes from raising her two sons in rural Marin County to becoming a San Francisco swinger.

McMillan & Wife (1971–77): Cop show featuring Rock Hudson and Susan Saint James as crime-busting socialites. In the final season, the title became *McMillan* after the Saint James character was killed off, reportedly because of a contract dispute.

The Streets of San Francisco (1972–77): A homely old cop (Karl Malden) gets teamed up with a handsome young cop (Michael Douglas).

Trapper John, M.D. (1979–86): A spin-off of the popular *M*A*S*H* movie–TV franchise, starring Pernell Roberts as the likeable chief of surgery at San Francisco Memorial Hospital.

Hotel (1983–88): Based on the 1965 Arthur Hailey novel, this upscale soap opera starred Anne Baxter, James Brolin, and Connie Sellecca. During its five-season run, the show became a virtual employment agency for actors, featuring several hundred famous guest stars.

Full House (1987–95): Sitcom about a widowed father raising his three daughters with a little help from his friends. The cast included Bob Saget, John Stamos, Candace Cameron, Lori Loughlin, and the Olsen twins. Although set in San Francisco, the series was taped in Burbank.

Charmed (1998–2006): Three sister witches (Alyssa Milano, Holly Marie

Combs, Shannen Doherty/Rose McGowan) put the hurt on local demons and wear sexy outfits.

Monk (2002–09): Former cop with OCD and 312 phobias (Tony Shalhoub) goes around the city catching bad guys, straightening pictures, and avoiding ladybugs.

Musical Milestones of 1967

Music lovers were treated to some of the greatest rock and pop albums ever in 1967, including *Sgt. Pepper's Lonely Hearts Club Band* by the Beatles, *Surrealistic Pillow* by Jefferson Airplane, and landmark albums by the Doors, Jimi Hendrix, Pink Floyd, the Byrds, the Who, the Mamas & the Papas, and other influential groups. Here are twenty-five of the hit singles. They're listed in no particular order and reflect the author's preferences. A few of the songs were released in late 1966 and remained on the charts in 1967. Surprising to many, some of the best-selling albums and singles of 1967 were recorded by the made-for-TV band the Monkees.

- "San Francisco (Be Sure to Wear Flowers in Your Hair)," Scott McKenzie
- "White Rabbit" and "Somebody to Love," Jefferson Airplane
- "All You Need Is Love," The Beatles
- "For What It's Worth," Buffalo Springfield
- "A Whiter Shade of Pale," Procol Harum
- "Light My Fire," The Doors
- "Purple Haze," Jimi Hendrix
- "Good Vibrations," The Beach Boys
- "Dedicated to the One I Love," The Mamas & The Papas
- "Kind of a Drag," The Buckinghams
- "Respect," Aretha Franklin
- "Happy Together," The Turtles
- "Groovin'," The Young Rascals

- “Brown Eyed Girl,” Van Morrison
- “I’m a Believer,” The Monkees
- “Massachusetts,” The Bee Gees
- “Get Together,” The Youngbloods
- “Gimme Some Lovin’,” The Spencer Davis Group
- “I Can See for Miles,” The Who
- “Ruby Tuesday,” The Rolling Stones
- “There’s a Kind of Hush,” Herman’s Hermits
- “Soul Man,” Sam & Dave
- “Ode to Billy Joe,” Bobbie Gentry
- “Up, Up and Away,” The 5th Dimension

Acknowledgements

Special thanks go to my editor, Verena Rose, whose suggestion that I create a third "Music & Murder Mystery" prompted me to develop this story, which draws on some of my own experiences. Thanks as well to the other talented staff members at Level Best Books who helped bring this novel to the page. Also, thanks to my excellent proofreader, my wife, Janice, and to my savvy website manager, my son, Evan. Finally, thanks to San Francisco resident and aficionado Mark Hugh Miller for his insightful comments.

About the Author

Paul Martin is a former book and magazine editor with the National Geographic Society. His writing assignments have taken him around the world. The author of twelve books of fiction and nonfiction, he has also edited or contributed to a dozen other books on history, science, and travel. An amateur luthier and onetime vineyard owner and winemaker, Martin lives near Washington, D.C. For additional information about his work, visit www.paulmartinbooks.com.

Also by Paul Martin

NOVELS

Dance of the Millions
Killin' Floor Blues
Lost in Saigon
Far Haven

POETRY

Strange World

NONFICTION

Secret Heroes
Villains, Scoundrels, and Rogues
American Trailblazers
Land of the Ascending Dragon

FOR YOUNGER READERS

Messengers to the Brain
Science: It's Changing Your World

CPSIA information can be obtained
at www.ICGtesting.com
Printed in the USA
BVHW081019080223
658058BV00006B/159

9 781685 121686